Praise fo

Fighting Gravity

"In this rare look at divorce from the male perspective, Michael Godin takes readers on a heartfelt and humorous journey of one man's struggle to rebuild his life after heartbreak. As he stumbles through the ups and downs of the online dating scene, Nick's hilarious escapades reveal the challenges—and unexpected joys—of moving on."

—Ashley Farley, USA TODAY Bestselling Author

"An entertaining novel about second chances in life and love. Godin narrates Nick's adventures in warm, observant prose that captures the indignities of dating in middle age. This gentle, breezy novel has much to offer." Our verdict: GET IT

—Kirkus Reviews

"Fighting Gravity goes down as smoothly as a Sazerac. The novel's snappy dialogue, finely drawn characters, and compelling plot will capture your imagination and hold your attention until the end. Laissez les bon temps roulez with Fighting Gravity! I highly recommend it—I could not put it down!"

—Heath Hardage Lee, Author of
The League of Wives and The Mysterious Mrs. Nixon

"Godin crafts a compelling protagonist in this delightful romcom...a refreshing change of pace for the genre. Comparable titles: Nick Hornsby's High Fidelity, Lucy Score's Forever Never."

—BookLife Reviews

"Raw, unfiltered, and tragically hilarious...A brilliant story that examines the human cost of maintaining a façade—and the grace required to drop it. Godin's latest novel is a darkly funny, emotionally honest portrait of a man on the verge...The book's pacing is deliberate, and humor is in abundance."

—The Prairies Book Review

"The perfect follow-up to Godin's debut hit, The Big Prick, the novel Fighting Gravity delves into Nick's life twenty years later, exploring the trials and tribulations of divorce, single life, and dating...an exclusive, behind-the-scenes look at the world of plastic surgery, and a perfect balance of conflict, suspense, humor, and love. Falling in love with Nick's character is inevitable..."

—Autumn Woods, author of Nightshade and His Secret Gift

"Fighting Gravity is a smart, heartfelt take on midlife romance from a man's point of view. Think chick flick charm viewed through a guy's desperate and hilarious perspective."

—Joni Davis, author of Feng Shui Love

"Fighting Gravity is a funny and sexy romp which takes the reader from the consultation room to the bedroom of a successful but emotionally scarred New Orleans plastic surgeon as he attempts to lift the lives of his patients with the best part of himself---his big heart."

—Irene Ziegler, author of Rules of the Lake and Ashes to Water

"Godin has a sharp eye for psychological insight. What elevates this novel is its cast of finely etched supporting characters, rendered with intelligence and autonomy. The narrative balances forward momentum with frequent introspective pauses, allowing readers to breathe deeply into Nick's world. Lovers of fine literary fiction, taut medical drama, and character studies will find much to admire."

—BookView Review

"Michael Godin delivers a sharp and funny take on modern dating, while managing to keep things light without ever being cynical or mean-spirited. I found myself laughing out loud more than once. Nick is a great character---this book has a lot of heart. What makes this book stand out is how it balances comedy with deeper emotions. Fighting Gravity is a fresh, funny, and surprisingly heartfelt look at mid-life reinvention that I recommend."

—K.C. Finn for Reader's Favorite Reviews

"Fighting Gravity is a thoughtful and entertaining reflection on resilience, second chances, and the unpredictable nature of human relationships. Michael Godin is a brilliant writer! He makes Nick an interesting and relatable protagonist that all readers will root for. The narrative is engaging and sharp, striking a perfect balance between humor and emotional depth."

—Rabia Tanveer, Reader's Favorite Reviews

"Godin's attention to detail shines through...a profoundly relatable origin story. I found Fighting Gravity captivating and highly recommend it to readers seeking a romantic drama that breaks from convention."

—Essie Asian for Reader's Favorite Reviews

"...subtle, witty, and engaging...a dynamic reading experience...a relatable and enjoyable reading experience that resonates with the audience."

—Amanda Hanson for The US Review of Books

5-13-26

FIGHTING GRAVITY

For Jennifer,

Please enjoy with my best wishes,

Michael Goodwin

FIGHTING GRAVITY

A NOVEL BY

MICHAEL GODIN

This book is a work of fiction. The names, characters and events in this book are the products of the author's imagination or are used fictitiously. Any similarity to real persons living or dead is coincidental and not intended by the author.

Fighting Gravity

Published by Uncommon Sense Publishing, LLC

Library of Congress Control Number: 2024945951

ISBN (hardcover): 9781662964152
ISBN (paperback): 9781662957437
eISBN: 9781662957444

To my family and friends who help me fight.

"O, do not pray for easy lives. Pray to be stronger men! Do not pray for tasks equal to your powers. Pray for powers equal to your tasks! Then the doing of your work shall be no miracle. But you shall be a miracle...."

Phillip Brooks, "Going up to Jerusalem,"
Twenty Sermons (1886)

Contents

Disclaimer

This is a story, but it's not my story. To create an engaging work of fiction, an author must "raise the stakes" and create events that are much more dramatic than real life. So, as you read it, please keep in mind that this book is NOT an accurate account of my life some years back. And please, don't visualize the guy in the photo on the back cover as Nick Jordan. Choose someone handsomer. A fifty-ish George Clooney, perhaps. Yes, that should do nicely. Now please enjoy...

MG

Prologue: 1993

Nick heard it again in the darkness—metal on metal, a knocking, scraping sound. He lay on his small, hard bed in an on-call room at Charity Hospital of New Orleans. He was tired because he'd been up all night and felt angry that the little bit of sleep he'd been allowed was being disturbed. He knew his fellowship year would have rough spots, but this was ridiculous.

The noise seemed to be coming from across the hall. Nick rose slowly from the bed, his fatigue making the room sway a bit. He could see nothing but a dirty strip of yellow light beneath the door. He shuffled his way toward it.

The furtive scraping sounds were louder now. He turned the knob noiselessly and cracked the door open enough to look out with one eye.

The hallway was weirdly lit. A fluorescent bulb sputtered fuzzy light from above, throwing shadows onto gray walls. Just down and across the hall, Nick saw the back of a man. He immediately recognized him as one of the volunteer high school students—medical scholars they called them. This one was breaking into the narcotics cabinet.

Nick considered confronting him, but weariness and fear pushed him in a different direction. He shuffled back to the bed and dialed security. In whispers, he described what was happening. He gently replaced the receiver and lay back down. He closed his eyes and sleep came quickly.

He never even heard the kid being arrested.

Part One
Trauma

"Injuries are most difficult to repair when
pieces are lost."

—Terry Johnson, MD to his residents, 1993

1

New Orleans, 2010

As Nick Jordan slowly regained consciousness, he became aware of a stinging pain in his face. "Please keep your eyes closed, sir," a deep voice said from what seemed like far away, "there's broken glass on your face." He felt a hand brush debris from his closed eyelids and forehead. He could taste blood in his mouth. While the hand worked, he silently inventoried his facial bones—mandible, maxilla, zygomas, frontal sinus—and wondered if any were broken. He ran his tongue over his teeth. None seemed loose or fractured, but he could feel a cut on the inside of his cheek. He must have bitten himself during the wreck. He wondered what he had hit. He clamped his jaws together gently, and his teeth seemed to fit together normally; that was a good sign. He said a silent prayer that he hadn't hurt anybody. "That should be okay," the voice said, and Nick slowly opened his eyes.

From the driver's seat of his convertible, he saw a streetlight hanging over him at a strange angle. It was leaning badly but still lit the streetcar tracks and neutral ground of this part of St. Charles Avenue. Next to the light appeared the face of a large policeman leaning over the crumpled door of his car. He wondered if the cop could smell bourbon on his breath. Nick felt something in his right hand and with horror realized it was a prescription bottle. He fumbled to put it into his shirt pocket. It hurt to move his arm. The officer reached down and gently tucked the bottle away. Even through his mental fog, this struck Nick as strange. He saw the officer lean closer and heard him whisper, “Don’t worry, Doc. I got you.” He felt even more confused.

He struggled to release his seatbelt. The cop opened his door and helped him to his feet. Nick still felt dazed but better, and he brushed bits of broken glass from his button-down shirt and jeans. He stood up straight to his full six feet and stretched, looking around in the darkness. Traffic had slowed in both directions, as rubberneckers stared at him and his wrecked car.

Nick Jordan was fifty years old but looked younger. He had a lean, athletic build and a full head of black hair, just starting to gray near his ears. He was always amused when women called him handsome; he thought maybe it was the deep-set hazel eyes he’d inherited from his mother. He knew he must look like crap now, and the thought made him self-conscious.

Nick heard a familiar voice behind him say, “You okay, Boss?” and turned to see Lesli, his office manager, approaching him. He was shocked to see her there and taken aback by her appearance—the jeans, t-shirt, and flip-flops she was wearing were far more casual than the business suits and heels he normally saw her in.

"Lesli. What are you doing here?"

"Oh, just out for a little drive," she said, peering at him. He could see concern in her face.

"At this hour?" He looked at his watch, "it's four-thirty in the morning."

She shrugged back at him. "Only when I have to."

"You clean up nice," he said, grinning at her.

"Shut up," she said, flashing him a look, and then the concerned expression returned. "Oh, my God, look at you. You're all scratched up and you've got blood on your mouth."

Nick wiped his lips with the back of his hand. "It's nothing, just a little cut on the inside of my cheek. I think I'm okay. My shoulder hurts a little."

"Well, the EMTs are here, and they're going to check you out," she said, looking over her shoulder. "But let the policeman talk to them first." Nick followed her gaze down the grassy median where the streetcars ran, and saw the cop in what appeared to be earnest conversation with two emergency workers. He turned back to Lesli. She was on the short side; five foot three or perhaps four, slender, and attractive. Piercing black eyes, twin clues to her Sicilian heritage, rested beneath bleached-blonde bangs. She was smart and excellent at her work; over the years, Nick had come to value her fierce loyalty to him and learned to avoid her equally fierce temper. He supposed that came from her Sicilian roots. A stirred-up Lesli was like a hurricane, and in New Orleans that was never a good thing.

They were standing on the downtown section of Saint Charles Avenue, close to the Garden District, where office buildings gave way to spreading oak trees that lined the street. The policeman had finished talking with the EMTs, who now approached Nick, one of them carrying a clipboard. “Uh oh,” he whispered to Lesli.

“I think it’s okay, Boss. Just let them do their job.”

“But I’m a little over the limit. This could be bad.”

She turned and gave him a look. “I know, just relax. I’ve got this covered.”

Nick couldn’t imagine what she meant, but he greeted the emergency workers and gave them a version of what had happened in the accident. He heard himself say, “I was on my way to pick up some groceries. I had no dog food for the morning, and I need to feed my little guy before I go to work.” He knew this was an outright lie. The liquor store was his only stop that night, and they didn’t sell pet food. “…and a cat ran out in front of my car. I swerved to avoid it, and I guess I jumped the curb and hit the streetlight. It happened so fast.” Nick knew he’d hit his head and blacked out, and for a moment he considered letting them take him to the ER for a brain scan. That would be what he’d tell a patient to do, every time. But he knew he couldn’t risk it. He might end up with a drunk driving citation or worse. “But now I feel fine, really. I just want to get home.”

The man with the clipboard took notes, and neither one of the EMT’s interrupted him. When Nick was finished talking, they thanked him and asked no more questions. One of the men looked him over, suggested he ice the shoulder and keep the cut in his mouth clean with saltwater rinses, and told him to see a doctor if either injury bothered him after a few days. They wished him a good night and left. Nick looked at Lesli with relief, and she gave him a little wink.

A wrecker came for the car. The driver used a winch on the front of his truck to separate the convertible, a turbocharged BMW 1 series, from the base of the streetlight. A loud wrenching noise, like a metal rake scratching a chalkboard, made Lesli cover her ears as the car came free. Nick felt his stomach turn when he saw the damage; the hood had buckled, and the front bumper was barely hanging on. "That's going to take some fixing," he said, leaning towards Lesli and putting his head on her shoulder. "Still, I guess I was lucky."

"I know how much you love that thing," she said, patting his cheek.

At length Nick straightened up. "My own fault entirely," he said. "I'll have him bring it to the dealer's shop, and they'll give me a loaner until it's repaired, I guess."

"Sounds like a plan, Boss," Lesli said, then waited while Nick gave the tow truck driver instructions. When he returned, she gave him a little push and said, "Let's get you home. I want to get a little nap before I've got to get ready for work."

"What time is it?" He asked.

"A little after five. We see patients in three hours." She looked at him. "I'll tell you what; I'll call the early ones and push them back until later in the day. We'll start you at ten. That should give you time to get some sleep and clean up."

"I'm so sorry, Lesli." He knew she hated inconveniencing the patients. Screwing up the schedule was her pet peeve.

"Normally I would tear you a new one, but you're way too pathetic for that this morning. Just don't make a habit of it," she said, unlocking her car.

They made the quick drive through Uptown to Nick's house, passing the wrecker that was going in the opposite direction with his car attached. "Bye, baby," Nick said with a whimper. Lesli smiled.

On the way to Nick's house, she handed him a large tan-colored envelope. "I picked this up from the floor of your car," she said, handing it to him. His head hurt, and he closed his eyes. He gripped the envelope, remembering it contained his divorce papers. He supposed that was what had set him off. He knew the divorce was inevitable, but seeing it stated in print, having to sign off on it, had pushed him over the edge. He had known the pills and booze would ease his pain, and he had overindulged. When the whiskey ran out, he'd decided to get more, and his early morning run had ended in disaster.

Nick felt the car spin and opened his eyes to make it stop. He wondered for a moment if this was an effect from the accident, but knew it was more likely from the Percocet and bourbon. He felt ashamed and wanted to never take either again. The realization that he was too weak to stop made him feel worse.

They reached a stoplight and Lesli turned off St. Charles onto State Street. It was still dark and very quiet. The substantial Victorian houses looked peaceful with just a porch light here and there to illuminate their front doors and steps. She dropped Nick off on the driveway of his house. A gas lamp near the sidewalk threw a faint light on his face, which accented the scratches. She winced, then her look softened as she said, “I’m glad you’re okay. Get a little rest, hear?”

“I will. Thanks so much for tonight. I’ll get my act together, you’ll see.” Nick gently closed the car door and turned away. Before she could drive off, he ran back and knocked on a window. She lowered it and he leaned in to ask her, “You never answered my question. How in the world did you know to be there?”

Lesli laughed, “I was wondering when you’d get around to asking me that. So smart and yet so dumb.” She raised the window and pulled away, leaving her boss confused.

2

Much later that morning, Nick leapt up the stairs that lead to his office two at a time; not with boyish enthusiasm today, but from force of habit. He lingered on the front porch for a moment and composed himself, as he had done each day for the last several months. He made slow, circular motions with his arm, trying to work out the soreness in his shoulder. He knew he would have to function at a high level, and do so cheerfully. He took the anxiety and fear that he constantly carried around these days and pushed it all to a corner of his mind; he could deal with it later. He had always been good at compartmentalizing. He'd been doing it for a long time now and knew he'd have to keep it up. If something had to give, it sure as hell wouldn't be him. *At least not here*, he thought. He was never allowed to have an off day.

Before entering, Nick once again admired details of his office's workmanship. He considered the porch he stood on to be spectacular. He looked up at perfectly preserved mahogany slats bound in intricate curlicue molding that gleamed above him. They ran at angles to a colorful mosaic of small tiles, laid carefully and expertly 150 years ago, that formed the floor. The beauty of the place had always impressed him. His office occupied an 1850's era mansion on St. Charles Avenue, his favorite street in the world. *Still my favorite street* he reflected, remembering last night's fiasco a few blocks down. Opening the crystal-cut glass door, he stepped into a large and unexpectedly modern waiting room.

The woman at the front desk looked up at him expectantly. "Good morning—right on time, as usual," Ginger said with a sarcastic smile. The smile vanished as she saw the cuts, coated in shiny antibiotic ointment.

"Good Lord, what happened to your face?" she asked cocking her head to the side. The motion made her elaborate hair bun shift dramatically. Nick grinned at her. "A little trouble shaving," he said, "but you look nice."

She smiled; she always liked to be complimented on her appearance. Ginger was tall and, Nick thought, rather glamorous, with lustrous brown hair that featured a wide streak of blonde swirling up from above her right eyebrow. He knew she had a tendency to gossip and could at times be quite judgmental. But when it came to the office and its patients, she was perfectly discreet and kept her opinions to herself, at least while the patients were there. She dressed in well-tailored, expensive clothes that were always a little provocative and flattered her excellent figure. She was in her early 40's and had modeled and done some acting in her youth. She stood up to look at him more closely; she was a little taller than Nick in three-inch work heels. There was a flirty intelligence in her large brown eyes as she silently evaluated him. Nick remembered his mother describing one of her friends as "not book-smart but shrewd," and thought that the characterization fit Ginger nicely. "You're not going to tell me what happened, are you?" she said, arching a perfectly manicured eyebrow.

Nick hung his head in mock shame. "Not to worry. And I'm sorry to hold you up this morning," he said. "I was born twenty minutes late, and I never made it up. But starting two hours late is ridiculous." He gave her a warm smile and turned towards the long hallway that led to his office.

On the way, he looked into Lesli's office to say hello. "She'll be here soon; she's running a little late today too," Ginger called after him.

"I understand," he replied, continuing up the hall.

The spacious hallway was part of what had once been a grand home. The ground floor featured ten-foot ceilings topped off with impressive crown moldings. Most rooms contained fireplaces surrounded by carved marble mantles. He had installed an elevator and state-of-the-art operating rooms on the second floor. Using a talented interior decorator for guidance, Nick had chosen mainly antique furniture and mostly contemporary art for the office. To him this symbolized a coming together of old and new—a metaphor for what had happened to the building, and, for that matter, what happened daily in his practice.

He took off his coat and looked at the schedule. A full boat today. That's what he wanted, of course, but he knew it would make for a long day. He'd be on stage for eight hours. He pressed a button on his phone that got him the front desk. "Ginger, could I please have a coffee? A *grande* today, I think." Ginger would know that *grande* meant he hadn't gotten enough sleep last night. Most days she went to Starbucks to fetch him the life-giving fluid. This was an office ritual; Nick always ran a little late, and after he arrived, she would walk the two blocks to get his coffee. He knew she enjoyed the brief trip, especially on nice days like today.

"I'll go get it as soon as Lesli comes in," she said through the intercom, and he thanked her.

Nick walked down the hall to the first exam room and saw Sandra sitting in the big chair looking at a magazine. He smiled, relieved that he'd start his day with her. She was a pretty strawberry blonde with a warming smile that relaxed him immediately. He gave her a little hug and sat down on a rolling stool with her chart.

"What happened to you?" she said, registering alarm.

"I was in a fender-bender last night; no big deal, really, but I came away with a few scratches."

He could see she was concerned. "Thank goodness it wasn't worse."

He patted her hand. “I’m fine, really, I am. But what about you? How are we going to make you even more beautiful today?” he asked.

She laughed—a lovely tinkling sound—“Just some Botox, I think.”

“Okay.”

“So other than car wrecks, how’s life treating you, Nick?”

He knew she was referring to life after Elizabeth. “It’s getting better,” he replied, “I’m just glad to start the day with you. What’s Dave up to?” Dave was one of Nick’s best friends. They’d been at college together and kept in close touch while Nick endured a decade of medical training. Dave had gone to business school and then founded a successful real estate development company. He had a reputation as a fierce competitor in business but was a lot of fun to be with—a bit on the goofy side in fact. Nick knew that marrying Sandra was the best move his friend had ever made.

She smiled and sighed, “Working his butt off as usual. He just got back from China.”

“Ah, yes, our Dave is a captain of industry. Tell him we need to get together for scotch, soon. He’s one of my oldest friends, and I never get to see him anymore.”

“Oh, you’ll be seeing him soon,” she said, suppressing a smile.

Nick gave her a quizzical look. “Is something up?”

She shook her head and turned an imaginary key to lock her lips together, then threw it away.

"Hmmm. Well, let's focus on you today. Show me what you can do with your forehead. How about a frown?" Sandra complied, creating tiny branching lines between her eyebrows. "Good, now raise your brows like you're surprised." Three horizontal lines appeared across her forehead as the brows arched up. "And how about a squinty smile?" Sandra wrinkled her nose at him and scrunched up her eyes, causing tiny wrinkles to radiate across her temples.

"Well, they're not bad yet, but we don't want to let them get that way, do we?" Nick said, taking a small glass vial from a countertop. He drew up a syringeful of clear fluid and attached a tiny needle to it. He asked Sandra to repeat the forehead movements again and injected the liquid at intervals along the lines and folds, raising tiny red bumps.

"That always stings, dangit," she said, when he finished.

"I know from experience it does. Do you remember that the first person I did it to was me? That time I did half my forehead in the mirror, and I looked like I'd had a minor stroke for two weeks? I had to do the other side, just to even it out."

She giggled, "I do remember that. Why in the world did you do that to yourself?"

Nick thought back to that time; Botox had been used to treat wrinkles in Europe for years, but was new for that purpose in the United States. Injecting himself in the mirror had been painful and awkward; the needle seemed to go in the wrong direction as he moved it. After a few days the medicine had taken effect. Elizabeth hadn't noticed so he brought the change to her attention. He remembered she laughed and told him he looked cock-eyed. Served him right, he had supposed. His mind returned to the present. "I just wanted to see if it worked before I put it into a patient."

Sandra laughed. "I call that going the extra mile, Nick." She drew a little closer. "Now remember this is our little secret. Dave doesn't like it when I treat myself to your services."

"I've never understood that," Nick answered. "He's strange that way."

She nodded. "In other ways too," she said, then rose and gave him a hug and bustled down the hall to check out with the ladies up front.

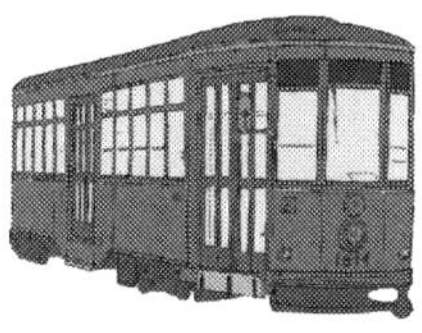

3

Lesli and Ginger had been with him eight and six years respectively, and he treasured them. They were not only excellent at their jobs, but were also great friends to each other and Nick. They helped make the office a happy place. Ginger met him in the hall, her bright green nail polish contrasting nicely with the white paper coffee cup. "Thanks, you're a lifesaver," he said, and sipped foam from the top of his mocha.

The busy Monday morning wore on. Nick went from room to room efficiently, giving each patient the time they needed, thankful for the surge of energy given him by two shots of *espresso*. He saw a fresh post-op facelift patient and showed Greg, the practice's new medical assistant, how to take out some, but not all, of the stitches behind her ears.

When he had finished seeing the patients in his morning schedule, Nick entered a large room near the back of the hallway, lined with floor to ceiling bookcases. He reached behind a row of books to where he'd concealed a stack of prescription pads. In doing so he accidentally knocked over a small wooden picture frame and took a moment to look at it as he picked it up.

The photograph had been taken in front of the big tree at Rockefeller Plaza in New York several years ago. It was Christmas time, and he and Elizabeth had been shopping up and down Fifth Avenue on a windy, cold afternoon. Their cheeks were flushed in the photo, and they were holding hands as they always did back then. They looked happy—*really* happy. Nick sighed and sat down. It used to be so easy between them, so natural, he reflected.

Still, he remembered, there had been things about her that annoyed him even then. On that day, they'd been shopping together, and, as always, Elizabeth just seemed to disappear, leaving store after store without telling him, as if she weren't even with him. Then he would have to search the adjacent shops until he found her. It made him feel like she didn't care about him; like he was just an accessory, taken for granted. He had chalked this behavior up to her ADD, knowing that the moment she became bored with where she was or saw something that attracted her, she was gone.

He also knew that her carefree mindset was one of the things he loved about her. It made her fun and free in a way that other women were not. He loved her so much at the time that her lack of consideration simply didn't matter to him. She had been more than worth it. Nick wondered if, on some level, he could have known even then that her love for him was not as deep as his for her. He took a deep breath and carefully tucked the photo back behind the books, where he wouldn't have to see it, then turned to write the prescription.

Nick brought the script up to the front desk and then returned to his private office to check email. There were the usual investment newsletters, messages from medical societies, and one from a Nigerian banker who wanted his assistance moving large sums of money out of his country. Nick continued scanning down his in-box list and found an email from Fiona Espinoza. *Hmmm.* He leaned back in his chair and thought of Fiona for a moment. In his eyes, she was basically the perfect woman: gorgeous and brilliant with a great sense of humor to boot. She was an excellent dermatologist, and over the years they had worked together as close colleagues, sending patients to one another whenever they could. He trusted her as a doctor and admired her as a person. He wondered what she could want. He found her email, went directly to it, and clicked:

From: Fiona Espinoza DrEspinoza@NewOrleansDermLaser.com
To: Nick Jordan MD
Re: Interesting email

Hey Nick—I saw this online. I have to say I was surprised. I know you've been through quite a lot lately, and frankly it just doesn't sound like you. Are you okay? I'm available to talk any time you need to.

Hang in there, Fiona.

What the hell? Nick thought, and scrolled down from her email to find the message he had sent to her. There it was, written at 5:32 AM. It looked like a Match.com profile but without some of the graphics. Then with a sickening feeling, he remembered doing something on his computer at home the night before. Unable to sleep after the car wreck, he had been online, and he *had* been trying to sign onto the dating site. There had been lots of questions to answer and he now recalled typing in his credit card information. In a panic Nick read what he had written:

NJMD_NOLA	Move Photo Here
His details	
Relationship:	Divorced (almost)
Have kids:	No
Wants kids:	No (not anymore)
Ethnicity:	White / Caucasian
Body type:	Athletic and toned
Height:	6' (183cms)
Faith:	Jewish (light)
Smoke:	No
Drink:	Moderately

Nick digested the introduction to his profile. The name he had given was a dead giveaway. How many doctors with the initials NJ could there be in New Orleans? "*Ugggh,*" he said to no one. He wished he could take back the "not anymore" after "Wants kids." It was nobody's business, and it touched a tender spot within him. The rest of the details seemed okay; "moderately" was an outright lie. He couldn't believe he had done this. He read on:

In his own words:

I'm a nice guy whose looking for a great woman to be with. My ex totally screwed me over and left me after being unfaithful. the bitch. I just want to have fun with being with a woman again. Just to be looking forward to being with her. Going out to dinner or whatever. And since I a aplastic surgeon looks are important to me. I need an attractive woman. It's the truth. But most of all I need someone nice and honest who won't screw me over.

Nick cringed. Aside from the drunken grammatical mistakes, the words embarrassed him to his bones. He sounded bitter and needy. And stupid. He didn't consider himself a bitter person, but he also knew he hadn't been the best version of his true self these days. *Maybe deep down I am that guy right now*, he thought. If he was, he certainly didn't want Fiona to know about it. *Why had he sent this to her?* He read on:

His interests	
Sign:	Sagittarius
Political views:	Middle of the road
Favorite hot spots:	Galatoire's, Rosie's Riverside Bar Bayonna
	Acme Oysster House
	Eddie Marquez's Po Boy shop
College:	Tulane University
Favorite things:	Faithful women that don't leave me
	Roquefort – my French bulldof
	Doing beautiful cosmetic surgery
Last read:	Confedracy of Dunces

Nick recognized more drunken grammatical mistakes, and what was worse, more bitterness. Feeling like he was facing a firing squad, he took a deep breath and continued to read.

Sports & exercise:
I exercise 5 or more times per week: Cycling, Football, Golf, Running, Skiing, Swimming, Tennis / Racquet sports, Walking / Hiking, Weights / Machines

Well, he thought, *that wasn't so bad.*

My idea of a great date:
We stroll together, hand and hand on the levee, looking out on the river, and have a piknic lunch and a good bottle of wine. Then I take you home and we make very passionate love. I kiss you all over bringing you to climax many times, and you do the same to me.

Nick sat up straight and stared. *Oh God, Fiona read this*? A wave of nausea hit him, and he pulled a wastebasket closer to him, in case he actually threw up. Why had he done this? And why had he sent it to her, his friend and colleague? He wondered if he wanted her on some deep level that the pills and bourbon had brought to the surface. Maybe this had been his way of reaching out to her. If so, he recognized that it was misguided and insulting. And so mortifying. He had no choice but to keep reading.

More about him		
APPEARANCE		
HIM:		WHAT HE IS LOOKING FOR:
Height:	6' 0"	5' 3" to 5' 10"
Body type:	Athletic and toned	Slender, Athletic and toned
Eyes:	Brown	Black, Blue, Brown, Grey, Green, Hazel
Hair:	Dark brown	Auburn / Red, Black, Light brown, Dark brown, Blonde, Dark blonde, Platinum

Even when drunk, Nick recognized, he knew what he liked. The height, body type, eyes, and hair were all in accordance with his sober preferences. He read on.

Lifestyle		
Smoke:	No way	No way, Occasionally

Aside from its disastrous health effects, Nick thought, smoking was an unattractive habit in women. Still, if the woman was attractive enough, he knew he could live with it occasionally.

Drink:	Social Drinker	Social Drinker, Moderately
Occupation:	Medical / Dental	Administrative /Artistic / Creative / Executive /Legal...

The list of occupations that she could have was extensive, and Nick didn't bother to read it all. He knew he really didn't care what a woman did professionally provided it was lawful, productive, and satisfied her. He liked that he hadn't divulged plastic surgery as his own profession; he recognized that the glamorous and lucrative nature of what he did might attract the wrong kind of women.

Income:	$150,001+	No preference

Well, that was probably right. He knew he could more easily relate to a woman who was out in the world making a living as he was, but recognized there could be circumstances in which a wonderful person was retired or taking a break; maybe volunteering her time or working full-time for a non-profit organization that couldn't pay her much. It dawned on him that he was looking at the profile more carefully now, and that he would most likely fix it, removing the drunken, bitter parts, and then actually post it on Match.com. Even in his current state, the thought excited him.

Relationship:	Divorced	Never Married, Widow, Divorced

Nick sat back in his chair and looked at the line. It was the first time he had seen the word "divorced" next to his own name. He considered that even in his stupor of the evening past, his mind had finally accepted the fact. That had to be a good thing. He looked at the manila envelope on his desk containing his unsigned divorce agreement. Maybe he was finally ready to sign.

Have kids:	No	Yes, and they sometimes live at home, No, Yes, and they live away from home
Want kids:	No	Probably not, No

Nick knew his responses were true, but they saddened him. What if she had kids, he wondered. *That would be kind of neat.*

He continued to read:

Background/Values		
Ethnicity:	White / Caucasian	Asian / Black / East Indian / Latina / Middle Eastern / Native American / Pacific Islander / White /Caucasian / Other

Wow, Nick thought, he was more open-minded than he knew. That was probably good; he was on the market now or soon would be, and he could cast the widest net possible. He wondered what "other" could be.

Background/Values		
Faith:	Spiritual but not religious	No preference
Languages:	English, Spanish	English

Nick found it interesting that he had put "Jewish" under his preliminary description and "Spiritual, but not religious" in the section he was reading. He had to admit that he almost never got to temple, and that Judaism was not a part of his daily life. Still, he respected his heritage. His mother, who was more observant than he was, had called him "Jewish light," and he supposed that fit. He said prayers in English every night before falling asleep and believed in a higher power. He felt he had gotten this part of the profile right last night. *In vino veritas*, he thought, smiling slightly. He knew that claiming Spanish as a language was misleading. He had taken in in school and knew only a few words and phrases.

Education:	Graduate degree	Bachelor's degree / Graduate degree / PhD / Post Doctoral

Nick realized this was a bit snooty of him but knew it was probably correct. He had spent so much of his life in school and in training that knew he had to be with someone who was well-educated.

He finished reading and leaned back again in his chair. At that moment a horrible thought occurred to him: Had he already posted this on Match.com? Maybe he had, since he remembered entering his credit card information last night. That meant that all of the singles on Match in New Orleans were reading about some asshole named NJMD. *Yikes.* He resolved to take the profile down right away and change it before re-posting.

But Fiona had written that she had received it as an email. *How the hell could that have happened*? And then with a crushing feeling, like the building was about to fall on him, Nick began to realize what had happened. The pieces of the puzzle moved into place in his mind like events in a Greek tragedy.

He must have known last night that he was drunk or high or whatever and that his writing ability was shit. So, it made sense that he would have wanted to edit it later when he was sober. He had never used Match.com before and didn't know how to edit his profile on the site, so he must have made a copy of what he had written and saved it as a document on his computer. And now, with his stomach turning, he vaguely recalled checking his email and responding to a few messages. But why had he sent the profile specifically to Fiona? *Was he in love with her?* He had been so wasted that he couldn't remember doing it.

Nick clicked on his Sent folder and scrolled down to the message he had sent at 5:32 AM. Following "To:" was a list of email addresses, beginning with the A's, which spanned seventeen pages. His profile was there as an attachment. He leaned forward, pressing his forehead against the desk and emitted a long, low whimper.

He had sent the profile to his entire address book.

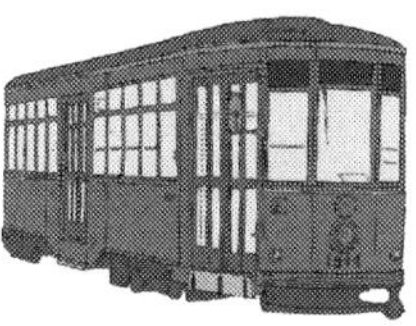

4

Late that night, Nick was in his study at home, sipping a beer and reading the *Wall Street Journal.* He looked across the room at a row of floor to ceiling bookcases, and for the umpteenth time admired the workmanship. The wood was Louisiana bald cypress that had been stained to a warm golden color and crafted into these shelves perhaps 150 years ago. The once great indigenous cypress stands were long gone from the state, but the wood they had provided endured; it had been some of the best ever harvested. Much of his house, which he treasured above most things, had been constructed from it. It's strength and beauty grounded him.

He was exhausted. The day had been an exercise in humiliation. Almost immediately after realizing what he had drunkenly done online, there had been a tapping at his office door. It was Ginger, looking like she was trying very hard not to laugh. Nick had hung his head. "You saw it in your email, huh?"

She handed over a small stack of mail and looked at him with a twinkle in her eye. "I don't know what you mean, Doctor."

Nick recalled breathing a small sigh of relief. Maybe she'd been laughing at something else. Maybe it hadn't gone through to everyone. He hoped not. He thanked her, and she turned to leave.

She had hesitated at the doorway, then said, "Maybe later we could go for a walk on the levee." Then she burst out laughing and kept on walking, not even looking back. Nick put his face in his hands and groaned.

The rest of his office staff had avoided any mention of his *faux pas*. Greg had given him what might have been an appraising look—it was hard to tell with Greg—but he knew better than to say anything. Lesli just rolled her black eyes at him and then gave him a hug; that said it all for her. Felicity, the practice's master aesthetician, giggled with her head down and eyes averted every time she passed him in the hall.

Nick figured that fully half of the patients he saw that morning must have seen the email. He hadn't realized that so many of them were in his address book. Their reactions had ranged from politely, but obviously, not mentioning his indiscretion to outright teasing. Two women said they had friends they wanted him to meet, and one brought in a printout of his profile with suggestions on its shortcomings handwritten in the margins. "*Less bitter – you're better than this*." He thanked her, wishing the floor would open and swallow him whole. The *coup de grâce* had been a call from his mother, encouraging him to keep his chin up and telling him that any girl would be lucky to have him. He had wanted to cry from embarrassment.

Nick put the newspaper aside and reached for his laptop. With a sense of foreboding, he opened his own email. There were triple the usual number of messages. Some were from friends, congratulating him on getting back out there and wishing him luck. Nick sighed. He had gone to great lengths to keep his separation and divorce a very private matter, but now, reading between the lines, he could see that the demise of his marriage was not the closely kept secret he had thought it was. He found another email from Fiona:

From: Fiona Espinoza DrEspinoza@NewOrleansDermLaser.com
To: Nick Jordan MD
Re: Interesting email

Nick – On reflection, I'm guessing that I and the three thousand other recipients received this by mistake.

OUCH! But hey, now it's out there, so go get 'em, Tiger. I mean it—call me if you want to talk,

Fiona

Nick shook his head and kept reading. He was horrified to see that many of the emails were replete with commentary on his dating likes and dislikes, hopes and dreams. *People actually thought he had sent it to them on purpose.* Two women wrote that they would be interested in going out, and one sent him a long response saying that while she thought he was a nice guy with many fine qualities, she was in a committed relationship and had no interest in dating him. Then with fresh horror, he realized that Elizabeth had gotten the email too. He moaned softly and put his face against the cool smooth wood of the desk, wishing it would all go away.

A grunting, gasping sound emanated from beneath the desk in his study. Nick knew that Roquefort must be dreaming. The mostly white French bulldog had a few dark spots; the color combination had suggested the cheese and hence, the name. Nick looked down at the pudgy animal; he was lying on his side with four stubby legs sticking straight out beyond a bulging belly. There was another loud grunt and then the legs began to twitch at once, as if Roquefort were trying to run or swim. Nick smiled and rubbed the soft belly with the toe of his shoe, reflecting that his pet looked more like a pig than a dog.

He closed the laptop and gave Roquefort a more forceful push, which woke the slumbering beast. They left the study and walked across a large, beautifully decorated living room and then through a high-ceiling central foyer to the formal dining room that he had long ago converted into his den. He turned on the big flat screen TV, and taking another sip from his beer, surfed through the channel guide until he found a movie he liked.

It was *The Quiet Man* with John Wayne and Maureen O'Hara, one of his mother's favorites. He thought about calling her to tell her it was on, but knew that she would be asleep by now. He could remember watching it with her in their house growing up.

Nick remembered the tired, patient look that his mother's face almost always wore in those days. His father had been a machine shop foreman who worked hard and late for not a lot of money, and made a practice of going out for beers most nights with the men from his work. That had left his mother with the task of looking after him and his brother and making ends meet to keep their home going. He rarely saw her happy; mostly, she seemed worried and exhausted. Being the oldest, he did what he could to bring in a little extra income and help her with the more strenuous household tasks, and he knew she loved him even more for it. He had sensed that the bond between him and his mother was strong; in many ways stronger than her ties with his younger brother and even his father.

What did bring her happiness was going to the movies. Nick recalled that she would take them to the theatre as often as she could, usually to comedies or musicals, and that on those days she'd become excited and energetic. He could remember sneaking a look at her during the movie sometimes. She seemed so much younger with the light of the screen reflected on her face. He thought, for her, it must have been the feeling of escape that worked the magic. The ultimate perfection of life in those comedies, how all the obstacles were overcome, and the heroes triumphed, and the loose ends were tied up at the finale; that produced in her a joy, almost a rapture that touched her soul and rejuvenated her features. And at those moments he wanted so badly to give her the happiness she saw on screen, so that the exhausted look would never come back. Thinking about it now, he realized that he hadn't had the power to make her life perfect; but he was certain that he had made it better.

He thought about his own life now. His marriage was over, and he was suddenly single at the age of fifty. If this were a romantic comedy a woman would appear; she'd be spunky and irreverent with a heart of gold. And beautiful—of course, beautiful. And she'd make everything right for him. He knew this was pure fantasy. He wasn't living in a movie, and he'd have to make things right for himself. He knew his life would never be perfect, but maybe he'd find a way to reconnect with all of the good there was in it. That was hard for him right now; he felt wrongly abandoned and alone.

His cell phone rang, and he looked to see who was calling so late. It was Joel of course. His younger brother had no regard for other people's need to sleep. Nick supposed that this was partly due to his lack of a schedule. Joel was currently, *no continuously*, Nick thought, between jobs. These days he got by on disability payments and what income he could make from selling magazines for a multi-level marketing outfit. The disability, a strained back, had long since healed. And, of course, he could always hit up his older brother. Nick knew Joel was calling to ask for money. It was the only time he ever heard from him.

Nick sighed and pocketed the phone, then shook Roquefort awake. The sleepy bulldog looked up at him in a disoriented way, drool spilling from a corner of his hideous mouth. "You're a mess, you know that?" Nick said, reaching down with a napkin. He turned off the television and the two of them walked upstairs to the bedroom.

An hour later, Nick sat up in bed looking at an empty wall. It was close to two AM, and he was having trouble sleeping. He reflected that this had never been a problem for him in the past; during his residency training he could fall asleep almost instantly. He had done it standing up in elevators, and even once during surgery while retracting a brain for the supervising surgeon. He glanced over at a stack of books on his bedside table; normally he read for a few minutes before turning out the lights and that did the trick. But not lately.

His bedroom was large and now looked empty to him. The movers had come and removed all of Elizabeth's things—really, *their* things that she had negotiated for and won in the divorce settlement. Aside from their large antique bed, only a bedside table and a small chest of drawers remained. Gone were Elizabeth's large dresser, the beautiful antique armoire, and the overstuffed sofa on which they had cuddled and watched TV together in happier times. Nick looked at dark rectangles on the floor, where the pieces had blocked sunlight from reaching, and thought they looked like shadows. The one bright spot was the dog; Roquefort slept on his back in his little bed; his stubby legs now extending towards the ceiling. His breathing was the only sound in the dark empty room. On the walls were more blackish squares, corresponding to paintings and photographs that his wife, *no ex-wife*, had taken with her.

He sighed and took another sip of bourbon. The Percocet was kicking in, and he knew he'd be able to sleep soon. It seemed this was the only way now. He remembered killing half a bottle of Maker's Mark last night and it not being enough. That was what had compelled him to go out so late to get more. It must have affected him, the divorce papers coming in the mail, he thought. He didn't remember hitting the streetlamp. He guessed he had just passed out. He took another sip. He knew he couldn't continue like this; it would destroy him if he did. He would have to get his act together soon. But alone in this big room, surrounded by shadows and memories of his great love that had died, he didn't feel up to it. He let the feelings of sadness and abandonment wash over him and looked straight ahead. Framed by the posts at the foot of his bed was a dark square on the wall where Elizabeth's wedding portrait had hung. He could picture it perfectly in his mind; her lips curved into a hint of a smile, her beautiful fingers rested lightly on stems of her wedding bouquet, her eyes looking straight at him. Another sip. He looked above the space to where the ceiling's crown molding met the wall. There was a distinct slant at the juncture where it should have been straight. The house was old and the wall, the roof, or both must have shifted as it settled. He squinted at the odd angle they made, coming together. It should be straight, *perfectly straight*, but it wasn't. The thought irritated Nick as his eyes closed and the empty glass rolled out of his hand, spilling bourbon onto the blanket beside him.

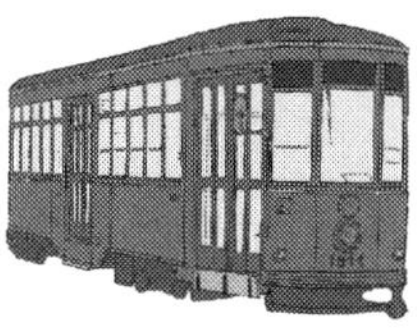

5

The next day, Nick walked to the front desk and handed Ginger a stack of notes from the morning, then went into Lesli's office. She looked up at him from a patient chart. He could tell she was surveying his face, assessing the scratches and bruises. He let out a deep sigh and collapsed into one of two chairs across the desk from her. "Well, that's the morning."

"Are people still asking you about your face? It looks better, by the way."

"Thanks. Yeah, and they're also still talking about the Match thing."

She couldn't suppress a smile. "You did have yourself quite an evening, didn't you?"

"Yup, and I am paying the price."

She looked again at the healing cuts and then into his eyes, "So how are you doing? You were in pretty bad shape the last time I saw you."

Nick nodded, "We haven't had time to talk, but I meant to thank you for everything you did. You and that cop saved my ass. How did you even know to be there?"

Lesli smiled, "You still haven't figured that out? Don't you remember my brother Robert, the guy whose chin you sewed up when he was at the police academy? They called three plastic surgeons, and you were the only one who would see him."

Nick's eyes widened, "That was him?"

"One and the same. He called me as soon as he realized it was you. He also called for the tow truck and ambulance, and then sent the paramedics away when we knew you were going to be OK."

"So that's why no hospital..."

Lesli looked at him meaningly. "Right...and no blood test, and no DUI."

"Oh my God, I owe you both, big-time."

"Happy to help, Boss. Just don't make it a habit."

"Believe me, I won't. I'm just, well, you know, I've been going through stuff with the divorce. The last papers for me to sign came the other day. She already signed them. Once I do, that's it—the marriage is dead."

"It was dead a long time ago; you know that."

He closed his eyes and nodded. "You're right. But it's still upsetting to see it in black and white. Anyway, I'm determined to get myself together. I talked with a supposedly very good therapist a while back, and she said it's just going to take a long time."

"Before?"

"Before I get over it. You know, before I'm happy again."

She looked at him and Nick could see a rare tenderness in her eyes. "Time heals all wounds, Boss. But if you ever want to talk, you know I'm always here for that."

"I know. We're doing it now. And I'm grateful to you for it."

"So, how's your car?"

"It'll be another week. I'm looking at about eight thousand bucks there."

"Will insurance help?"

He shook his head, "I could try, but it would raise my already high rates through the roof or get me cancelled. I've gotten a few speeding tickets lately."

She made a clucking noise. "I didn't know about those."

"And anyway, this was my fault, and it could have been so much worse. I could have killed somebody. I feel like I need to pay for it."

"I get it. Catharsis through financial pain." She closed the chart and leaned back in her chair. "Hey, while I've got you here, can we talk about something?" He saw her look towards the open door and recognized the cue to get up and close it, which he did.

He settled back down into the chair, "What's up?"

"It's Greg. I'm not sure he's a good fit for us."

"Really? He seems to be working pretty hard. And he's only been here a couple of months so he's still finding his feet." Nick paused, "Why, did something happen?"

She shook her head. “Nothing in particular. But he’s very odd, don’t you think?”

“Well, he’s no George Clooney, but neither am I.”

“Yes, but you’re a fairly normal, presentable human being. And you always seem to know the right thing to say.”

“And Greg?”

“Well, he’s got that high nasally voice, like he’s whining whenever he talks. It gets on my nerves. And he’s got a weird smell. I can’t put my finger on what it’s like, but it kind of grosses me out. Maybe like milk that’s just starting to go bad.”

Nick laughed. “He can’t help his voice, Lesli. And as for his… aroma, I noticed it too when he first got here. I took him aside and asked him if he showered in the morning before coming to work. He said he did. Then I asked him if he used deodorant. He told me he did that too.”

“Oh, my God. Was he offended?”

“I don’t think so. I got the impression he’s been asked those things before.”

She laughed and Nick continued. “Besides, having a medical assistant, even a slightly stinky one, is good for me. He speeds me up. When it comes to mixing the injectables, the guy knows what he’s doing. He used to do most of the injections himself where he worked before.”

“I know. I just wish we had a different guy. Forgetting about the other stuff, the way he says things pisses people off.”

"What do you mean?"

"He's kind of condescending, but not directly. It's hard to know how to take some of the things that come out of his mouth. I'm not sure if he means to be nasty or not."

Nick cocked his head toward his sore shoulder. "Can you give me an example?"

"Okay. Today he told me that I'm extremely bossy, but in a good kind of way."

Nick resisted the urge to laugh. "Well, you *are* bossy in a good way. You know that."

She flashed him a look. "Yeah, but he barely knows me. It's not his place to say that."

"Maybe he meant it as a compliment. Has he offended any of our patients?"

"Not yet that I know of. But he sure pissed off Felicity."

"Uh oh. What did he say to her?"

"He told her that an outfit she was wearing was—let me remember exactly what he said—oh yeah, he said her dress was old-fashioned, but that it suited her."

Nick rolled his eyes.

"And there's something else; his attitude. He acts like he's above everyone else. He's been okay with patients so far, but when he's talking to the staff, and that includes me, it's like he thinks it's his practice, not yours."

Nick's stomach growled, "Well, you're right; if he gets too far above himself, we might have to let him go. He might feel underused or even disrespected because I do all the filler and Botox injections here myself. But I always have. I explained that to him very clearly when I hired him."

"I remember; I was there."

"So, one of us should have a talk with him about his attitude and watching what he says. I can't have him offending our patients. Or you. And certainly not Felicity—I don't want to hear it from her. Do you want me to talk to him?"

She sighed. "No. I'm the office manager. I'll handle it."

"Ok, be firm but fair with him. If he realizes he's finally working with good people, it may instill some loyalty in him and make him a better employee."

"I will, but I want you to consider that we may have hired the wrong guy. You know you tend to hang on to people for way too long, even if they're not good for you."

He looked at her sharply, recognizing this was a reference to the lengths he had gone to trying to make things work with Elizabeth. Lesli had fiercely taken his side throughout the separation and divorce, and had no love for his ex.

"Sorry," she said, in a softer voice.

"It's ok; I know you've always got my back. But Greg's situation is completely different. He got a raw deal at his last job, and I feel sorry for the guy."

"I know you do. Have you ever thought about why?"

"What do you mean?"

"I think he reminds you of Joel."

Nick thought of his brother and nodded, "You may be right; I hadn't even thought about that. But the main reason I feel bad for him is that he got put out on the street through no fault of his own. The doctor lost his license for a year; the state medical board nailed him. The whole practice had to shut down. I think the doc is trying to start over now, but who the hell would go to him after what happened? Anyway, you can't blame any of that on Greg."

"I won't argue with you there. Imagine old Doctor Rose fondling a patient during surgery, and a male patient at that. I wonder how he got caught?"

"Didn't you hear? They were using a new anesthesia service, and the anesthesiologist saw it and reported him."

"Wow," She paused, and then said, "I wonder what their former anesthetist saw and didn't report through the years."

"What a scary thought. I hadn't even considered that."

"You know me—always looking on the bright side."

Nick shifted in his seat. "Speaking of the bright side, I hope, how are we looking for the month?"

"Good, actually" she said, opening a scheduling book on her desk to the current month. "We've got surgeries every Tuesday and Wednesday except for the fourth week." Surgeries were how the practice made the bulk of its money. Injectables helped—they brought in a steady cash flow, but were themselves expensive to buy. Still, in months when surgery was slow, Botox and facial filler treatments kept the business profitable. Nick liked to joke that they were the bar that sometimes floated the restaurant.

"That's what I want to hear," he replied, "Just get Greg in line, and all your ducks will be in a row."

"I'll cut him down to size. Not that he needs to be any shorter."

"Be nice." He grinned at her. "Just take him down a peg or two. Nobody's perfect, but he's good at what he does, and a help to me. Remember this," he said, pointing to a small bronze rectangle on the wall next to her desk. It was almost lost among the framed photographs and certificates.

The plaque read:

PERFECT IS THE ENEMY OF GOOD.

Lesli looked at it. "You know, you put that up there years ago, and I've never fully understood it. If good is good, isn't perfect better?"

"Yes, but it's a reminder that by chasing perfection, we can destroy the good. It can happen in life and in surgery."

"Are you worrying about me destroying Greg?"

Nick laughed. "A little yes, but not by trying to perfect him. We both know he'll never get there. None of us will. Not even you."

"Sure, I will."

"You're close, but no, not even you."

"So, tell me why that's hanging there."

"That plaque was a gift from my mentor, Dr. Johnson. He gave it to me the day I graduated from my fellowship with him. It's meant as a reminder that when the patient has a very good result, it's time to stop."

"I see, so you don't overdo it."

"Right. Aggressive surgeons tend to push a result too far by chasing perfection. They keep on cutting or injecting when they should put down the knife or needle. There's a fine line between a good result and an unnatural looking one."

"Lord knows you've had to undo some of the overdone ones."

"I have. The surgeon who over-operates puts his patient on a slippery slope. At the bottom of that hill is freakishness."

"Is that why so many of the Hollywood people come out looking strange?"

"Yup. It even happens to patients of very talented plastic surgeons. My theory is that the celebrities and their agents push for perfection and the star-struck surgeons get intimidated and operate against their better judgement."

"Wow. I never thought of that. Let's keep that saying up there."

Nick grinned, "I wasn't about to take it down."

"And let's both keep an eye on Greg."

"Will do," he said, rising. "I'll start right after lunch."

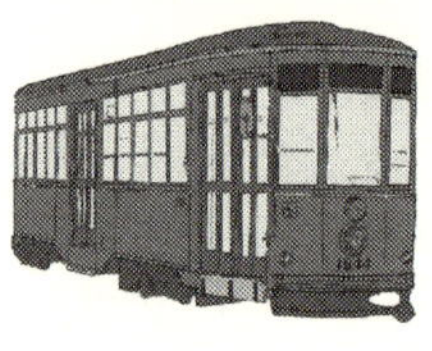

6

Back in his office after a quick bite, Nick looked over the schedule for the afternoon and smiled. Charles Monroe was his first patient. Nick always thought of Charles as a *bon vivant,* a pleasure seeker with means. Charles had sold his commercial real estate company and divorced his wife of many years some time back. Having shed those substantial encumbrances, he lived his life with the energy and zeal of a college freshman setting out on his first spring break. Nick always enjoyed talking with him.

"Now here is someone to watch out for," Nick said to Greg as they entered the exam room. Charles grinned, displaying beautiful dental work. As always, he was elegantly dressed. "Doctor, whatever could you mean?" he asked, rising to shake Nick's hand. "I'm just a mild-mannered retiree trying to enjoy some peace and quiet."

"Right," Nick said, chuckling as he pulled up a rolling stool and sat. "You know I live vicariously through your adventures. So please, Charles, tell me how you've been enjoying your peace and quiet lately."

"Well, Doc, I have to admit I did have a little adventure recently," the older man said in a mischievous tone.

Nick winked at Greg. "Here it comes." He turned back to Charles. "Don't make me beg. What have you done?"

"Well, me and a few buddies had a race."

"I didn't know you ran."

"No, God forbid," Charles laughed. "See we were in Vegas, and we rented these Lamborghinis, there were four of us."

"Go on."

"And we sort of raced from one end of the strip to the other and back. Twice."

Nick laughed out loud. "And nobody got killed or arrested?"

"No, but two of the guys got tickets, and I had a little problem with one of the fountains at Caesar's Palace. Our racecourse called for a few detours along the way. Anyway, I'm hoping insurance will help with that. You'd be surprised how expensive those cars are to repair."

Nick laughed again. "Charles, nobody I've met but you would even know what it costs to fix a damaged Lamborghini. As always, you are living the dream."

"It's the single life, Nick," he said, giving the doctor a conspiratorial smile, "and you can't beat it."

Nick looked over his shoulder toward Greg, who had wandered back out in the hall, then said in a quiet voice, "I don't know if you've heard, but I'm about to live that life again myself. My divorce goes through this week."

Charles' smile faded and he looked at Nick closely. "I did hear something about that. And I'm sorry if what I said sounded flippant. Are you alright?"

"I'm getting there. One day at a time you know."

Charles nodded. "Well, I'm going to tell you what a good friend of mine told me when I was in your shoes."

Nick met his gaze. "Which is?"

"I'm sorry… and congratulations."

Nick nodded. "I guess that covers it. I'll be okay." He cleared his throat, "But enough about me. How can I help you on this fine spring day?"

"I think, no I know, that it's Botox time. And let me know if I need any filler."

Nick performed the Botox treatment, and they made plans to inject a long-acting filler into the older man's cheek folds in a few months. "That should hold you for a while, Charles. I don't want to make you too good-looking. It would just get you into trouble."

Charles laughed and extended a hand. "You're the man, Doc."

"Well, I'm lucky to be doing something I love," Nick replied. "I don't think for one minute that I rank up there with the real doctors who save lives, but people seem to enjoy the results, and that makes me happy."

"I disagree. What you do is important—you make people feel good about themselves." The men shook hands again and Charles walked out to the reception desk.

Nick smiled, shaking his head and began to write a note in the chart. When he was finished, he turned to Greg, who was tidying up the room, "Now there's a guy who's really living life. Still having adventures."

The assistant paused, "That's kind of pathetic at his age, don't you think?"

Nick looked at him sharply. "Pathetic? No, I wouldn't say that. He went through some tough times, and now he's living large for a while. I think it's fun to see him enjoy it so much. Most people wouldn't have the energy or the nerve."

"I could see where you might feel that way," the assistant said and left the room.

7

The following afternoon, Nick was at his desktop computer, taking a short break between patients. He glanced at a few emails and pulled up the schedule. The next patient was due in five minutes: *Botox touch-up. Patient says it didn't do enough*. Following were two facelift consults booked for the same time block; probably friends coming in to talk about surgery together. Women sometimes did that. Men never did.

Nick rose and walked up the hallway to an exam room. Pausing at the door, he overheard Greg say to a patient, "I see why you're disappointed with your Botox treatment. It's really not Doctor Jordan's fault. It sometimes happened to my patients when I was doing treatments at Dr. Rose's office. But honestly, not that often."

Nick entered the room immediately, resisting the urge to tear into his assistant on the spot. There could be no doubt that he had overheard what Greg had just said. The practice's new medical assistant stared up at him unapologetically. He was a short, pale, wiry man in his forties with close-cropped red hair and a weedy moustache. His baggy gray surgical scrubs accentuated the thinness of his physique. Nick wheeled on him, his back to the patient. He gave the smaller man a look that could have melted sand and said, "I've got this, Greg. Why don't you go organize your mixing area?" The assistant shrugged and left without a word.

Nick turned and greeted the patient, a pleasant woman in her 60's. "I'm sorry about that—he's new and just learning the ropes here." He picked up a syringe from the counter and spoke in a reassuring voice, "It's always best to be conservative, especially with a first-time treatment." He carefully injected the folds running horizontally across her forehead. "If I were to do too much here and your eyebrows dropped, you'd look exhausted for 3 months. I know that's not what you come to me for."

"No, I certainly don't," she replied, in a voice that assured him that she was glad to be in his hands.

He dabbed at a tiny dot of blood above one of the brows. "That's why I wanted to see you back today, two weeks after your first treatment. I'll always do what I think you need, but if I'm off, it will be on the lighter side. That's why I do free touch-ups for patients when they need them. This way I don't have to overdo it, and you won't ever be over-treated, which I think is worse than no treatment at all. Does that make sense?" The patient agreed that it did, gathered her coat and purse, and walked out of the room with him.

Nick bid her goodbye and walked across the hall to the procedure room, where Greg was working. "We need to talk," Nick said, approaching the counter where they mixed injectables.

"Yes, sir?" Greg asked, not looking up from the small glass bottles he was arranging.

Nick pushed Greg's shoulder hard, making him turn and drop a Botox vial. "Look at me, dammit." He was towering over the assistant now, and his body language suggested imminent homicide.

Greg looked up at him, fear showing in his watery eyes. "What's the matter?" he said innocently, almost in a mocking tone.

"I know you're not stupid, so you fucking know what," Nick shouted. He had clenched his hands into fists, and for an instant the thought of crushing Greg's nose crossed his mind. He could see the bones shattering.

The tone was respectful now; Greg apparently had survival instincts, "I don't. Really."

"I think you do, but let me spell it out for you. When I hired you, I made it clear that I'm the only one in this office that does the injections. I know you did them for Doctor Rose, but that's not the way we do things here. I'm very different from your last employer. I don't fondle patients when they're asleep, and I do all the injectables myself. And my staff sure as shit doesn't talk about how much better they are at it than me in front of patients." He was still shouting. "Now do you fucking understand?"

"Yeah. Sorry."

Nick took a deep breath and backed up a step. He controlled the level of his voice with effort. "I want you to really understand, Greg. Botox and fillers are expensive for me to buy, and they only last for a few months, which means they're a significant recurring cost to our patients. That's why I do them myself. Everything in this business is about gaining the patient's trust and giving them good service and results. And in my mind getting treated by the doctor is top of the line service. Do you get that?"

"Yes, I do. I didn't try to inject her."

"I know you didn't, but you told her that you were the injector at another doctor's office. What's worse, you said you rarely got her type of complaint from your own patients. You were implying that you got better results than I do."

"I really wasn't."

"I think you were. And that makes me look bad. Can you see that?"

"Yes. I mean, if I did. I guess." Greg muttered.

Nick didn't think he was making his point. He spoke louder, looking directly into Greg's eyes. "I don't want you mentioning doing injectables yourself here, and I sure as hell don't want you talking to my patients about what goes on in other offices." He lowered his voice a bit. "You haven't been here that long, and I need you to do things right and say the right thing. If I ever hear anything like that again, you're gone. Do you understand?"

Greg met his gaze directly, "Yeah I get it," he said.

"For your sake, I hope you do. I want things to work out for you here. I'm pissed off right now, but I'll get over it."

“Thanks. I’m sorry.”

“Just don’t do it again,” Nick said. He turned towards the doorway where Lesli, hearing yelling, had appeared. She had never heard her boss shouting before and was staring at him. Nick motioned towards her. “Lesli also tells me you need to work on your behind-the-scenes communication skills. You might not mean to, but you’re offending our staff with some of the things you say. She’s going to talk to you about that.”

“I don’t know what she’s talking about,” Greg answered. He shot Lesli a puzzled look.

Nick felt the anger rising in him again. “Oh, she’ll make it clear, don’t worry. The fact is that this is my practice, not yours, and you’ll do things the way I want here.” He leaned toward Greg and tapped his chest hard with a finger. “You’d better listen to what she says and take it to heart, or you’ll be out of here like shit through a goose. Is that clear enough?”

Greg looked away and bowed his head. “Yeah,” he said softly.

“I didn’t hear that.”

“Yes, sir” the assistant said more clearly, still not looking up.

Nick had finally cowed the man and his voice was suddenly gentler. “Look, I want you to succeed here, Greg, I really do. I’ll go see the facelift consults. Why don’t you talk with Lesli, then see what we have coming up next and get ready for it?” He thought about giving the younger man a pat on the back as he left but didn't. Lesli nodded at him on his way out. She said nothing, but her black eyes burned with satisfaction.

A few minutes later, Nick returned to the procedure room. Lesli and Greg had left and were presumably having their talk. He looked for the Botox bottle Greg had mixed and then dropped. He searched everywhere, but couldn't find it.

8

Back in the hallway, Nick almost ran into Felicity, the practice aesthetician, who shot him a pirate's smile. At forty she was ten years younger than her boss, of medium height and weight, and all in all very pretty, he thought, with her auburn hair pulled back by a bright purple bow that set off exquisite blue eyes. She had been doing skincare in New Orleans for close to twenty years and was excellent at it. Her skills and exuberant personality had combined to give her a large and loyal following in the city. Although she had moved to the States right out of college, she still maintained a British accent, as if she'd never left England at all.

"Buy a girl dinner first, would you, sailor?" She said, giving him a pat on the back very close to his rump.

He chuckled. "Felicity, you know that's sexual harassment. Am I going to have to fill out another complaint form on you?"

She laughed and flashed those blue eyes at him, "Throw it on the pile, Boss." She gave his arm a squeeze. "But, hey, I did want to talk to you about the facial machine in the second room. It's on its last leg; it's time to order a new one."

Nick sighed. "OK. I'll cancel my trip to Paris next year so you can have a new toy. Would that make you happy?"

It was Felicity's turn to laugh. "Sweetcakes, I know you're good for it." She turned to walk down the hall but stopped herself. "By the way, I'm seeing your friend Dave soon."

Mark stared at her "Dave McGloughlin? For what?"

She giggled. "A facial. His wife is making him come to see me."

Nick smiled and shook his head "Sandra did that? Huh…well, Missy, you've got your work cut out for you."

"Don't worry, I can handle you boys," Felicity called back winking at him. "Not that I want to."

Nick was still grinning when he walked into an exam room and was met with a disapproving look from the woman seated in his procedure chair.

"She's certainly familiar with you, isn't she?" said Muffy Williams. Nick looked at her. Muffy was a trim, petite, and attractive woman in her early fifties. Her gunmetal gray hair was pulled back into a severe bun, and she wore the tailored slacks and sweater set that was the daily uniform of her social sphere. She was his neighbor and came from a family that had lived in New Orleans for several generations. It occurred to Nick that Muffy was pretty much the polar opposite of Felicity. "She should be more respectful."

Nick nodded. "I can see what you mean, but if you know Felicity, you know she means well. She's a lot of fun. Always makes me smile."

Muffy wrinkled her nose. "It's your office; run it as you will. I suppose it's the British sense of humor. Their television's like that too. Now about my lips…"

The rest of the afternoon went by quickly. Office days usually did, Nick thought. There was a rhythm to his day, going room to room, which he enjoyed. He was keenly aware of how fortunate he was to have chosen as his life's work something that fit him so well.

The next patient for the afternoon was Jane Meadows. She had been coming to him for years and was ten years his senior. He always thought of her as perfectly put-together; a true Southern lady, who dressed beautifully and always seemed to carefully consider what she said. Her perfectly highlighted hair was never out of place, and Nick knew that she must have been one of the most beautiful women in New Orleans in her youth. Still beautiful, he thought, just in a different way.

He entered her exam room saying, "Hello, Jane. How are you?" Nick was astounded to see her usually composed expression contract into a mask of pain as she looked away from him. He saw a tear form at the corner of her eye, and then watched it run down her face, tracking along a little furrow in her cheek. Nick felt momentarily paralyzed, like a young boy looking at something he knew he shouldn't see.

He grabbed at a Kleenex box. "Here, Jane, take some tissues." He sat down on the rolling stool in front of her. "Just breathe dear—take your time; I'm in no hurry."

She dabbed at her eyes and then gently blew her nose, making a tiny bleating sound. When she finally spoke, her voice was soft and plaintive. "Doctor Jordan, I've known you a long time, and I know I can count on you to be discreet." Her eyes were glassy with brimming tears.

Nick nodded. "Of course you can, Jane."

The words rushed out, "Alan's leaving me. He told me this morning." She sobbed for several seconds and then took a deep breath before speaking again. "I'm sorry."

Nick patted her hand. "There's no need to apologize."

"It's just that I had this appointment with you, and I figured I'd come anyway."

"I'm glad that you did."

She paused to dab at her eyes again with the tissue. "It happened out of the blue. We've been married 32 years." She tried to smile at him. "I guess I can use a lift now more than ever."

Nick wanted desperately to reassure her. "I'm so sorry, Jane. This must be a big shock." He moved closer and patted her shoulder; he didn't know what else to do. "Do you want to talk about it? You're right, you know; you can trust me not to say anything to anyone."

She sighed. "He just met somebody, and now he's in love. She's younger, of course. Much younger. And he's got his mind set. He says he respects me, but he doesn't love me anymore. And he wants out."

They were quiet for a while, and then Nick said softly, "Jane, this is not the first time I've seen this. Believe me, in my line of work, I've witnessed it quite a few times; watched it happen to women and to men. And sometimes a marriage can survive something like this, if that's what you both want."

"I don't know what I want."

"I understand. I'll do anything I can to be of help—you know that, right?"

Jane sniffed and looked into his eyes. "You're very kind; thank you." She straightened up in the chair. "I was thinking on the way over here that since things are this way, maybe it's time that I fixed myself up. I'd love to deal with this darn turkey neck," she said, touching the loose skin under her chin.

Nick shook his head gently. "Now's not the time, Jane."

"But why?"

"First of all, you look great; you always have. And second, I'll help you with that at the right time if you want me to." He took her hand again. "But, Jane, please let me help you now as best I can. You're going through something extremely emotional, which makes now the worst time to have elective surgery. This is not cancer; it doesn't have to be done tomorrow. Going through a facelift would put additional stress on you, and you don't need that now." He released the hand.

"I can't believe you talk your patients out of surgery," she said, smiling a little.

He returned the smile, "I'd go broke doing that all the time, but I try to do the right thing for each patient at the right time. And now is not that time for you."

"Because I'm an emotional wreck?" she said, and the pain was back into her voice. He looked in her eyes and recognized a kind of pitiful anguish, like she could break at any moment. "I can't help it. I just feel so…betrayed."

Something inside of Nick responded powerfully as the word "betrayed" seemed to echo in his head. He felt anxiety, like the worst kind of heartburn, rising in his chest. He spoke quickly. "Look you're not a wreck, okay, but you are emotional right now which is completely understandable."

"I know," she said quietly.

Nick was silent until he felt his composure return to him. At length he said gently, "And there's another reason that surgery's not a good idea now. One that you probably haven't considered."

"What's that?"

"If you do end up getting divorced, the lawyer on the other side could use the fact that you had cosmetic surgery against you. I've seen it happen. He could say that it was a frivolous thing to do with assets that hadn't been divided yet. And worse, he'll say that you're obviously not really upset or affected by the end of your marriage, since you're off getting a facelift. Like you don't have a care in the world. Trust me Jane, I know what I'm talking about. Now is not the time."

She gave a little sigh, and then smiled. "I didn't think of all of that, but, of course, you're right. Thank you for advising me so well at your own expense."

"This is about you, not me," Nick said, rising. "And I want you to know I'll be here when you need me. In the meantime, Felicity can do some skincare, and I can do minor treatments to help you maintain your considerable beauty and feel a little better if you'd like."

"You saying I have considerable beauty makes me feel better already."

He chuckled. "Just stating a fact. And I've got one more idea; my own masseuse is just down the street, and she gives a great massage, which I highly recommend. I defy you to feel tense after she's done with you. You've been a wonderful patient through the years, so I'm going to treat you to one."

Jane dabbed at her nose with the tissue once more and stood, finding a small trash can to throw it in. "Doctor... May I call you Nick? You're a true friend. And at a time like this—I can't thank you enough."

"Of course you can, and it's my pleasure," he said, giving her a little hug. She gathered her things, and he walked her out.

Nick instructed Ginger to arrange a massage for Jane, and then returned to the exam room to write a quick note in her chart:

Patient with aging face concerns, discussed possible facelift in future. Have agreed to defer due to her current emotional state. Return for skincare and injectables as desired.

He looked at what he had written. Given what Jane was going through her emotional state was perfectly normal, he thought. At least she was letting some of it out; he'd been surprised in how forthcoming she'd been with him. Nick had kept his problems and all the anguish that went with them to himself. He'd shared some with his friend Eddie, but except for that he'd kept it all bottled up.

Nick thought about what a bastard Jane's husband had been. To dump one's life partner, the person he'd raised kids with, for a younger model was unforgivable. Jane had used the word *betrayed* and it fit. The one person who had promised before God and the world to love her forever had thrown her away like garbage. Was there anything worse than betrayal, than being hurt so badly by the one you trusted the most; the one who had sworn to honor and protect you?

He felt anxiety, like a tide, rising within him again and took a deep breath to dispel it. He was used to these waves of feeling by now. He'd experienced them throughout his separation from Elizabeth, but this one was stronger. Nick felt overcome by a certain realization that something terrible was happening. He tried to shake it off by standing up, but the feeling wouldn't go away. He felt light-headed, as if he were rising from bed too fast after a night of heavy drinking.

Nick sat back down on the stool. Something was definitely wrong. He suddenly noticed that he couldn't feel his hands. The chart fell from them onto the floor, making a surprisingly loud noise. Lesli appeared in the doorway, attracted by the sound as she passed by in the hallway. "You throwing things, Boss?" she asked playfully, then looked at his face.

"Oh my God, what's wrong? You're white as a sheet."

Nick was breathing fast and sweating. "I don't know. I was feeling fine, and then I don't know."

She came forward and put two fingers on his neck. Beneath them his pulse raced. "Do you have any heart trouble that I don't know about?"

"No," he said, gasping for air. It scared him that his chest was hurting. "I'm in good shape. Always pass my physicals. EKG's have been perfect."

She could feel he was sweating. She went across the hall and got two icepacks, then returned and put one on the back of his neck. "Does that feel better?"

He nodded and tried to control his breathing. "I just got this feeling, like something horrible was going to happen."

"Impending doom?"

He nodded, “Exactly.”

After a few seconds she said, “Boss, have you ever had a panic attack before?”

“No.”

“Well, I’ve seen them. My dad used to get them. They look a lot like this.”

Nick didn’t say anything. His head was bent down to his chest and his eyes were closed.

“Just try to breathe a little deeper and slower.” She moved the icepack to his forehead, and he straightened up on the stool a little. She noticed his color was better. “That’s it. Nice and easy.”

They stayed like that for a while, and gradually Nick felt better. At length he sagged back against the cabinet and let his head rest against the countertop. The light-headed feeling was gone, but now he felt nauseated. He opened an eye and looked at Lesli. “I guess I’m your patient now.”

She smiled, “Your color is better. Just take it easy. Did something happen to upset you?”

He nodded, bumping his head. “I think it was Jane Meadow’s situation. Her husband left her, and she was just so hurt, and I think it affected me.”

“That’s right—you just saw her.”

“Yup. And she just got dumped hard. I guess my mind went back to all the pain I had with Elizabeth. How hard I tried to save it. How frustrating and sad it was; like I was trying to breathe life into something dead. And I ran out of breath."

She patted him on the forehead. "Why don't you go back to your office and rest? There are just a couple of patients left, and I'll reschedule them; tell them you've been called away on an emergency."

"I know how much you hate doing that."

"I do. But you're in no shape to see them right now."

"Thanks."

"Don't mention it. But get some help, okay? A therapist or something?"

He raised his head and looked at her. "After couples therapy, I've had enough of therapists to last me a lifetime. Anyway, Eddie is kind of my therapist now."

She rolled her eyes, "The prince of po-boys is your therapist? Then we are in big trouble. But seriously, if that's not enough, get some help. There are medicines, you know, antidepressants and stuff. And maybe get your heart checked too. Just to be sure."

He got to his feet, slowly and said, "I hear you, Lesli." They left the room together. He knew what the problem with his heart was.

9

Nick drove his newly restored convertible under the spreading oaks of Saint Charles Avenue. He had made it through the remainder of the afternoon without another panic attack and was looking forward to meeting his friend Eddie Marquez for a cold beer, probably several. As he headed uptown towards the neighborhood known as Riverbend, he saw the stately stone buildings of Tulane University lined up on his right. Gibson Hall was the centerpiece and nestled behind it was the law school, where Elizabeth worked. Whoever she was screwing worked there too.

Nick found parking in a shell lot across the street from Rosie's. Rosie's Riverbend Bar stood in a run-down part of the city that was experiencing a slow and fitful renewal. It was a quiet neighborhood where tourists rarely ventured. Most of the buildings were small, single-story homes and businesses. The houses were all different and many were charming in their own way. They were too small and close together to permit driveways and garages. The bars and stores were old and had crushed oyster shell parking lots that crunched when you walked on them.

Inside, Rosie's looked like most old New Orleans bars. The large main room featured a long bar on one side and a column of brown vinyl booths against the opposite wall. Tables with red and white checked cloths occupied the middle. The walls were decorated with football memorabilia; LSU, Tulane, and Saints posters hung everywhere. Bumper stickers, license plates, and Mardi Gras beads occupied the spaces in between. Wide wooden planks weathered from the footfalls of a century of patrons formed the floor, and the ceiling was a sea of stamped tin squares punctuated by slowly turning ceiling fans. The place was filling up, and the energetic vibe felt good to Nick.

Eddie was at the bar playing a trivia game for twenty-five cents on an electronic console. Nick pulled out the stool next to him and sat down. "Hey there, buddy," Eddie said, not looking away from the screen. "What was the name of the girl who played Mary Ann on Gilligan's Island? Was it Natalie Schafer?"

Nick signaled the bartender for a beer "No, Dawn Wells. Natalie Schafer was Lovey. You want oysters, Eddie?"

"Yeah sure. Damn, you're right. Game over—I win."

Eddie swiveled away from the console, picked up his beer, and grinned at his friend. Eddie Marquez was a short, thick balding man of about 50 with an infectious smile and a voice loud enough to easily carry over the din of the crowded room. Nick had met him almost seven years ago, when Eddie, enormously intoxicated after enjoying a Saints victory, had fallen off a concrete staircase at the Superdome and fractured his cheekbone. Eddie owned a popular po-boy shop in the Garden District, and, as it turned out, had excellent medical insurance. Nick first met Eddie in the emergency room at Tulane Hospital and brought him to surgery, where he screwed three titanium plates into Eddie's face. They had become friends during the recovery. Nick discovered that despite his impulsiveness and overindulgence in women and drink, Eddie was highly intelligent and had a philosopher's soul. This put him in sharp contrast to most of the trauma patients he had met through the years. Nick also learned that Eddie was a distant relative of Tommy Robichaux, a friend and colleague he had trained with in San Diego. Eddie reminded Nick of Tommy in many ways, and the association reinforced their bond.

The two shook hands. "Where y'at, doctor?" Eddie said, with a heavy New Orleans accent that could only belong to a life-long resident of the Crescent City. Nick looked up at the bartender. "I'll have an Abita, and let's get a dozen oysters to start." She nodded and was gone.

"So, Nick, are you a Ginger man or a Mary Ann guy?" Eddie asked, taking a long sip from his mug.

Nick laughed. "Well, growing up I was definitely a Mary Ann guy. At least I thought she was the type of girl I wanted to marry. But I always had a thing for Ginger too; especially when she got all sexy around Gilligan and made him do whatever she wanted. I guess you could say I was conflicted. How about you?"

"I would have liked them both, especially at the same time. The answer to my thirteen-year-old dreams!" Eddie howled slapping the bar counter with an open palm. His face became more serious. “So how are things going with you?”

Nick took a long drink from the icy mug that had appeared before him. “The divorce papers came in the mail. I’ve been carrying them around with me. I can’t bring myself to sign them yet.”

Eddie nodded slowly. “You’ll get there, my friend. It takes time. Believe me, the first one is the hardest. By my second divorce I couldn’t wait to sign the damn papers.”

“I guess you’re right. But, man, I never want to go through this again.”

Eddie took another sip from his beer, “Look, you guys did couples therapy and gave it your best shot. Were you ever able to figure out what happened?”

“I don’t know—sort of. Faults on both sides and that kind of thing. The therapy was doomed from the start. Nothing was going to move her dial.”

Eddie gave Nick a contemplative look. “I also remember when you two used to be all over each other. The first time you came into my shop, I thought I was going to have to turn the hose on you to make you behave.”

Nick hunched over his glass, peering into it. “I’ve thought about it a lot, of course. I think at some point I just lost her. And it really could have been a long time ago – I don’t know. I mean, we’d had our ups and downs just like in any marriage. There were times when I was working really hard and couldn’t give her the time or energy I should have. And when she got really stressed out at work or home she got mean, *really* mean, to the point where I couldn't stand to listen to her or be around her. Stuff like that. But then after a while the clouds would always lift, and we'd be having fun again."

"Believe me, I know," Eddie said. "I've had those ups and downs in three different marriages. It's made me the penniless bachelor I am today."

Nick shook his head. "I can't even imagine what you've been through," he said. "But you know, I always thought we could recover from the downs. I know I did. But Elizabeth couldn't. Something deep inside her wouldn't let it happen. She says she can't even remember what it felt like to love me. She can't access those feelings."

"Really?"

"Yeah. And I remember exactly how I felt when we were dating, but Elizabeth can't. Even the therapist had never heard of that." Nick looked up from his beer. "At some point along the way, she put me on the other side of a wall, and once I was there, I couldn't get back over, no matter what I did. I stayed on my side of that wall for as long as I could, waiting for her to come around. But she never did."

"So, did you do everything you could think of? Pulled out every stop?" Eddie asked, putting down his beer.

"I really think I did, Eddie. I failed. And it's still tearing me up. I practically passed out from anxiety today."

"You did?"

"Yeah. Lesli said I had a panic attack. She says her dad used to get them, so she knows what they're like."

"Damn. Are you okay now?"

"Uh-huh. Between talking with you and the beer starting to take effect, I'm feeling pretty good."

"I'm glad. And I know what your problem is."

"Do tell."

Eddie looked him in the eye. "You haven't failed before. You're a straight A student, BMW driving, world class plastic surgeon with an eight handicap at golf. And now something in your life has gone down the tubes, and you have no idea how to handle it."

"You're probably right."

"Let me tell you this, my friend," Eddie said, giving Nick's shoulder a squeeze, "You're going to have to realize that you haven't failed. It takes two people for a marriage to work. And I believe you did everything you could to make it right." He took a swig of beer with his free hand. "It's a dance, you see. And if your partner can't keep dancing, it's not your fault. If you pick her up, throw her over your shoulder, and carry her around, then you're doing it all by yourself. It's not a dance anymore."

"I know."

"You haven't failed. You did what you could, brother. It's out of your hands."

Nick looked at him "You know, you're right. And I guess the feeling of failing at something so important, really the most important thing, messes with my ego, big-time."

"Of course."

They were quiet for a moment, drinking their beers. Eddie turned to his friend. "So, are you still taking the pills?"

"Yeah"

"You know that's not a good long-term solution. It leads to bad things."

"I know. I think I kind of hit bottom the other night." Nick told him about the car wreck.

Eddie shook his head. "Listen, I know you're in pain, but prescription pain pills and booze are just going to make that pain worse."

"I know. I'm working on it."

"Work hard, man. You can lose everything going down that road."

"I will."

"Good. And besides, you know she's in pain too, right?"

"I guess. She never shows it."

"Uh huh. Well, let me tell you, cheating on your spouse and breaking up your marriage is not something you overlook. It weighs on you. It weighed on me at the end of my first marriage. Still does today."

"You never told me you cheated."

"Well, I did. And at first it was great—the freedom, the fucking pleasure of it. But the pleasure is fleeting, and the guilt builds up. It built up in me until I couldn't hardly function."

Nick drained his glass. "I wonder if Elizabeth feels that kind of guilt."

Eddie pushed both of their empty glasses across the bar. "You'll never know, but I bet she does."

Nick looked at him. "I hope she does. She deserves to feel that."

"Yes, she does."

"And you know, there's also a feeling of loss. We had something really great that I'll never get back. I think that's what I was fighting so hard not to lose. The possibility of getting it back."

Eddie nodded. "We all have to deal with loss—you can't get around that. But the good news is that time makes it better. Always. It's the great healer."

Nick smiled. "And I know a thing or two about healing."

"That you do, pal."

The oysters arrived on a dented aluminum platter accompanied by two fresh beers. Nick picked one up. "You're a good friend, Eddie. I guess I'll be all right in time. But it's too late for these poor fellows."

Eddie laughed and they dug in.

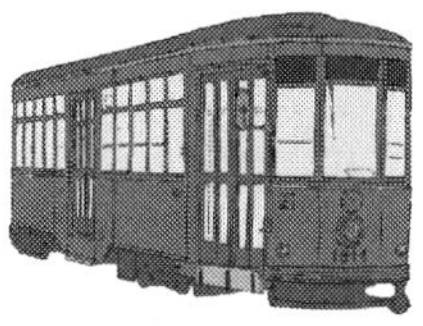

10

The following morning broke clear and sunny. Nick parked behind his office and then walked around to the front of the building, along a brick path lined with ferns and azaleas. Ginger looked at him with surprise as he entered the large reception area. Sunshine glinted on a dangly purple and gold earring that reached almost down to her shoulder. "Fifteen minutes early and you got your own coffee! Is the world coming to an end?"

"No, I don't think so. This morning's just an aberration, that's all."

"So, I still have job security?

He smiled at her. "You know you do," he said and headed back to his office. Nick tossed his briefcase on the desk and opened it revealing a stack of papers. At the top of it was the large Manila envelope. He felt a momentary sense of dread and then re-opened it and removed a thick stack of white papers. He read the first line:

Divorce Decree – State of Louisiana

He sat down behind his desk and read the first page again, then flipped to the last, where a blank line awaited signature by a judge from the Civil District Court of Orleans Parish. At the bottom was the state seal, which featured a mother pelican in her nest, feeding her young. He fished an old Montblanc pen out of his pocket and signed on the line next to the seal. The baby pelicans didn't look up from their meal.

It was official; he was getting divorced. He sat back in his chair and took a deep breath. There was no going back. The good, *no great*, old days with Elizabeth, maybe the best days of his life, would never return. But deep down he knew this was for the best; that it had to be. And when he searched his feelings, he was surprised to find that he wasn't more upset. This moment had been a long time coming. He'd been carrying the envelope around for weeks. He was grateful not to feel the panicky feeling, and thought that maybe his conversation with Eddie had helped him.

He looked back at the birds in their nest. The words UNION, JUSTICE, and CONFIDENCE surrounded them. Well, his union was at an end. He saw no justice in the failure of his marriage, but at least he was trying to get his confidence back. *One out of three ain't bad* he thought and smiled to himself.

What struck him was how anticlimactic this was—just a few sheets of paper telling him he was divorced, like an announcement that he'd been gifted enrollment in a fruit of the month club. There'd been no trips to court, no judges banging gavels, just this. He felt grateful for the lack of drama. He and Elizabeth had chosen the collaborative approach to their divorce, and that had been the way to go.

Nick carefully replaced the sheaf of papers into the envelope, sealed it shut, and pushed the intercom button on his phone. "Ginger, could you please ask the staff to meet me in Lesli's office in five?"

"It shall be done, my lord," was the response from the speakerphone.

Five minutes later he walked down the hall and found Lesli sipping coffee and chatting with Felicity and Ginger. Greg appeared just behind him in the hall and the two men entered the room.

"Thanks for coming everybody. I want to talk with you all before the patients get here."

Nick sat on the edge of Lesli's desk and looked at them all quietly for a moment. Greg slouched against the wall near the door behind him. Ginger returned Nick's look with mock alarm. "What's up? Am I getting fired?"

He smiled. "We already went over that today. Not a chance."

"I don't know," Ginger replied, turning to Lesli. "He got his own coffee today. Maybe he doesn't need me anymore."

Nick shook his head and then looked at the women sitting before him. "Nope, I love you all, and you're not going anywhere. But I do need to tell you what's happening." He took a deep breath.

"You're scaring me, Boss," Felicity said, scanning his face for clues.

“No reason to be scared. It’s just this: I know patients ask all of you about my personal life. Up until now, the party line has been that Elizabeth and I have separated.” He glanced down at the envelope in his hand. “That’s changed. These are the divorce papers, and I’ve just signed them. Elizabeth already did. So, it’s official. We’re divorced.” No one spoke for several seconds. The women looked at Nick with concern.

Lesli spoke up, “It happens, and I think it’s usually for the best.” She looked at Ginger and Felicity. “Two out of three of us have been through it; me twice. Life goes on. And you know we’re here for you.”

“Whatever we can do, Sweetcakes,” Felicity chimed in.

“That’s right,” Ginger added. “We’re your work family.”

“You all are tremendously kind,” Nick said “I knew I could count on you. One thing I need you all to do is to keep this as quiet as possible. No need to feed the gossip machine even more. Especially after my email fiasco.”

The three women smiled at each other and had the grace not to laugh.

“You know,” Lesli said, rolling her eyes, “once it does get out that you’re officially divorced, even more of the patients are going to be in love with you. They’re going to be all over you.”

Felicity made a growling cat sound. “He’s not half bad. If men were my thing, I’d be all over him.”

Nick laughed. "Well, there won't be any of that; I will not be dating our patients. To be honest, I really don't even want to think about dating."

Ginger winked at him. "You say that now, Boss, but you're a man. Sooner or later, you'll think about dating. Believe me."

They all laughed. "Group hug," Lesli said. Ginger and Felicity rose and the four of them embraced across the desk. Greg remained against the wall.

"I don't know what I'd do without you all," Nick said, then turned to leave the room. As he walked out, he thought he saw a smirk on Greg's face.

Nick stopped in his tracks. "Something humorous about this to you, Greg?"

"Naw, Man…I just think it's funny how y'all love each other so much."

"We do. We've been working together a long time, and that creates a bond. Understand what I mean?"

"Sure. Maybe someday I'll be lovable too." His face creasing in an ugly smile.

Nick gave him a quizzical look. He felt angry with the guy and sorry for him at the same time. He heard Felicity mutter, "I doubt it" under her breath.

He gave Felicity a come-on-really look and slapped his assistant on the shoulder. "We'll work on that Greg," he said and left the room.

A few minutes later Nick was back at his desk, sorting through a clutter of papers he could never seem to clear away completely, when Ginger spoke to him through the telephone intercom.

"Doctor Espinoza on line two for you."

"Thanks, got it," Nick said, reaching for the blinking button on the phone.

"She's single, you, know."

"Thank you, Ginger," he said, shaking his head and pressing the button. *She is?,* he thought. "Good morning, Fiona."

"Good morning yourself, Nick. How are you?"

"I'm good. To what do I owe the pleasure?"

Fiona Espinoza's laugh tinkled through the telephone speaker. Nick pictured her at her desk with a cup of tea. She was a trim, auburn-tinged brunette with large dark eyes, and she was really lovely in every way, he thought. She had a playful, quick mind and, he suspected, some fire in her temper as well, handed down from her Irish mother and Chilean father. He always enjoyed talking with her. "Do you always find it pleasurable to speak to dermatologists?"

"I do when they're you, Fiona. How can I help you today?"

"I wanted to talk with you about a mutual patient, Charles Monroe. You know him, right?"

"Sure, I've known him for years. What's up?"

Nick could hear her flipping through a chart. "I'm not sure yet. I was doing his yearly head-to-toe skin check, and I found a lesion on his scalp that I don't like. It's in the hairline behind his right ear and it needs to come off. I'd say with at least a five-millimeter margin around it. I offered to do a biopsy, but he wants you to do it. Can you do me a favor and get him in soon?"

"Does it look bad to you?"

"Yeah. Could be a melanoma."

"Okay, Fiona. I'll call him, and get him in. We'll do it in the next couple of days. I'll have the biopsy results back in a week and I'll let you know where we stand."

"Sounds good, Nick. Thanks."

"Right back at you. I'd say he's lucky to have such a thorough dermatologist." He took a quick sip of his coffee. Remembering what Ginger had told him, he asked, "So what else is going on? Are you and Tom travelling this spring?

There was a pause, then she spoke, "You didn't hear? Tom and I split up. The divorce went through two months ago."

Nick gulped. "Oh, Fiona. I'm so sorry. I had no idea."

He heard her sigh through the speaker. "You might be the only person in New Orleans who hasn't heard. You know how this city is; once word got out, it was everywhere."

"I know, believe me. Are you okay?"

"I am now. It was no fun at the time, but you get through it, and then life sort of starts over. You don't really get a clean slate, but you get to put yours through the dishwasher."

He paused for a moment, wondering if he should talk about his own divorce. He decided to keep the conversation focused on her. "Well, it sounds like you've got a great attitude about it, Fiona. I know this is after the fact, but if there's anything I can do to help—anything at all, like help you move something or just talk—will you please let me know?"

"Thanks, Nick." She chuckled "You're a good guy, no matter what anybody says."

He laughed. "That's a very backhanded compliment, my friend."

He could hear her chuckle on her end. "Hey, speaking of my backhand, I'm going to start playing tennis again. I remember you're good, so when I get my form back, maybe we can play together."

Nick's mind warmed to the thought of Fiona's form, imagining her in a short skirt. Playing together sounded great to him. *Was she flirting with him?* In a cracked voice he said, "That would be great."

Part Two
Reconstruction

"The wound will heal best if as little tension as possible exists between the surface and what lies beneath."

—Terry Johnson, MD to his residents, 1991

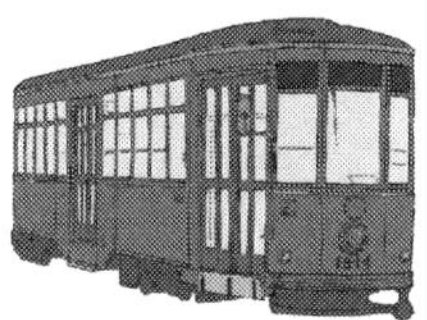

11

On a steamy Tuesday morning the following week, Nick was at his desk early checking email. Lesli gave his office door a rap and entered. "Good morning, Boss. Nice to see you bright and early."

Nick looked up at her. "Good morning yourself. What do we have today?"

"One facelift—Jane Meadows."

Nick's eyebrows went up. "You're kidding! She scheduled fast, didn't she?"

"Yup. We talked about it, and it's something she really wants. And get this—her husband—the jerk who left her, encouraged her to do it. I think he feels guilty. He brought me the check himself."

"Interesting," Nick said. "So how is she emotionally? The last time we talked she was pretty broken up about the whole thing. We both know she's got to be stable enough to recover from her surgery, especially if we run into any problems afterward. Do you think she can handle it?"

Lesli sat down in a chair across the desk from him. "I do. We talked for a long time. She's definitely sad about her situation, but she seems determined to get on with her life. And she wants to do it with a better neck and jawline."

Nick nodded. "I can understand that. Okay, let's do it. What else is going on?"

"I added on that biopsy for Charles Monroe. How long will it take?"

"Shouldn't be more than half an hour."

"Perfect," she said, rising to leave. Then she thought of something and sat back down. "By the way, are you doing more Botox touch-ups lately?"

"I'm not sure. I never charge for them, so they're popular. Maybe, I guess. Why?"

"Well, we really seem to be flying through the stuff. We're still making money on it, but we're using more, so profits are down. And we need the income. We're not as busy with surgery as we usually are this time of year."

Nick nodded, "I know; it's strange. But this business is cyclical, and it doesn't always make sense when we're slow." He looked her in the eye. "It will pick up. The work will be there, I know it."

"I hope so."

He rose from his seat. "I know so. Maybe I'm getting more generous with the Botox in my old age. Do me a favor and keep an eye on that going forward. Let me know if it doesn't improve. But remember, the most important thing is to keep the patients happy. Speaking of which, where is the soon to be single Mrs. Meadows?"

"She's in the first exam room. The anesthesiologist just finished talking with her."

"OK. I'm on it. Keep me straight, Lesli," he said, patting her on the arm as he passed.

"That's my job," she replied, following him out of his office.

Nick walked down the hall to a room where Jane sat in a large examination chair. She was wearing thick socks and no shoes and looked at him anxiously through small horn-rimmed glasses. He thought she looked like a scared little rabbit.

"Good morning, Jane," he said. "Are you ready for our big day?"

"Good morning. I guess so."

"Are you excited or nervous or both?"

She gave a tiny smile. "A little excited. More nervous."

Nick gave her a reassuring smile. "That's normal. I've done over a thousand of these, but this is your first one. Once Doctor Shear gets a hold of you, you won't be nervous anymore—in fact, you'll be the happiest person in the zip code. I guarantee it." Her smile returned, a little bigger this time.

He turned her chair towards the open doorway. "Why don't you come with me, and I'll show you what we're going to do today."

They walked the short distance to Nick's private office where he asked her to sit in a chair very close to a large mirror. He stood behind her and gently placed a hand on each side of her neck, just below the earlobes. "Now Jane, look at these bands hanging down in the middle of your neck. I know you don't like them."

She nodded "I hate those—please get rid of them."

Nick pulled back on the sides of her neck, and the sharp lines disappeared. "They're the edges of a muscle called the platysma. What I'm going to do is sew them together in the midline first to make them smooth, then pull hard from the sides to give you a nice firm neck." He pulled a little more and the neck became more defined.

"It looks 15 years younger," Jane chuckled "That would be great."

Nick let the neck relax. "Well, it's not pie in the sky; that's what we're going to get. Keep in mind that I have to overpull a little because necks always relax. So, the first couple of weeks, it's going to feel tight, especially when you turn your head."

She smiled. "For a neck like that, I can put up with it."

"That's the spirit," Nick said, moving his hands gently to her face, the tips of his fingers resting lightly on the skin in front of her ears. "Now, in the face it's different. If I pull too much, it might stay that way. So, I have to put the tissues right where we want them." He moved the skin and tissue underneath gently upward. The jaw line became straight and the jowl, which had been gathered along it, disappeared. "Notice how the pull here is more vertical and gentler," he said. "The fold near the corner of the mouth is gone and the one between the cheek and the mouth is still there but not as deep. Most important of all, the corner of the mouth doesn't move much at all. It looks natural."

Jane sighed. "I love it. If you can do that, I will be one happy woman."

Nick released her skin. "Well, that's what it's all about today. My goal is to end up with a happy Jane." He walked her back to the examination room. Once there, they encountered Herb Shear, Nick's anesthesiologist of many years, in the hallway. "Jane, have you met Dr. Shear? He'll be your bartender today."

Herb was a thin Jewish man in his 60's who wore a colorful surgical cap and a perpetual smile. He had the air of a kindly grandfather. Nick knew him to be both extremely intelligent and superb at what he did. A colleague had once called him unflappable, and Nick thought the word fit his anesthesiologist well. In the rare instances when things got scary in the operating room, Herb Shear was solid as a rock.

The older man smiled his big toothy grin. "Oh, yes, we had our talk. Thank you, Doctor Jordan, for giving me such a nice healthy patient today."

"My pleasure, doc," Nick replied as Jane settled back into the big exam chair. He reached for a purple skin-marking pen and sat on a small rolling stool directly in front of her.

"Look over my shoulder at that painting across the hall," he directed.

He made two thick marks along the vertical bands in her neck. "Lift your chin a bit." He made another smaller mark transverse to the others, just under the point of her chin. "Here's the place I'll go through to get to those muscles. Lots of people have a scar under here from falling on a curb or a coffee table when they were kids, anyway." She made a tiny grimace. Nick patted her hand reassuringly. "You'll be in La-La Land and won't feel a thing, don't worry."

"I have faith in you, Nick."

"I know. And I promise to live up to that. Now I'm going to lay you back," he said, pressing a button on the side of the chair. She was lying almost flat now. Nick drew out the incision lines, in front of and behind the ears, and then reached for a safety razor. "Now I'll trim just a little bit of hair, in the sideburn area and in the hairline behind the ear. It might seem like a lot, but it's not. Maybe a quarter of an inch. You'll never miss it." He gently stroked the razor in front of her ear. He knew she could hear the hairs being scraped away.

"You didn't know I was a hair stylist, did you?" Nick joked. He repeated the process on the other side so that the purple marks were symmetrical. He then reached for the first of two lengths of surgical masking tape and directed Jane to gently lift her head off the chair. "I'm going to gather your hair and tape it up. This will protect it during surgery and keep it out of my way when I'm working. Let me know if it pulls too much." He secured the tape in a turban-like band around her head, then placed the second piece over it for reinforcement. Nick pressed a button on the chair, and it returned her to an upright position. "OK, Cinderella, you are ready for the dance," he said and gave her a hand as she rose from the chair.

Jane walked across the room to a mirror on the wall and looked at herself. "Don't be offended, Nick, but I don't think I'll be hiring you as my permanent hair stylist."

Nick smiled at her. "I understand," he said, glad that she seemed more relaxed now.

Lesli entered the room with perfect timing, derived from years of experience. "Time for the restroom?" she asked, smiling at Jane.

"Yes, we'd rather do it before than during the surgery," Nick chimed, walking across the hall into the office's operating room. This was his favorite place in the world to do surgery. In the beginning of his career, he had operated exclusively in the hospital. Having a surgical suite in his office allowed him to set it up exactly as he wanted. Over the years he had collected the best instruments, equipment, and especially people. He had recruited Herb to do his anesthesia after working with the older man for several years. All their cases were done under intravenous sedation, which was lighter and less risky than general anesthesia. He knew that giving sedation was an art, and in its execution he considered Herb to be Michelangelo and da Vinci rolled into one person.

He had also managed to recruit a superb scrub nurse to assist him with the surgeries. Virginia was a pleasant and attractive African American woman in her 40's whose skill and demeanor had impressed him in the hospital. She had a way of calming him; he often told her his blood pressure went down ten points just seeing her in the room when he walked in. Herb and Virginia were his "A Team," and he was grateful to have both working with him in the office.

Lesli appeared at the door with Jane in tow. Herb rose to greet them. "Come right this way," he said, directing her to lie on the operating room bed. Nick moved to the bedside and stood over her, as Herb prepared to place an IV in her hand. "Jane, we'll take great care of you, and I'm going to do my very best for you," he said, giving her other hand a squeeze.

"I know you will," she said, taking a deep breath.

Nick asked her to choose the music she wanted to hear as she was going off to sleep. "I've got Pandora on the iPod. What'll it be?"

Jane looked up at the ceiling. "Oh, I don't know. Something relaxing. Can you play Michael Bublé?" she asked.

"Absolutely—I like his stuff," Nick replied, using the touch screen to find the crooner's digital station.

"A little pinch," Herb said, using a small needle to introduce the IV into Jane's hand. "I barely felt that," she said as music filled the room:

I'm not surprised. Not everything lasts.

Nick thought for a moment of Elizabeth and a wave of anxiety hit him hard. He took two deep breaths to calm himself. During their separation, when things were so uncertain and he had felt like his world was falling apart, the office, especially the operating room, was the one place in his life that he could escape to. Small things like a photograph or a lyric from a song still brought the painful feeling back sometimes. He looked up and saw Virginia peering at him with concern. He gave her a little wink to signal he was OK and walked back to the bedside. Jane's eyes were beginning to glaze, and she was smiling.

"Starting to feel relaxed, dear?" Nick asked.

She looked at him hazily "My husband paid for this, you know. He is such an…." she took a deep breath and then let it go in a slow exhale "…. asshole." Her eyelids fluttered and closed.

Herb looked up at him; Nick could tell the older man was smiling under his mask. "Ready to inject," he said.

The procedure lasted three hours and went smoothly. Face-lifting was the most common surgery they performed, and Nick and his team functioned like a musical band that had been together for years, each knowing what the other would do in advance and working in unison to get the job done.

"I wish they all were like this; much easier than doing one on a larger woman or a man." Nick said to Virginia.

She nodded and said, “thank Goodness for small-headed women.”

When the surgery was finished, Nick rose and removed his gloves and paper surgical gown. Lesli came to the OR doorway. “Charles Monroe is here, Doctor J. I told him you were just finishing up and would need a few minutes to catch your breath and get a snack.”

Nick moved past her, tearing off his surgical mask and cap. “You know me well. I’ll see him in five.” He turned back to Herb and Virginia, who were watching over Jane as she slowly regained consciousness. “Thanks, you guys. Great day.”

He walked down the hall to the break room and found some cheese, crackers, and a Diet Coke. An old *People* magazine caught his eye. On its cover a photo of a celebrity couple had been digitally torn in half. “Marriage on the Rocks?” proclaimed the headline. He had to laugh. He rose and walked down the hall to find his next patient.

12

Charles sat in the exam room chair looking dapper as ever. Clad in a sky-blue golf shirt, salmon-colored khakis, and brown suede loafers (minus socks of course), Charles looked like he was relaxing in an exclusive departure lounge, waiting for his Palm Beach flight to depart. He rose and extended his hand to Nick, giving him a big smile that exposed perfect white teeth. A vague smell of musky cologne wafted through the air. "What's the good word, Doctor?" he said, returning to his seat.

"Good to see you, as always, Charles," Nick replied, opening the chart and taking a seat next to him. "Doctor Espinoza says you've got something on your scalp she wants me to remove."

"Ah, Fiona," Charles said, "What a fine, fine woman she is. And single too, I hear. If I were ten years younger…" he said, looking at Nick with meaning.

"Oh, I agree, she's beautiful, no doubt. But more relevant to our little get-together today, she's also an excellent dermatologist." Charles chuckled and Nick continued, "If Fiona says you've got something that needs to come off, then you probably do. Let's take a look."

Charles turned his head away and pulled the top of his right ear forward with the tip of a finger. Amid the recently trimmed (and dyed, Nick was sure) hairs behind the ear was a raised, dark skin lesion. Nick looked at it carefully through a lighted magnifying lens. “Let me measure that and get a picture, Charles,” he said, reaching for a skin-marking pen to carefully draw a purple circle around the area. He then took a stainless-steel caliper from a drawer behind him and measured the lesion and then its distance from the outside edge of the circle at several points along its circumference. He reached for his camera and took a photo. “Charles, let’s go back to my office and take a look at this,” he said, heading out into the hall with the older man following behind him.

They settled into chairs in front of a large computer monitor. Nick took the digital memory card out of the camera and inserted it into his desktop computer. A photo of a black and purple lump filled the screen in high-definition sharpness. It looked like a multicolored scab. “Yuck,” Charles said, then added, “Get that off of me, Doc”.

“I will,” Nick replied. “Fiona was right. This definitely needs to come off. I don’t like the look of it. The purple circle is where I’ll make the cut. You won’t feel it because I’ll numb the area first. But taking that amount off should give us a safe margin around it.”

Charles whistled. “That seems like a lot, Doc.”

“Well, it is a generous margin. I measured a full centimeter around it at every point. That’s a reasonable amount to take and for the pathologist to look at to make sure we're clear. We're lucky that it's behind your ear. Your hair and your ear will hide it when we're done. Sometimes these crop up on a cheek or forehead or somewhere worse."

"What do you think it is?"

"I can't be sure until the pathologist looks at the specimen we're going to send. But it has pigment in it, and it's raised and irregular in shape. There's a chance it's a melanoma."

"That's bad, isn't it?" Nick had never seen Charles look concerned before.

"Sometimes yes, sometimes no. It depends on several different things, like how deep it goes and especially what levels of the skin it's in. But we're getting ahead of ourselves. It might be something else. That's why we're going to take it off and send it to the lab."

Charles blew out a deep breath. "Well, you know what you're doing, and you have my confidence. What will it look like when you're done?"

"In the beginning, it'll just be a hole that we'll cover with a bandage. After we get the all-clear, I'll repair it by making some cuts and moving nearby skin in or maybe by taking a graft of skin from behind your other ear and putting it there. Sometimes I do both. The main thing is for me to get it off now and see what it is."

"And what if the edges, I'm sorry, margins, aren't clear?"

"We'll cross that road if we come to it, but I'd probably have to take another centimeter or so around it and send that to the lab."

Charles leaned forward and clapped Nick on the knee. "Ok, then. Let's do it. You da man, Doc."

Nick rose and went to the door. "Step into my parlor," he said, gesturing for Charles to follow.

Forty-five minutes later the procedure was completed, and a disk of flesh the size of a silver dollar floated in a plastic jar half-full of formaldehyde. Nick stood and put the last touches on the bandage he had created on the right side of Charles' head. "You okay?" he asked.

"I'm fine, Doc. It didn't hurt a bit." The older man's jaunty demeanor had returned during the procedure. He'd been talking with Nick about sport fishing and golf destinations while the doctor was working.

Nick gave his patient a printed sheet describing wound care instructions. As he was preparing to leave, Charles stopped and looked Nick in the eye. "So, how are you handling the divorce stuff? Are you alright?"

"To tell the truth, it hasn't been a whole lot of fun. But I'm hanging in there."

Charles nodded. "Let me tell you something, Doc. I've been through the whole nine yards, and I know it's an emotional wringer. But I also know there's a light at the end of the tunnel. And I'm not talking about wild sex with girls half your age, although there is that." Charles grinned. "I'm talking about something else. Peace, I suppose. Less drama—less of the crap you've been going through. More time to yourself to relax and take stock of things."

"That will be nice," Nick agreed.

Charles straightened up. "Good things are coming to you, Doc; I know it. Because you deserve them; because of who you are."

Nick bowed his head, humbled by the compliment. "You're too kind, Charles. And you always seem to make me feel better." He looked up. "That's supposed to be my job."

"I guess we help each other," the patient said softly. Then in an upbeat voice he added, "By the way, I'd like you to come to a party I'm giving in a few weeks at my home. I live at Fleur de Lis. Do you know it?"

"Sure, I know it," Nick said, "and thanks, I'd love to come. He rose and peered at the bandage to be sure it was in the proper position. "So, getting back to the hole in your head, I'll have your result in four or five days, and we'll go from there. In the meantime, I don't want you to worry too much about this. I'm on it, and I'll do my best for you."

13

That evening found Nick pushing a red plastic shopping cart down a brightly lit aisle at the Veterans Avenue Target store. Still wearing his surgical scrubs and tired from the day's exertions, he had finally made time to shop for the house. He had a list of necessities; things Elizabeth took that needed replacing sooner rather than later.

He smelled vaguely of massage oil—lilac and peppermint. Seven years ago, he had begun getting a weekly massage at the end of his busiest operating day. After performing surgery for five to ten hours, a painful tightness often crept into his neck and shoulders. Heather, his massage therapist, knew how to break up the knots and get him feeling human again. In addition to making him feel better, the weekly massages could well extend his career, Nick thought. Neck and back problems were an occupational hazard for surgeons, and he knew of a few who had been obliged to retire due to unmanageable pain or nerve damage from slipped discs compressing their spinal nerves. Heather was like a disability policy, and he never minded paying the premiums.

Nick saw a sign indicating that he had reached the bathroom section. Heaving a sigh, he reached for a soap caddy, and further down the aisle, a toilet plunger. He found a shower curtain with matching rings—a brightly colored plastic affair with a penguin motif—probably meant for a kid's bathroom. It was bright and cheery. *Might as well*, he thought, tossing it into the basket.

His mind went back to the other times in his life when he'd done this. He remembered shopping for his dorm room in college and his utterly divey apartment in med school, and yet again for a slightly better apartment when he started his residency. The focus then had been on price, the cheaper the better. He thought back to shopping with Elizabeth for their new home—*that had been fund*. They'd been so excited to start their new life. He was more of a shopper than she, but they had enjoyed doing it together. The stores they chose were more upscale too; Wal-Mart and the Dollar Store had given way to Crate and Barrel and the Pottery Barn. Now he was back at Target, not so much to save money as for the convenience of getting everything at once. He felt embarrassed and sad to be doing this again at the age of 50, but here he was.

Might as well get fun stuff, he thought – colorful things to brighten the mood in his empty home. He threw a hopelessly bright bathmat into the cart, wondering if Roquefort would be able to see the color. He heaved a heavier sigh and headed to the kitchen section.

On his way down the glistening main aisle of the store, he stopped in Electronics and bought a seven-season box set of one of his favorite TV shows, an ensemble comedy called

Scrubs that was set in a hospital. *Perfect for what I'm wearing,* he thought and chuckled. The power of good entertainment, especially comedies, to take his mind off troubles had always amazed him, and here in this box were about two hundred hours of distraction.

Nick heard his name and turned to see a couple waving at him. He felt trapped and resisted the urge to thrust the cart behind the nearest display and disappear. Not that he didn't like these people; they were his neighbors, and normally he enjoyed their company. He just didn't want people to know about the divorce yet. He'd been trying to keep his private life a secret for so long that it had become instinctual. Was he ashamed to be divorced, he wondered? *They'd probably seen the moving truck anyway.* He turned to them and smiled. They approached side by side, pushing their cart together. They seemed to have the kind of close-knit marriage that Nick knew he had long ago, and the thought filled him with sadness.

"Buddy," The man, whose name was Alex said, extending a hand. Nick shook it, and then gave his wife, Sasha, a hug. "Hey, y'all. What are you two up to?"

"Just picking up a few things," Sasha said, moving her shopping cart from the center of the aisle.

"What about you Nick?" Alex asked, picking the plunger out of his basket and pointing it at him like an imaginary microphone. "It looks like you're getting ready to set up house somewhere."

Nick's mind raced for an explanation. He stalled for time "You caught me; I'm moving to Alaska to beat the heat and just thought I'd need a few things." He grabbed the plunger from Alex and put it back in the cart. He thought of something more plausible. "Actually, I'm helping my niece get her dorm room set up. She's starting at Tulane this year."

"Oh, is she here?" Sasha asked, looking around. "I'd love to meet her."

"No, she gave me a list," Nick lied. "She's at some orientation thing."

"Really? In April?" Alex said, giving Nick a quizzical look. "They sure are getting started early for next semester, aren't they?"

Nick shifted his feet and prepared to lie again. He searched for a reply. "It's a special thing for transfers, I guess." *Why couldn't he have thought of something else? A vacation home. That would have been more believable. You have to buy new stuff for that. Damn.*

Alex turned to Sasha., "Baby, why don't I meet you over at the groceries? I want to catch up with Nick for a minute."

She looked at her husband with complete understanding. "Sure, Honey," she said, then suddenly reached out and squeezed Nick's hand. Their eyes locked for a moment. "Nick, if you need anything at all, you ask us, understand?"

Nick realized they knew the whole story. Probably everybody on his street did. He smiled and squeezed back. "Thanks, Sasha."

Alex put an arm around Nick's shoulder and steered him into the pet food aisle. "Buddy, I drive by your house every morning on the way to work and every night on the way home. Your car was missing for like six months. Now you're buying bathmats and shower curtains." They stopped mid aisle. "It doesn't take a genius to figure out, you know."

Nick looked down at the floor again then directly at Alex. "You're right. My car was never there because we were separated. I was living in an apartment during that time. I ended up keeping the house in the divorce settlement. Elizabeth moved out a few weeks ago and the movers took her stuff when she did. So now I'm living alone in the house."

"Are you holding up okay?"

"Yeah, I am. My work keeps me busy during the day, so I don't have to think about it."

"Well, then let's have you to dinner some nights as well. I'll get Sasha on it."

"You guys are great. I'd love that. Do me a favor though and keep this under your hat. I'd like it not to get around for a while. I'm just adjusting to it myself, and I don't want to have to talk about it all day long."

"I understand," Alex smiled. "Sorry for being such a nosy neighbor. But you hadn't been around and when I saw your shopping cart, the penny dropped for me. Sasha's got a sixth sense about these things. She told me months ago that something was going on. There's no way to keep anything from her."

Nick chuckled. "Yeah, I guess I've got to find stupider friends. But thanks. I really appreciate it."

“Like she said, anything you need.” He clapped Nick on the shoulder and left to find his wife. Ashamed of being caught in an obvious lie, and filled with the certain knowledge that all his friends and many of his neighbors must already know about the death of his marriage, Nick headed back towards the kitchen section swallowing hard.

14

A few days later Nick was finishing a chart note in the reception area when the front door burst open and Dave McGloughlin strode into the office. Ginger looked up to see the movie-star-handsome man in his early fifties dressed in a sport coat and tie gazing down at her. Seeing them regarding one another, Nick was struck by the symmetry; two very good-looking humans with physiques that in an earlier time would have been called heroic, face-to-face. Coincidentally, Dave's pocket square matched the color of her scarf perfectly.

"And whatever can I do for you?" Ginger asked, in a voice that Nick hoped was far flirtier than her usual one. He stepped forward.

"Ginger, have you met my friend, Dave McGloughlin, Sandra's *husband*?" he said, emphasizing the final word.

"Umm, no, I haven't," she said, whisking a platinum forelock away from in front of her eyes. "Pleasure to meet you, Mr. McGloughlin."

"Oh, it's no pleasure, believe me." Nick said.

The visitor smiled at her, flashing extremely white teeth. "Don't pay any attention to him, darling. In his addled mind, that's what passes for courtesy. And call me Dave, please. I'm charmed to meet you."

Nick rolled his eyes. "Okay, Don Juan; did you get lost or something? This isn't a cocktail bar, you know."

"Nope, I'm here with a purpose, buddy." He fished inside his sport coat. "My wife made me an appointment for me with you all, but it's not my thing. I'd like to return this gift certificate for a refund." He handed the envelope across the counter. "She got me this at a charity ball. It's for a deluxe European facial, whatever the hell that is."

Ginger reached for the envelope and extracted the card. She read it then looked towards Nick for guidance. Nick shook his head and said, "Explain it to him, Ginger. No big words; he's a little slow." Dave adjusted his lapel with his middle finger extended, making sure Nick caught the gesture.

Ginger smiled at Dave, "Of course, Mr. McGloughlin, I mean, Dave, we know Sandra well, and I know that you and Doctor Jordan are friends. I normally would refund what she paid, but this was purchased at a charity auction, so we didn't receive any money for it. There isn't anything for us to refund."

"Huh, I see," Dave said taking back the card and looking at it as if for the first time. "A deluxe European facial—I think that'd be a waste of time on an ugly mug like mine. I cultivate the weathered look, you know." He smiled at Ginger, scratching his head.

“I’m sure you’d enjoy it, sir. Our aesthetician does a wonderful job.”

“Well, I suppose I could give this back to Sandra for her to use, but that might hurt her feelings. She bought it for me. And anyway, she’s beautiful enough. She’s away on a girl’s trip with some friends. But usually she’s in here a lot, isn’t she?”

Ginger smiled. “Now sir, you know we can’t talk about what we do for other patients.” Nick nodded his approval. She was back in professional mode.

Dave looked at her, “Even to their husbands?”

“Especially to their husbands,” Ginger said, giving him a conspiratorial smile.

“I see what you mean,” Dave replied, “If all of us husbands knew what Dr. Jordan here was costing us, we’d form a mob and burn the place down.”

Nick laughed. “I’ll tell you what I tell all husbands: If it makes her happy, it will make you happy.”

Dave chuckled. “And I suppose it’s cheaper to fix up the old one than to get a new one.”

“You talk awfully brave when your wife’s out of town.”

Dave looked up at the ceiling, then pursed his lips and exhaled. “So do you even do deluxe European facials for men?”

“Of course! Skincare isn’t just for women these days,” Ginger replied. She looked at her computer monitor; “You have a treatment scheduled now, so why don't you try it? I think you'll like it—everyone does. Felicity will be out in a moment to get you."

"Felicity, huh? Sounds like a…"

"Sounds like a what, darling?" Felicity said entering the reception area. She gave him a critical look up and down. "You must be Dave. I've been taking care of Sandra for years. She's told me *so much* about you." She gave him a big smile and extended her hand.

Dave shook it and smiled back. "I hope some of it was good."

"Right, bits and pieces were very good," she answered, shooting him an eyebrow. "So, are you ready for your facial?"

Dave looked at his watch. "Umm, yeah, I guess. I'd hate to see my money go to waste." Nick was going to point out that a donation to the Children's Hospital of New Orleans wasn't really a waste, but he held his tongue.

"Do you think you can do anything with this?" he said, pointing at his face.

"Oh, I've seen worse, love. Come along," Felicity giggled, taking his hand and leading him down the hallway. "Step into my parlor, said the spider to the fly."

Dave turned back to Ginger and Nick and said, "If I'm not back in an hour please come save me." They laughed.

"No mercy for you, hotcakes," Felicity said giving his hand a yank.

Nick passed the door of the aesthetics room. It was slightly ajar, and he could hear laughter coming from inside. He heard Felicity say, "Now I'm going to treat your décolletage," and Dave respond, "I thought you said there *wasn't* going to be a happy ending." There was much more laughter. Nick shook his head and continued down the hallway.

Forty-five minutes later, Nick encountered Felicity in the break room. She was stuffing an armful of towels into the laundry hamper. "So, how did it go?" he asked.

"Your friend is really something, you know," she said, giggling.

"Was he completely inappropriate?" Nick asked, fearing the worst.

"No, not really" she said, leaning in closer and lowering her voice. "But midway through the facial he got an erection, and it, ummm, stayed that way for quite some time."

Nick laughed out loud. "That's my boy."

They walked down the hall to join Dave, who was chatting with Ginger at the checkout counter. "You sure know your stuff, Felicity," he said louder than necessary for effect. "Somebody ought to give you a raise."

"That's enough out of you," Nick said, scowling.

Felicity patted Nick on the back. "He pays me okay, mostly with sexual favors."

"That can't be much pay at all," Dave said, then pointed at the shelves full of skin care products. "Does he even know what all of this stuff is?"

Felicity shook her head. "No. He just lets me order what I need and signs the checks. When I try to teach him about skincare, he puts me off with his caveman imitation—you know, 'Me surgeon, me cut, me no understand skin stuff.' I can't get him interested in the details."

"Well, he's lucky to have you. Let me know if you ever want to make a change and come work for me."

Nick cleared his throat. "I'm standing right here you know."

Felicity stepped in between the two men and gave Nick a mock scowl. "Dave has shopping to do. He wants to keep his skin beautiful with a program at home. So, leave him alone." She turned and gave her new client a bottle of water adorned with the practice logo. Ginger looked up at him with a twinkle in her eye. "So, it wasn't so bad after all, Mr. McGloughlin?"

"No, not bad at all," he replied. "Now I know why my wife's been getting facials all these years." He turned back to his beaming aesthetician. "Felicity, what do you recommend?" He made a dismissive motion to Nick, and then put a hand to his newly smooth cheek. "I want to keep this going."

Nick rolled his eyes. "Now you're going to become a regular. I think it's time to retire."

Ginger smiled and winked at him, “The magic of Felicity, I guess.”

Felicity raised her arms over her head in triumph. “Yes! A convert!” She walked behind the reception desk to where bookshelves displayed rows of colorful boxes and bottles. “Let’s see, you need a good basic cleanser. Here’s one,” she said, reaching for a tall green bottle. “And I highly recommend you get the Vibratonic device to help you clean your skin. It does a much better job than you can on your own. Sandra has one, but in my experience, wives do not want to share them.” She began to pile boxes on the desk next to Ginger.

“Whatever you think; load me up,” Dave said, and threw his credit card on the counter.

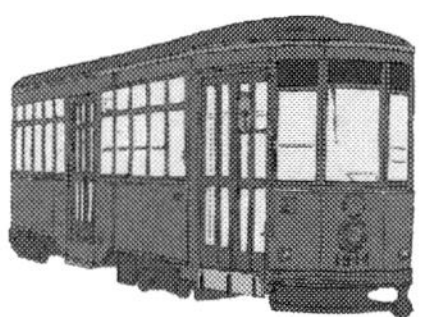

15

A few nights later, Nick stepped from his car into the warm New Orleans evening. It was the middle of May now, and the air was thickening with humidity. He entered an enormous building beneath an illuminated sign that read DIAMOND GYM. The interior, with its busy rows of machines, looked like a fitness supermarket. Being in New Orleans, its walls were loudly adorned with team banners and posters; the purple and gold of LSU and black and gold of the Saints predominated. A splash of green and blue for Tulane appeared here and there. Nick had joined the club recently, fully aware of how stereotypical it was for a newly divorced person to do so. He waved his membership card beneath the laser reader and nodded at the front desk girl.

Even though it was dinnertime, the place was crowded. The steady hum of treadmills, bikes, and elliptical machines was punctuated by the percussive crash of weights and weight stacks being brought back to earth. Bright lights and brighter Lycra workout clothes gave the place an almost festive air. This was the place to work out in New Orleans, especially if you happened to be single.

Nick accidentally made eye contact with a cute blonde speed walking on a treadmill. He gave her an awkward half smile then turned and walked quickly away. He wasn't ready to flirt, let alone date. *Just here to get a good workout,* he thought, as he walked to the entrance of the "Cardio Workout Theater". He opened the door to darkness and a large movie screen. The room was about half the size of a normal movie theater and full of exercise equipment. People were exercising in the dark, looking up from their machines to watch the entertainment. Nick selected an elliptical machine in the back row. It took him a while to figure out the touch screen controls in the dark, but at last he pressed the right combination of buttons and began his workout.

On the big screen, a hockey player was learning to play golf so that he could win enough prize money to reclaim his grandmother's house and get her out of a nursing home. It was silly escapism, but Nick enjoyed the movie as he worked. At intervals his mind went back to the divorce, how alone and abandoned he felt, and the thought made him anxious and angry. For a moment he felt the panicky feeling swell up in his chest. He pumped the pedals of his machine hard and fast, making a loud mechanical whine. People on either side of him looked over briefly. After half a minute at Superman pace, he slowed to his regular rhythm. He was breathing hard, and his chest was pounding.

People came and went around him. Nick kept watching the movie and working the machine, pausing occasionally to wipe sweat from his face with a wad of paper towels. The hockey player was the new tour champion, grandma's house had been saved, and the title credits were rolling on the screen. The anxious feelings were gone, and he felt better. He knew he'd have a glass of bourbon when he got home, but didn't think he'd need a Percocet to sleep tonight. It was amazing how strenuous exercise calmed him down and made him feel better, he thought. *Not really amazing*—after all he was a physician and understood the physiologic effect. It was just that it always worked so well. Someone ought to write a book, he thought: *The Divorce Workout*. He grinned and kept pumping.

An unseen hand had re-started the movie and now Nick was getting bored with it. He looked down at the machine display, which read 1249 in glowing orange numbers. *How is that possible? The place closes at midnight* he thought. He looked at his watch; it was a quarter to ten. He'd been working out for almost three hours. Then it hit him—*those were calories*. He was in better shape than he'd realized. He chuckled to himself reflecting that even the misery of divorce had a bright side.

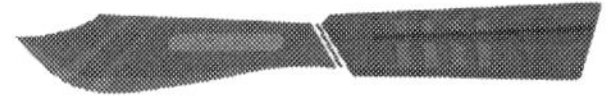

The next morning Nick saw patients in his office, going from room to room as usual. He stopped at a closed door to one of the exam rooms and took Charles Monroe's chart from the rack. He opened it and quickly re-read the pathology report, then gave two short raps on the door and walked in.

Charles was nattily dressed as usual. Except for the bandage behind his ear, he wouldn't have looked out of place in the member's bar at an exclusive country club. He rose from his chair with a smile and gave Nick a warm handshake. "Hey there, Doc. How are you?"

"I'm good Charles, thanks. Have a seat." Nick replied. He gently lifted the bandage and examined the silver dollar-sized area of raw tissue, which was clean and coated with ointment. "This looks fine for now; you're taking good care of it," he said settling into the chair next to his patient. "How are you feeling?"

"If I were any better, I'd be twins. But what about you? How's the single life treating you?"

"I'm getting along all right. I bought all the essentials, you know toilet paper and such, and I'm having some new furniture delivered tomorrow. It's a little lonely at times, but like you said, it's also peaceful."

"Hang in there, buddy; it gets better. If I can be of any help, or you ever just want to get a beer and talk, call me. You've got my cell number right?"

Nick looked at the number on the first page of Charles's chart and nodded, "I sure do. Thanks."

"And don't forget about that get-together at my place. I'll introduce you to some of my friends. There will be a lot of nice folks there." He winked at Nick. "And some very attractive single women, believe me."

"Charles, I don't doubt that for a second. I haven't really dated yet. I think I'm going to take it slow and do that when I'm ready. It just doesn't feel right to me now. But I'd love to have a drink with you at your place and meet your friends, so count me in."

Nick opened the chart. "Now let's talk about your head for a minute." He flipped pages until he came to the pathology report. "I sent your specimen to the lab, and it did turn out to be a melanoma. The margins were clear, meaning we got it all out with a generous rim of surrounding normal tissue around it, which is good." He looked up at his patient. "Before you get too worried, I can tell you that it's not very deep and not a particularly aggressive one. It's what they call intermediate grade."

Charles looked uncharacteristically serious. "And that means…"

"That means that you'll most likely be okay, but there's a chance that it could have spread, so we have to make sure it hasn't."

Charles nodded. "And how do we do that?"

"I'm going to call Larry Donato down at Tulane and have him schedule you for a sentinel node biopsy."

"Which is…?"

"It's a procedure where they check the lymph nodes to which the melanoma could have spread and make sure they're clean. You see, that's how melanoma spreads—through the lymphatic system. It's like a second circulatory system for your body. And the nodes are tiny filters that collect what flows to them through the lymph fluid. You with me?"

Charles nodded again.

"So, for any given spot on the body, there will be nodes or filters where the lymph drains to first. What Doctor Donato is going to do is find these nodes, take one or more of them out and send them to the lab to make sure they're okay."

Charles shifted in his seat. "And how does he find them?"

"He'll inject a radioactive fluid into the area where the melanoma was, around the hole I made in your head, and then right after, have you scanned to find out where the fluid collects. Those will be the sentinel nodes. Does that make sense?"

"Yup. And then he cuts them out?"

"That's right. And before he does, he'll inject that same area where I took out the melanoma with blue dye. It will follow the same path and end up in the sentinel nodes. That will make it easier for him to find and remove them through a small cut right over the lymph nodes."

"Got it. And then the pathologist looks at them?"

"That's right. And if they're clear of melanoma cells, that's it, you're good. If there are some in the sentinel nodes, then he'll need to remove all of the nodes around them. Because of where your melanoma was, that would mean a neck dissection, which is kind of like a larger version of the sentinel node biopsy through a bigger incision. Donato will do that too, if you need it. "

Charles nodded. "Well, let's hope that's a bridge we don't have to cross, Doc."

Nick rose and put a hand on the other man's shoulder. "I agree, Charles. There's no sense even thinking about that unless the biopsy comes back positive. I just wanted to let you know what could lie ahead. I'm cautiously optimistic that it's going to be negative."

Charles rose. "I understand, buddy. Me too. Can you set it up soon?"

"I think so; Larry's an old friend of mine, and I'll call him right away to get you in."

Charles rose. "You're a gentleman and a scholar, Doc. I'll buy you a drink at the party."

Nick smiled. "Let's get you figured out first, OK? I'll get you on Larry's schedule, and when he's done, I'll need to reconstruct the hole I made, probably with a graft of skin from behind the other ear. I'll work around his schedule, but let's aim to get both done next week."

"You got it, Boss." Charles said, offering his hand. Nick shook it.

16

Nick walked to an exam room near the end of the hallway and entered to find Greg putting numbing gel on a woman's face. "Good morning, Muffy," he said. She smiled at him through the clear goo.

Muffy Williams was dressed in the summer uniform of the New Orleans elite. She wore a brightly floral Lilly Pulitzer silk blouse and khaki capri pants that showed off surprisingly nice calves and ankles. Pink Tory Burch ballet flats, worn sockless, completed her ensemble. Her hair, a deep brown with lighter highlights, was pulled back in a bun, which seemed less severe to him today in harmony with her summer look.

"Greg, let's do a syringe of Juvederm®," he said to his assistant, who nodded and retreated through the doorway.

"So how are you?" Nick asked, picking up her chart.

"Blech… fine till this goop on my tongue," she said, making a face at him.

"I know. That gel is strong—I have it compounded for us in California. If I'm going to put a needle in your lip, I don't want you to feel it," he said.

"I won't argue with that, seeing which end of the needle I'm on."

Nick moved closer and looked carefully at the area around her mouth. "So how can I serve your beauty today?" he asked.

She smiled, "My lip lines are back. Can you fill them in without making me look like a duck?"

He laughed. "OK, no duck lips for you today," he said, putting on a pair of latex exam gloves. "I'm using one of the best fillers for working in the lip area, especially for softening those tiny lines around your mouth."

She sighed, "You know they call those smoker's lines, but I got them and never smoked. It's not fair."

He dabbed the numbing gel away from her lips with a gauze square. "It's true that smoking can bring them on or worsen them, but you can also inherit them. If your mom or dad had them, then you have a good chance of getting some as well."

Greg brought a syringe into the room, and Nick started by making a small injection at the corner of the mouth on each side. "This filler has lidocaine mixed into it, so it will numb you as we go. These two injections help bring the corners of the mouth up and out a bit and also get the numbness going." He put a gloved finger in her mouth and gently pinched each corner, smoothing the small lump of material. "I'll be massaging the filler as we go, kind of like a sculptor does with clay. That way it goes just where I want it, and you won't have any irregular areas."

Next, he injected a thin line of filler along the upper edge of the lip and repeated the smoothing. "Now I'll do the center of the upper lip, what we call Cupid's bow," he said, moving to the area directly under her nose. The needle went downward then upward following the natural contours of the lip. Muffy tensed in the chair. "I know, that's the most sensitive part," Nick said soothingly. "But it's done now, and it looks great. That was the low point of our relationship."

She rolled her eyes and gave him a playful punch in his side. "Don't hit the guy with the needle," he said, continuing down the other side of the upper lip and injecting evenly to make the treatment symmetrical. "You're going to like that," he said. Nick talked constantly to his patients during these treatments, mostly to distract their minds from the discomfort.

He took a step back and studied what he had done. "Good. Peroxide please," he said, and Greg wiped the area with a wet gauze sponge. The liquid made the surface of the skin slippery, which was ideal for feeling the material he had just placed underneath it and working it around using his gloved fingers. He looked up from the lip into Muffy's eyes. "You're doing great, my dear. I'm feeling the area I've treated to make sure it's perfectly smooth. No lumps or bumps for you." Greg wiped the area again to moisten it, and Nick took the center of her upper lip between the thumb and index finger of each of his hands and slid them both outward, feeling the filler just beneath the skin slip through them like a tiny eel.

When he was satisfied with the contours of the upper lip, Nick removed the needle from the syringe and replaced it with a shorter one of the same tiny gauge. "OK, now we're going to go after those lines you don't like," he said. "You've got a deep one on each side."

She gave him a crooked smile; the lidocaine not only numbed the lips, but also affected their movement temporarily. "The one on the right is James, and the one on the left is Kevin," she said.

Nick laughed, "You've named them?"

"Yes, they were the men I married. One passed away, and the other left me. But they both made their mark."

"Well, let's see if I can erase them," Nick said, checking the level of filler in the syringe.

"Oh, I know you can't get rid of them completely," Muffy said. "They were important, even vital to me, and now they're gone. The point is to accept that and move on."

A little shudder went through Nick. He hoped she hadn't noticed. "Are we talking about wrinkles or past loves here?"

"Both, I think," she said. He wondered if she knew about the divorce. Since gossip spread like wildfire in New Orleans, she probably did.

Nick continued the treatment. He inserted the tip of the miniature needle into the end of each tiny wrinkle and advanced it under the line, using a gentle sawing motion to lift the skin from the adherent muscle beneath. When he had created a tiny tunnel under the wrinkle, he slowly withdrew the needle, injecting the filler continuously. The indented line, filled from beneath the skin, looked noticeably shallower. When both lines were filled, he completed the treatment by giving the lower lip more shape to match the improvement in the upper one. He then went over each area, smoothing the material again, getting just the effect he wanted. He reached for an icepack and applied it gently to her lips. "Okay, Muffy, you're even more beautiful now," he said.

"Thank you, I think," she said. "My lips feel like they're the size of garage doors."

Nick laughed. "I wouldn't do that to you, my dear. You're much too pretty for garage door lips," he said, handing her a small mirror.

"There was local anesthetic mixed into the filler we used, so your lips are numb, and you won't be able to move them normally for about half an hour. Don't worry about how you're holding them right now. Everybody gets a little snarl like Elvis had for a while after this treatment." He wiped away a bit of numbing cream that had gathered near the corners of her mouth. "They're also a bit puffy right now. But by tomorrow morning I think they'll be beautiful."

Muffy looked closely at her mouth in the hand mirror. "They're definitely better, Doctor. Thank you."

"My pleasure," Nick said, pointing to Greg. "My assistant will clean off the remaining gel and bring you to Lesli."

The assistant nodded and Nick left the room.

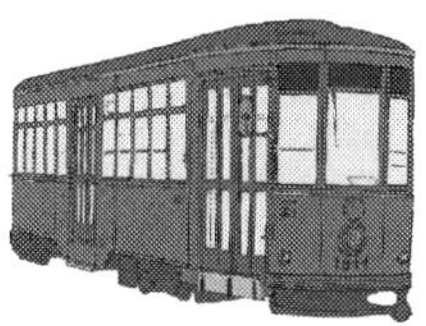

17

Nick entered the exam room across the hall and greeted Jane Meadows. It had been six days since her surgery. He unfastened the Velcro of her elastic bandage and unwound it. Underneath was a lighter cotton gauze wrap, placed to be comfortable against the skin, which he also removed. He stepped back and appraised her for a long moment.

"Well, Michelangelo?" Jane asked nervously, uncomfortable with the silence.

"You look just as you should. Actually, you're a little better than you should be for this point in time." He handed her a mirror. "Of course, you've got some bruising here and here," he said, pointing to her neck and the area behind one of her ears. "But that's par for the course." He ran a finger gently over the side of her neck. "And you're a bit swollen here."

Jane nodded, still looking at her reflection "I noticed that. And it's tender too. That won't stay, will it?"

Nick took the mirror from her. "No. The tenderness is temporary. And everyone is swollen at this point, especially on the sides of the neck. It's where the real work of lifting is done. There are sutures in the connective tissue and muscle there that hold everything in its newly youthful position. I call this swelling 'linebacker neck.'"

Jane smiled. "Then I'm glad it won't stay. I'm too small for football."

Nick grinned, "We're going to take out some stitches today. This is your first step towards becoming a civilian again."

"Thank goodness," Jane said. "I know you've done your best, and it's going to turn out great, but let me tell you, Nick, this is not a trivial thing."

"I know. Not like the way they tell it on TV. You did *not* have a lunchtime peel."

Nick took a small surgical forceps and scissors from a counter drawer. "Let's get some of these stitches out. That always seems to make people feel better." He used the forceps to gently grasp the end of each stitch in front of one ear, pulling the knot away from the skin. This revealed the suture beneath, which he cut on one side, allowing the blue nylon loop to slide easily from the skin. He repeated the process until the line of stitches in front of her right ear was removed, revealing a razor-thin scar. "Jane, I have to tell you, this is healing beautifully." He smiled at her. "I really appreciate it, too. The one thing I can't do for you is heal."

She beamed back at him. "I aim to please."

He gently cleaned and dried the area with more peroxide and a gauze pad. "So how are things going in general? You seem pretty upbeat for this stage in the recovery process."

Jane nodded slightly. "I am. Our attorneys got together, and it seems Alan is going to be generous with my settlement. I mean, he can afford it, but still, it's a relief. I think his guilty conscience is guiding him."

"That's good news."

"It is, but that's not all. Since I'm to be a woman of means, I've decided to enjoy it. So, some of my girlfriends and I got together and decided to take a Mediterranean cruise."

"Wow."

"They also divorced well, so we all can afford it. We're calling ourselves the 'First Wives' Club.'" Nick chuckled as she continued. "We leave in three weeks. Will that be a problem for me?"

"Not at all. You're healing well, and that will make it about a month after your surgery. I usually tell people they're good to go back to work in two to three weeks, so I think you can be on a cruise ship in four." He gave her back the hand mirror so she could see her profile. "You'll need to cover this area in front of your ears with makeup, since the redness in the scars will still be fading, but otherwise I think you'll be very presentable. I want you to wear a big hat and sunscreen when you're out in the sun, Okay?"

"Understood, Doctor. I'll be good."

Nick smiled at Jane. "It's great to see you doing so well. I think you're going to feel beautiful inside and out."

She gave him a hug and there was warmth in her voice. "Thank you, Nick. I think so too."

An hour later, Nick was passing the door to Lesli's office when he heard Felicity shout, "He's such a dick!" on the other side of it. He entered quickly.

"Ladies! I can hear you out in the hall. What in the world is going on?"

Lesli looked angry, "Have a seat, Dr. J. You should hear this."

Nick took the empty chair next to Felicity and looked at his office manager. "What's wrong?"

"Felicity was just telling me how Mr. Wonderful made one of our patients cry."

"What?"

"That's right," Felicity said. "Greg hurt Muffy Wilson's feelings and made her cry. He's such an asshole!"

Nick's face registered shock. "And how did he do that?"

"By basically telling her that she's old and that there's not much you can do to make her look better."

"Huh? That makes no sense. I just *did* make her look better. Tell me what happened."

Felicity blew a stray bang away from her eye, something Nick knew she only did when she was upset. "I was coming up the hallway when I saw Muffy just standing there with tears streaming down her cheek. She was trying to dab at her eyes with an icepack, and I was afraid she might scratch her cornea. I took it from her and brought her back to my room. When she finally calmed down, she told me that Greg had said that no amount of treatment was going to give her the skin of a younger woman. He said—and these are his exact words—that she'd never look young again, because for her the ship had sailed, and she wasn't a chick anymore."

"He said that?"

"What an idiot," Lesli added, shaking her head.

"Oh, and that wasn't the worst thing he said," Felicity continued.

Nick put his face in his hands. "Go ahead. Hit me."

"He said she was in denial. That she should face the fact she wasn't in her forties or even fifties anymore."

Lesli added, "And she's only fifty-two."

The surgeon looked up at the ceiling. "Oh, boy. Not good. So how did you leave it with her?"

Felicity shifted again, "Well, I took her over to the makeup bar and fixed the mascara, which had run all over her cheeks. I did my best to cheer her up. I told her not to listen to Greg and that she's actually quite lovely. Which I think she is. She felt better when she left, I think. She gave me a hug and said she's going to come to me for a facial."

Nick gave his aesthetician a grateful look. "It sounds like you saved the day. You handled this perfectly."

"Thanks, I did my best. I'd really like to tear Greg a new one."

Nick looked at Felicity for a moment, and then said, "You know, I think you should. Let me know how it goes and how he responds."

"Oh, you won't have to wait long. I'm on it."

Lesli held her hands in front of her as if in prayer: "Can't we just fire him?"

Nick rose to leave with Felicity trailing behind him. "If this becomes a pattern, believe me, we will. But if we have to do that, we'll need something in writing in Greg's personnel file. In this day and age, if you're going to fire someone, you need a paper trail. If you don't have one, they'll turn around and sue you for wrongful termination."

The office manager stuck to her guns. "Boss, I think you can fire him right now for what he just did."

Nick nodded, "I suppose I could, but it would be less likely to come back and bite us if there's a paper trail. Just trust me on this. And it is helpful to have him around on busy days."

"We could get somebody else."

"I know. But he got screwed at his last job, and I'd like to help him out if we can. Hopefully he can learn from this."

Lesli rolled her eyes, "Boss, sometimes you're too nice for your own good."

Felicity reached over and poked him, "Inside that meaty chest, you're a big marshmallow."

Nick chuckled, "Lesli, take Greg aside and get his side of the story about what happened with Mrs. Williams. Then write a memo to his personnel file. Make sure it reflects that you allowed him to explain what happened, and that he was definitely in the wrong. Be sure to write that he was reprimanded, put on probation, and told that another incident like this would result in us firing him. Have him sign it, okay?"

"My pleasure," Lesli replied, reaching for her keyboard.

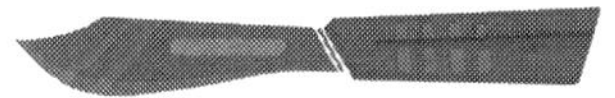

Nick stood aside to let Felicity walk up the stairs ahead of him. She made a beeline for the break room, and since it was lunchtime, he realized that the confrontation with Greg would probably take place now. He thought better of listening outside of the lunchroom; instead, he went to his office, closed the door, sat down at his desk, and pushed the intercom button for the break room, which he knew would allow him to hear what was being said there.

He heard a chair scrape on the floor, then Felicity's voice came through clearly.

"Greg, you are such an asshole."

There was a pause, and then Nick heard his assistant say, "Whaa?" probably through a mouthful of sandwich.

"You know what you did; what you said to Mrs. Williams. You really hurt her feelings."

He heard Greg laugh, "You mean *Muffy*? You *would* like her."

Nick cringed, hearing the obvious dig at Felicity's sexual orientation.

"Yeah, well it's guys like you that make women a preferable option. You know what you are? You're a wanker."

It sounded like Greg was laughing, then he said in a high-pitched voice, "No yankee my wankee."

"*What?*"

"Hello? Long Duk Dong? *Sixteen Candles*? Ring any bells?"

Felicity sounded angry. "You would say something completely idiotic like that."

"I don't know what you're talking about. I was perfectly nice to Mrs. Williams. Anyway, I don't care what you think."

"You'd better care. You know what you did, and it's bad for business. That's not how to treat anyone, let alone one of our patients. Lesli and Dr. Jordan are pissed."

"You told them?"

"Yup."

Through the intercom, Nick heard Greg say in a nasty voice, "You should worry more about *your* business and less about Muffy's muffin. Anyway, it's my word against yours about what happened in there." The surgeon bit down on his lower lip; he was getting angry.

Felicity sounded calmer now. "That's right, Greg, it is my word against yours. And if I tell on you, who do you think they're going to believe? You've been here what, a couple of months? I've been with them for four years."

Nick heard a chair scrape, "Yeah, but you're forgetting you're just an aesthetician. I'm the medical assistant, and that's more important. I help the doc make big money. And money talks and bullshit walks, so they can't afford to get rid of me."

"So, you think you can't be replaced? That's called having delusions of grandeur. What a wanker you are."

Nick heard Greg's laugh fade through the telephone; he must have been leaving the room. In a high voice, the assistant repeated, "No yankee my wankee..."

18

The city of New Orleans forms a North-facing crescent moon; Lake Pontchartrain lies at its belly, and a long slow curve of the Mississippi river flows against its back. Running along the river, Tchoupitoulas Street is the spine of the city. Nick was driving down it on his way to meet Eddie. On his right was the grassy green levee with its massive container cranes perched over the river. On his left, a variety of small buildings, most of them old and in decline, housed a myriad of businesses: small grocery stores, manufacturer's offices, nail salons, some of the best bars and music clubs in the city, and at least one massage parlor.

Nick saw Eddie's car and pulled up to an old yellow single-story house badly in need of paint. He was embarrassed to be there. *Why on earth did I let him talk me into this?* he wondered, as he climbed the porch steps and was greeted by a faded poster in the window showing someone's back being rubbed by female hands with very long nails. Next to it was a bright neon sign that read "OPEN". He tried the front door, which was locked, then pushed the doorbell button and heard a buzzer go off. The door unlocked and he pushed it open.

"Buddy!" Eddie enthused, as Nick walked into a dimly lit front room. He looked past his friend at two middle-aged Asian women who were regarding him with interest. Eddie turned and gestured toward them. "Nick, let me present Suki and YoYo." Nick stepped forward and shook their hands. One of them giggled and said something to the other in a language he didn't understand.

"That's Japanese," Eddie said. "Don't even try to understand what they're saying to you." He punched Nick in the shoulder. "Or about you!" he howled and broke into laughter. Nick thought he smelled scotch.

"Have you been drinking, Eddie?"

"Oh, just a little bit, to take the edge off, you know."

"I thought that's what they're for."

This brought more laughter. "Truer words were never spoken, pal!"

Nick felt uncomfortable in the extreme. "I'm leaving. You can have both of them."

He turned to walk out, and Eddie grabbed his arm. "Hey, listen man, there's nothing to worry about here. You'll just get a relaxing massage, and then we can go out and get a drink and something to eat. Besides, I already paid for both of us."

Nick was touched. "You didn't have to do that, Eddie."

"I know. I wanted to. You've been stressed out with good reason, so this is my gift to you."

Nick turned back and looked at his friend. "Okay, I'll stay."

Eddie slapped him on the back, "Good. Now pick one."

"What?"

"Pick who you want to massage you. YoYo or Suki."

Nick looked at the two women and felt embarrassed. He didn't want to hurt either one of their feelings. "They both look like good masseuses to me, I guess."

The women giggled and one of them stepped forward and put a hand gently on Nick's arm. "I'm YoYo. I massage you today." And with a smile over her shoulder at her colleague, she took the doctor by the hand and led him to a door at the end of a narrow hallway.

He stepped into a small room with no window that featured a massage bed in its center and not much else. "You want table shower?" Yoyo asked him.

Nick had no idea what that was, but couldn't imagine it happening in this room. "No thanks. I took a shower before I came."

Yoyo giggled. "Okay, you take off all clothes, lay on table."

"All clothes?"

"Yes."

"Do I lie face up or face down?"

"Start face down." She giggled again and left the room.

Nick undressed, looking at a watercolor print of a bridge, which hung on the bare white wall above the bed. A clock radio played cool jazz. He laid down on his stomach and sniffed at the sheet covering the table. It smelled freshly laundered, which reassured him. He put his forehead on his crossed arms and closed his eyes.

A moment later there was a soft knock at the door, "Ready?"

"Yes," Nick said loudly, and the door opened.

Yoyo entered wearing a silk robe and flip-flops. "Comfortable?" she asked and turned the volume on the radio up a little.

"Yes," he answered. He heard liquid being squirted and her hands rubbing together. Then she touched his back with a long, smooth stroke starting up near his neck and continuing all the way to the top of his buttocks. The feeling was amazing. He let out a slow deep sigh.

"Good?" YoYo asked, continuing to stroke him.

"Good," he replied, and relaxed into the massage bed.

"Mr. Eddie say you plastic surgeon."

Fucking Eddie, Nick thought. The man had no concept of discretion.

"That's right."

She stopped rubbing. "What I need?"

"Hmmm?"

"What I need plastic surgery?"

He raised his head and looked around at her. His standard line came out with no thought involved. "You don't need a thing. You look great."

She gave him a look, "I need something. Maybe nose?"

"Your nose is fine. It's a cute little nose."

She giggled. "Okay. I no make you work." She pushed gently on his neck and his head settled back onto the bed. He sighed contentedly as she continued to work him, her hands gliding over the thin coating of oil. She rubbed his calves and his thighs and his buttocks, alternating between firm pressure and light strokes. Every once in a while her hand would stray to an upper, upper thigh, and the feeling was fantastic. Without thinking he spread his legs apart slightly and her hands lingered there longer. He let out a little gasp.

"You like?" YoYo said softly.

The massage was now completely erotic, and Nick knew it. He didn't want it to stop. "Yes," he whispered back.

He heard her squirt more oil on her hands and then she was working his thighs and buttocks again, but lightly grazing other areas with every stroke. His body started to move in rhythm with her manipulations.

"You turn over now."

Nick knew what would happen if he turned over. He hesitated for a moment and considered asking her to stop. But what she was doing to him felt so good, and he reflected, it had been so long since anyone had touched him in that way. *Where is the harm, really*? he thought. This was her business, this was what she did, and he was going to tip her very well. It was two people getting what they wanted from each other; a win-win. He rolled over.

She ran her hands over his body, teasing and stroking him until he was fully hard. "I'm sorry about that," he said, acknowledging his erection.

"No sorry. Is good, is natural," she said, letting a fingernail play gently over one of his nipples.

"I guess you're right."

She took a step back from the table and loosened her silk robe, revealing nice breasts and a slim waistline. "What you want?" she asked, smiling at him.

"Huh?"

She giggled, "You want mouth or…" her hand moved lower over her body.

"Uh, no thank you. Just hands, okay?"

She nodded but left the robe undone. "Okay, you boss," she said and moved in to finish him.

Minutes later, Nick had come, and YoYo had brought in a warm, wet towel and cleaned him thoroughly. A sheet now covered his lower body, and she sat on a pillow above him, rubbing his scalp and temples. Nick couldn't remember feeling more relaxed. "This is wonderful", he said. "Thank you."

"My pleasure," came the soft reply from somewhere above his closed eyelids.

They heard loud grunting and raucous laughter coming from a room nearby. YoYo giggled, "That Mr. Eddie."

Nick grimaced and shook his head. "I don't even want to know. Can you turn up the music, please?" She did so, but the noises from across the hall grew louder too, and he had to listen to his friend climax. Eddie was apparently very vocal at such times. So was Suki for that matter. There was more laughter and then silence.

"They done now." YoYo said.

"Thank goodness" Nick replied, and turned his complete attention to what she was doing to his neck and shoulders.

Eddie nursed his third J & B Scotch and watched Nick finish another bourbon and ginger. Rosie's was crowded and they were at one of the small tables tonight. The waitress set down two steaming dishes of spaghetti with daube and took their order for another round of drinks. Nick speared a piece of tender roast beef dripping with red gravy and tried it. "Man, that's good," he said.

"Was the massage good for you too?" Eddie asked, his mouth half full of meat and pasta.

"Yeah."

"Did you enjoy your happy ending? It's been a while for you, hasn't it?"

Nick looked at him innocently, "What are you talking about?"

Eddie grinned, "You know what I mean. Did she blow you or what?"

Nick shook his head, "Just a straight up massage. That's all."

"Uh-huh."

They kept eating. Nick silently wondered why he'd just lied to his friend, *Am I that scared to have someone know something personal about me? Just like with the divorce. No one can know. What the fuck is my problem?*

Nick took a pull from his drink. "I'm sorry. I don't know why I lied just then."

"It's okay. I knew you were full of shit. Suki told me you got off."

"Did she now?"

"Yup. She also told me you tipped YoYo two hundred dollars." Eddie laughed, "You really made that girl's night. I'd already tipped her a hundred."

"Good. She can probably use the money."

Eddie nodded, a bit of red gravy showed at the corner of his mouth, "I'm sure she can." He wiped his face. "You care too much about what other people think, you know."

"I was just thinking that too."

"I mean, I know doctors have to have a squeaky-clean image and all. But you're not perfect; you're still a human being. And I'm the last person you need to impress."

“I know.”

Eddie looked at him. “I suppose we all try to fool the outside world in our way,” he said, “but what’s important is that we don’t bullshit ourselves.”

“Are you going somewhere with this?”

“I was thinking about those panic attacks you were having. You usually keep it together pretty well, so there must be something inside you that’s not right. Maybe something unresolved. And if you’re not truthful with yourself, whatever that thing is, you might never make it right. It might stay unresolved, which is probably not good for you. It’s just a thought.”

Nick took another bite of the daube, “You know, you’re right—I’ve always cared too much about what other people think of me. Remember how you felt in middle school? How hard you tried to fit in and be liked? I think I’ve always been that way.”

Eddie nodded. “So, you build this idea of what you want the world to see. And that becomes you. But if it’s not in line with your true nature, then there’s a conflict. Like tonight—you were lying on that table with beautiful little YoYo’s hands all over you—the real you had to come out.”

“Well, I could hear the real you coming through the damn wall.”

They both laughed. “Sorry about that pal. But really, I’m not.”

“No apology necessary.”

Eddie looked him in the eye, "Nick, the way you act and carry yourself is spot on. To the outside world you're the perfect doctor. But you sure as shit aren't perfect. You got to keep it real, man; especially with yourself. Feel what you gotta feel. Do what you gotta do. That's all I'm gonna say about it."

Nick leaned back in his chair. Sometimes Eddie amazed him. He'd talked to therapists, and none could get down to the truth the way his friend just had. He took another long pull from his bourbon and felt the world loosen up a little.

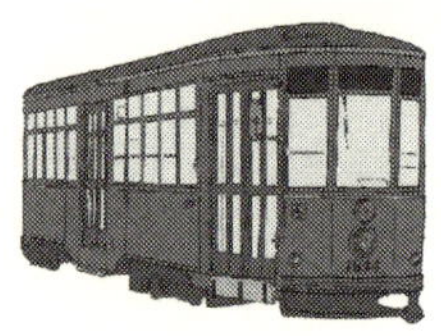

19

The next morning, Lesli tapped on Nick's office door and entered. He raised his head from the desk and gave her a bleary look.

"You okay there, Boss? You don't look so good." Nick rubbed his eyes.

"Don't start with me." He took a sip of his coffee. "Long night with Eddie. Anyway, what's up?"

She gave him a knowing smile. "Lovely is here. She wanted to say hello before you start seeing patients."

Nick stood up and stretched then tucked in his shirt. "Sure. I'll say hi to her."

"You might want to fix your hair before you do, Dr. J.," Lesli said, leaving the room.

Nick walked to the mirror he used for consultations and smoothed errant tufts of his thick brown hair. He straightened his tie. *It was always good to see Lovely,* he thought. Her parents had nailed the name. Maybe calling her that had been a self-fulfilling prophecy. Then he remembered something. *She's in my address book too.* She had seen the damn profile.

There was a soft tap at the door, and something positively gorgeous bounced into the room. Lovely Pendergrass was tall and blonde and had a slim athletic body. She dressed better than any pharmaceutical rep he had ever known. The yellow dress and black patent heels she was wearing accentuated her figure perfectly. She had a movie star's smile and big brown eyes that seemed to sparkle with good humor. As a facial surgeon he admired her perfect, slightly upturned nose and flawless bone structure. "Hey, Doctor Jordan!" she said in a bright southern accent. She came close and gave him a hug. She was a hugger.

"Hey, Lovely, how are things?" Even in his current dismal mood, she raised his spirits. The sun came out from behind his mental clouds when she entered the room.

"Fine," she replied, settling into an armchair across from him. "I'm always busy, you know. My territory is the whole state, and my poor little car is tired." She set her beautiful lips in a playful pout.

Nick chuckled. "So how many of us boring doctors do you have to see in a day?"

"I visit up to four practices every day I'm on the road." She shifted in her chair recrossing long, toned legs. Nick felt his mouth get dry and swallowed hard. "So, some days I see quite a few doctors. They're not all boring." She grinned at him. "But of course, you're my favorite, Doctor Jordan."

"Ha," he replied, in a slightly cracked voice. "I'll bet you say that to all the docs. And, hey, please call me Nick when we're not around patients or staff."

"Thank you. I'll do that, Nick. So how have you been?"

He loosened the knot of his tie a little. "The practice has been a little slow, but I'm sure it will improve, thanks in part to your wonderful products. Personally, I'm okay. I've just gone through a divorce, which was painful." He sighed. "Actually, you might have seen something in your email related to that."

She leaned forward and smiled at him. "I did get something from you some time back. But it didn't seem like you."

"Thanks for saying that. I think I was legally insane when I wrote it."

"So, I gather you're a free man these days?"

"Free as a bird, but you don't want to hear about my non-existent love life."

"Sure, I do; tell me about it."

"I was, uh, overserved one night and somehow logged onto Match.com. I'd been trying to keep the divorce private, so I think that even in my drunken stupor, I tried to fill out the profile anonymously. You know, no photo or information that would allow people to find out that it's me."

"Uh huh. Like NJMD?" She giggled.

He hung his head, "Like I said, I wasn't thinking clearly…"

"I'm sorry, go on."

"So, long story short, I filled out the profile and then somehow I sent it to my entire address book."

She covered her mouth and laughed. "Whoops. I guess that let the cat right out of the bag!"

He nodded somberly. "We can safely say that it did."

"It might turn out to be a good thing for you. A lot of women must know you're single."

"I don't know; the whole thing was pretty damn embarrassing."

"I'm sure it was, and I don't mean to make light of it. I'm sorry if I did."

"I know. It's okay."

Lovely leaned forward and put her left hand on his. The feel of her fingers on his skin sent a warm shock through him. "Nick, in my opinion you have nothing to be embarrassed about and certainly nothing to worry about. You're a nice guy, you're good-looking, and you're interesting. Women will be falling all over themselves to get a date with you."

He gave her a warm smile and made no move to withdraw his hand. It felt great under hers. "You're too kind, Lovely. But if you really think I'm attractive, we're going to have to get you to the eye doctor."

She giggled. "All this and modest too. I think any single girl would be lucky to go out with you, Nick." He looked down at her hand. There was no ring on it.

They chatted for a while longer, and eventually spoke about the products she sold to his practice. Ginger broke in over the telephone intercom to let him know that the first patient for the morning was waiting for him. They rose and Nick got another hug, a little longer this time. "See you soon," Lovely said, as she left the room.

He took a few moments to collect himself and then went to see the patient. Afterwards he wrote a short note in the chart and then walked into Lesli's office. She looked up at him from her surgery-scheduling book. "Hey there, Lesli-Lou," he said, using his nickname for her. He said it so often that some of their patients thought it was her actual name.

She finished writing in the book and closed it. "Hey yourself. What's up?"

He sat down across the desk from her. "I was talking with Lovely about my little email mistake."

She chuckled, "Oh, yeah, that was the hot topic of conversation around here for weeks. You know, I think it turned out to be a good thing for you. At least you don't feel like you've got to keep the big secret anymore. It's definitely out there."

"Lovely said the same thing. We had a nice talk. She tells me we're tops in the state with her products."

Lesli raised an eyebrow and looked at him. "Yeah, we burn right through them. We should be some of her favorite people."

He reddened slightly. "Funny, she said that too."

Lesli smiled. "Uh-huh. So, what did she think of your dating profile?"

"She was very nice about it. Complimentary."

"Like flirty complimentary?"

He shifted in his chair "No. A little, I guess. I don't know."

"You should ask her out."

"You think so?"

"Sure. Strike while the iron's hot."

"I've always liked her. Maybe I will." He rose from the chair. "On a far less tantalizing note, are the financials getting any better?"

She looked at her monitor screen and clicked a few keys.

"Still down from this time last year. Some of our regulars aren't returning, which is weird. And the Botox profit numbers are still low. Are you comping all the hair and nail people?"

"No. I give them a break because they refer clients, but I never comp anyone except family and staff."

"We're below our targets, but I'm hoping things will improve. The whole thing is kind of baffling."

"I know," he said, turning to leave. "Stay on it and keep me posted."

"Will do." Lesli answered, flipping the scheduling book back open. "Ask her out!" she called after him as he headed out the door.

In the hallway Nick almost ran into Muffy Williams, who was coming from the spa area. Her face displayed the shiny pink glow that clients always had after getting a facial or light peel. "Hello, Ms. Williams," he said, making way for her to pass. "Have you just been buffed and polished?"

"Muffy, please, doctor. I have, and it was wonderful. Felicity gave me a terrific Silk Peel."

"I'm glad to hear you enjoyed it." He leaned closer and said in a conspiratorial whisper, "I thought you didn't approve of Felicity. You said she was too—what was it, informal with me—wasn't that it?"

Muffy smiled. "You have a good memory, Doctor. But she was very kind to me recently, and now she's taking wonderful care of my skin." Her voice dropped to a whisper that matched his own, "Let's just say my views on the subject have changed."

Nick cocked his head and watched her walk away. He could swear she was humming.

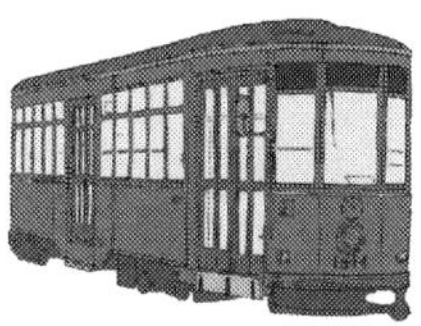

20

It had now been over a month since his email fiasco, so Nick was surprised when a patient commented to him: "Doctor, I want you to know that I received your dating profile. I assume that was sent to me by mistake?"

Nick sighed and looked at the heavyset sixty-five-year-old woman, whose sutures he had just removed and nodded. "It was. Much to my dismay, that document went out to about thirty-five hundred people. It's been very embarrassing."

She chuckled "Someday you'll look back on it and laugh, but maybe not for a while. Still, I can't imagine a man in your position needing to do online dating at all. I would think you'd have women knocking down your door to go out with you."

Nick shook his head. "It's really not that way."

She smiled. "I'm sure you're just being modest, Doctor. I bet you've got a hot date tonight."

He recalled the conversation as he separated a cardboard takeout box from the stack and looked over the salad bar. He was in a grocery store near his office, and it was getting dark outside. He noticed a few other middle-aged singles shuffling around the bar, peering at the available veggies through glass sneeze guards. He came here a couple of times a week, and it always made him feel sad. After all, if you had an intact family, *or at least an intact marriage*, you'd be home, having a glass of wine with your wife, talking about the day you'd both had. What you wouldn't be doing is scooping your dinner into a box, having someone weigh it, and then driving it home to eat by yourself in front of the television. *Welcome to Loserville,* he thought as he made his way down the aisle.

He was beginning to recognize faces; the man in the gray sweatshirt always seemed to be here, and a dour-looking woman in her fifties looked familiar. It occurred to him that he was becoming a fixture of the place as well. And he knew that living this way was okay for a while, but he wanted the glass of wine and the conversation again soon. The way it had once been with Elizabeth it would have to be with somebody else. He would have to go out there and find her. The thought made him fearful—what if he never found her? A wave of sadness hit him, and the idea of feeling sorry for himself made Nick feel ashamed.

Arriving back home, he found a hand-addressed envelope in a pile of letters and magazines in the foyer beneath the mail slot. He opened it. So, Charles was having his party, even with a hole in his head. Screw his own pity party, he thought, this was a real party. As he sat down to eat his salad, Nick smiled thinking of what Charles had said. *You can't keep a good man down.* Words to live by.

21

On a Friday evening several days later, Nick eased his convertible through the main entrance of *Fleur de Lis* apartments and found visitor parking. The massive building, known to locals as "Red Square," occupied an entire block on St. Charles Avenue, at the point where the stately Victorian homes of the Garden District gave way to more commercial establishments closer to downtown. The all-brick structure was a four-story-tall quadrangle with a charming central garden and a large underground parking deck. Nick lingered in the BMW for a few moments, gathering his thoughts. He recognized that, in a sense, this was his coming out party—the first time he'd been out socially since his divorce went through. He recognized the earliest signs of anxiety beginning to stir within him and consciously fought against the feeling. For a moment he considered starting the car again and leaving. He looked at himself in the rearview mirror and saw weakness in his eyes. He hadn't taken a Percocet in the last two weeks, and he wanted one to fight the nervousness now. He closed his eyes and took a deep breath, then opened the car door.

He found the elevator and pressed the button marked **3**. Nick had been surprised to learn that Charles lived on the third floor of the four-story building; he'd always just assumed it would be the top floor and best view for his high-flying patient. He arrived at number 301 and noted it was the only apartment he'd seen in the building with double doors. He rang the bell and was greeted by a tall and beautiful woman in a black halter-top. She wore a Chippendale-style white collar and dress cuffs which showed off tan, bare shoulders and arms. "Welcome. Please come in," she said, flashing Nick a brilliant smile.

Stepping into the foyer, Nick stopped short at the sight that greeted him. The far wall seemed to be one enormous window that framed the twinkling lights of New Orleans' downtown skyline. It seemed impossibly tall.

He felt a hand grip his shoulder and turned to see Charles Monroe grinning at him. His host was dressed in a charcoal gray suit that Nick knew had to be custom tailored. Charles had selected a black dress shirt, blue silk tie, and matching pocket square to complement the outfit. He wore a Sinatra-style black felt hat tilted at a rakish angle, which effectively covered the area where Nick had done the biopsy. "Bigger than it looks from the hallway, isn't it, Doc?"

Nick wasn't aware that he'd been staring at the huge apartment in amazement. "These ceilings must be twenty feet high, Charles. How did you do this?"

"Well, I wanted a nice view and plenty of space, so I bought the corner apartments on the third and fourth floors. I brought in an architect and a contractor, and they figured out a way to turn them into one big home for me."

Nick shook his head "Unbelievable. The building let you do that?"

"It took some persuasion and a structural engineer to convince them the roof wasn't going to cave in, but yeah, I managed it."

"How many bedrooms?"

"There are four, but I use one as an office. Both original apartments had three bedrooms, but we reconfigured the space to make the big gathering room here." He took Nick by the elbow and led him down a set of wide, polished stairs to a large, square living room, where most of the guests were gathered. The ceiling seemed even higher from this lower level.

Nick accepted a glass of champagne from the silver tray of another gorgeous server and turned back to Charles. "Fantastic. I should have known you'd have the mac-daddy pad here." He lowered his voice, "So how did it go with the node biopsy?"

Charles moved his shoulder in a slow circle. "I had it done a few days ago. They found the lymph nodes that the hole you made drained to. It's still a little sore. They said the nodes looked normal when they took them out, but that I'd have to wait for the pathologist to say if there's any melanoma in there."

Nick nodded. "I'll call Monday and get your result. When do they want the stitches out?"

"They said Wednesday."

"All right. Give the office a call and tell them to get you in with me on Wednesday. I'll take care of the node biopsy area for you, and I'll give Dr. Donato a call and let him know I'm doing it. I've got a few tricks up my sleeve—don't tell Larry I said so, but you might end up with a better scar that way."

"Thanks, Nick, I appreciate it." Charles looked up at the entrance and his face brightened. "Ah, there's the lovely Tiffany. I'll make sure you two meet." He walked a few steps and turned back to Nick. "And at some point, check out the deck. It's pretty cool."

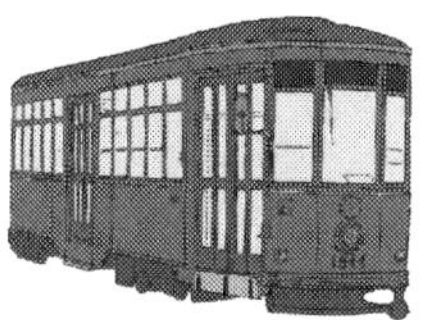

22

Nick looked around the room and marveled at how well decorated it was. He had expected a modern theme in what he knew would be a bachelor pad. A tasteful blend of classic period furniture and modern and postmodern art gave the room a comfortable and inviting feel. Charles had hidden depths, he thought, or at least the brains to hire a very good interior designer. Any visitor, especially a first date invited up for a cocktail, would be positively impressed. He reflected, not for the first time, that Charles did bachelorhood right.

The room filled as more guests arrived. Models in collars and cuffs continued to circulate, serving hot hors d'oeuvres. Smooth jazz played in the background, controlled by a futuristic-looking Bang and Olufsen stereo system that was custom installed into a large stone fireplace. Near the center of the ceiling, an enormous skylight opened electronically to give the party guests a spectacular view of the night sky. One of the largest men Nick had ever seen stood next to a grand piano topped with trays of sushi. He recognized him as a defensive lineman for the New Orleans Saints. The acoustics of the large room made it sound like a crowded New York restaurant. The party was in full swing.

Nick wandered through a doorway off the main room and found himself in a comfortably furnished study. He examined a framed photo of Charles with golf buddies at a course that looked to be in Ireland or Scotland. He was studying a small black and white photograph when a voice behind him said, "That's me and my parents, just before they divorced." He turned to see Charles holding the hand of a gorgeous blonde. "I was about ten when that was taken," he said.

"I bet you were so cute," the woman said, giving him a hug.

Charles chuckled, "Still am, right?"

Nick turned to greet them, but as he did, his attention shifted to a framed shadow box. It displayed military dog tags with Charles's name on them. A weathered wooden tag had been mounted beside the metal ones on a rusted chain. The writing on it was faded and smudged. "What does this tag say?" he asked.

"Those are my dog tags from Vietnam," Charles answered. "I made that wooden one from a piece of an old crate. It's a Winston Churchill quote. It was appropriate at the time, believe me."

Nick could just make out the first few letters "If you...."

Charles looked him in the eye, and for a moment his perpetually jovial demeanor vanished. "If you're going through hell, keep going." Then the smile returned to his face. "It was a tough time for me. I was just a scared kid, really."

"I can only imagine," Nick said. "Charles, you never cease to amaze me."

"Well, I'm like an onion. I have layers," he laughed. "On a much happier note, Nick Jordan, let me introduce you to Tiffany Hunter."

She extended a beautifully manicured hand, which Nick noticed felt great in his. "I'm pleased to meet you, Tiffany," he said and meant it. Her eyes were large and blue and seemed to sparkle as he looked into them. Charles had been right; she was a knockout. Looking at her with the critical eye of a plastic surgeon, Nick could only admire her lovely neck and high cheekbones. Her lips were full and beautifully shaped, a model of what he tried to achieve with filler. She was wearing a brightly colored dress made of a sheer material that accentuated a beautifully formed and maintained body. Her exceptional beauty was turning him on; Nick was suddenly embarrassed to realize he was beginning to get an erection. He released her hand and sat down quickly in an armchair.

Tiffany gave Charles a puzzled look. He grinned at her. "It's OK honey. Nick is a brand-new bachelor. He's forgotten how to talk to beautiful women who aren't his patients. Be gentle with him, will you?" He turned and started to leave.

"I'll let you two talk," he said as he closed the door to the study on his way out.

Tiffany sat in the chair next to Nick. "So, you're a plastic surgeon?"

Nick's composure returned to him. "That's right. I do work you obviously don't need."

She gave him a smile, exposing two rows of bright, perfect teeth. "You're sweet. What's your favorite operation to do?"

He took a sip of his drink. "Well, I specialize in facial work. Neck up only."

She looked down at her breasts and then back up at him. "That's too bad. I may need your help someday."

"Not anytime soon. You look great."

She smiled again. "That's quite a compliment considering your specialty."

"It's an honest one, believe me," he said. "But back to your question. I'd say the most challenging surgery I do is rhinoplasty, reshaping the nose. It's probably my favorite. But I do more facelifts than anything else. And I really enjoy them, because you see the neck and jaw line transform right before your eyes."

She nodded. "That must be very satisfying."

"It is, and it pays the bills." He took a sip of his drink, "And what about you, Tiffany? What do you do?"

She smiled. "Nothing really, but I stay busy at it." Nick chuckled politely, "I divorced my husband three years ago. He was a crappy husband but a good businessman, so I don't have to work. We didn't have any kids. So mostly I renovate my house." She told him where in the Garden District it was.

"That's a beautiful street."

"Thanks, I like it. I've just started re-doing the kitchen again. Not that there's anything wrong with it, I just like shaking things up. I remember one time when I was married to my husband, the poor slob, and he asked me when we'd be done renovating. I gave him the sweetest look and said, "Why, never, dear." She laughed at the recollection. "I spend my days looking at tile."

Nick couldn't think of a response. At length he asked, "Do you travel?"

"I find a beach to lie on occasionally. Usually Gulf Shores or Pensacola," she said, referring to resort towns on the Gulf of Mexico within driving distance. They talked about Nick's medical practice and the hobbies he never had time for—golf, sculpture, and classical guitar. Searching for something they had in common, he found out that she exercised every day. "I don't particularly like to work out, but I'm a realist. If my body doesn't look like this, how am I ever going to find a man who can afford me?"

"I'd say it's what's on the inside that counts, but that would sound wrong coming from a plastic surgeon."

“We both live in the real world, Nick. I know how things are.”

They regarded each other in silence. Finally, Nick spoke, “Well look at that, our glasses are empty. Why don’t I go refill them?”

She smiled and he looked into her eyes again. The chemistry wasn’t there for her either. He opened the door from the study to the crowded main room. She patted him on the back, and her lips were very close to his ear as she whispered, “I’m fine, but you go on. It was nice talking to you, Nick.” Then she was gone.

Nick joined the throng of guests in the main room and talked with two of his patients who were friends with Charles. He could never attend an event of any size in New Orleans without running into at least one patient; he’d been practicing in the city for far too long. Their reactions to seeing him varied. Some pretended they didn’t know him, especially if they were with husbands or boyfriends. Nick knew many of his patients hid the cost of their procedures from their spouses, and he supposed that some wanted their beauty to be considered completely natural. Other patients went to the other extreme and would hail him across a crowded restaurant, or praise him and his services in front of their friends: “You must meet Dr. Jordan. He did my facelift!" These uninhibited and vocal advocates of his work were lifeblood to the practice, and he treasured their support.

He decided to give the champagne a rest in favor of bourbon and walked to the kitchen, which was just off the main room opposite the study. The room was bright and invitingly modern with gleaming white granite countertops and commercial-quality appliances. A caterer was arranging caviar-topped toast points on a platter, and Nick asked her where he could get a glass of water. She gestured with her head towards a bar set up in the far corner of the room. He looked in that direction, and what he saw astonished him.

Two women were drinking wine and talking with their faces very close together. One of them had her arms around the other's neck, resting them on her shoulders. They were giggling about something, and Nick could tell instantly that they were in love. He didn't know what to do. His first impulse was to flee, but he knew that would be childish. He walked around the large central island close to where the couple was. They were absorbed in one another and hadn't seen him.

"Hello, Felicity," he said, in a pleasant voice. She turned her head to him, and her bright blue eyes went wide with amazement. She opened her mouth, and something between a scream and squawk came out. Her lover turned to look at the source of the interruption and looked even more shocked than Felicity had, dropping a wine glass in surprise. With a quick movement, Nick caught it in mid-air, spilling only a little of the wine. He smiled at his patient, taking in the complete change in her appearance. Gone were the severe bun and sweater set, replaced by a tight pink dress short enough to show off nice legs. Her hair was down and, Nick noted, recently highlighted with auburn streaks. "How are you, Muffy?" he asked.

Muffy Williams looked flustered. "Dr. Jordan! Hi! I was just, ummmm, helping Felicity with her necklace." She turned back to her partner with a look of frenzied appeal in her eyes. Felicity was chugging her glass of wine. When she saw the look, her cheeks puffed out in a blowfish-like attempt to avoid laughing and keep the wine in her mouth. "Felicity, swallow!" Nick yelled. She got the wine down and gasped for breath. They all burst into laughter.

Nick put a hand on each of their shoulders. "So, you two are a couple, huh?"

Felicity hung her head. "I'm afraid so, boss. Am I fired?"

Nick looked at her seriously for a moment. "Well, normally I don't approve of my employees fraternizing with the paying customers." He looked at Muffy. "But Felicity's a first-time offender so I'll let it slide. Besides, you two are grown-ups; you know what you're doing."

Felicity squeezed his hand. "You're the best, Doctor J."

He smiled at her. "It's nice to see a romantic relationship that's working. It gives me hope."

Felicity looked up at him and this time it was she who looked serious. "Can I tell you something, Boss? Good things are coming to you in life. Because of who you are. You deserve them."

He gave her a hug. "You're the second person to tell me that, and it's one of the nicest things anyone's ever said to me, sweetie. Thanks." He looked back over at Muffy. "It was good to see you both. You two have fun."

"Thank you, doctor," she said, as Felicity slipped an arm around her waist, and he could tell that she meant it.

Nick accepted a glass of bourbon from yet another stunning server and re-mingled with the guests in the main room. The sushi had been cleared from the piano, and an Asian woman in a red gown was playing Gershwin and Cole Porter songs. Nick's mind flashed back to his mother humming some of them when he was little. Next to the pianist sat a singer he recognized from the New Orleans Opera. She was dressed in a vintage tuxedo, doing a wonderful job with “Someone to Watch Over Me,” one of his favorites:

Won’t you tell her please
to put on some speed, follow my lead, oh how I need
...Someone to watch over me.

The words hit him as they never had before. Elizabeth was gone, and he knew he’d have to find someone new to share his life with. He realized it might take a long time. But he knew that he wanted a love in his life, and when he found her, he hoped she’d put on some speed.

Nick looked from the piano to a sliding glass door framed by curtains. He thought it must lead to the deck Charles had mentioned. The door was closed against mosquitoes and other winged creatures of the Louisiana night. Nick opened it and stepped out, sliding it closed behind him.

The view from the enormous platform on which he was standing was astounding. Given the deck’s size, he was surprised that he’d never noticed it protruding from the building. Gazing towards downtown, he could see the illuminated monument to Robert E. Lee, the general’s arms crossed defiantly as he faced the North. Behind him rose the buildings of the Central Business District; illuminated rectangles resembling rows of glittering boxes. The deck itself was a feat of engineering; a slab of glistening glass, steel, and wood, suspended in the night air by massive cables and hidden girders.

A woman leaning against the rail at the far end of the deck turned her head and looked at him. For a moment he didn't breathe. She was beautiful. The short, sleeveless dress she wore revealed athletic arms and legs. Her pretty face was framed by long brown hair made wild with blonde streaks. There was warmth in the big green eyes that looked over at him. In the moonlight, she struck him as a marble statue, suddenly come to life.

"Hello," she said.

"Hi."

"This is fantastic. I wonder why we're the only two out here."

Nick took a sip of his drink and moved closer. "Because after a long period of cruelty, the fates have finally decided to be kind to me."

She smiled and took a sip of her wine. "Or maybe it's just a little break in the torture before the eagles return to peck out your liver."

He chuckled appreciatively; she knew the story of Prometheus. "I haven't stolen fire from the gods. All I took was a couple of hors d'oeuvres and this glass of bourbon."

She smiled at him, and he could tell she liked that he had gotten the classical reference. *Beauty and brains* he thought as he extended his hand. "I'm Nick."

She clasped it; her skin felt soft and warm. "Hi, Nick, I'm Rachel."

They stood for a moment with their hands touching and Nick felt it. Chemistry. Two or three sentences and here it was. His mind flitted back to his recent talk with the lovely but vacuous Tiffany and the contrast amazed him. What a tiny miracle. He searched for something to say and then noticed a large woven chaise for two at the end of the deck. "Would you like to sit down?"

She followed his gaze. "That looks more like a lie down kind of thing, but okay, as long as you behave yourself." Then she laughed and grabbed his hand again, pulling him along with her.

They lay on their backs, heads resting on outdoor sofa cushions, looking up at the night sky, and talked of their childhoods and families. She had grown up on a ranch outside of Jackson Hole and went back to visit several times a year. He told her about growing up in California and then moving around the country as he acquired the various pieces of his medical education. They talked about living in New Orleans and how they had both come to realize that nothing ever changed much in the Crescent City. They talked about their careers. Nick was impressed to learn that Rachel had founded and now ran a non-profit that collected and distributed food to the city's soup kitchens.

"My congratulations for actually doing some good in the world," he said.

She sighed. "We do our best, which is rarely enough, but thanks."

He took another tug on his drink. "Is the Ozanam Inn on Camp Street one of yours?"

She looked at him with surprise. "I'm amazed you've heard of it."

He nodded. "I've worked there a few times."

"Well, that's very good of you, Nick."

He chuckled. "It's not as altruistic as it sounds. I lost a bet."

"Really?"

"Some friends and I wanted to lose weight a few years back, so we got together and called ourselves the Fat Boys Club."

"Phat with a 'P'? As in pretty hot and tempting?"

He grinned. "No, the regular spelling of fat, signifying obesity or at least pudginess."

She laughed and sat up, drawing her knees toward her. "Go on. This is fascinating. I've met thousands of volunteers over the years, but this is new."

"So, it really was a bet. We had a weight goal every month and would have to meet it on the first Friday or suffer the penalty. We started with money, but that didn't have much effect. I came up with the idea of public service. At one point a few of us were wearing yellow vests and picking up trash on St. Charles Avenue."

She giggled. "So, how'd you get hooked in with the Ozanam Inn?"

"Someone who works in my office knew about it and suggested the losers, or actually non-losers, help out there."

"And is this a regular thing? Should I look out for your fat boys the next time I'm there?"

"No, we disbanded the club. Before we did, a couple of my idiotic friends got into trouble for eating the sandwiches they were supposed to hand out. It defeated the purpose on multiple levels."

She laughed and Nick thought it was a delightful sound. "That is priceless. With your permission, I'll tell that story at our next board meeting. Of course, I'll leave out your name to protect the innocent."

"There are no innocents in this scenario, but please do keep my name out of it."

Nick realized they'd been talking over an hour. A hint of chill had crept into the early summer air, and he saw Rachel shiver. "Cold?" he asked. "A little." she said, looking down from the now spectacular night sky into his eyes. He extended his arm above her head. "You have no reason to know this about me, but I'm an excellent radiator of heat." She seemed to hesitate for a moment and then inched closer to him. She put her head on his shoulder, and he gently pulled her to him. Her hair smelled of coconut, and her body felt warm next to his. He let out a long sigh. "This is heaven," he said. "Balm for my tortured soul."

She rested an arm on his chest. "Is your soul tortured?"

He took her hand is his. “I’m afraid so.” He told her about his separation and divorce from Elizabeth and about the paralyzing anxiety he’d felt while going through it.

She patted his hand. “I’m sorry, Nick, I really am. I’ve been there and done that years ago. It sucks, but you get through it, and then things are okay, maybe even better than ever.”

He closed his eyes and pulled her a little closer. “This is the best moment I’ve had in a long time, Rachel. Thanks.”

She massaged his hand with hers. “Don’t mention it,” she said. They lay there together looking up at the stars. Nick’s last conscious thought was of how relaxed he felt.

He woke to the sound of two couples chatting together on the other side of the deck. He looked around in the darkness for Rachel. She was gone.

23

Several days later, Nick paused in the damp summer heat and looked across Tulane Avenue at Charity Hospital. The mammoth grey structure stretched upward from a vast concrete slab like a monolithic sphinx rising from the desert floor. Its massive wings and central tower dwarfed all who went near it and engulfed them as they entered. It was at once hideous and strangely beautiful.

There were several entrances, but Nick always took the main one in front. Entering the mouth of this building never failed to impress him. He could still remember how he had felt walking through it the first time as a medical student; it seemed calculated to intimidate. The central lobby was a cavernous concrete, wood, and glass space full of patients, their families, and medical staff. The acoustics of the room made it sound like a crowded train station. High on the central wall, a severe-looking nun in a winged cap looked down from her painting onto the throng. Carved into the wall beside her were the words every visitor saw first:

WITHIN THESE WALLS LIFE BEGINS AND ENDS

The sentiment had always struck Nick as poorly chosen, for it made him think of the unfortunate sick people who had to read it. Logic dictated they'd already been born, so to him the words implied that death, the only other outcome mentioned, was all that was left to them. Of course, this wasn't nearly as depressing as the legend he'd seen carved in stone above the door of the rehabilitation adjacent to the hospital:

NEW ORLEANS HOME FOR THE INCURABLES

How would it have felt to be gravely injured and read those words while being wheeled through that door? Sensitivity to the feelings of patients was not a priority for hospital builders back in the day, Nick mused. Still Charity was both terrifying and majestic; the same could be said for what went on in it. The hospital was awful and necessary, full of grandeur, desperation, courage, and unrealized potential, in perfect harmony with the city it served.

Nick stood to one side of the entrance and waited for his team to arrive. A professor of his had once called this hospital a circus without a tent, and the description fit it well. The lobby smelled of hot box lunches, cleaning fluid, and human grime. Groups of young doctors and medical students hurried past the sick, the homeless, the anxious, and the bored. Nick recognized which university (Tulane or Louisiana State) the students were from by the colorful patches on their white coats. Charity was so big that it easily accommodated doctors in training from the two medical schools that flanked it on either side. The hospital was a major selling point for the schools; there was no limit to the amount of experience that an enterprising young doctor could get on its floors and wards. Of course, the same medical specialty services from each university competed for the most interesting cases. The young doctors from opposite ends of Tulane Avenue were friends and rivals at the same time. Nick recalled the feeling and recognized that this place had helped to shape him as a physician and a person. It had become part of him. And deep down he didn't want to give it up. All the hard work and the absolute necessity of staying calm in the middle of chaos had helped him grow; perhaps it still did. Coming here kept him grounded and connected to a world that had nothing to do with social position and privilege.

He remembered being here at the beginning of his medical career. First, he had worn the short white coat of a medical student, then years later the longer one of a fellow in training. The suit and tie he wore now set him apart as an attending physician. His official title was Clinical Professor of Otolaryngology/Head and Neck Surgery. The head and neck service, also called ENT for ear, nose, and throat, was where he had gotten his start. After four years of dealing with everything that could go wrong in the human head and neck, he had decided to do a fellowship in facial plastic surgery. Now he had a busy private practice in cosmetic surgery and could easily turn his back on Charity. But he remembered where he started and felt a responsibility to help the young doctors who had taken his place. The academic departments at Tulane, like those at all medical schools, couldn't hold on to cosmetic surgeons for long; the money to pay them what they were worth in private practice just wasn't there. The departments relied on community doctors, usually alumni, to come in and help when needed.

Nick was happy to help. He was fully aware that he had chosen to use his training and education in a relatively frivolous field of medicine. Sometimes the fact made him feel guilty. Almost all of his classmates had to contend with real disease—with death and dying and devastating sickness affecting good people. He respected and admired their efforts, but had no desire to share their burden. He'd seen plenty of medical misery, which invariably left him feeling frustrated and sad, during ten years of training. Cosmetic surgery made people feel happier and more confident; the specialty was positive and creative and suited him perfectly. He knew that helping people to look their best wasn't as important as the vital work his colleagues did. Working with the doctors in training at Charity was his way of giving something back to that world.

He spied the head and neck team coming his way. The chief resident, a tall man in his early thirties from Upstate New York, shook his hand. "Thanks for coming, Dr. Jordan. We've got a nice mandible fracture for you." Behind him stood three other residents and a pair of medical students.

Nick nodded to their leader. "Lead the way, chief."

They rode the elevator to the surgical floor and entered the pre-op area. A row of gurneys against the wall held patients waiting for surgery. The chief resident led the group to the third one down, where a thin, disheveled man in his twenties with a swollen face was sitting up in bed. "Dr. Jordan, I'd like you to meet Mr. Henry Erskine." Nick extended his hand, and the patient shook it. The chief continued. "Mr. Erskine was involved in an interpersonal conflict last night and presents with a fractured mandible. His jaw is broken at the left angle and right subcondylar region," he said, referring to two commonly broken sites along the jawbone.

The patient smiled, revealing three remaining front teeth. He looked at Nick. "Son of a bitch cold-cocked me. I never saw it coming. Lucky for him 'cause I would have kicked his ass."

Nick smiled, thinking that Charity never changed. "I'm sure that's true, Mr. Erskine, but let me ask you this: if I fix you up, are you going to go out there and make more work for me? Take your revenge?"

"Naw, Doc, I'm a pussycat at heart."

"I'll take your word for that."

Nick changed into green scrubs in the surgeon's locker room and walked to the O.R. On the way he passed the infamous bullpen and looked through the window in the door. It was exactly as he remembered it—the product of a bygone era in medicine, a bowl-shaped operating theater covered completely in faded beige tile. It functioned as a crucible of pain and embarrassment for medical students. Nick remembered presenting cases to surgery faculty members there on several occasions, and more often than not, left cut to ribbons by their questions and criticism. He involuntarily shuddered and kept moving.

Two hours later they had repaired the broken jaw and wired Mr. Erskine's teeth together to help the bones heal. Nick changed back into his street clothes and met the team at the entrance to the O.R.

"Would you like to eyeball our patient before you leave?" the chief asked.

"Sure, he's on my way out," Nick assented. The chief resident bid the rest of his team goodbye, and he and Nick set off down the long tile hallway to the elevators, which took them down several floors to the patient's ward.

The wards at Charity hadn't changed since Nick was a medical student there twenty-five years ago. Every ward consisted of a row of ten beds on each side of a narrow aisle. The beds were so close together that if adjacent patients stretched out their arms, they could hold hands. The nurses' work area occupied one end of the long room, looking like an oversized teacher's desk. The arrangement guaranteed a complete lack of privacy for all patients. Nick remembered feeling sorry for them as a student on rounds. He and a dozen or more doctors would be gathered around one of the beds and a resident or intern would recite the facts of the case: "Mr. Chambliss here is a forty-eight-year-old man in hospital for complications of syphilis." The other patients found the information about their roommates fascinating and made no secret of straining to hear every word. At some point the hospital had installed hanging curtains that could be pulled around each patient's bed. They cut off the view but did nothing to block the sound, in effect turning the ward occupants' favorite soap opera into a radio program.

Nick reflected that he'd seen it all at this hospital as he entered Mr. Erskine's ward. As always, Charity had more to offer. His jaw fracture patient, sitting up in bed, gave him a big, bloody smile as he approached. On the bed were an open pizza box and a set of wire cutters. Mr. Erskine bled freely from his mouth as he chewed. Nick could see small pieces of wire all over the beige blanket. A thin trail of blood ran down his patient's neck. Another man sat at the foot of the bed. They both seemed to be enjoying the pizza. The doctors stared at them, stunned.

Mr. Erskine looked at them quizzically, and then through a full mouth said, "What?"

The chief looked angry. "Sir, we've just spent two hours fixing your jaw and wiring your teeth together, so it stays fixed. What the hell have you done?"

Mr. Erskine swallowed and looked contrite. "My bad, Doc. I got back here, and they gave me a crappy milkshake to drink, but I was still hungry. So, I called my brother-in-law here." The other man nodded at them amiably and continued chewing. "And I told him to bring over a pizza. I knew there was no way I could eat it with my teeth wired together, so I asked him to bring the wire cutter too." He explained this to the surgeons in a patient tone of voice, like someone speaking to confused children.

Nick tried not to laugh and failed; this was a new one. He pulled the flustered chief aside. "Let them finish then have one of your residents come back and re-wire the arch bars on his teeth back together. Then I want you to sit down with Mr. Erskine and his brother-in-law and explain to them what the wires are for and that if his jaw doesn't heal right, he'll be an oral cripple for the rest of his life. Got it?"

The chief shook his head. "Yes sir. I can't believe some of the characters we get in here."

"Always did, son, always did."

Nick escaped the building with the familiar feeling he always had when leaving Charity—like the night watchman at an insane asylum finally going home.

24

Nick walked into Cure on Freret Street and stopped to admire the décor. The old brick building had been converted into one of New Orleans's most chic cocktail bars. Behind the gleaming black counter stood a huge, illuminated back bar that soared eleven feet to the ceiling and contained hundreds of bottles of all shapes sizes and colors. The crowd looked hip and young, and Nick hoped he hadn't made a mistake in coming. Then, remembering that it was Dave who had arranged for him to meet a girl here, Nick sighed, realizing he probably had.

Nick looked around for someone matching the description Dave had given him. At length he saw a woman waving at him from the corner of the bar, and he moved to greet her. As he approached, he saw that Dave had been right; she was beautiful. Nick noticed with a sinking feeling that she also appeared to be young enough to be his daughter.

"Are you Mick?" she called when he was halfway across the room moving towards her. He waited until he was seated on the bar stool next to her before saying, "Actually, it's Nick."

"I'm Shelley. It's nice to meet ya," she shouted, in a high-pitched New Orleanian accent. Nick knew it was unfair, but he always felt that the local way of speaking sounded even more bizarre coming from women. As harsh as her accent was though, there was nothing wrong with the way Shelley looked. Big dark doe eyes peered out at him from beneath a tumble of long auburn hair that framed an impossibly delicate neck. She had not spared the makeup; her full lips glistened with gloss and her cheeks glowed with color. Further south was a clingy mini dress that advertised a wonderful body.

Nick took it all in for a moment before speaking. "Thanks for meeting me. Did Dave threaten to fire you to make you do this?"

She smiled and shook her head, sending gleaming auburn strands flying. "Naw, nothing like that. Mr. McGloughlin knows I'm not dating anybody now and that I'm up for meeting new people." He could tell she was looking at his temples, and it dawned on him that it was the gray in them that was attracting her attention. *Had Dave told her his age*? he wondered.

They each ordered one of the bar's signature craft cocktails. Nick supposed he enjoyed the current fascination with complicated drinks made with fancy ingredients. The bartenders now did their own consultations, then whisked and shook and muddled ingredients for their patrons, all at a premium price. Good old rum and Coke was out of fashion.

As they drank and chatted, Nick was struck by how uninhibited Shelley was. They tried different specialty drinks, mixing cucumber-infused gin and single batch bourbon with the vodka and rum they had already consumed. Nick felt himself relaxing quickly and warming to the girl. In stark contrast to the calculating and expensively bored Tiffany from Charles's party, Shelley's mindset was wide open; she was living for now. After their third round, she became more animated and, he noticed, started touching him more when she spoke. They talked about her decision to drop out of college and about the apartment she shared with two other girls uptown near the University.

"So how long have you worked for Dave, I mean, Mr. McGloughlin?"

"Its alright, sugar, we all call him Dave. About five years now."

"You like it?"

"It's fine. It pays the bills. And that lets me be me."

"Well, let's toast to that."

She clinked his glass hard with hers. "Damn straight."

He took a sip. "You know, don't tell him I said it, but Dave's actually a pretty good guy. I imagine he'd be fun to be around at work."

"Most of the time he is. But like all guys, he can be a prick sometimes…" she stopped and looked up at him, "whoops."

Nick laughed. "Don't worry, sweetie. I know what an asshole he can be every now and then. And I swear, nothing you say to me tonight will get back to him."

She looked up at him with large, intoxicated eyes and laid a hand on his thigh. "You're nice, you know that? You want to get out of here?"

He let the hand stay where it was. Finally, he picked it up and held it. "Tell me something, Shelley. How old are you?"

"How old do you think I am?"

"Oh no, I never play that game with women. There's no way to win. Dave told me you were in your mid-thirties."

She laughed. "Did he? Fuck him. I'm twenty-five."

"The man lies. And how old do you think I am?"

"He told me early forties."

Nick chuckled, "Another lie. Try fifty."

"I thought so." She reached out and stroked his temple. "The gray gave it away." She stroked his hair again. "You like that?"

"Yes."

"Good." She leaned closer and gently pulled his head towards her until her lips were touching his ear. He smelled bourbon on her breath. "I'm okay with our ages, darlin'. We're both adults."

Nick knew what he had to do, but lingered there a few seconds, feeling her hair, her hand, her breath against his skin. With an effort, he pulled back from her. "You're right, Shelley, but you're still young enough to be my daughter."

She leaned in closer; her lips now very near his. He longed to kiss them. "Your call," she said softly in a teasing voice and then leaned back with a satisfied smile on her face.

Nick could tell that she sensed her power and that if she pushed it, she could probably make him cave. "Wow," he exhaled. "You make it hard to do the right thing." He picked up his glass and took a long pull.

"I can make it hard, period," she giggled, returning her hand to his thigh.

"Let's get out of here."

"Okay," she said, and they finished their drinks. Nick paid the bill, and they left the bar. Shelley walked unsteadily on high heels and would have fallen onto the sidewalk a few steps from the door, had Nick not moved quickly to catch her. He propped her back up and put his arm around her to help her walk. "You're not driving like this," he said. "Leave your car parked here, and I'll drive you home."

Her arms were around his waist, and she gave him a squeeze. "No argument from me, baby."

He put her in his car, fastened her seatbelt, and let himself into the driver's seat. She looked around the BMW dreamily. "This is nice, Doctor Nick."

He grinned and put the car in gear. "Thanks."

"Can I ask you something?"

"Sure."

"Do you think my nose is ugly? I think my nose is ugly."

He took a right and glanced towards her. Sweat had smeared her makeup a little. "No, not at all. It's a pretty nose."

"I think you're just being nice. I want a rhinoplasty." She reached out a hand and began rubbing his shoulder. "Will you give me a rhinoplasty, Doctor Nick?"

He laughed. "Honestly, I wouldn't change it at all. You're beautiful the way you are."

She brushed hair away from her face. "I've never liked it. But thanks, you're sweet."

He heard her hiccup and then burp. An unpleasant smell filled the car. Nick knew that smell. He pulled over quickly and looked for a place to stop.

"I think you'd better get out and get some air," he said, hurrying to find a parking place.

She turned to him and said, "No I'm…" and vomited.

At the nearest gas station, Nick cleaned his pants and the car interior as well as he could using paper towels and water in the dark. Shelley sat on the hood of the car next to him, looking very relaxed, watching traffic go by. "I'm hungry," she said, smiling at him.

"You lost your dinner so that makes some sense."

"Hey, I'm sorry about..."

"You already apologized. Don't worry about it."

"Let's go to Camellia Grill, my treat. I would love an omelet."

He stared at her in disbelief for a moment, and then smiled. “Sure, what the hell.”

An hour later they had eaten their fill of greasy, satisfying diner food, and Nick was searching for the address Shelley had given him. He looked over at her. Her head was on her shoulder, and she moved it a little as she slept, probably having a dream, he thought. She looked very young to him now, and he was glad that he had decided not to sleep with her; that his better self had prevailed. At length he pulled up to a duplex off Carrolton Street, and was relieved to see that the lights were on. At least one of her roommates was home to take care of her. Then he noticed a flight of steep concrete steps and sighed, knowing he'd have to carry her up them.

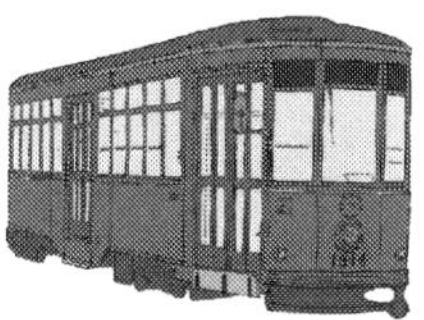

25

It was lunchtime at the office. The staff was upstairs eating, except for Ginger who lunched at the front desk, watching the phones. Greg was off somewhere; he always went out for lunch.

The doctor was looking at email. He'd cancelled his Match.com membership immediately after the dating profile debacle. But he soon found that he missed the daily email listing twelve potential matches, each with a photo and written description, so he'd created a far more anonymous profile and rejoined the site. After viewing his "daily dozen" for a few weeks, he'd become better at reading between the lines. So many of the profiles began with extensive lists of what the writer required in her ideal mate—attributes she was looking for and traits she wanted to avoid. Nick instinctively found this approach off-putting. He much preferred the profiles in which the woman first described what she herself had to offer. *It's nice to see a menu before you get the bill* he had mused, a little embarrassed at the crassness of the thought. Still, he was a man looking at women, and an attractive set of photographs could more than compensate for apparent self-involvement on the part of the writer.

Nick of all people understood the value of beauty. He was pleased to find that intelligence and wit attracted him just as powerfully; if the woman had a good sense of humor and her profile was well written, it invariably drew him in.

His interest was more voyeuristic than anything else; he'd posted no photos and so got very little interest from women on the site. He was there mainly to look. Some of the women on Match attracted him, most did not, but it was interesting to see what the offerings were each day. A few had enticed him enough to reach out in the form of an email, but so far, no dates had resulted. There was one in the works; he'd start with that one and see how it went.

The woman he'd corresponded with seemed funny and was undoubtedly smart; she'd graduated with a degree in electrical engineering from Yale and ran her own technology consulting firm. She looked wonderful in her photos, and her profile assured him that her pictures were recent and accurate. They'd emailed back and forth on what to do and where to meet for their first date, finally deciding on a sushi restaurant in the Garden District. It looked over-the-top in every way; a Japanese palace inhabited by wildly creative sushi chefs.

As Nick worked through his emails, he became aware of an appetizing smell, and realized that the staff must have brought in lunch. He had thirty minutes before his afternoon began, more than enough time to go up and eat. He went upstairs to the break room and saw Lesli and Felicity sitting with Lovely. At the dining table's center were several foil dishes filled with heaps of different types of pastas and salads. Felicity looked up at him as he came in. "Hey there, Boss. Lovely brought us lunch."

Nick smiled. "I can see that. And it smells delicious. Salmonella?"

Lovely rose from the table and extended her hand to him. He noticed she didn't hug him in front of his office staff. "Very funny, doctor. I was told by usually reliable sources that you like Semolina."

Nick beamed at her; she looked great as usual. "You were told right, Lovely—that's just my pet name for the place. I love their pastas. It was so nice of you to bring us lunch."

She pulled out a chair next to hers. "It's my pleasure, Doctor Jordan. Come sit down, and let me get you a plate." She turned to him and put a hand on his arm. An electric shock went through his body, and he shuddered slightly. He didn't even have to look at Lesli to know she was smirking at him. "You're getting so thin; we're going to have to fatten you up."

Lovely made him a plate with two types of pasta and salad. Conversation flowed among the four of them; they talked about how the weather was getting increasingly hot and the latest celebrity gossip. Lesli looked at her watch. "Five minutes to one. We'd better wind this party up." Everyone rose and cleaned their places, then Lesli and Felicity left to start their afternoons. Nick and Lovely were alone in the room. She was putting away leftovers in the refrigerator. He looked at her and smiled, then looked quickly away.

She turned to him. “So, Nick, how’s it going? The last time we spoke you were thinking about getting out there and dating. Have you met anybody special yet?”

“Not really. I’m taking my time with all that. To be honest, it’s been so long I don’t even remember how to do it.”

She laughed. “You’ll be fine. Just be yourself. You’re perfectly charming when you talk to me.”

He looked into her eyes and felt warm. “That’s nice of you Lovely, but you’ve got to be kidding.” He paused, “The truth is, I sometimes feel tongue-tied around you. Maybe you’ve noticed. You’re so beautiful that I get distracted and can’t think of anything to say.”

She gave him her brightest smile. Nick thought it was like looking straight into the sun. “Awww. You say the nicest things. I think you’re making that up, just to be sweet.”

“I’m not honestly.”

She took a step closer to him, “Then that’s quite a compliment, coming from someone I admire so much.”

“You’re always such a cheerleader for me.”

She cocked a perfectly plucked eyebrow at him. “I was one in high school and college. I guess you could say old habits die hard.”

He chuckled nervously. Now was the time and he knew it. *Here goes nothing*, he thought. In a dry voice he said, “Maybe I’m rusty—it could be I need practice talking to a beautiful woman. One who’s not my patient.”

“Uh-huh.”

"So…since you were nice enough to feed all of us, how about if I take you to dinner one night?"

She drew a little closer and looked right into his eyes. "I thought you'd never ask." She put a hand on his shoulder. He felt himself getting warmer. "I'd love to have dinner with you."

His throat felt tight. "That would be great, Lovely." Then another inspiration hit him. "Would you like me to cook for you? We could meet at my place, and I'll do my best to make something edible. If it doesn't work out, we can send out for pizza."

She giggled—a beautiful sound. "That sounds great. And I'll bring the wine. Just let me know if you want red or white." She drew closer and hugged him. Her embrace felt wonderful.

"Okay," he croaked, and then recovered his voice. "I'll call you and we'll set it up. Maybe next week?"

She released him and picked up her purse. "That sounds great, Nick. I'll talk to you soon. She looked away, and he could see she was blushing. "See you later," she said through another giggle and fled.

Nick stood in the middle of the room sweating. He looked down and saw that he was fully erect.

26

On Friday night of the following week, Nick checked himself one last time in the mirror. Roquefort sat at his feet and sniffed the air appreciatively; it was rare these days for the scent of cologne to reach his wide, flat nostrils. "This will have to do, boy," Nick said, and led the small bulldog to the sunroom. He turned the TV on so that Roquefort would have sound and something to watch while he was gone. The portly canine knew he was being left alone and gave him a reproachful look. Nick made sure the water bowl was full and the light turned on. "Wish me luck, Rocky," he said, and softly closed the door.

The shadows of the trees that lined St. Charles Avenue were lengthening as Nick drove towards the Garden District. He reflected that he was about to have his first date courtesy of the internet, where he had encountered and communicated with the woman he was riding to meet. The idea of it felt foreign to him. Online dating technology didn't exist when he and Elizabeth had met. Nick took a deep breath and prepared to participate in this brave new world. He found a parking spot on cracked asphalt under a spreading magnolia tree just off Magazine Street and took it.

The woman's name was Nancy, and this was her favorite restaurant in the city. The building itself was impressive, a sort of futuristic pagoda set among ordinary-looking businesses and homes. She'd suggested they arrive thirty minutes before their seven o'clock reservation to have a drink in the bar and chat before dinner. He'd gotten a text from her while he was driving over, letting him know that she was running late, so he decided to go inside and have a drink. Nick felt nervous and hoped a cocktail might settle him down.

He entered the restaurant and was greeted by a tall and beautiful Asian woman in a long, black dress who escorted him to a bar area overlooking the restaurant. Nick had to admit it was spectacular. There was a large central atrium bordered by golden staircases that lead up to different levels, each with a cluster of tables perched on glossy black tiles. In the middle of the ground floor sat an immense Buddha covered in antique gold leaf and adorned with clusters of fresh flowers. Servers clad in black uniforms moved from table to table, getting them ready for diners. The place was over-the-top cool, and just what Nick had expected.

A cocktail waitress greeted him and gave him a drink menu. His cell phone buzzed in his pocket. He retrieved it and found Nancy's text. *Thirty minutes out. Sorry, N.* He knew she was coming from across Lake Pontchartrain. Traffic must be bad, or maybe there had been an accident on the Causeway, one of the world's longest continuous bridges over water. Nick opened the menu and looked through the specialty drinks. He thought he might as well try one. The waitress returned, and he asked her advice. They settled on the Samurai-In-Your-Eye, a pomegranate, sake, and lemon concoction. He'd always been able to tolerate sake well and enjoyed the gentle buzz it gave him. The drink arrived in a stylish glass with a tiny blue paper umbrella. He looked around the restaurant and sipped deeply, noting that he was still the only customer.

Half an hour later he got another text. She was getting frustrated: *Fifteen minutes out. Fucking traffic. N.* The first Samurai had left him unfazed, so he ordered another. They went down extremely well, and now Nick was aware of a pleasant inner glow. The noise level in the restaurant was picking up as the seven o'clock reservations began to arrive. The waitress returned and asked if he'd like another cocktail. He wasn't sure how much more sake he could drink and remain sharp enough to be charming with his date—*whenever the hell she arrived*—so he decided to shift gears and nurse a bourbon instead. He ordered a Maker's Mark and ginger ale with a cherry in it, which was his old reliable.

The drink and the next text arrived at the same time. *Pulling up to the restaurant now, N.* Nick took a swig and looked at the entrance to the bar. This was it; his first date courtesy of the internet. What would it be like? She had sounded smart and witty on the phone, and her pictures were terrific. What if the date went really well? Could he sleep with another woman yet? *I'm divorced, so why the hell not?* he thought. Nick took a deep breath and looked again.

The light from the doorway was suddenly blocked. He could only see a backlit silhouette, but the outlines of the woman standing in the doorway arrested his attention. Her shape was amazing—long legs flowing into a perfect hourglass figure. A soft spotlight, from where Nick could not tell, played up her body and illuminated her face. Her features were exotic and model-perfect. She looked at him and smiled, then pursed her lips in a mock kiss that made him hold his breath. There seemed to be some sort of breeze in the room, because her long blonde hair was blowing back off her shoulders, heightening the dramatic effect her beauty was having on him. Her shiny silver topcoat fell open, and he was thrilled to see that she was wearing a pink bikini beneath; the bright color of the swimsuit contrasted beautifully with the golden tan of her toned midsection. Nick lowered his head, and his eyes found the cocktail in his hand. The cherry floating on top seemed to have developed a face. It smiled at him and winked. *What a crazy daydream. Maybe sake does affect me after all,* he thought. Startled, he looked up towards the doorway again.

In it stood a short, stocky man. Then he realized it wasn't a man; it was a woman, and she was looking at him expectantly. Nick smiled pleasantly and, in that instant, he realized *it was her*. He felt his insides clutch. Whatever libido that remained in him through the nervousness and alcohol vanished like a bird fleeing towards the horizon. She started forward toward him. The smell of her perfume, a strong scent he immediately disliked, filled his section of the bar.

He rose to his feet and as he did her roundness and general dumpiness became even more apparent. *Athletic and toned my ass,* he thought.

In creating her online profile, Nancy had described her physique as "athletic and toned." She had correctly declined to call herself "slender" or to use the more accurate designation of "a few extra pounds". Nick now thought that the remaining Match.com classification, which was "curvy," would have been more accurate and to use it was still being kind. He extended his hand to greet her and reflected that there ought to be a way to make people describe themselves accurately. He imagined a weighing and measuring station for online daters in every major city, where the romantic hopeful's statistics would be collected and reported on his or her profile. A nice feature to add to the site would be a body mass index calculator. He dismissed these thoughts; aware that they were superficial and probably meant he was a bad person.

As they shook hands, Nick was careful to avoid looking at her body. Nancy, on the other hand, was obviously scanning him up and down. "Sorry to keep you waiting so long," she said, as they sat. She eyed his drink. "I hope you're not drunk. I might have to have my way with you."

Nick let this nauseating intimation pass. "No problem. I know what traffic coming into the city can be like. I'll go and let the hostess know we're both here."

He did so and was told that because they had surrendered their seven o'clock table, they would have to wait an hour for the next available one. He returned to the bar and ordered Nancy a drink. As he walked back to the table, he chided himself. *Grow up - you're not going to be attracted to everyone you meet on an internet date.* This was an opportunity to learn about the online singles scene and dating in New Orleans in particular. He might as well relax and enjoy the evening. Nick took a deep breath and settled into the booth next to Nancy.

The problem was that there really was no small talk. In an alarmingly short period of time, she was asking him pointed questions about his marriage and Elizabeth.

"So, Nick," she said, receiving a martini from the waitress. "What part do you think you played in the demise of your marriage?"

He was taken aback. "Well, I'm not sure. I guess I'll have to think about that."

She sipped and nodded. "You should. I'm sure you have some personal flaws that contributed to it. You need to figure those out, so you can avoid making the same mistakes again."

Offensive as her remark was, he recognized there was truth in it. "I guess we all have flaws," he replied, taking a big tug at his bourbon. "I'll have to work on mine. But I also think it takes two people to make a marriage, and sometimes you grow apart, and it just doesn't work anymore, no matter how much both of you want it to."

She rolled her eyes and chuckled. "Men. Never taking ownership of their problems."

Nick took this latest insult in stride and peeked at his watch. Time seemed to be standing still, and he felt the need to move things along. "You know, I'm on my third drink now, and I've had nothing to eat since lunch. Do you think they'd feed us here in the bar?"

She shook her head. "No. It's such a beautiful restaurant. I don't want to eat in the bar. See if they'll bring you a cracker or some nuts."

"Good idea—I'll see if they have something," Nick said, rising to consult with the bartender. He was relieved to get away from her.

He was informed that regrettably food was not served in the bar. Nick eyed the drink garnishes longingly, and the bartender, understanding his predicament, handed him a stack of napkins. Nick picked out a selection of olives, pickled onions, and celery stalks and returned to the table. Nancy had finished her first cocktail and ordered another. "You're hilarious," she said, eyeing the pathetic snack he had assembled.

He ate an olive. It was the best one he'd ever had, or at least the olive he'd needed the most. She reached out and grabbed his left hand. "You're still wearing your wedding ring?"

He looked at it. "Yup."

"Don't you think that's a little weird—to be out on a date wearing your wedding ring?"

He thought about that. "Well…maybe you're right. I've worn it so long that I don't even realize it's there. I never thought about taking it off."

"Is she still wearing hers?"

"I really don't know."

Nancy laughed again and the sound grated on Nick's nerves. "I bet she's not, dude. Anyway, it's a dating no-no. Sends the signal that you're still hung up on your ex-wife. Are you?"

"No, I wouldn't say I'm hung up on her. I've accepted the divorce."

"Well, it's a real turn off," she said, looking around the room.

An eternity later, the hostess came to bring them in to dinner. They descended a staircase to the first floor and took a table close to the Buddha. Nick couldn't help noticing that Nancy's body type pretty well matched the statue's. The thought that a little asceticism might do her good made him giggle to himself. A trim and elegant waiter brought menus. Nick glanced at the prices and realized that he might be at the most expensive restaurant in New Orleans, which was saying something. *This just keeps getting better,* he thought. The waiter returned.

Nancy re-opened her menu. "I'll have the tasting experience."

The server nodded. "The six-course or the nine-course menu, Ma'am?"

"Don't call me Ma'am. It makes me feel old. I'll do the nine-course one. And another martini."

"Yes, Miss," the waiter replied carefully, "Just to let you know, the nine-course experience takes a minimum of two hours to complete."

“Fine with me,” she said smiling at him. “That will give the gentleman and I more time to talk.”

Nick ordered a seared tuna salad and the waiter departed, giving him a look in which amusement and commiseration were nicely blended.

Over the course of the next two and a half hours, Nancy continued to question him about his married life, his business, his upbringing, and whatever else occurred to her. She spoke about her own ex-husband with contempt. Apparently, all of the flaws that had led to the demise of their marriage had been his. The conversation was interrupted at intervals by the arrival of fantastical creations from the kitchen, each a component of Nancy’s tasting menu. The most memorable was a thick slab of ice that required two servers to carry. In its center lay two small slabs of fatty tuna sprinkled with shavings of gold and caviar. Surrounding the pieces of fish, a ring of fire somehow blazed from the ice. Eventually Nick’s salad arrived as well.

He didn’t mind the money so much—Nancy’s sushi extravaganza was going to cost about as much as a lip filler treatment cost one of his patients—but her personality made him want to leave. He’d downed two more bourbons, but they weren’t helping. Nick considered inventing an emergency call from a patient but didn’t feel up to the playacting. He toyed briefly with the idea of faking a heart attack, but knew the restaurant would have to call the paramedics, causing a waste of their valuable time which was probably illegal.

Now she was going on about her love of animals and how she knew she'd be a wonderful vegetarian if she didn't like steak so much. Nick felt like an animal himself; one that had lumbered into a trap. He heard her say something derogatory about hunting and his attention returned to her. He had hunted as a boy with his father. "Besides, all those hunters are just stupid rednecks anyway. They probably like their big guns because their dicks are so small."

Nick had heard enough. Something in him snapped a little. "I don't know about that Nancy," he said in a slow, quiet voice. "I used to hunt a good bit. It was really pretty cool." He looked her in the eye. "I mean, when you stare down the barrel of your rifle at a beautiful animal and slowly squeeze the trigger, well that's quite a feeling. A hell of a damn feeling." She was staring at him, mouth open. "Do you know you can hear the thwack of the bullet hitting the animal's hide before it even falls to the ground?" Her eyes were cartoon-character wide now. It was like she was dining with Charles Manson, and he was casually describing the Tate-Labianca murders to her.

The effect was magical. There was a long period of silence during which she chewed her food. And then, outrageous as it was, like a blessing from on high, the check came.

They walked out together. The cool night air felt wonderful to Nick, especially since he knew he was almost free of her. "Would you walk me to my car?" she asked.

The suggestion caught him off guard. He wanted to be rid of her, but the gentleman in him won out. "Of course," he replied, telling himself it would be over soon.

They walked several blocks to where her car was parked in a handicap-reserved space. Nick was disappointed to note that she hadn't received a ticket. She chuckled. "Got away with it again." She reached into her purse for her keys. He stepped aside to let her get to her door and she did something that surprised him. Before he realized what was happening, she had placed her hands on his shoulders and guided him firmly backwards against the car. His back pressed up against the driver's side window. Her hands slipped to the doorframe on either side of his arms, effectively locking him in.

"What are you doing?" he asked.

She put her face close to his. "I like you, Nick. Call me next week, and we'll go out again."

Now Nick was a trapped animal. "Okay," he lied. She looked at him, saying nothing. He could tell she expected a kiss. He decided to give her a peck on the cheek and leaned forward slightly to do so. And in that instant, she was on him like a lion on a gazelle.

She practically threw herself onto him, and her lips were on his. Her surprisingly powerful hands pulled his face into hers. Her tongue thrust past his pursed lips into clenched teeth. There was saliva—lots of it. Nick thought briefly about dropping to the ground and escaping to the underside of the car. He knew there was no way she could fit into that small space. Then a perfectly goofy thought crossed his mind: *Nobody's wanted you like this for years, man. Just go with it.* And so, he did—for about a minute. When he could stand no more, he placed a hand on each of her shoulders and slowly but firmly bench-pressed her away from the car.

"Nancy, I have to go now. I've got an early morning. Get in your car and let me make sure it starts." She did as he asked and he tottered out onto the sidewalk and into the humid night, not looking back.

He heard her yell, "Call me," but didn't turn around.

Nick drove quickly to his house, breathing hard. Once inside, he immediately opened the windows to let in the night air. Roquefort was interested in the unusual activity and stared up at him with a puzzled expression, waving his stubby tail. "You wouldn't believe it if I told you boy," he said, and went upstairs to brush his teeth much longer than usual. He gargled with mouthwash and welcomed the stinging feeling on his lips. He decided a shower might help wash away the dreadful scent of her perfume. *Go screw yourself internet,* he thought, as he stepped in.

27

Nick slept fitfully that night and woke the next morning with a sake-bourbon headache. He looked at the televised morning news in a detached sort of way, and then heaved a deep sigh and got out of bed. He felt like crap. He also felt the need to expunge all memory and any trace saliva from last night's fiasco from his body and mind. He took a long hot shower, and then feeling better, headed out to the park for a run.

It was a gloriously sunny New Orleans morning. Audubon Park was full of walkers and joggers, many accompanied by their dogs or pushing strollers along the oval track that surrounded the park. Nick saw Alex stretching against the base of a huge oak tree and went over to say hello. The two neighbors shook hands.

"Did you just finish running?" Nick asked.

"Yeah, a couple times around the park."

"Good man."

Alex chuckled. "At our age, we've just got to keep it going. So how are you? Did you get settled into your place okay?"

"I did. I'm all set. Things are pretty good. I had a date last night."

"Really? Was that your first since the divorce?

"My first from Match.com."

"Wow. How'd that work out?"

"Not great, terrible really, which I guess is the reason I'm out here jogging first thing in the morning."

Alex grinned. "Instead of enjoying morning after sex."

"Exactly."

"Well, my friend, you got back on the horse, and that's something." His face brightened, "Hey, I've got an idea for you."

"What?"

"Sasha says there's a new dog park on a lot off Henry Clay Avenue near here. Do you know it?"

"Yeah. I think I've driven by it before."

"She brings Frankie over there all the time now and says it's full of cute women. I remember she said a lot of them are single."

"Really? I might have to check that out."

"It wouldn't hurt to try, right?"

"That's what I was thinking. And anyway, Roquefort could use the exercise. Plus, he's kind of a chick magnet."

The two men chatted for a short while longer, and made plans to get together for dinner, then Nick took off to run.

As he plodded along the warming asphalt, he thought about Roquefort's appeal to women and of his own.

Thirty minutes later he was perched on a stool in his kitchen, researching the dog park on his laptop. He found its Facebook page easily and scrolled through posted photos of people and their dogs playing there. Nick was pleased to see that several of the women pictured were indeed attractive. He cleaned up and put a leash on Roquefort. The bulldog seemed excited and confused; he was accustomed to being taken for walks early in the morning or in the evening, but almost never during the day. "C'mon boy, you're my wingman today," Nick said, and gave him an affectionate pat on the butt as they headed out the door.

Nick noticed immediately that it felt quite a bit hotter outside, and he gave Roquefort a wary look. The bulldog always started their walks with a great deal of swagger and energy, but Nick knew it couldn't last for long. All bulldogs fare poorly in heat, and his Frenchie was no exception. Within half a block the energetic panting had given way to a gasping, wheezing sound. Nick considered that the park was only two blocks away, and the online photos had confirmed that it featured water bowls. He slowed their pace and a block later stopped in the shade of a small tree. Roquefort collapsed like he'd been poleaxed. His purple tongue lolled from the side of his mouth and undulated in time to each gasping breath. The dog's eyes met Nick's, and the message was clear. "You know me, Daddy, I'm up for anything, but this walk will probably kill me—just so you know."

"All right," Nick said and stooped to gather the slobbering animal into his arms. He carried Roquefort the rest of the way to the park, aware that a steady stream of saliva was flowing down the back of his shirt. "Here we are, boy," he said, placing the dog down carefully beside a large metal water bowl. Roquefort wagged his tail and dove in, collapsing in its center and displacing most of the water.

"That's dangerous, you know," said a voice behind him. Nick turned to find the source of the comment sitting on a bench, a book in her lap and a yellow lab curled up at her feet. She appeared to be about thirty and extremely fit. She might even be pretty, Nick thought, if she weren't scowling at him. "Bulldogs can't take the heat; it has to do with their breathing. They have trouble getting enough air in because of their flat faces. They're called breakyo kefalic breeds."

Nick nodded, "Brachycephalic. It means short skull."

"Oh, so you know that, but you don't know to keep him out of the heat? Or maybe you're just trying to kill him? Either way, it's completely irresponsible."

Wow, this girl was really giving him shit. "Look, I know you mean well, but I love this dog and I wouldn't hurt him. I live, like two blocks away, and once I realized how hot it was, I carried him here. I knew the park had water. He's doing fine now."

She looked at Roquefort who was lying contentedly in the water bowl, regarding a squirrel with casual interest. "Yes, and preventing any other dog from getting a drink."

Nick sighed and walked over to where Roquefort was lying. He gingerly lifted him out of the bowl, trying unsuccessfully to keep streaming dog water off his shoes. Roquefort licked his arm once and then collapsed in the shade, nose to nose with the retriever who seemed amused by the proceedings. Nick found a hose nearby and refilled the bowl.

"See, he's already starting to pant again," the woman said, looking at Roquefort. "Poor baby."

Nick stood up and looked around. There weren't any other women in the small park, and he didn't want to spend another second with this one. "Guess we're out of here," he said, and bent to pick up Roquefort again. The dog was hot and wet in his arms, and seemed to have doubled in weight. He started toward the street when suddenly there was a retching noise and Roquefort vomited. Nick could feel the warm, sticky mess on his neck.

From behind him he heard laughing. "Serves you right," said the voice.

Nick didn't turn around. He patted his dog and whispered, "That's okay, Rocky," and walked quickly home.

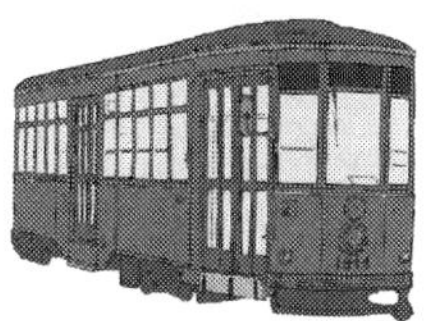

28

Nick got Roquefort cleaned up and settled, then stripped off his clothes and showered. He put on boxer shorts and a t-shirt, sat down at the kitchen table, and turned on his laptop computer.

During his run earlier that day, Nick had resolved to save something from the wreck. Yes, last night had been an epic catastrophe, and the dog park had been a humiliating bust. But tonight was Saturday night, and he was single. He resolved to go out somewhere and talk to a single woman. One who wouldn't accuse him of trying to murder his dog. *It doesn't even have to lead to anything,* he thought, *but I want something good to happen.* There was no time to find someone on Match.com and, anyway, last night had soured him on the site. He considered researching the popular bars and going to one hoping to meet somebody. But he knew that meeting people at bars, especially loud, crowded ones, wasn't his strong suit; in fact, he didn't even like being in them.

Not sure what he was looking for, he Googled "upscale dating New Orleans." A variety of matchmaking and personal introduction sites came up first. Clicking on one, he found himself looking at a page of headshots of gorgeous models. The site revealed that all of these women wanted to meet him provided he had a net worth in excess of ten million dollars. He chuckled and returned to the search page. There were articles from local news outlets on the best places to meet women. He followed the links and read a couple of them, which listed hot bars and restaurants where single women could supposedly be found. *Not my scene*, he thought, and returned to the search page. Near the bottom, a link caught his eye: "Speed Dating Party—NOLA Singles."

He followed the link and read about how speed dating was the best way for men and women to meet into today's fast-paced society. The author, someone named Stacy, told him she had met her husband at one of her company's parties. She assured him that love was just around the corner waiting for him, and that to find it, all he had to do was sign up to attend an event. Nick smiled and thought, *well, if it worked for Stacy…* He clicked on the site's "events" tab.

A long list of speed-dating opportunities came up immediately. Nick was impressed not only by the number, but also the variety and specificity of the events the company hosted. There was speed dating for Jewish people over 35, for Hindus looking for love, and for hot people. To get into the latter event, he would have to post his photo on the site and other singles would rate him as either "hot or not." He would then be informed if New Orleans singles considered him attractive enough to attend the event. *Yikes*. There were also parties for college-educated daters, for tall people, fit and trim people, travel enthusiasts, postgraduates, for the chunky and funky, and many other highly specific groups.

Nick modified his search to list the events by calendar date. There was, in fact, something tonight, and it seemed to be open to anyone: "Rooftop speed-dating party for 300 upscale singles—meet up to 150 women in 3 hours." "Geez," he said out loud to no one. He read the description making sure he understood. Yes, there were, in fact, going to be three hundred single people on a rooftop overlooking the Mississippi River, all trying to meet each other as quickly as possible. Male and female hosts would act as "love catalysts". Nick tried to imagine what that meant. The accompanying photo showed two attractive and obviously drunk girls that were young enough to be his daughters. He read the event description again and confirmed that the party was open to speed daters of all ages. The thing was so outrageous that it had to be fun, and if not, he'd just leave. He entered his information and credit card number and reserved his place at the party.

He spent the rest of the day catching up on paperwork and puttering around his house, which was remarkably satisfying. Later he went to the gym and had a light upper body workout, then returned home for his third shower of the day. Wrapped in a towel, he groomed especially carefully. He clipped his fingernails and toenails. He used an electric trimmer to keep offensive hairs in his nose and ears at bay. It had been a gift from Felicity; he still remembered how that had come about. Months ago, she had been lying on her back in his exam chair while he did a small procedure for her. She looked up at him as he was working and said: "Boss, you've got a forest growing in your nostrils there." He smiled at the recollection. One of the many great things about turning fifty, he supposed. He finished clipping the tiny black hairs and switched the trimmer off.

He went to the closet and retrieved the outfit he had decided to wear to the party. He wanted to look good, even a little hip. He put on dark blue jeans, a black form-fitting dress shirt, and a shockingly expensive Zegna blazer. It was probably the nicest piece of clothing he owned. He checked himself in the mirror and thought he looked okay. As he got in his car, he realized he wasn't at all nervous about tonight—it was a circus, plain and simple.

29

Nick drove to the French Quarter and found parking in an open lot near the old JAX brewery, which had been converted to a shopping mall for tourists. He located a large, ivory and white building overlooking the water with a sign that read: RIVAH CLUB. It was fifteen minutes before the party was scheduled to start—the online instructions had been very clear about the need to arrive early. He entered and ascended a three-story staircase, climbing past mostly empty restaurant and bar space. He opened the door to a huge rooftop deck, and was treated to a glorious sight, the Mississippi River aglow in the setting sun. While it wouldn't set for another hour, the sun was already low in the sky, backlighting the buildings of Algiers and Gretna and illuminating the clouds above in gold and purple streaks. The dark buildings and fantastic colors reflected in the river's undulating surface presented an enchanting impressionist vision. Nick smiled. The view alone was worth the price of admission.

He spotted an attractive African American woman at a table covered in name tags and walked over. She flashed him a broad smile. "Hello, I'm Jayla. Are you here for the speed-dating event?"

He felt nervous for the first time, but returned the smile. "Yes, I am. Nick Jordan."

"Welcome, Nick. Thank you for being on time. Let's find your name tag." She sorted through a stack and handed Nick's to him. "The number on your tag is the table you'll be starting at." She handed him a printed form and a pen. "Each time you speak with a woman, write down her name, then check the box according to how you feel about her." Nick looked at the form. The possible choices were: "Invite for second date, Friendship, Business, and No."

"You'll have seven minutes to talk to the woman at that table. When time is up, I'll ring this bell," she said, pointing at large metal gong. "And you'll move on to the next numbered table, going up. The ladies stay seated, the gentlemen move each time."

Nick had a question. "So, if each speed date takes seven minutes, it would take me until tomorrow to meet one hundred and fifty women."

Jayla laughed, "You don't speed date a hundred and fifty women, sir. You'd have to be hospitalized if you did." Nick grinned.

"You'll have one-on-one with about twenty women. And we'll take a break somewhere in the middle, so you'll be able to talk with anyone else who catches your eye."

"I see. And is that when the love catalysts do their stuff?"

She laughed again. "Oh, yes, indeed. The bar is open now if you'd like a shot of courage before we begin."

Nick thanked her and walked over to the bar. To the west, the sun was a little lower in the sky, and the colors it produced in the clouds and on the water were even more spectacular. A crowd of nervous singles surrounded the bar. Nick waited his turn, weighing the idea of ordering a Tequila shot to take the edge off a bit. In the end, he decided to remain sharp enough to speak to twenty women with some degree of charm and ordered a beer instead. His Miller Lite arrived costing eight dollars. Nick threw the bartender a ten, understanding why the owner allowed his club to host these cheery little events.

He checked the number on his badge—42—and looked across the giant rooftop to a table bearing a sign with that number. A pleasant-looking woman sat there, absorbed in her smart phone. He could tell at a distance that she wasn't his physical type. He relaxed a little, realizing that they would just chat and there was no chance of a future date. He was struck by the oddity of physical attraction. Here he was fifty feet away from the woman; she wasn't obese or badly dressed, and yet he instinctively recognized he wasn't interested in her physically. He knew that for most men physical appearance was an instant elimination factor; they only dated women they were initially attracted to. Some of the women in his practice operated in the same way, but others spoke about being drawn to men over time, not by virtue of their looks, but by the force of their personality and character. As was his habit when pondering the fundamental reason behind peculiarities of human behavior, Nick searched his mind for an evolutionary reason for the difference. He supposed that the caveman needed a healthy mate to bear his offspring and knew instinctively that a woman's fitness could be judged by a visual inspection. The cave woman needed a good provider and protector who would stay with her so that she could raise her children; that characteristic was learned over time from repeated contacts with a man. *Nick Jordan, cultural anthropologist*, he thought, smiling to himself.

He drained the rest of his beer, relishing the cold sting. Next to him, a short thin man gulped a shot of something and looked in his direction. Nick was momentarily taken aback by his bizarre appearance. The man, whose nametag identified him as Andrew J., wore a spotted bowtie, bright red silk vest, a long black topcoat with tails, and a shiny top hat. He also sported a handlebar moustache, waxed upward at the ends, which somehow connected via facial hair bridges with mutton chop sideburns. Nick thought the overall effect made Andrew J. look like a demented Vaudeville magician, circa 1900. He looked hopefully at the man's nametag for a table number. It would be ideal to follow this odd little fellow in the rotation bringing relief to every woman he sat with. Nick saw that Andrew followed him by several tables and sighed.

He heard the gong being struck and saw the crowd at the bar begin to move en masse to the numbered tables. He walked over to his assigned table and took the chair opposite the woman he had spotted. His assessment at a distance had been correct; she was a pleasant-looking brunette, but not his type.

"Hello, I'm Nick Jordan," he said, extending his hand.

She shook the hand. "I'm Darlene, and we're not supposed to use last names."

Nick winced. "That's right—no last names, no phone numbers, no identifying information. I forgot."

She chuckled, "So you did read the instructions. We only exchange information through the website after the event if we both want to." She took a sip of red wine. "Is this your first speed dating party, Nick?"

"It is. Yours as well?"

"My second," she said.

They chatted until the gong sounded, and Nick looked around to see the daters scribbling notes on their forms. It was getting dark now, and he had to put on his reading glasses to see, which embarrassed him. "These make me look old, I know," he said, looking across the table for a name tag. He wrote "Darlene P" into the first line of the printed chart, and then making sure that she wasn't looking at his paper, put an X in the column under "No."

In succession, Nick met Lori P., who ran clinical drug trials for a large hospital, Francesca E, a recently emigrated Italian woman with an MBA in marketing, Anna M. and Trisha B. who were licensed massage therapists that worked together, Lily S., a personal assistant at a hedge fund company, Machiko N., a ballet dancer turned graphic designer, Liza O., a paralegal trying to break into young adult fiction writing, Kelly P., who worked in tech support for a hospital and played guitar in her spare time, Janice S., a painfully dull accountant with a lazy eye, and Nora R., a recent arrival from Hungary, who spoke broken English and worked in a frame shop. Several of the women told him it was intimidating to be seated across the table from a plastic surgeon—they were certain he was evaluating their looks and finding flaws. Nick assured them that he was off duty and looking at them like any other guy would. All of them said this was either their first or second speed dating experience. Given the obvious popularity of the event, Nick wondered if some of the women didn't want to admit to serial speed dating. Perhaps they felt there was a stigma attached to it. But he quickly realized that most of them were nice, intelligent, and overall, not bad looking. He was surprised to realize that even the ones who didn't attract him became more appealing after he had spoken with them for several minutes. His surgeon's eye automatically focused on their most beautiful facial features rather than their flaws; the shape of their cheekbones or the curve of their lips, for example. He wondered if other men experienced their mini dates in the same way.

"This is the last date before the break," Jayla shouted over the noise of the crowd. Nick moved to the next table and found a very attractive African American woman jotting notes on her form. He sat down and she looked up at him. She was stunning, actually; the best-looking woman he had seen at the party. "Hi, I'm Nick J.," he said. "Please take your time; they hardly give us any time to write between dates."

She smiled. "Oh, I'm done with that one," she said, rolling her eyes for effect. He chuckled appreciatively. "I'm Melissa T., at least for tonight," she said.

They began talking easily. Melissa was an Ivy League-educated lawyer, who had left a large, prestigious New York law firm to become in-house counsel at a local shipping company. "The pressure and the hours were insane," she confided, "and all the associates were unbelievably competitive. I felt like I had to watch my back among people who were supposed to be my colleagues. It was beyond a rat race. It was a rat stampede."

Nick nodded. "I felt that way sometimes in college. A professor would get up at the beginning of the term and tell a class full of pre-meds that he would only be giving out two A's. We all knew we needed them to get into med school. So, it was the same situation; I felt like I was competing with my friends."

"I know, right? It's so unnecessary. In both situations, everyone's motivated to do well going in. It should be about mastery of the material to be learned or the work to be done, not about beating out the people around you. It's just archaic thinking. Someone did it to them, so now they're going to do it to us."

"Exactly."

They talked a little about hobbies and backgrounds and the gong went off. Their eyes met and Nick could feel the warmth of Melissa's gaze. Jayla's shouting broke the spell. She let them know that there would be a thirty-minute break, and that the bar was open. "If you have your eye on someone you didn't get to speak with, now is the time to say hello," she said, finishing her remarks.

Hoping Melissa would do the same, Nick checked "second date" on his form, then left the table and headed to the bar to order a Diet Coke. He found the rapid-fire dates exhausting and hoped the caffeine would perk him up. He looked around and noticed that the crowd seemed looser—ninety minutes of speed dating had really taken the edge off. He hadn't known what to expect in terms of his fellow attendees, but as he gazed about him, most of them seemed attractive and outgoing. *Why the hell did they all need to be here?* he thought, and then reflected that even in a large city with an unlimited pool of people to date, it was hard to make a lasting connection.

Nick heard a loud voice behind him and turned to face an energetic young man in a bright yellow t-shirt bearing the dating company's logo. "You, sir", he yelled, "come join the fun." *Oh, God, this must be the love catalyst* Nick realized. With a feeling of dread, he took a long final pull from his diet soda. *What the hell, I'm here to have an experience.* "OK," he responded, "What kind of fun are we having?"

The party host reached into the crowd and grasped the hand of a bemused-looking brunette, whom he guided toward Nick. "This is Rhonda. You two are going to play a game together."

Nick looked at Rhonda. She gave him a big smile and said, "Sure! I'm up for it."

The catalyst produced a blue plastic ball and instructed Nick and Rhonda to keep their hands behind their backs and pass it back and forth using their chins and necks primarily. "Don't let it hit the ground or the game is over! If you drop it, use your bodies to keep it from falling and then one of you can go down and get it.

"Dirty dancing with a dog toy," Nick quipped. Rhonda giggled. The host leaned in close and whispered loudly, "Keep doing it, and maybe your ball won't be so blue."

"I heard that!" shrieked Rhonda. Nick was laughing so hard that he dropped the ball.

The break came to an end and the partygoers resumed their speed dating. Nick met a few more women who were interesting for various reasons, but so far, he considered Melissa T. to be the pick of the night. A tipsy pharmacist named Sharon surprised him when she said, "I've worked with lots of plastic surgeons. I think you're all a bunch of narcissistic players."

Nick laughed. "Trust me, I'm as far from that as you can possibly get. It took all my courage to even come to this event."

"You know, I was wondering about that. I'm surprised that a plastic surgeon would even be at one of these things. You must have women all over you in your practice."

Nick shook his head. "They're not all over me, and even if they were, I couldn't date a patient."

She smiled. "Uh huh, I see. Well then, how about a colleague? And I don't mean me. I can tell you and I aren't happening."

Nick felt embarrassed. "Umm, okay. Yeah, I guess I could date a colleague."

The gong sounded. She looked at him and her features softened. "You seem like a good guy. I'm sorry for what I said about being narcissistic."

"It's okay."

She winked at him and motioned toward the next table with her head. "I think you'll like the colleague who's coming up next, Nick. She's pretty great."

"Really?"

"Yup. She's one of the good ones. Best of luck."

"Thanks," Nick said and rose. He looked over to find his next date, but a large potted shrub obscured his view of the table. All he could see was a shapely lower leg extending past the foliage. He took out his chart and checked "No" next to Sharon's name. "Last speed date," Jayla yelled from somewhere. Nick took a deep breath and stepped around the plant.

It was Fiona. Nick couldn't believe it. She was sipping wine and looking infinitely bored. After the initial surprise, his overwhelming emotion on seeing her was relief. "Dr. Espinoza, I presume," he said, stepping up to the table.

She turned to look at him. "Oh no, this can't be happening."

He laughed and took the chair opposite her. "What?"

"I'm mortified. I didn't even consider that you might be here." She was wearing a floral print dress, cut low in the front.

"You look great."

She took a generous swig of wine. "Thanks, you too."

"I gather you're embarrassed?"

"Yes."

"Nothing to be embarrassed about. Besides, it's a perfect night to be outdoors, and the view of the river is just beautiful."

"All true, but it's the circumstances, not the setting, that embarrass me."

He nodded. "I guess I can see that. Is this your first time speed-dating?"

She chuckled. "Yes, and my last. I got talked into it by a friend."

"Would that be Sharon, the intoxicated and quite outspoken pharmacist?"

This drew a big smile from Fiona, "Very perceptive, doctor. Yes, we're friends alright."

"I can tell. She has nice things to say about you."

"Good to know." She saw him eyeing her wine glass. "Want a little?"

"Yes, please," he said. She handed him the glass, and he took a long sip, not bothering to avoid her lipstick mark. He let out a long sigh. "Thanks. It's so good to see a friend here."

"I know what you mean. Some of the guys have been nice, a few have been weird, but this is the first time I've felt truly comfortable."

Nick thought about that word, *comfortable*. He wanted to say something to her. "You know, that's how I feel too. And it's so great. Because, aside from a few people at work, you're the only woman I really feel that way with."

"I'm sorry. But that's nice to hear."

"Can I have another sip?" She gave him one. "So, look Fiona, we're both single and you must know, or at least sense that I'm attracted to you. I have been for a long time."

She looked at him keenly, "Yeah?"

"Yeah. And if you were willing, I don't know why we couldn't date. There's nothing stopping us."

She smiled. She was way ahead of him, "Except for?"

"Maybe except for common sense. I value our friendship; you're one of my favorite people. I don't want to screw it up."

"And you think dating would do that?"

"I think it could. I'm in full rebound mode from the divorce now. I really don't know what I want going forward. I know I want comforting arms around me and a warm body next to me in bed at night. But those are very basic needs. It's like I have to evolve again from some lower life form."

She laughed. "Make your way out of the primordial swamp?"

"Yeah, I guess."

She finished the wine. "Well, Nick, I think that's very self-aware of you. And..."

"And?"

"And I might have some of those feelings for you too." His hand was on the table; she reached out and covered it with hers. "But you're a smart man, and I agree with you; now is not the time."

He turned his hand over and took hers in it. "Maybe someday?"

She hesitated, then gave him a warm smile and freed her hand, "Maybe."

Nick drove to Houston's, one of his favorite spots for a late dinner, and ordered a steak and baked potato at the bar. He ate ravenously, and drank cold Japanese beer. From time to time, he caught the bartenders giving him curious looks and didn't know why. When the bill arrived, he reached into his shirt pocket for his reading glasses and felt paper on his chest. He looked down and saw his name tag. All night he had been sporting a fluorescent yellow rectangle bearing the speed dating company logo, which read: "Hi, My Name is: Nick J." and below it in block letters: LETS DATE!!" He grimaced and tore the sticker from his chest.

Nick hardly noticed the drive back home. He felt that something important had happened tonight and the feeling energized him. He hadn't stayed home and sulked after the previous night's disaster; instead, he had made the best of things and gotten right back out there. He didn't know if his encounters tonight would lead to anything, but he did see the experience as proof that things could work out for him in the end. Screw the divorce, and screw his missteps in the dating world. If he just stayed positive and kept trying, the universe would provide. And as he stepped out onto his driveway, like a benediction, a misty rain began to fall. It felt wonderful on his face in the warm summer night.

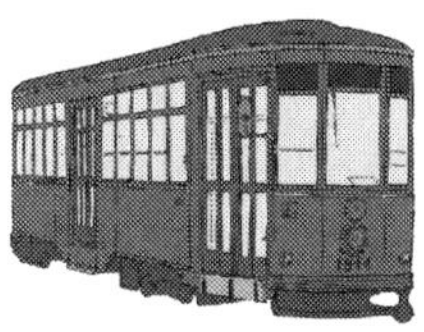

30

Nick woke the next morning, feeling refreshed after nine hours of sleep. He went to the window and rolled up the blackout shade to review a stunning view of his street bathed in morning sunshine. He was happy to have this Sunday to relax. He dressed and went downstairs to get a bowl of cereal and check email. A follow-up message from the speed dating service urged him to enter the badge ID's of anyone he had met the night before and wanted to see again. He entered the name of the lovely lawyer and was told he would be notified if she wanted a second date with him.

In the email's sidebar was an intriguing ad. Beneath the photograph of a gorgeous woman in a low-cut blouse was written: "You wouldn't do your own brain surgery, so why find your own dates?" *They have a point*, Nick thought, as he read that the company, Rare Beauty VIP Dating, could arrange for him to meet exactly the type of woman he was looking for. They were based in New Orleans, so on a whim he called the number. To his surprise he got an immediate answer and was able to schedule a "free consultation" with their local advisor for later that morning. Pleased with himself for discovering yet another facet of the NOLA singles dating scene, Nick rinsed out his cereal bowl and headed upstairs to shower.

Two hours later he took an elevator to the 32nd floor of an office building in the Central Business District where the offices of Rare Beauty were housed. A receptionist took his name and gave him an extensive questionnaire to fill out. Ten minutes later he heard a voice behind him say, "Doctor Jordan?" and turned to meet his advisor.

"I'm Emily," said a tall, blonde woman, extending both hands. Nick accepted a hug from the stranger, not knowing how to avoid it. She smiled at him. "Don't worry, doctor, we're going to get to know each other so well in the next two hours that a hug is totally appropriate."

Emily's gleaming wooden desk sat in front of floor to ceiling windows that commanded a spectacular view of the French Quarter and Mississippi River. "Please take a seat."

Nick sat in the substantial glove leather chair she pointed to, transfixed by the panorama.

"I love your view."

"I do too, but I don't spend enough time enjoying it. My back's to it almost all the time."

He transferred his gaze to her and took in her features. He was surprised and pleased to see that she was about his age, perhaps a few years older. He could tell that her eyes had been done. He also knew immediately that she had undergone at least one facelift and more recently filler to the lips and cheeks. The effect was a bit overdone for Nick's tastes, but not overwhelmingly so. Their eyes met and he saw that she was intelligent; she knew he was cataloging the plastic surgery procedures and injections that her face had endured. She smiled her understanding and left what was obvious unsaid.

Nick shifted in the deeply comfortable chair and said, "Thanks so much for coming in on a weekend, Emily."

She gave him a warm smile, "It's my pleasure. You're a busy guy, so we needed to meet at your convenience. You're going to like what we have to offer."

She carefully reviewed the form he had filled out, asking questions periodically. "Any chance of you and the ex getting back together?" she asked.

"None."

"If I'm getting too personal, let me know, but can you tell me in general terms what went wrong between the two of you? It seems like your relationship started out great; that you were very attracted to her."

"I was madly in love with her in the beginning. I suppose through the years we changed. I wasn't as crazy about the person she became. I respected her in certain ways, but after a long time, I didn't want to listen to her. I must have changed too, because in the beginning I couldn't get enough of her. Anyway, we both changed in ways that made it impossible to be together."

She nodded compassionately. Nick liked her. She exuded empathy.

"I hear that a lot. Marriage takes hard work, but in my opinion, it also takes luck. Everyone goes into it with good intentions, but half the time they can't stick it out. It gets so they shouldn't. Life is short, and there's no point in being miserable. The best thing is to part as amicably as possible and move on."

"That's exactly what I'm trying to do."

She smiled, "I'd like to help you do that, Nick."

Emily told him about the basic setup of the operation. In addition to a big advertising budget, the company spent an impressive amount of money each year recruiting new women. "Our girls are chosen to be beautiful, what would be considered at least an eight on a ten-point appearance scale," Emily related, "and they're also selected to be wonderful on the inside as well."

"That's good to hear."

"We'll get to the physical attributes, Nick, but what would you say are the most important internal factors for you?"

He thought about that for several seconds, "I'd have to say a big one is character. Loyalty and honesty; they're both very important to me." He stopped, wondering if she'd guessed that Elizabeth had been unfaithful.

"Uh-huh. Go on."

"Intelligence is very important. I have to be able to talk with her and be interested in what she has to say."

Emily nodded, making notes.

"A sense of humor is important to me. And above all a good heart. I want to find someone who is kind. Kind down to her soul."

"Age range?"

"I'm fifty, so I guess, what, late 30's to early 50's? I don't want to date any twenty-somethings. It'd be like going out with my daughter. Probably the 40's are my sweet spot I guess."

She looked up at him. "I'm glad to hear you say that, Nick." She sighed, "You wouldn't believe how many guys I get in here, your age and older, sometimes much older, who want twenty-year-olds. They've got more money than brains if you ask me."

"Speaking of money?"

"We'll get to that at the end." She smiled, "I have to get you hot and bothered with the picture books first." He laughed.

She came over to his side of the desk and reached for a large leather album. "Now, Nick, all the women in this book are beautiful. Most are rated nine or ten for appearance. But you'll find some attract you more than others. I'd like you to tell me which ones attract you most, and if you can, why. Given that you're a plastic surgeon, I'm interested in how you're going to analyze them."

For the next half hour, they looked through three large albums together. Emily had been right; most of the women were spectacular. Still Nick preferred some to others and would point out small facial flaws, a slightly droopy nasal tip or eyes set too close together for example, which fell short of the ideal. Emily took copious notes as he went through the photographs. When he had finished, she looked at what she had written. "So, you like women who smile, especially if there's a warmth in their appearance that comes through in the pictures. You don't like pouters. And you seem to prefer brown-eyed girls, Nick."

The statement surprised him, "I do?"

"Oh yeah. All of your "wows," your favorites as you expressed them to me, had brown eyes, and that is the minority of our women. Also, it doesn't seem to matter if they're Caucasian, Asian, Black, or Latina, you like brown-eyed women."

"Huh. I never realized that."

"Any idea why? Often, it's something from your past—your first crush or an important person in your life, even your mother."

"No, her eyes are green."

"Um-hmm. And what color are your ex's eyes?"

"Brown."

"See? I think you definitely prefer brown-eyed women. Not that the right blue-eyed girl couldn't knock you on your ass." They both laughed.

She reached for a stack of papers, each in a clear plastic sheath. "So, let's look at some actual women that are available to date in our area. By the way, we have offices in other cities, so you might want to consider dating some of our Miami women as well. We have so many knockouts there."

"Hmmm. Food for thought."

She laughed. "Nick, the feeling I'm getting is that you'll be happiest with someone bright, certainly college-educated, maybe even with an advanced degree. We have some like that in New Orleans and even more of those types in New York."

"I'll keep that in mind."

"Let's start with New Orleans." They looked through the stack. In addition to one or more photos, each page contained a short biographical sketch of the women. "Make a "yes" pile and a "no" pile," Emily said, clearing space on the desk for him to begin.

Nick worked his way through, noting many of the women were in their twenties. He put each of them in the "no" pile, sometimes shaking his head as he did so.

Emily smiled. "It's hard to say no to a beautiful woman, but I wanted to see if you were serious about the age range."

He had to admit, as he looked at the bios, that many of the women were accomplished as well as beautiful. Several had MBA's or law degrees. "I'm seeing lots of women I would date. I'm amazed they have to use a service," he said. "I wonder why?"

"For the same reason you're considering it—because it's hard for busy professionals to meet someone special. We save you time."

"Uh-huh," Nick replied, reading the bio beneath a gorgeous picture. "This one seems a bit shallow. She's only twenty-eight, but listen to this: "I'm looking for a gentleman who can pay for me to finish college and will take me traveling all over the world. Together we'll enjoy the best restaurants and shopping. I prefer older men up to and including those in their sixties, because they tend to be more generous than younger men. I don't mind dating Jewish men as long as they're not stingy."

Emily winced. "Youch. I'm wondering how I missed that."

"Beautiful outside, but maybe not within, I would say."

"I take your point. We try not to let the gold diggers in, but occasionally, one gets by our screening process."

Nick chuckled. "I do plastic surgery and screen my patients carefully, so I understand. We have an expression: 'don't let crazy slip through the net.'"

"Words to live by." Emily smiled and removed the gold digger's file from the pile of sheets on her desk. She turned back to Nick. "So, now's the time we talk about money."

"Hit me."

"Depending on the package you choose, a one-year membership costs between twenty-five and fifty thousand dollars."

"Wow. I didn't mean that hard."

She smiled, "I think you can see the value here, Nick. We provide as many introductions as you would like, at least one per month, until you find that special person or a year passes."

"And the women pay what?"

"Nothing. But remember, we only recruit beautiful ladies who are looking for a long-term relationship. And in your case, we would only introduce you to women who are here or willing to re-locate."

"I understand. And the packages?"

"Most of our clients go for the basic package. It's all they need. We do have some members who are very particular in what they're looking for and don't mind paying for it. For example, nine-point fives and tens guaranteed to be print models. That kind of thing."

"I see. I was impressed with almost all the photos you showed me. I think the basic package would suit me fine."

"Great. Can I get the paperwork started?"

Nick shook his head. "No, I need some time to think about it. I'm really impressed at what you're offering, and I wouldn't waste your time if I weren't interested."

"Okay, I believe that."

"But I'm also not impulsive by nature. I like to mull things over for a while. You should see how long it takes me to buy a car."

"I understand," Emily said. Nick could tell she was disappointed, but to her credit he noticed she remained upbeat. "I think you'll come around eventually. You won't find this caliber of service and women anywhere else."

"I believe that," Nick said, rising. They shook hands and she walked him to the elevator and assured him she'd be in touch by email. She left him with a nice compliment. "You'll do great in our service, Nick. You have a high street value."

He grinned. "Thanks," he said, turning to leave. *Like a gram of cocaine*, he thought.

On his way home, Nick thought about what he had seen and heard during the meeting. Rare Beauties had some extraordinary women, no doubt. It bothered him that the men paid an exorbitant fee, that they had skin in the game, while the women paid nothing. They had to know going in that they'd be set up with wealthy men who had paid a lot for their company. It wasn't exactly the way he saw a partnership for life beginning. *But then again*, he reflected, *what the hell do I know about relationships*? He was glad to know the service existed and filed it in his mind as a last resort; something to try if he felt he had to.

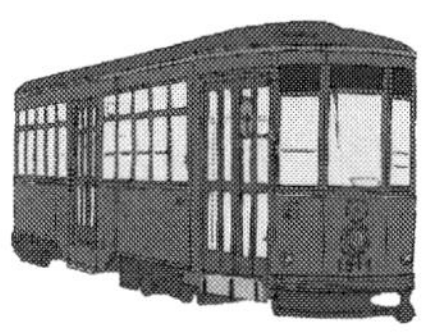

31

Nick looked at the morning mail. At the bottom of a stack of envelopes lay a letter marked "PERSONAL" with no return address. *That's strange,* he thought. He reached for a letter opener and carefully slit the envelope open, holding his breath just in case anthrax powder came spilling out. Printed on a single sheet of plain paper was the following:

DOCTOR JORDAN,

WE HAVE WORKED IN THE SAME TOWN FOR YEARS, AND ALTHOUGH WE DON'T KNOW EACH OTHER WELL, I HAVE ALWAYS RESPECTED YOU AND YOUR PRACTICE.

THAT'S WHY WHAT YOU'RE DOING NOW COMES AS SUCH A SHOCK TO ME. IT IS BOTH ILLEGAL AND POOR BUSINESS PRACTICE, AND PUTS PATIENTS AT RISK.

IF YOU DON'T STOP IMMEDIATELY, I WILL REPORT YOU TO THE STATE BOARD OF MEDICINE.

I MEAN WHAT I SAY. THIS WILL BE YOUR ONLY WARNING.

A COMPETITOR

Nick set the page down and leaned back in his chair. *What the hell?* A competitor? It had to be another plastic surgeon, he guessed. *But who? And why?* He wasn't doing anything new in the practice that would cause this type of reaction, so it made no sense.

It could be a prank. Probably is. Dave maybe? No, it wasn't his style. Thinking he'd worry about it later, he folded the letter and put it away in a drawer.

Later that day, as Nick leaned against the check-out counter finishing a chart note, the front door flew open. and a man strode into the waiting room. "Good morning, Mr. McGloughlin," Ginger said to him, smiling. Nick looked up from the chart and nodded at his friend.

"Good morning, my dear," Dave said, advancing to the long slab of polished granite. He took in Ginger's tall, elaborate hairstyle and large hoop earrings. "You look gorgeous today."

She batted long dark eyelashes at him. "Why thank you, kind sir."

Nick rolled his eyes and continued to write. Dave glanced at the wall of products behind her. "I'm in a bit of a hurry, but I want to pick up a few things."

Ginger consulted her computer monitor. "Felicity just went in with a client. She won't be free for about ninety minutes. Do you need her to help you pick them out?"

Dave shook his head. "No, I think you can help me. I really like the stuff she put me on." He put a hand to his face "It's only been a couple of weeks, and my skin already feels better."

Nick muttered under his breath, "Anything would be an improvement."

Dave turned to him and said pleasantly, "When I want crap from you, I'll squeeze your head."

The receptionist looked up at them from her chair behind the granite counter. Dave's face was shiny, and his skin had a pinkish glow. "It's important not to overuse the products," she said.

Dave wasn't listening. "I'd like to try some new stuff. What's that ACE BOMB over there?" he said, pointing.

Ginger chuckled. "That's the bomb of antioxidant creams. It's super strong. The ACE stands for vitamins A, C, and E."

Dave looked interested, excited. "Really? Give me one of those."

Ginger cocked a carefully plucked eyebrow at him. "You should really check with Felicity first. Why don't I have her call you when she's done with her treatment?"

"Nah, I'll just use it sparingly. Let me have one of 'em." He was looking at the bottom row of the shelf now. He pointed at the retinol pads. "I seem to remember Felicity saying that the one she gave me was *only* two percent. Do they come in higher strengths?"

The receptionist gave him a dubious look. "Yes…they make a five percent and a seven-point five percent, but you have to be very careful going up. Felicity always tells her clients to start a new strength every other night and see how it goes. If they're not too irritated, they can go to every night, but only after a while."

Dave smiled at her. "Wise and beautiful. So that's what I'll do. Give me a tub of the seven point five."

"We recommend that you go up one level at a time. The seven point five would be too strong for your skin."

Dave nodded, looking thoughtfully at the little jars, "Well…what strength does my wife use?"

Ginger consulted her monitor. "Sandra uses the seven point five."

Dave looked at his watch. "OK, let me have a five percent for me and a seven point five for her."

Ginger stood up and retrieved the ACE BOMB and the pads. She put them in an elegant bag and handed them across the counter. "Just be careful with these, and *please*, stop them and call us if any irritation occurs. You're a handsome man, and we want you to stay that way."

Dave smiled and pushed across a credit card. "I bet you say that to all the guys. Don't worry, I'll be careful." He looked at Nick. "I feel like I'm trying to buy beer underage here."

Nick closed the chart he'd been working on and handed it across the counter. "She's being kind. The truth is, if you get any uglier, we're going to have to put you in a home."

Dave turned to him. "Not very nice, NJMD."

Nick winced.

"Too soon? You're still not over that?"

Nick walked his friend to the front door. "If I live to be a thousand, I'll never get over that."

"Understandable. But at least it got you back out there. I pity the single women of New Orleans." The two men shook hands and Dave left.

Ginger turned to her boss and shook her head. "He's way too excited about skincare."

Nick nodded. "Did you think his skin looked a little red?"

Ginger went back to looking at her monitor. "Yep. Red and shiny. I'm sending Felicity an email telling her what he bought. She should probably check in with him."

32

Nick took a chart from the rack and read it in the office hallway. A new patient named Lolly Boudreaux. After seventeen years of practice, he could tell a lot about people from the small amount of information they gave him when they filled out their forms. Age was important; patients tended to think generationally, and their needs changed as they matured. Lolly was seventy-two—two decades past that first early morning glance in the mirror that had revealed the shocking image of her mother. The early fifties were when signs of aging usually became undeniable. It was then that many of his patients found both the resolve and financial resources to reverse them.

Nick liked doing primarily facial work; his client base tended to be a little older than that of a general plastic surgery practice, where mostly body work was done. As a rule, his patients kept themselves in good physical shape and dressed well, but that was as far as it went; butt lifts and tummy tucks were not on their radar screens. The face was different from the body—you couldn't cover it in Armani. So, they came to him to make the telltale signs of aging go away.

He returned to the chart and looked at marital status. He liked when new consults were married; it reflected a certain stability that made for a good patient. And if they had a challenging personality, which many but not most did, it meant that at least one person on the planet could stand to be with them. Nick recognized that there were plenty of nice single adults out there—*hell, I'm one of them now*, he realized, so he worked with most of them. But he also knew about the subset of single people that were lonely, deeply bitter, and generally pissed off at life. There was no way to make those types of patients happy and they could make his life hell after surgery. It was much better to part ways without touching them. On the other hand, some married people were difficult too. It was kind of a crapshoot.

His screening process, which started with the perusal of a new patient's chart, was vital. Everyone was a little crazy in his or her own way, and if he didn't take care of eccentric patients, he wouldn't have much of a practice. He didn't mind most kinds of oddness, but he did his best to weed out people who were toxic. He'd lived through the experience of trying to help such people, of getting a good result, and still not pleasing them. Nothing made them happy—certainly not cosmetic surgery. And after the operation or treatment, they'd done their best to make his life miserable. Experience had taught him that it was far better to avoid working with these types of patients. It wasn't worth any amount of money to operate on them.

Nick looked over the chart. There were other telling items: what they did for a living and who employed them. What meds they were on. What neighborhood they lived in. Even their handwriting told him something. Maybe the most important piece of information was what their goals were. Lolly had written, "do something about my neck" in that space. Nick closed the chart and entered the room.

Lolly Boudreaux sat in the large examination chair. From a distance, Nick could see that she'd had quite a bit of work done. He noted the telltale sweeping lines from the corner of her mouth to her earlobes signifying that her facial skin had been pulled too tight or too many times or both. She was elegantly dressed, wore beautiful jewelry, and smelled of perfume. This was another generational thing; women her age tended to use perfumes far more often and abundantly than their younger counterparts. Nick had needed to speak to a few of them about it, since both he and many of his patients were allergic to strong scents.

Sitting next to her was a distinguished-looking man in a wheelchair. He too was elegantly dressed; in fact, Nick noticed that the colors of his cashmere sweater-vest and corduroy slacks matched Lolly's own ensemble perfectly. He wondered if she dressed them both. He appeared to be several years older than his wife, and his face had a forlorn look, like a basset hound denied its dinner. As the doctor entered the room, he rose awkwardly from the wheelchair to greet him. Nick strode over to him and shook his hand, then greeted Lolly.

"Hello, Mr. and Mrs. Boudreaux. I'm Nick Jordan. How can I be of help?"

The woman extended a tiny hand to him. A sizeable diamond solitaire glittered against bones and veins. "Lolly, please. And this is Douglas," she said, nodding towards her husband.

"I'm pleased to meet you both."

Lolly smiled at him, displaying excellent dental work. "Nick, may I call you Nick?" she said, and then continued, not really asking for permission to address him informally. "We know a lot of the same people. And in the circles that I travel in, you come highly recommended." She raised an eyebrow and looked to be sure he caught her meaning. Social standing was a priority for Lolly.

For a moment, Nick thought back to his own upbringing, which was less than modest compared with Lolly's social strata. He had grown up one of two children in a lower middle-class family. When the gang situation at his public middle school got bad, his parents had sacrificed to scrape together the tuition to send him to a middling private school. They selected this for him over his brother Joel because his grades were better. They simply reasoned that he could benefit the most. Nick had always felt guilty that he was given an opportunity that was out of necessity denied to his sibling.

His parents had never complained to him, but Nick knew that even the cost of his school uniforms had been a stretch. At school he could afford none of the extras, like the extravagant hobbies and vacations that the other students took for granted. Almost all his classmates got new cars when they turned sixteen. Nick got on his bike and made spending money by riding to their houses to wash and detail the new vehicles for them. For years, this was as close as he came to driving. Eventually, he saved enough to buy an old Ford beater that got him around.

Nick nodded. "I'm glad I've been able to help some of your friends, Mrs. Boudreaux. Please go on."

She leaned towards him, and her face took on a conspiratorial look. "Lolly, please, Nick. And yes, I have been talking with people. I understand you're one of our city's newest and most eligible bachelors."

Nick reddened slightly. "I doubt that very much, Lolly." He paused, then continued, "But back to you—what can I do for you?"

She straightened up in the chair. "As I wrote in your chart, it's my neck. I can't stand it. I look like a damned turkey."

Nick gazed at the only skin above her collarbones that wasn't stretched tight as a drum. He nodded again.

"So, I want to know what you can do about it. It needs to be cut out or tucked or something."

He looked down at her chart. Under "past surgical procedures" she had listed only "gallbladder out approximately 30 years ago."

"Well, Lolly, there's no mention here of any past cosmetic surgeries. Can you tell me what you've had done?"

She looked surprised. "You mean you can tell I've had plastic surgery?"

Nick told a kind lie. "It's my job to notice these things. I'm sure most people can't tell."

She seemed to accept this. "Well, I did have my eyes done in my early forties. And a couple of years after that, I had a brow lift in New York. I think he might have done a chin tuck then too."

Nick moved closer to examine her scars. "Uh-huh. May I feel the chin area?"

"Yes. Oh, that's right. I had an implant put in there. But that was when I had my second lift."

He felt the firm piece of silicon rubber fixed to the center of her jawbone. "And when was the second lift done?"

"I did that for my fiftieth birthday. Oh yes, and my eyelids again and a temple lift too."

Nick's hands moved to hair, gently brushing it away from her ears. Looking at the traces of other surgeons' work always interested him. It was a bit like archaeology; divining what had happened in the past by clues left behind.

He could see extensive scarring behind the ears and a migration of her hairline upward and backward. He also saw several small scars close to the earlobes and underneath the jaw line on each side. He considered what might have been done through the healed openings. "It looks like there may have been some other work done. Tell me about that."

Lolly gave him an approving look. "You're good. Last year I went to this doctor who was charming but, honestly, a bit of a quack in my opinion. He did what he called a 'string lift'. It didn't work, and he had a hard time getting the strings out."

Nick nodded. "I can imagine. Most surgeons have moved away from those, but some still do them. String lifts showed promising early results and were very popular for a while, so I don't think you can blame your doctor for trying to help you with one." He moved to her other side and lifted her hair to examine her scars. "The procedure involved using permanent or long-lasting sutures that had barbs on them. The idea was to make a small incision under your earlobe, and then create a tunnel from there to the center of your neck on both sides. Then they would put the barbed strings in. When they pulled the strings, the barbs caught the skin and soft tissue and moved it in the direction they wanted it to go. There were technical problems with getting it right and getting it to stay. And if the sutures had to be removed, it was difficult to get them out because of the barbs. I'm guessing that's what all these little scars are," he said, touching one behind her ear.

"You're correct, Doctor" she said heaving a sigh. "It was a mess, and it didn't work. After I'd healed from him removing the strings, he did another lift, to smooth out my neck. That lasted for a while, but now the gobbler is back."

Nick walked over to a table next to Douglas, who regarded his wife with a patiently interested look. He picked up a camera and helped Lolly move to a swiveling stool in front of a blue photographic background. "Now, I know it's hard not to smile when someone is taking your picture, but please just keep a relaxed expression on your face." He quickly snapped front, side and oblique views of her face and neck, periodically asking her to tilt her chin slightly up or down to keep her head level. When he was finished, he removed a tiny memory card from the back of the camera and placed it into a small device on the desk. Lolly's photos came up immediately on a large, bright monitor.

"I know these aren't the most beautiful photos you've ever taken," he said to her, "but they do show areas we're talking about in precise detail, so they're helpful."

"They're ghastly," Lolly said, grimacing. Douglas said nothing, but looked supportive.

"Well, I didn't let you smile, and the camera was right on top of you, so they're sort of like mug shots," Nick replied. "Believe me everyone hates these. Even models." He reached for a cordless controller and moved the monitor's cursor over the screen to emphasize points as he spoke.

"If we look carefully, we see your jaw line is nice and firm. You've had four lifts including the string one, and your face doesn't need to be any tighter. There's no sagging. Your eyelids healed beautifully, and you certainly don't need any skin or fat removed from them. And the eyebrows are at a nice level from the brow lift you had all those years ago."

He looked at her. "Do you agree with what I've said so far?"

She nodded.

"So that brings us to your neck. If you look carefully, you see that one side, your right, hangs down more than the left. You can see it more clearly on the side view." He showed her each side, using the cursor to point out the difference. His eye was drawn to something on her left temple. He looked away from the monitor towards the patient.

"Let me take a look at something," he said, reaching into his pocket for a magnifying lens. He held it close to the hairline above her left ear. The smooth skin was thickened into a nickel-sized mound in this area. It was not discolored but had a waxy appearance, and there were small blood vessels running across its surface.

"What is it?" Lolly asked. He could tell her antennae were up.

He knew what it was. He'd seen this type of lesion a hundred times at least. "There's an area near the hairline here that doesn't look normal," Nick answered." I'm suspicious that it could be a skin cancer." But before you get worried, I want you to know that if it is, I'd bet the ranch it's a basal cell carcinoma. That's the best kind to have."

He was surprised to hear her chuckle. "I'm not worried, Doctor." I've had half a dozen of those taken off."

He was relieved that she was taking it so well. "Well, then you know they're not the kind of cancer that tends to go to the lymph nodes and cause major problems. Still, they do need to be taken care of, so they don't continue to grow."

She turned to him. “So can you take it off when you do my neck?”

Nick sat down in front of her. “Well, here’s the thing. I’m not sure it’s a good idea to do a neck lift right now. You’ve had a lot of surgery, and there’s quite a bit of scar tissue in your neck already. It might be best to let it continue to heal a while longer before operating.”

“But...”

“Mrs. Douglas…”

She cut him off, “Lolly.”

“Right, Lolly, in plastic surgery you can only go back to the well so many times. It’s important to do the right thing at the right time; otherwise, you get that over-operated Hollywood look. And it does not go over well in most places. Do you hear what I’m saying?”

Nick could see Lolly’s lips pursing and her brow drawing inwards. She gave the overall impression of a darkening sky getting ready to pour fourth its contents. From the wheelchair came a sound like steam escaping from a kettle as Douglas performed a long, slow exhale.

Nick hurried to reassure them both. “I do see what’s bothering you, and we agree that one side is hanging more than the other. I recommend we wait until the entire neck sags a bit more. Six months to a year, maybe. Then we can do a nice correction, and everything will be in sync. Otherwise, I’m afraid one side will always be tighter than the other, and we’ll spend the next few years going from side to side, like a dog chasing its tail.”

Lolly glared at him. “But I want it fixed now.” She added triumphantly: “And I’ve been to another plastic surgeon who’s already agreed to do it.”

Nick nodded. “I’m sure you can find any number of surgeons in this town who would operate on you. But I don’t think it’s the right thing to do. Not yet. I don’t just want to take care of you this week or this month. I want to help you for the next ten years if you’ll let me. So, we have to be smart and do the right thing at the right time. What you should do now is see your dermatologist and have that area near your left eye biopsied. If it does turn out to be a basal cell, I can help you with the removal, the reconstruction, or both. Just let me know if you and your doctor would like my help.”

Lolly drew a deep breath and looked at the ceiling. “I must tell you I’m disappointed, Dr. Jordan.” She looked straight at him. “But I’m also grateful to you for finding this suspicious area that the other doctor overlooked. I admire your attention to detail. I’ll do as you say and get the biopsy. When that’s done, I’d like to talk with you again about my neck.”

Nick rose. “I understand, and that’s perfectly fine with me.”

She rose and shook his hand. “We have to get home. It’s time for Douglas’ swim.”

Nick looked at the man in the wheelchair, who now looked morose. “You swim, Sir?”

Lolly chuckled, "Oh, yes. You see, Douglas here was quite the man about town in his day." She gave her husband a withering look that seemed to go right through him. "That is before he had his stroke." She turned back to Nick. "Now it's up to me to care of him. So, every day before lunch, I dress him in his swimsuit, wheel him down to the shallow end of the pool, and just sort of dump him in. He can't really swim, but he flounders around and gets lots of exercise." She smiled sweetly at her husband, and then looked back at Nick. "He hates it…but it's good for him."

33

Nick stood naked in his bathroom, regarding himself in a full-length mirror. *All in all, not bad for fifty* he thought. Athletics had always been part of his life; he'd played team sports growing up and had been working out regularly since college. He was solidly built but a bit on the thin side lately. The stress of the divorce had affected his appetite for food; at the worst times he had simply forgotten to eat. That combined with the longer and more intense workout sessions he used to combat the anxiety of a dying marriage had trimmed off his extra fat. He was as lean and strong as he'd been in twenty years.

What had changed was his hair. There was more of it, and to his growing alarm, some of it was gray. He looked at the light patch of hair in the middle of his chest and was reminded of his French bulldog, whom he could hear snoring in the next room. Roquefort was mainly black but had a white tuft of fur in the center of his wide chest.

Nick reached for the electric trimmer he had bought earlier in the day. Its packaging advertised it as "perfect for trimming body hair." The idea of cutting hair anywhere but on his head (and more recently in his nostrils and ears) was foreign to Nick. He had heard and read about "manscaping" and knew that men, like their female counterparts, were now expected to groom their intimate body hair. He reflected that things had been much simpler years ago, when he had never given it a second thought. But now, here he stood, trimmer in hand, wondering what to do.

There were no guidelines, at least none that he knew about. How much do you trim, he wondered. What do women like—a little chest hair or none? And what about down lower? *Should I shave down there and if I do, can I avoid nicking myself?* The thought gave him a chill. He decided to approach it the way he would a new surgery. *I'll just be conservative and get a nice improvement.* It was like he was talking to a patient. He giggled to his reflection in the mirror and began.

Nick collected and threw away a surprisingly large amount of hair, then cleaned and put away the trimmer. He took a long hot shower, then groomed and dressed carefully. He looked at himself in the mirror and took a deep breath. *This is as good as it gets,* he thought. He was excited because Lovely was coming to dinner.

His thoughts were interrupted by a text letting him know that she was five minutes away. All was in place, including Roquefort, who now lay snoring in the middle of the dining room. The tiny beast was on his back with his legs askew, potbelly pointing heavenwards. The Frenchie had always struck Nick as comical; half dog, half pig with a bit of wombat thrown in. Roquefort's breathing was consistently noisy, and he was unbelievably gassy at times. As if to illustrate the point, the small dog snorted and then coughed in his sleep, sending the velvety jowls on one side of his mouth flapping.

Lovely would be here any moment now. Suddenly, Nick noticed his wedding ring. Should he take it off? Why not? Elizabeth wasn't wearing hers anymore. And his date, *his date*, was coming now and anything could happen. *Anything! Jeez, I could get laid.* It had been so long. The fact that it could happen almost didn't seem real to him.

With an effort he twisted the plain gold band from his finger. He felt a small wave of sadness pass through him. The feeling made him angry. He rolled the ring between his fingers, and then placed it in a side table drawer, which closed with a surprisingly loud bang. He looked at his bare left hand, and felt the base of his ring finger with his thumb. He could feel a thick callus, where the ring had rubbed his skin. He knew that the ridge would remain, reminding him that the ring was gone. He guessed it would go away with time.

There was a knock at the door. Nick answered it to find Lovely looking perfectly smashing on his doorstep in a short skirt and heels, a wine bottle in each hand.

She gave him a hug, which caused the bottles to clink together loudly. "I didn't know what we were having, so I brought red and white," she said. Roquefort let out a high-pitched bark and scrambled to his stubby legs, rushing forward to sniff the visitor.

Lovely knelt to pet the quivering beast, who gave her knee a lick and then fell to his back, all four paws waving in the air. She accommodated his obvious desire for a belly rub. Nick had never envied Roquefort until this moment. The dog responded with a kind of loud purring punctuated by gasps for breath.

Lovely rose and made a full turn looking around the home's entrance. "So, this is your place. It's beautiful."

"Thanks," he said. "I really do love it. I'm glad I was able to keep it in the divorce."

"I can see why," she said, running a manicured fingernail along gleaming doorframe molding.

He walked her into the living room. "There's a nice view of the side garden through these windows."

She joined him at the ten-foot floor to ceiling windows that opened high enough to let them walk through if they wished. "That *is* a great view," she said, admiring flowers and plants in the early twilight. She was quite close to Nick now, and a shiver went through him. He couldn't think of anything to say. He grabbed at the cord to raise the blinds and give her a better view, but missed and put his hand through the blinds becoming entangled in them. There was the odd noise of flexible slats bending and Roquefort barked.

Lovely giggled. "Are you nervous, Nick?" she said, looking up at him.

He freed his hand from the window shade. "Yeah, I am. Pretty obvious, I guess."

She moved closer and put a hand on his waist. “Then let’s get rid of your nervousness, all right?”

He nodded, unable to speak. She pressed her body into his and kissed him lightly on the mouth. She looked straight into his eyes. “You okay?” He nodded again and put his arms around her. They kissed again, still gently, this time together. He pulled her closer and felt the tip of her tongue on his lip. He could feel the contours of her back, light and strong, through her blouse. She pressed into him again, and his hand moved down to her skirt. Her ass felt perfect to him. He squeezed and she gave a little moan, her hands moving up and down him now. He was rock hard and without realizing it he was moaning too.

She stopped, took his hand, and led him back out into the foyer. “Maybe we should see the rest of the house,” she whispered, “Does it have bedrooms?”

He smiled. “It does.” They walked up the central staircase together and he led her to a large door at the end of the second-floor hall and stopped.

“Are you ready for this?” she asked turning to him.

He bent his head down to give her another kiss. “Yes, please,” he said softly. She giggled and led him into the room. They fell onto the bed together in an embrace, kicking off their shoes. She was on top of him now and his hands were all over her. He realized that it had been such a long time; years, in fact, since he’d wanted anyone like this. They fumbled with their clothes, unfastening and stripping them off each other. Then they were half undressed, and she seemed to fit perfectly into his arms. To Nick it felt like the most natural thing in the world.

He rolled on top of her, and she guided him in. He felt the soft skin of her legs as her feet slid down the backs of his, locking him in. He pumped slowly and gently at first, then harder and faster. Her fingernails traced light circles on his back and sides. She was moaning loudly now, and they were both breathing hard. Her fingers went lower, and his mouth was on her neck. They seemed to come together in an explosion of pleasure, both wailing loudly in the moment of ecstasy.

"Thank you," he whispered, and rolled onto his back, pulling her close "so much." She put her head on his shoulder.

"Don't mention it," she answered, cuddling up against him, "I've been wanting this too." She felt so soft and warm, *so right*, beside him. Instinctively he knew this closeness, this intimacy, was what he needed to heal. Nick closed his eyes feeling deeply relaxed. Together they slept.

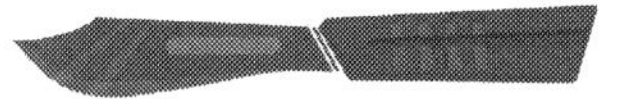

After about two hours, Lovely kissed his ear lightly and said, "How you doing there, Doctor Jordan?" She was still in his arms, and one of her hands was gently cradling him, encouraging along the erection that had returned. His hands began to trace the curves of her body and she responded, pulling him closer and caressing his chest. As if in slow motion they removed each other's remaining clothes. Then he was inside her, moving slowly in the delectable warmth. He rolled to put her beneath him and the intensity of his need for her exploded; it was fast and hard and consumed him completely. He came loudly within minutes, thrilled beyond anything he could remember.

He kissed her deeply and they rolled together, side by side again, looking into each other's eyes. "That was wonderful," he said.

She smiled at him. "I gather this is your first time since the break-up?"

"Yup," he said, pulling her back to him.

"Well, I'm glad I was the one to pop your cherry." They both laughed.

He rolled onto his back and looked up at the ceiling. "Till the day I die, I will always be grateful for that."

She chuckled and kissed him on the shoulder. "It was my pleasure too. You were really something; like a rocket going off."

He laughed, and they were quiet for a while. She followed his gaze to the ceiling across the room. "What are you looking at?"

"My crooked wall," he answered. "See how it pulls away from the molding there?"

Lovely looked. "That's a beautiful old molding. They don't make them like that anymore."

"I know, but it bothers me."

"Because it's not perfect?"

"I suppose."

"It's an old house, Nick. How could it be? That's part of the charm, right?"

He turned to her. "I guess you're right. Still, it bothers me."

She was looking at the empty wall beneath the ceiling now, "What was there?"

He sighed, "My wife's wedding portrait."

She turned and kissed him lightly on the lips, "time to get some new art."

He smiled at her, "You're right. And speaking of imperfection, I realize that was a little fast. I feel like I owe you an orgasm."

She chuckled, "I accept your I.O.U."

"It was like I was the escaped convict, and you were the warden's wife."

They were both laughing now. "We could dress up like that if you want," she said. He pulled her on top of him and they made love again, this time longer and slower. He paid his debt.

They showered together and got dressed. Nick poured a tomato, basil, and sage sauce he had prepared in advance into a frying pan and put it on the gas range to warm. He opened one of Lovely's bottles, a nice *Valpolicella*, and soon they were drinking and chopping vegetables for a salad. He put a pot of water on to boil, then added salt and olive oil along with a generous fistful of uncooked pasta. When the pasta was *al dente*, he dumped it into the frying pan and stirred the sauce into it. Lovely found two shallow bowls, and he poured a steaming portion into each. Nick sprinkled freshly grated *Parmigiano Reggiano* cheese on top of the pasta mounds and then plated their salads. They sat down at the table and Lovely refilled their wine glasses. They toasted each other and dug in.

The conversation flowed easily over dinner. They talked about their families, their businesses, and where they'd like to travel. Nick poured the rest of the red wine, and then opened the bottle of white. There was something he wanted to ask her, and he felt that now was the time. He took a sip of the *Orvieto* for courage. "Lovely, I'm not quite sure how to ask this, so I'm just going to say it: does this mean we're a couple?" He looked into her eyes. "Are you my girlfriend?"

She giggled. "That was smooth."

"I know. I'm a real smoothie."

She sipped from her glass. "Nick, I think you and I have had a crush on each other for quite some time."

He nodded, "Yup. At least on my end."

She squeezed his hand. "And what happened tonight was wonderful. I don't regret it." She took a deep breath and looked into his eyes. "But long term, I don't think we're right for each other. We're at different stages in our lives, you know?" At this moment, as if to underscore her answer, Roquefort emitted a long squeaky fart from under the table, filling the air with noxious bulldog gas. Despite what was going on above the table, they laughed.

There it was, Nick thought, their age difference. He was fifty, and she was in her thirties. He knew she wanted to have children; she'd mentioned it before. And while he'd certainly consider having a family with the right woman, he knew that it would come at quite a cost for her, and for that matter the kids themselves. He'd be a much older dad for her children and a husband who'd eventually become old well before she did; who'd probably die and leave her a widow for far too many years. Sad as it was to realize, she had a valid point, and he knew it.

He reached over and took her hand. "I'm disappointed, but I guess you're right. You're a fantastic woman, Lovely. I'm going to hate losing you."

She got up from the table and leaned down to hug him, then kissed him on the ear. "Thanks for understanding, Nick." She ran a hand down the front of his shirt then whispered, "but hey, there's no reason we can't see each other until I meet Mr. Right, right?"

He smiled and kissed her on the lips. "That is definitely a silver lining." He rose from the table and took her hand. They would clean up the dishes later.

34

The following Thursday was a surgery day. Nick walked into Lesli's office wearing his usual blue surgical scrubs and running shoes. "What have you got for me today, Les?" he asked dropping into a chair in front of her desk.

She smiled up at him. "Not much. Just an earlobe repair."

"No kidding? And we're doing it under sedation?"

Lesli chuckled. "Yup. It's Muffy Williams. She was so skittish about the whole thing that she decided to pay for an hour of anesthesia, so she wouldn't feel it or remember it."

"Huh. Well, that's a first. And that's it for the day?"

"Yes." She looked unhappy. Her primary job, which she took very seriously, was to keep the surgery schedule full.

He nodded. "Another light day—I guess I'll be able to get other stuff done." He rubbed his temples; it felt like he wasn't as busy at work these days. "So how are we doing this month?"

She clicked a few keys and looked at a screen. "We're still down compared to this time last year—less surgeries, fewer consults. Injectables are down too. Ginger says she's getting about as many calls as always from new patients. Greg is helping her with the overflow so she can get her other work done. But less patients means less revenue."

"How is Greg on the phone?"

"Good, I think. I haven't heard any complaints."

"Well, keep an ear out for any problems with him." He looked her straight in the eye. "More and more I'm thinking he's not a good fit for us."

Lesli's face lit up. "Thank goodness. I agree one hundred percent."

"So, we agree. Good. Just document any missteps he makes. I want to have a robust paper trail when we let him go."

"I've been doing it, and I'll keep doing it."

"Great. As for the financials, you know we get a report card every month in terms of what I take home. And, lately, I've been failing. The last few months, I've had to take money out of savings to pay my personal bills. I've been in such a funk over the thing with Elizabeth that I haven't really focused on it."

She gave him an understanding look. "I know. Are you still helping your brother out?"

"Yeah, now and then."

"I think you should stop that. Let him stand on his own two feet."

Nick sighed. "You're probably right. It's just that he's my little brother. I feel like I have to help him."

"He's a grown man. I don't think you're doing him any favors by being an ATM whenever he needs one."

"It's not like that. Well, not quite like that anyway."

They were quiet for a moment. Lesli added, "I've done my best to handle things around here myself and not bother you about them."

"Thanks for that."

"But you should know I've spoken to our accountant, and if things don't improve, we're going to have to make some cuts."

"Like?"

"Like less hours for Ginger or me, or maybe move to cheaper office space."

"Really?"

"Yup."

Nick shook his head slowly. "I've got reserves, and I'm not going to let that happen. We'll figure out what's going on, and we'll fix it. I've been practicing in New Orleans for seventeen years, and people know us. We have a good reputation here. It's going to be okay."

"I hope you're right," she said softly, then turned back to her computer. "Now go fix Muffy's ears."

"I'm on it," he said and left.

On the way into the operating suite, Nick ran into Felicity in the hall. She gave him a warm smile.

"Good morning, gorgeous."

"Good morning, yourself."

"You doing Muffy's ears this morning?"

Nick was momentarily surprised; Felicity usually had no idea who or what was on the surgery schedule. Then he remembered that she had been helping Muffy with skincare. And presumably other things.

"That's right."

"She was nervous to have it done. She told me she's having sedation."

Nick smiled, "Yes. First time I've fixed ear lobes with the help of an anesthesiologist."

"I hope Muffy doesn't spill any state secrets."

"You never know."

She grinned and gave him a little tap on the butt, "Well, get in there, sweet cheeks. Take good care of her."

"That's harassment, you know. I'm going to fill out an HR form on you."

She was already down the hallway. "Throw it on the pile, darling."

Eighties pop music played in the operating room. Muffy was already sedated, snoring softly. Nick greeted the OR team, then took a stool next to her and looked at an earlobe. The human ear was not designed to hold metal, he reflected. Years of wearing earrings, especially heavy ones, often resulted in lengthening of the holes. They got to the point that small earrings dangled or fell out and larger ones hung too low, stretching the ear in an unattractive way. In extreme cases, the elongated holes eventually tore through the edge of the earlobe, resulting in a wedge-shaped defect. Nick thought this made the earlobe look like a Pac-Man icon. The weight of the earrings and time were the usual cause, but sometimes a grasping baby or a slipping cell phone completed the tear by inadvertently ripping an earring out.

Muffy's holes had not stretched all the way through her lobes, so Nick was able to preserve the edge of the ear. Using a number eleven blade, which he selected for its extremely narrow tip, he cut away a tiny rim of skin from the edges of the opening, creating a small ellipse. It was like removing the center of a bagel and leaving the rest of it undisturbed. Doing this positioned raw tissue at the edges of the hole for him to sew together, which was necessary for healing to occur. Muffy would end up with a small vertical line where the hole used to be. Six weeks after the repair, Nick would re-pierce the ears in a higher and more central location. He would make Muffy promise to wear light earrings from that point forward. If she followed his directions, she would be set for life; earlobe-wise.

Nick looked at Virginia, his scrub nurse of many years, who was using a small Q-tip to dab antibiotic ointment onto the tiny stitches. Her intelligent eyes peeked out from between her surgical hat and mask, watching everything. He held the ear forward so she could apply the goo to the back of the lobe. "That's a nice difference, Dr. Jordan. She'll be pleased."

"Thanks," he said reaching out a hand. She gently placed a small pair of scissors in his palm. He never had to ask. "One step ahead of me as usual, Virginia. I love that. I swear, just having you here lowers my blood pressure by ten points."

Her eyes crinkled with a smile beneath her mask. "Not my first day, Doctor."

He cut the temporary sutures that held the sterile towels to tape that protected Muffy's hair and kept it out of the way during surgery.

Herb Shear sat next to the patient writing on a clipboard. "Are you finished, Nick?"

"I'm done, Herb. Just need to put a dressing on."

"Then I'll wake her up."

The patient stirred. "I'm already awake," she said softly.

"Are you feeling any pain?" Herb asked.

"No. I'm very relaxed. This is wonderful."

Nick reassured his patient. "Everything went beautifully—you're going to love your result."

She smiled in a lopsided way, still sleepy from the sedation. "That's what I want to hear."

"Just relax and let me put a bandage on for you," Nick said. Muffy responded with a light snore.

A few minutes later, she stirred again. Nick was putting the finishing touches on the gauze bandages that circled the patient's head. For the next 48 hours they would protect the earlobes and keep the ears in the ideal position for healing.

"Are we done yet?"

"We are indeed. Everything went well. You're going to love it."

"Was I good?" she asked in a dreamy voice.

"You sure were, Sweetie," Herb answered.

"Did I say anything embarrassing?"

"No, you were fine."

There was a silence as Nick continued to tape the edges of the dressing.

Her eyes opened halfway. "Did I talk about my experiences when I was a hooker?"

Nick stopped taping. He looked at Herb whose eyebrows had shot up. He could tell the anesthesiologist was grinning beneath the mask. Virginia looked utterly shocked. There was silence. Finally, Nick spoke up: "No, you didn't."

Muffy sighed deeply and smiled. "Good," she said, and her eyes closed again.

Nick saw Herb dial up the IV, a clear plastic tubing through which a white fluid was running into the patient's arm. The drug was Propofol, the so-called "milk of amnesia". It was one of the main medications they used to keep patients relaxed during cases. Muffy began to snore softly. "She won't remember a thing," Herb said, making a note in his chart.

"I can't believe she said that," Virginia said. "Actually, I can't believe she *did* that."

Nick chuckled. "Patients can say anything under sedation. You've heard the phrase 'what happens in Vegas stays in Vegas'?

She nodded.

"Well, our OR is like that times a thousand. This place is the vault. Nothing escapes."

Virginia took the tape roll from him and placed it on her tray. "Amen to that."

Nick walked back to his office and fell back into his desk chair. Even after short procedures, he liked to zone out quietly for a few minutes. His eyes closed and, as he started to dream, Ginger's voice came over his phone speaker. "Doctor Goldman for you on line two, boss."

"Tell him I'll call him back," he said sleepily. He knew he'd enjoy talking with Isaac Goldman, one of his closest friends. They had survived internship and residency training together at the beginning of the AIDS epidemic in San Diego. A moment later, Ginger's voice had returned.

"He says if you don't pick up now, he'll go to the police with everything he knows."

Nick smiled. "Okay," he said, fumbling for the correct button on his phone's console. He found it and forced himself to sound peppy. "Isaac, what the hell do you want?"

A Bronx baritone filled the room. "You sound tired, man. What are you doing sleeping during the middle of the day?"

"I just finished a small case and was resting a bit," Nick replied. "I seem to like to do that these days. What are you up to? It sounds like you're in the car."

"Fucking morons," Isaac grumbled, and Nick heard several car horns sound in the background. "People in this city need to learn how to drive."

"How is the big apple these days?"

"Same as always. Greatest city on earth. But right now, parking enforcement is pissing me off. I've got M.D. plates which are supposed to let me park anywhere, but they were about to tow me. Something about parking in the pickup lane of a nursery school."

Nick pictured Isaac's car, a large old Mercedes with New York plates that read SNOT DOC blocking a line of baby carriages.

"What was going on? Did you get called in to see a kid or a teacher?"

"Nawww. I was just parked for a few minutes while I ran down the block to the liquor store."

Nick laughed. "Very nice, Doctor Goldman. An errand of mercy, I see."

"For me it was anyway. But no, my practice is still minding the ears, noses, and throats of Manhattan's richest dipshits. Hold on." Nick heard the screech of brakes and several car horns blaring at once. "Sorry, that's not true, I take care of mostly good people I guess." Nick knew that Isaac was the go-to head and neck surgeon for New York's elite. It had started when he removed a thyroid tumor from a woman who turned out to be the mayor's sister. Since that time, politicians, diplomats, athletes, and actresses filled his Upper East Side waiting room daily. This was ironic because Isaac was stubbornly down to earth and disdained snobbery and pretension. He had a love-hate relationship with his lofty status, which was fun to needle him about. Nick was trying to come up with a suitable barb when Isaac broke in, "So how are you, man? You getting through the divorce okay?"

"I'm starting to see daylight, I think. I've had some good dates and some disastrous ones."

Nick could hear Isaac chuckling. "Welcome to the club, brother. There's a whole lot of fish in the sea and some of them are pretty scaly." Isaac had been divorced years before, and was a man about town. His name occasionally appeared in New York gossip columns.

"Yup," Nick said. "I'm more worried about my practice than my dating these days, to be honest. We're down compared to previous years."

"That's a shock. You've built a solid practice there. I wouldn't expect it to take a dive now."

Nick sighed, "Neither would I. But that's what the numbers are telling me."

"Huh. Let me ask you something—do you feel like you're less busy?"

"Maybe a little; not drastically."

"Then that's not it. Which means something else is wrong. Could somebody be stealing from you?"

"What do you mean?"

"Stealing means taking your money without your permission, dumbass."

Nick straightened up in his chair. "I don't think so. My staff up front handles the money and they've been with me for years. I trust them all. Nothing there has changed. But I did get a weird note that I didn't understand." Nick told him about the message from an unknown competitor.

There was more honking and shouting in the background. Isaac came back on the line. "That sounds bizarre, Nick. If it was me, I'd keep a sharp eye out. Sounds like something fishy is going on down there on the bayou."

"What's with you and the fish motif today? You hungry for sushi?"

Isaac laughed, "Maybe I am brother. I gotta run but, hey, keep in touch. You know I'm here if you need anything."

"I know, my friend. I'm doing alright. I'll try to get up to New York and see you this year."

"That would be great. Just let me know and we'll do it."

They said their goodbyes and Nick hung up. He sat back in his chair. *Something fishy. Huh.*

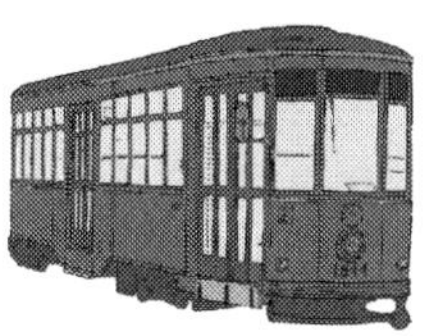

35

The following morning was bright and already getting hot at nine A.M. Nick was looking over Ginger's shoulder at the day's schedule. Felicity bustled into the office and hurried behind the counter, dumping things on her desk. "Greetings, my good people," she said, grabbing the small white coat she wore at work.

"Greetings, yourself," Nick replied, not looking up from the schedule.

"Darling Ginger, may I have *my* schedule please?" she asked, smoothing the tails of the coat.

"On your desk, darling," replied Ginger, with a smile.

Felicity turned and looked, "Ah, here's the little bugger. If it were a snake, it would have bitten me." She picked up the piece of paper and gave Nick a playful whack on the head with it. "I'm off to make people gorgeous," she said, starting for the corridor.

Ginger spoke up. "Oh Felicity, you should probably give Dave McLaughlin a call. He came in and bought more skincare products for him and Sandra. He seemed kind of overly excited about the whole thing. You might want to see how he's doing with them."

"Will do, lovebug," Felicity called over her shoulder and swept out of the room.

Ginger looked up at her boss. "Now *she's* in a good mood today," said Ginger. "And did you notice she's wearing the same clothes as yesterday?"

That drew him up short. "I did not notice that."

"Well, she is. I think our dear Felicity got lucky last night."

Nick cocked an eyebrow at her. "Walk of shame?"

Ginger giggled. "That girl's shameless." They laughed.

A moment later they were going over the schedule when Felicity returned, a cup of coffee in one hand and a blueberry muffin in the other. She collapsed into her desk chair and bit at the pastry. Through a full mouth she mumbled, "Ginger?"

"Yes, dear?" inquired Ginger.

"Before I forget, can you get Dave McLaughlin on the phone for me? I've got appointments all day, so I'd better talk to him now." Nick found a paper napkin and handed it to Felicity. She smiled at him, displaying bright teeth and crumbs.

"Sure" replied Ginger sweetly, "Are you sure there's nothing else I can get you?"

"Like what?"

"Oh, you know, like some aspirin, or a fresh change of clothes or something."

Felicity giggled. "Clever girl. Just get me Dave, please." There was a pause that gave the aesthetician time to eat half of her muffin and wash it down with a gulp of coffee. She would have preferred tea, but there was no time.

"He's on line two."

"Thanks, sweetie" Felicity said and reached for the phone.

A male voice greeted her, "Hello?"

"Good morning, Mr. McLaughlin, it's Felicity at Doctor Jordan's office."

"Oh, hey Felicity; Dave, please."

"Okay, Dave. The girls at the front suggested I give you a call to see how you're getting along with your skin care regimen."

"Just fine."

"Good. Are you using the products every day?"

"I am."

"And how's your skin looking?"

"Well, I think I see a little improvement. I wouldn't say it's rocking my world at this point, but, all in all, I think it looks a little better."

"Just stick with it, Dave. It's a gradual process. You must be patient."

She could hear him chuckle over the phone line. "Darlin', I know patience is a virtue, but it isn't one of mine."

"I understand," she said. "Just do your best."

"I will. Hey, while I have you on the line, can I ask you a question?"

"Sure. Fire away."

"I bought Sandra some products that are different than mine. Would it hurt me to use them?"

Felicity paused to think. "Sandra's been on treatments for quite a while, and some of her products are stronger, so yes, they could be too much for your skin. Just stay with what I gave you for now. I'll look at you next time you're here. After a few more treatments, maybe we can go up in strength a bit."

He sighed. "Okay, I'll be good."

"Right. Well, I've got to go start my day, and I'm sure you're busy too. Love to Sandra."

"Thanks, Felicity. Take care."

There was a click as he hung up. She wondered if he'd be good.

Nick was looking at the *Wall Street Journal* when Ginger buzzed him on the office intercom. "I've got the Chief Resident from Charity Hospital for you."

"What fresh hell is this?" he answered dramatically, then added, "Okay, I got it." He put down the paper and reached for the speaker button. "What's going on, chief?"

"Good morning, sir. Sorry to bother you, but we need your help if you can give it."

"What's up?"

"Remember Mr. Erskine, our pizza eating jaw fracture patient?"

"I'll never forget."

"Well, we re-wired his teeth and discharged him the next day. He went directly to the hospital parking lot and stole a motorcycle."

Nick buried his face in his hands. "I don't like where this is going."

The chief snickered on the other end of the line. "Neither did he. He might have been a little out of it from the pain medicine, who knows, but he drove the bike into our emergency room sign at the bottom of the garage ramp."

"No."

"Yes sir. Trauma Surgery's been taking care of him since he ruptured his spleen and broke several ribs."

"And you're calling me because he has new facial fractures."

"Yes sir. The jaw survived intact, but there's a right-sided tripod fracture involving the floor of his orbit, which also needs repair."

Nick knew that the chief was talking about the patient's cheekbone. The term tripod came from the fact that this bone connected to three different areas of the face. If all three connections were broken, the cheekbone became mobile and was usually knocked out of place. It was a common facial injury that Nick had fixed hundreds of times. The extension into the orbit meant that the thin shelf of bone on which the eyeball and the fat around it normally sat had been broken as well, to the point where it would have to be repaired to put the eye back in its normal location.

Nick sighed. “Well, that’s just smashing.”

“Pun, sir?”

“Nope. I’m not that quick this early in the morning. When do you want to do it?”

“He’s still pretty swollen and the trauma service has to clear him before we can operate, so I’m thinking tomorrow afternoon?”

Nick sighed. “Go ahead and set it up. Let me know when we can go.” He knew from experience that it was useless to tell Charity when it was convenient for him to operate. To help the Tulane residents he had to take operating room time whenever the hospital deigned to give it. “I’ll make it work with my schedule here.”

“Thanks so much, sir. I really appreciate it.”

“You got it chief,” he said.

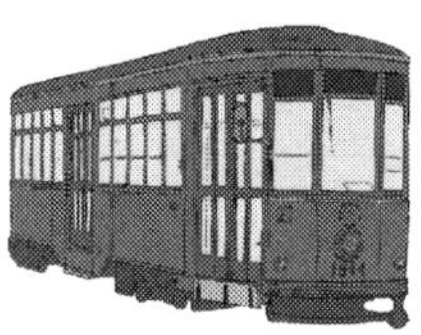

36

Nick walked into Rosie's Riverside Bar and spotted Eddie Marquez sitting at the end of it. He was doing the *Times-Picayune* crossword puzzle and drinking his usual Abita Turbodog beer straight from the bottle. Nick settled onto the stool next to him. "What's a nine-letter word for a harsh mixture of sounds? It starts with a C," Eddie said, without looking up.

"Cacophony." Nick spelled it for him and signaled the bartender for a beer.

Eddie counted the spaces in his newspaper, then filled them in. "Good one, Doc. I see that million-dollar education wasn't totally wasted."

"Not totally," Nick replied, accepting an ice-cold bottle. "Cheers."

Eddie folded the paper and lifted his beer. "Mud in your eye, brother." The bar was starting to fill with people just getting off from work.

Nick took a deep drink and let out a long, contented sigh. "Man, that's good. So how are things?"

"Pretty good. People gotta eat, and false modesty aside, I make the best po boys in the city, so I'm busy. What about you?"

"The practice could be better."

"I've never heard you say that before. What's going on?"

"I don't really know, but it's got Lesli worried. We'll figure it out."

Eddie nodded. "I'm sure you will. And what about your new life as New Orleans's most eligible bachelor?"

"Ha, if only. Why, have you been hearing things?"

"No, but it's time you got out and about a little." He called the bartender over. "Let's get a pitcher, Darlin'."

Nick turned to his friend. "Well, actually that situation picked up a little recently."

"Finally, some good news. What happened?"

"I'm not the kiss and tell type."

"So, there's been kissing—good. Go on."

The pitcher arrived and they traded their empty bottles for frosty mugs. Nick poured them full.

Eddie took a long pull from his, "So give."

Nick chuckled. "Okay. I've been seeing a drug rep that I've known for a long time. She's great to hang out with, but there's no future there."

"Why? You don't see yourself with her?"

"No, that's not it. I could see it, actually. She's really nice, and she's got a good head on her shoulders. I could see myself with her long term, but she doesn't see herself with me. She's in her thirties and while she hasn't come right out and said it, I know she wants a younger guy she can have kids with."

"Uh-huh."

"I can't blame her for that. We had a talk and agreed that what we have is strictly temporary."

Eddie nodded. "So don't make the mistake of falling in love with her. You've had enough heartache for a while."

"True. She'd be easy enough to fall in love with."

Eddie grinned at him. "You know you're a lucky bastard. Dating a thirty something. The sex must be something else."

"A gentleman never tells, but since you don't know her, I'll just say it's…" Nick paused for the right word, "mind-blowing. She's totally beautiful and in great shape. And she's really into it; when we get going, she's like a force of nature. I mean, I haven't felt like this in years, maybe decades. Maybe never."

Eddie laughed and raised his glass in a mock salute. "So divorce has an upside."

"It does for now, but once she finds what she's looking for it'll be over."

Eddie pointed to Nick's beer. "The glass is half full, not half empty. Enjoy it while you can, brother."

Nick took a deep sip. "You're right."

"Is there anyone else on your radar screen? What about that lady doctor you have a thing for? The dermatologist."

"You mean Fiona? Yeah, she's beautiful inside and out, but she's a colleague, and I've always thought of her as a friend. Not that I'd object to dating her—she's awesome. And she's just getting over a divorce herself."

"Interesting. So, she's on the back burner for now. Anybody else?"

"I did meet someone nice at a party a few weeks back."

"Did you ask her out?"

"No, I fell asleep, and she left."

Eddie laughed. "You're going to have to up your game, boy. Make an effort, you know?"

"Yeah, anyway, her name's Rachel, and she did tell me where she works."

"What's her story?"

"Very cool girl. She's a do-gooder. Her job is feeding the hungry if you can believe that. And she's really bright too."

"Maybe you should ask her out. She might soften the blow when your other girl flies the coop."

"Maybe I should." Nick refilled Eddie's glass, then his own.

Eddie sipped at the foam. "So, Doctor Jordan has been getting out a bit. Good."

Nick took another swig from his mug. "You know, talking to you is making me feel better, Eddie. Until now, I didn't realize I had all these possibilities."

"That's what I'm here for, bro." Eddie replied, and they clinked mugs again.

At that moment, the door to Rosie's opened, and a group of women entered. Nick recognized Rachel immediately and without thinking said, "Whoa."

Eddie turned his gaze to where Nick was looking. "What's up?"

"I don't believe it. Remember that do-gooder I told you about from the party? She just walked in."

"Which one?"

"Cute brunette, blonde streaks."

Eddie scrutinized the group. "Oh yeah—she could do you some good, buddy," he said, but Nick didn't hear him. He was already on his way over.

Nick grabbed a stack of menus and walked up to the corner booth. The four women looked to be in their early forties, and all were cute. "Welcome to Rosie's. Can I get you ladies something to drink?" he said.

Rachel, who was sitting on the near end, looked up at him. For an instant he could see her struggling to place him. Then her face flushed with recognition. "Oh, it's you," she said, with a smile. She turned to her friends. "This is not our waiter. He's a plastic surgeon; cute and tortured."

Nick smiled down at her. “Cute, huh? I like the sound of that.”

“Don’t let it go to your head. Still tortured?” she said, in a way that sounded delightfully flirty to him.

“Always. May we join you?”

“We? Did you become royalty since we last met?”

“No, me and my friend over there.” He pointed out Eddie, who waved at them from the bar, a big smile on his face.

There was a chorus of “sure” from the women, and Nick waved Eddie over, signaling him to bring the pitcher. Eddie settled into the big booth opposite Nick and introductions were made. The girls turned out to be a group of friends who all ran or owned businesses in the city. They knew Eddie’s restaurant and went on about how much they liked it. Eddie beamed. Nick didn’t think he’d ever seen the man smile so much. They ordered wine, more beer and food: oysters and fried shrimp, garlic toast and just salads for two of the women. Eddie charmed them all with a seemingly endless string of anecdotes about bizarre happenings in the city and the pitfalls and perks of running a business in it.

Rachel turned to Nick “Your friend is something else,” she said, sipping chardonnay.

“Oh, yeah. Eddie’s quite the raconteur. You wouldn’t think it to look at him, but he has a lot of depth to him. He’s got the soul of a poet trapped in the body of a sandwich maker.”

They both laughed. He picked up a shrimp from one of the platters. "I'm thinking back to the first and last time I saw you. You left me sleeping alone on a balcony."

She smiled. "You looked so peaceful, like you really needed the rest. I just decided to slip away."

"I wouldn't have minded you waking me up. Or, say, tucking a cocktail napkin with your phone number in my coat pocket or something."

"Not my style. Anyway, you knew my name and where I work. I'm findable, right?"

"Touché."

"So why didn't you?"

Nick looked her in the eye. "I've been busy with work and other stuff."

She looked back at him with big green eyes framed by wild wispy bangs. He thought she looked adorable. "So, Nick, are you still tortured?" she said, this time with meaning.

"Always. Isn't life supposed to be a struggle? P.G. Wodehouse had a line in some of his stories; about how we're not put on this earth for pleasure alone."

"Uh huh. Is he a favorite of yours?"

"My very favorite writer in fact."

She smiled at him. "I could see that. Jeeves and Wooster, big ensemble comedies, hijinks at country houses. I think his writing suits you."

Smart and beautiful, Nick thought. This girl was the total package. "That's one of the nicest things anyone's ever said to me, I think."

"Not at all. Just an observation."

Nick took a gulp of his beer to offset the spiciness of the shrimp. "So, what have you been up to, I mean, other than work?"

"Let's see. Oh, I was in Barcelona two weeks ago."

"Quite a place."

"Incredible. The food, the people watching, all that history, and great beaches to go with it. I could live there."

He nodded agreement. "I was there years ago with Elizabeth, my ex." Nick had no idea why he had mentioned her, but he immediately felt angry with himself for doing it. "Anyway, it was great. Did you go with friends, or your new lover or anybody?"

She laughed. "No, just little old me." She took a sip of her beer, "I don't mind traveling alone really. Still, it would be nice to share incredible places with someone."

Nick saw his in. "Does that mean you're not seeing anybody?"

She laughed. "That's direct."

"I'm sorry—too forward of me?"

She looked down at her wine glass. "No, it's okay. I've been on a few dates recently, but nobody special." She looked up at him; that flirty doe-eyed look that made his heart beat faster. "What about you?"

"Well, I've been seeing someone a little, but we've both agreed its temporary."

"Why's that?"

"She's too young for me."

Rachel laughed. "Good problem to have."

"Yeah, I know, but she's put me on notice that I'm not what she's looking for long term. As soon as she finds Mr. Right, I'm out of the picture."

"That's kind of harsh, isn't it?"

"A little. But it's also practical on her part. I get it. We're at different stages of life."

"I can see that. What about you? Is she what you're looking for?"

"I don't know what the hell I'm looking for, Rachel. I do know that being with someone beats the hell out of being alone."

She raised her glass. "I'll drink to that."

He clinked her gently with his mug. "Me, too."

The six of them talked and laughed, polishing off the food, another pitcher of beer, and two bottles of wine. They ordered desserts and six spoons. The check came, and Eddie grabbed it. "This one's on me. I don't know when I've enjoyed a night at Rosie's so much."

Nick took a credit card out of his wallet and flipped it across the table to Eddie. "That's nice of you, but I've enjoyed it just as much. Let's split this, okay?" His friend nodded and put his own card and Nick's together with the bill before handing it to a passing waitress.

They exchanged hugs all around in the crushed shell parking lot. Nick told Eddie he'd see him Monday at the restaurant for red beans and rice. He stayed close to Rachel and walked her to her car. The night was warm, and the sky was clear and full of stars.

"It was great to see you again," he said.

She turned to him, her back against her car. "For me, too."

They were very close now. The moon was bright against the dark sky, like a streetlamp hanging above them. Nick tried to think of something to say. She leaned forward and kissed him softly on the lips. He moved closer to her, not wanting the kiss to end.

Then she was in his arms, her body pressed against his. The first soft kiss turned stronger and more urgent; Nick felt the tip of her tongue flick across his lips. He kissed her deeply and his hands found the firm curves of her back. He could feel her fingers in his hair, caressing his neck and ears. They stayed together for a long time, making out in the parking lot. Nick heard the sound of shells breaking beneath their feet when one of them shifted. He was vaguely aware that he felt like a teenager again. Someone walked right by them in the lot; it could be a patient of his for all he knew. He didn't care. She felt perfect to him. And as far as he could tell, she was perfect *for* him; smart enough, pretty enough, *and* they had tons of chemistry. He went on holding her and kissing her, feeling in his bones how right this was, thinking: *this could be the one.*

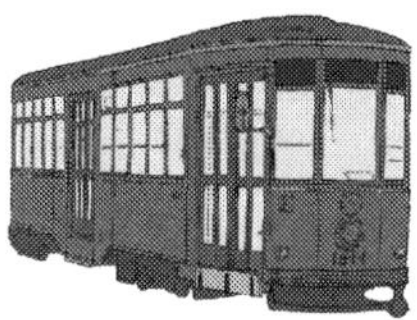

37

Nick parked in the faculty section of the Tulane Medical Center garage and took the concrete stairs down to street level. He walked quickly up a side street, passing the doorway of what had once been Joe's, a long-closed bar he had frequented as a medical student. It had been the place to go for happy hour on the few evenings he was lucky enough to be away from the hospital. He recalled that the management reserved a closet for all the white coats that students and residents left there after getting too drunk to remember them. The place had always had a frenetic vibe; mostly because the young doctors felt and behaved like escapees from their prison across the street.

Crossing Tulane Avenue, he noticed a pharmacy now took the place of Mike Serio's po boy shop. He had loved the jambalaya and spicy sausage lunch special there and was a regular for several years. He resolved to go by their place downtown sometime; he just wouldn't tell Eddie.

He found the chief resident waiting for him on the concrete plaza in front of Charity. They exchanged greetings and passed into the massive lobby.

"Are they ready for us?" Nick asked.

The chief sipped from a paper coffee cup. He looked like he hadn't slept in a while. "Should be soon. If you don't mind, I'd like to take you by the emergency room first. My team is there with a new patient. Human bite, I think."

Nick sighed then nodded. Charity never failed to provide. "Sure. Let me guess, an ear?"

"Bingo," said the chief, leading the way.

They arrived at the crowded E.R., which reminded Nick of an airport terminal in an overpopulated third-world country. They found the head and neck surgery team at the nurse's station in the center of the main corridor. "What have we got?" asked the chief.

"Human bite to the ear sir, about four hours ago" answered the senior resident, consulting a chart. "Marijuana and alcohol last used yesterday and nothing to eat for the last eight hours."

"Good," said the chief, looking at the chart. "His stomach's empty so we can bring him to the OR after the first case. What's he like?"

"He's a hard-core biker and not the friendliest guy in the world." The senior resident paused and looked up from the chart to Nick. "Also, he's got some pretty idiotic tattoos."

Nick and the chief looked past the nurse's station to the other side of the corridor. In the room directly across the hall sat a shirtless mountain of a man with his large back to the group. Tattooed over one shoulder blade in black and red ink was the image of a screaming skull wearing a

Nazi SS officer's cap. An eagle at the top of the hat clutched a medallion decorated with a swastika. Beneath the skull, on a banner that spanned his entire back, were the words: WHITE POWER. "Wow," said the chief.

Taken aback by the raw racism, Nick's mind cast back to something he had witnessed years before in this same hospital. He was new to New Orleans at the time, and his experience with racism had been limited to crass remarks he'd heard made about Mexican immigrants in Southern California. So, when a fat white nurse gave him a chart he was looking for and said sweetly, "She's the nigga woman dying in the last room on the left," he almost dropped it in shock.

The woman had advanced thyroid cancer, beyond curing. She'd been in the hospital for a long time, mainly to control her pain. He took a deep breath and went down the hall to find her.

A sickly-sweet smell had hit Nick from the open doorway; the odor that surrounds desperately ill people after they've been on the wards for a long time. He entered and pulled aside a curtain beside her bed and introduced himself. She was rail thin, and her head was turned away from him at an odd angle, forced that way by a large lump on the side of her neck. She tried to swing her eyes around to look at him, which made the whites of them look bigger. There was a vein over the lump that looked like the body of a snake turning upwards and disappearing behind her ear. Her skin was so dark that it seemed to make the vein stick out more. He could see it pulsing. She didn't speak at first, but there was recognition in her eyes; she could tell that her appearance shocked him.

She was a horrific sight, and he could tell she was in a lot of pain. But she tried to smile, a sort of distorted half-smile, and reached out towards a chair at the side of the bed. Her fingers grazed the back of it a couple of times; she was trying to move it toward him. She, in all her dying and pain and stink, wanted *him* to feel comfortable. That was who she was, what she was made of. It was probably how she'd been raised. And it amazed him—such grace in that situation. It was devastating.

Nick took the chair and sat beside her for a while. Finally, he told her he'd do all he could to help her with her pain and added, "I wish I could do more." She turned toward him as far as the lump would allow, and spoke with a voice that sounded like gas under pressure escaping from a rusted valve, "I know, baby."

Nick wrote new orders in her chart, adjusting her pain meds to make her more comfortable. He searched out the nurse who had given him the chart and handed it back to her. "See that this patient's orders are updated," he said, looking her in the eye, "and if you ever call one of my patients the N-word again, I'll do everything I can to make sure it will be your last day working here. Do you understand?"

The nurse looked surprised. "I didn't mean anything bad by..."

"Do you understand?"

"Yes, doctor," she said, lowering her eyes.

From across the hall, Nick studied the Nazi biker, looking up from his grotesque tattoo to the ear above it, which was partially covered with a gauze bandage. He turned to the team. "Take off your name tags, we're going to have a little fun with this guy."

Nick led the way into the room, holding the chart. He glanced at the name. "Hello, Mr. Hawkins. We're from the head and neck surgery service, and we're here to help you with your ear."

The large man turned to him and grunted. He looked angry.

Nick approached him. "May I take a peek?"

The biker gave him a nasty look. "If you gotta."

Nick put on latex gloves, then carefully peeled adhesive tape from the man's cheek, raising the gauze with it. "I'll be gentle," he said, slowly working the dressing free. It came off in a clump. Nick stood back and looked keenly at the site. More than half of the ear was gone. The lobe and the bottom had survived, but from midway up there was nothing but a ragged edge.

Nick confirmed that the residents had taken photographs of the damage, and then covered the wound with a fresh dressing. "I don't suppose you have the other part of the ear with you?" he asked.

The man grinned, displaying brown teeth. "In my coat."

Nick nodded at the Chief Resident, who picked up the coat from a side chair and handed it to the patient.

He reached inside and withdrew a bloody bandanna. Nick unwrapped it carefully and looked at the other half of the man's ear, stuck to the fabric with dried blood. He turned to the team. "This is great. The skin's of no use; it's been without a blood supply for too long, but we'll be able to sterilize the cartilage and implant it. That'll be a big help in the reconstruction."

He turned to the patient who looked completely disinterested. In simple terms, Nick explained how the team would clean and close his wounds. They would place the piece of cartilage under the skin of his scalp to use in a later operation to give his ear its normal shape. The biker appeared to understand and grunted again in a way that seemed to signify approval.

"We've got another surgery now, sir, but we'll be seeing you in a few hours. Please remember not to eat or drink anything from this point on, or we'll have to delay the surgery which will keep you in the hospital for at least an extra day." Nick turned to go, and then spun back to the patient, as if he'd just remembered something. "Oh, I forgot to introduce the team to you, forgive me." He paused, and then continued. "I'm Doctor Leibowitz." He pointed to each of his colleagues. "And this is Doctor Rosenbaum, Doctor Goldfarb, Doctor Cohen, and Doctor Silverblatt."

The patient no longer seemed disinterested; in fact, his eyes were wide with alarm. Nick could tell the residents were trying hard not to laugh, so he quickly led them out of the room. The chief came last and stopped, placing a hand on the patient's shoulder; his fingers closed on the Nazi skull. "Don't worry sir, Doctor Leibowitz is a real *mensch*."

Nick helped finish the first operation and then decided to run down to the cafeteria to get a bite before the next case. He found a clump of white coats hanging on the back of the O.R.'s exit door and grabbed one to put over his scrubs. As he was preparing to leave, he looked down the hallway to the pre-op area. There was his biker, lying on a hospital gurney. His massive bulk made him look like an iceberg, floating among the flat beds. The man turned his head towards the door, and even at that distance, Nick could tell he was nervous. He sighed, then walked over to his patient. The snack could wait.

The biker turned his head away to stare up at the ceiling tiles as Nick approached. Someone had written "HERE" on his neck below the mangled ear in purple marker. This was standard pre-op protocol, aimed at keeping surgeons from operating on the wrong side of the body.

"We're done with the first case, Mr. Hawkins, so you're next. They're just getting the room turned over and everything clean for you."

The patient gave a non-committal grunt. Nick said, "If you're nervous about this, you don't need to be. We have a first-class anesthesiologist who will make sure you're asleep while we do this, so you won't feel a thing and you'll be safe."

The biker grunted again, this time with some appreciation.

"Is there anyone you want me to call for you? To let them know what's going on?"

Mr. Hawkins turned to him. "Naw, doc. It's just me. No one to call. I'd think about calling my brother, but we're in a fight right now."

Nick looked at him. "Let me guess. Was he the one who bit your ear off?"

"Sure was, the little bastard." The patient shook his head. "Sometimes family is more of a pain in the ass than it's worth."

"I understand. Just try to relax. I'll do my very best for you."

The patient sighed. "Thanks, doc."

Nick turned to leave.

"Doc?"

He turned back. "Yes?"

The big man shifted on the gurney. "I'm sorry about the tattoo. I know it offends your religion."

Nick suppressed a smile. "I think it offends pretty much all religions."

"Yeah, I guess you're right."

Nick nodded. "I'd imagine that your head was in a different place when you got it."

The biker let out a big sigh. "Yup, I was young and stupid and the world's biggest badass. Or at least I thought so. I was full of hate."

Nick nodded. "I understand. We all go through stages; some of them we regret later." He paused for a moment, and then continued, thinking of Fiona, "I'll tell you what—I have a friend who might be willing to remove that Nazi tattoo with a laser. It would be at her office, and it would take several treatments. If you want it off, I'll ask her do it. If she agrees, I'll cover what she charges for it."

Mr. Hawkins looked him in the eye. "That's nice of you, doc. I'll think about it."

Nick patted the rail of the gurney. "Fair enough," he said, turning to leave. "I'll see you in the O.R."

The patient grinned. "Do your best in there. I want to have something that looks like an ear when you're done."

Nick was already on his way out of the pre-op area. Over his shoulder, he called, "I will."

38

Three hours later, Nick was back in his street clothes, exiting the elevator on the first floor of Charity Hospital. As he passed the ER, he saw something in the waiting area that stopped him in his tracks. There, on a plastic chair in the middle of the room, sat Rachel. He found the sight disorienting at first. Two different aspects of his life had bizarrely come together. She was reading a book with one of her feet up on a chair, wrapped in a towel. *What the hell?* he asked himself as he walked over to her.

He stood quietly behind her for a moment, watching her read. "We have to stop meeting like this," he said at last.

She jolted in her chair, and then turned around. The frightened look on her face gave way to a smile.

"What are you doing here?" he asked.

"I cut my foot," she said, motioning to the pink dish towel secured to her ankle and foot with duct tape. A few toes poked through at the end, their silver polish coordinating nicely with the color of the tape.

"I can see something happened to your foot," Nick said, taking the chair next to her, "but why are you at Charity?"

She chuckled. "That's the thing about working for non-profits; we're not awash in extra cash. I have what they call catastrophic health insurance; it only kicks in for really expensive medical problems. So, I end up paying for pretty much everything medical out of my own pocket."

"I see." He paused for a moment, looking around. "Did you sign in at the front?"

"Yes."

"Okay. Hold tight here for a minute. Let me talk to them."

She saw Nick disappear through a door beside the waiting room check-in counter and appear behind the desk moments later, talking with a tired-looking man in scrubs. At length the man handed him some papers, and she could tell Nick was thanking him. He returned to her. "You were never here," he said, handing her the papers and her insurance card.

"Okay…?" she said.

He held out his hand. "Come with me." She gathered her things, which included a flip-flop for the injured foot. Nick helped her hobble through the doorway and down a long hall to a small treatment room, where he lifted her onto a hospital gurney and put her injured foot up on a pillow.

"Now this is service," Rachel sighed. She looked great, Nick thought, stretched out before him in her shorts and tank top.

"Must remember I'm a doctor," he whispered to her, biting his lip.

Rachel giggled, "Later baby, not here."

Nick nodded and carefully removed the tape and towel. An inch long cut ran over the top of her foot, close to the ankle. "How did you do this?" he asked.

"It was the stupidest thing ever. My cat did it."

"Really? Her claws must need trimming."

"No. She didn't scratch me. It was the cat food."

He grinned, still eyeing the cut. "Elaborate please."

She rolled her eyes, "Okay, so I was feeding my cat, Butterball."

"Butterball?"

"Yes. So called because she is not svelte."

"No?"

"No. As cats go, she is definitely on the fatter side. She likes her groceries."

"Got it. Go on."

Rachel sighed and raised herself up on an elbow, "We were in the kitchen, and I had the TV on. I had just opened the can to feed her. And there was a show on about the Iditarod, you know, that long dogsled race in Alaska. And on the TV, one of the dogs barked, and it scared Butterball. So, she jumped into my arms, knocking the full can of cat food with its razor-sharp lid from the counter. And that is how I come to be in the emergency room tonight."

Nick laughed "And I thought I was the only one with a fat, idiotic pet," he said, thinking of Roquefort.

"Nope. She's all bulk and no brains."

He approached the bed. "Well, let's see what we have here." He gently lifted her foot and removed the pillow beneath it. "I'm going to have to numb it before I clean it and sew it up, and that is going to sting a bit. Do I have your permission?"

She nodded, biting her lower lip.

Nick had drawn up some local anesthetic while they were talking, and now he removed the cap from the needle. "Just a little prick," he said, sliding the tip beneath her skin at the wound's edge.

"Oww," she howled, and then laughed. "You're a little prick."

Nick smiled at her. "Don't antagonize the man with the needle," he said. He injected again. "Did that hurt?"

"No."

"That's because I'm injecting through the numb area. It's my beachhead of numbness. I was trained to inject stealthily, like a ninja."

"I guess I'm grateful for that. I hope it's the only way you're sneaky."

Nick was setting up his surgical tray with instruments and suture. "Don't worry. It is." When he was certain the area was numb, he carefully cleaned the cut, then sutured the edges of the wound together in two layers. “There’s a deep layer of absorbable stitches and then an outer layer that I’ll remove for you starting in about a week. This will mean you’ll have to come to my office and see me,” he added, smiling.

“Ewwww.”

“Ewwww about the sutures or ewwww about coming to see me?”

She shot him a playful smile. “The second one.”

He picked up her bandaged foot and ran his fingers over the sides and toes, massaging slowly, “I’m not so bad, really, am I?”

Her eyes closed and her head rolled back, “You have your moments. Please keep doing that.”

He did for a while.

Nick kept an arm around Rachel’s waist as he helped her back to her car, keeping her weight off the injured foot. They paused under a streetlight on Tulane Avenue.

“Thank you for taking care of me tonight,” Rachel said softly.

“It was my pleasure. I think if you could, you would have done the same for me.”

She took his hand and massaged it. “I would.”

"That feels nice."

"Good. Are you sure I can't pay you for this?"

"Don't be silly."

She looked into his eyes. "You're a good man, Nick."

"Nice of you to say. I guess I'm all right."

"No. You're better than just all right. You're compassionate. To me, that's a very attractive quality."

"I try to be," he said, lightly squeezing her hand, "but you're the do-gooder, not me."

She chuckled. "You do good things for people, too."

"Yeah, but I'm well paid for it. You wouldn't find me in the Charity ER waiting to be treated."

"Maybe not," she said, leaning against him. Her lips were close to his ear. "You're a good guy, Nick Jordan," she whispered, giving the ear a light kiss.

"You're a better person than I am," he replied, holding her a little tighter. He wasn't sure why he had said it, but he knew it was right. The recognition made him feel uneasy, as if one day, he might do something to prove it.

"Now you're being silly," she said, drawing closer to him. "Kiss me, doctor."

Nick did, and their bodies pressed together, as the kissing became more passionate. Struck by the oddness of making out directly across from the hospital, he started to laugh.

Rachel pulled away, "What's so funny?"

"It's just doing this here, with you, is, I don't know, strange, I guess."

"Because I'm your patient?"

"No, not so much that. We were romantic together before I sewed you up, so it's not like I used my doctorly influence to seduce you. It's just I feel like the hospital is watching me."

"I get it," she said, "not in front of the medical center." He helped her settle into the driver's seat.

"You're not mad, are you?"

"No. How could I be mad at my knight in shining armor?"

"Good," he said, reaching over her to buckle her seatbelt. As he did, he noticed her bandaged foot in its flip-flop. His mind flashed back to a trip he'd taken long ago with Elizabeth to California, shortly after they were married. Elizabeth had cut her foot hiking with him on the cliffs that lined the ocean. Nick had bandaged it for her at a pharmacy. Afterwards, he remembered entering an art gallery with her in Laguna Beach. She was wearing a floral sundress and sandals and hobbled a little from her injury. The image of her there, standing in the middle of the room regarding the art on the walls, came back to him with perfect clarity—her skin glowing from the sun, her hair wild from the sea and wind. He thought she was the most beautiful woman he had ever seen. But he knew now that there were imperfections even then, little cracks and seeds inside of her that would spread and grow, invisible to him in the glow of her beauty and his love for her, in the haze of his desire for her and their recent promises to love until death do we part. Or maybe it was more of a weakness in her, an inability to guard against the ebb of affection, the dying of the light? Had he sensed it even then? Maybe on some level he had. But now he knew with certainty that those tiny flaws had been there—nascent, disastrous, and embryonic; they had to be. And they would spread until they took over and she didn't love him anymore; until she became a person whom he couldn't even listen to, whom he couldn't stand to hear.

He remembered that the gallery owner, an older man with a gravely wise look, had come over. Nick had complimented him on the art and the man had thanked him and said, "But the most beautiful creation here is the one you brought in with you. She is special; hold on tight to that one." Nick remembered resolving to do just that; to fight hard to keep his love with Elizabeth strong and safe for the rest of their lives. But time and the world had done their work with the inevitability of water on stone. Now she was just a conflicted set of memories to him.

"You okay?" Rachel asked, looking up at him with a searching expression.

"Yeah, I guess. Why?"

"I'm not sure. I thought maybe I lost you there."

39

Nick spied a parking spot on St. Charles and maneuvered his convertible into it. He waited for a streetcar to pass, then walked across the tracks in the middle of the avenue toward the Columns Hotel. He saw that a crowd had already gathered in front. Pat O'Brien's in the French Quarter had the most famous patio in New Orleans, but the Columns had the most popular front porch. It was large and inviting and had even been featured in the movies. A high, overhanging second floor balcony formed a partial roof for the porch, which was bracketed on both sides by enormous, fluted columns. Ancient oak trees framed the building. Nick had always thought it a setting worthy of a scene in *Gone with the Wind*. Inside there was a cozy bar that stayed open late. The Columns had been a favorite place for New Orleanians to meet for decades.

This evening the Tulane Medical Alumni Association filled the porch and its bar. Doctors were drinking and chatting gaily, the women in cocktail dresses and the men in sport coats and ties. Several of the guys wore seersucker; *how very southern*, Nick thought.

He walked up the wide path and stairs to the porch and looked around. He was pleased to immediately spot Fiona

Espinoza chatting with a circle of older doctors; her bright auburn hair made her impossible to miss. He waited for the small group to disperse, then walked up and tapped her gently on the shoulder. She turned to him and her delicate features formed a welcoming smile. "Doctor Nick Jordan. *Now* it's a party."

He moved forward and gave her a hug. "Right. You know what a party animal I am."

"It's always the quiet ones you have to watch," she replied, taking a sip of something pinkish from a martini glass. "What's new with you, Nick?"

"Let's see," he said, "Oh, Charles Monroe's sentinel node biopsy turned out negative, thank goodness."

"That's great news. He's such a nice man."

"That he is," Nick replied. "I reconstructed his scalp last week."

"Did it go well?"

"It did. I created a couple of small flaps to close it." Nick had brought the skin around the wound together by making strategic cuts to allow it to move easily. "It came together nicely."

"I have no doubt about it," Fiona said, smiling. "You da man."

Nick stopped a passing waitress and ordered a Sazerac, a classic New Orleans cocktail made with Rye whiskey, absinthe, and bitters. The Columns made good ones. Turning back to Fiona, he was momentarily struck by her large dark eyes and reflected that the woman from Rare Beauty VIP Dating had been right; her really did have a thing for brown-eyed girls, especially this one. "What other patients do we have in common right now?"

Fiona considered this for a few seconds. "I know one, Lolly Boudreaux. You sent her over for a biopsy, remember?"

"Right. She's a bit of a character, don't you think?"

"I agree. Her husband seems scared to death of her."

"Maybe he has good reason. Did you do the biopsy?"

She nodded. "Yup. And the whole thing needs to come off. She's got a fairly aggressive squamous cell carcinoma. Good pick up by you, doctor."

Nick gratefully accepted his drink from the waitress. "Thanks," he said, moving his glass towards hers. "Cheers," they said at the same time and clinked the glasses together.

Nick took a deep sip; the cocktail tasted great in the humid Louisiana evening. "It was on her left temple, right?"

"Good memory. I'm going to send her for Mohs."

"Uh-huh." Nick knew this meant Lolly would have the tumor removed by a specially trained dermatologist. The technique was named for its originator, Frederic Mohs, who had developed it in the 1930's. Lolly's tumor would be frozen immediately after removal and looked at under a microscope. The Mohs surgeon would note any edges that still contained cancer cells and would make a detailed map of what to remove next. The process would continue until all the malignant cells were gone. The technique was more effective than simply cutting a circle around the whole area, sometimes repeatedly. And it saved normal tissue from being removed, which was enormously helpful in getting a good result with the repair. There would be a smaller hole to fix. "Would you like me to do the reconstruction?"

Fiona nodded. "I think both the patient and I will insist on it. You're really good at what you do, you know."

Nick smiled and looked away. "Some things, anyway."

Fiona looked at him with concern, then put a hand on his arm. "How stupid of me. I haven't even asked you how you're doing."

Nick took another tug at his drink. He was already feeling the effect. "I think you once told me news gets around New Orleans like wildfire. So, you know about the divorce."

She gave his arm a squeeze. "Yes, we talked about it on the phone. And remember, I also got your, ummm, email."

"My what?"

"You know, that profile you sent out."

Nick's head fell to his chest and he shook it slowly. "Oh shit, I forgot." She giggled.

He looked up and saw that her glass was empty. "Come inside, and I'll tell you about it."

They found a table with comfortable antique chairs. Nick went to the bar and got more drinks. He settled down next to Fiona.

“Here’s to new beginnings,” she said, and they touched glasses again.

Nick was again struck by how beautiful she was. It was like a trick his mind played on him, he thought; he was constantly rediscovering how attracted he was to her. In addition to her looks, he deeply liked her as a person. She really was the complete package. And she was single. So why, he wondered now, shouldn’t he act on his feelings and ask her out? There was his relationship with Rachel, of course; it was going well, and he saw no reason to rock that boat. *Did he prefer Fiona to Rachel?* he wondered. Anyway, they’d talked it over at the speed dating party and decided not to date. Fiona was a colleague and a referring one at that. He valued their working relationship and didn’t want to screw it up. Nick remembered a quote at that moment, served up from somewhere in his subconscious mind, “Of all the words of tongue or pen, the saddest are these: *it might have been*.” He told his subconscious to shut the hell up and turned his attention back to what Fiona was saying:

“…it was the strangest thing. She told me that she called your office and was told that you don’t do eyelid surgery anymore. She said the person on the phone referred her to Doctor Rose.”

Nick was feeling the effects of the Sazeracs. “That’s impossible. She must have been mistaken. Maybe she called a different office and thought it was mine.”

Fiona nodded. “Maybe so.” She took a sip of her cocktail. “So, give me the full story on how your very entertaining email found its way to my in-box.”

He told her about the night of too much bourbon and Percocet, and how the Match.com profile got sent to his entire database.

She looked concerned. "Are you still taking prescription narcotics to feel better?"

"No, I've stopped. After a while they stopped working and I didn't need them as much. Thank goodness I don't have an addictive personality, or I could've gotten hooked. Anyway, I've found that working out or running for long periods of time makes me feel better, too."

"I was going to say, you look great; really fit."

"Thanks. The anxiety seems to be going away now. I think signing the divorce papers made it feel more final. There's no more uncertainty. It's over."

"Do you want it to be over?"

He considered that. "For so long my mindset was to save our marriage at all costs. I think the reason I hung on so hard was because I remembered how good it was in the beginning, and I wanted to get it back. But the problem was, she didn't. She couldn't access those memories. She had no recollection of what it felt like to love me; I mean none. It's like she lost a sense. And if your partner doesn't have those kinds of memories, then how can you possibly come together when you've drifted apart?"

She shook her head. "I don't know. Bastard that Tom is now; I still remember how crazy I was for him in the beginning. I can remember exactly how it felt to kiss him. Your ex losing that must have been hard on both of you."

He took another tug at his Sazerac. "It was. I tried so hard, and in her way, I guess she did too." He looked into Fiona's lovely eyes again, "But what I came to realize was that I wasn't married to the same person I started out with. I guess nobody is if you get right down to it. People change; I'm sure I did, too. But the Elizabeth I divorced was nothing like the girl I started out with."

Fiona nodded. "There's truth in that. Lord knows Tom and I changed. I mean, kids, careers—how could we not?"

"Right," Nick answered, "so you either change together in ways that are compatible or you don't. And if you don't, you either stay together and strike a deal to be unhappy for the duration, or you split."

She reached out and took his hand. "And life's too short to be unhappy, at least for too long. You're such a good guy, Nick. You deserve better things."

He squeezed her hand. It felt nice in his. "Right back at you, doctor." He raised his glass. "Here's to the both of us finding happiness."

They clinked again and spoke of other things.

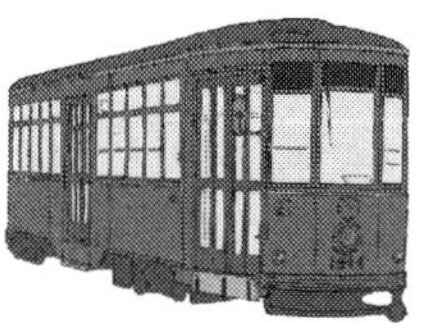

40

The following morning, Nick was passing the break room on the way to his desk when a buzzing noise attracted his attention. He turned to see a cell phone vibrating against the wood of the dining table. He went in and picked it up, then read the text on the phone's display:

Very good. Keep me posted Greg.

Nick went to the door and looked up and down the hallway. Seeing no one, he swiped the phone's screen to reveal more of the text conversation. What he read made him grab a chair and sit.

How is our project coming along?

Pretty good. I've been able to answer more calls and send them your way.

You're doing well. A few new consults have told us that Jordan referred them. Do you think you can send more?

I'm getting them to you as fast as I can, but I have to be very careful.

Do you think they suspect you?

No. These assholes aren't as smart as they think they are. But they're not stupid either.

I understand. Try to answer as many incoming calls as you can.

I will. You're keeping track and I get my cut, right?

Yes of course. How's your offsite venture going?

Good. A few new clients each week and some repeats too.

Wonderful. And they don't miss the Botox?

No. I only take parts of bottles that are already mixed. No unopened ones.

Very good. Keep me posted Greg.

Nick checked to see where the texts were coming from. He found a New Orleans number and wrote it down. He'd look it up, but he knew it had to belong to Dr. Leslie Rose, Greg's former employer. Nick felt stunned by the audacity of what his assistant was doing. He'd been planning to fire Greg any day now; Lesli had assembled enough of a paper trail that there could be no question of an unlawful dismissal.

As the shock abated, Nick thought hard. He flashed back to what Fiona had said about a patient being told he didn't do eyelids. Greg had been answering calls and sending people to his old boss. And he was probably, no, *certainly*, doing Botox treatments somewhere else using product that Nick's practice had paid for. A cold anger filled him. Simply firing Greg would not be enough. The snake would just get another job somewhere else. Nick wanted to ruin him, to make it so Greg would have to leave New Orleans or stay there in prison. Rising, he returned the phone to where he had found it on the table and left the room.

Nick called Lesli and Ginger into his office.

Ginger smiled at him, swaying slightly on high heels. "What's up Boss?"

"From now on, I want the two of you, and only the two of you, to handle all incoming calls."

Lesli nodded. "So, Greg…"

"Is not to be on the front desk anymore. Find other things for him to do." He thought for a moment. "Tell him that we're working on Ginger's phone skills, that we want her to be able to handle higher volumes of calls, something like that."

Ginger looked worried. "Don't I handle the calls well?"

"Of course you do," Nick replied. "That's why I want you answering all of them. When you're away, Lesli will take them."

"You're the big cheese," Ginger said, "and your wish is my command. Is that all?"

Nick stood up, "Yup. That's it for now."

The two women rose and headed out of the room. Lesli stopped and turned to her boss. "You'll fill me in on what happened later?"

"You betcha," Nick answered, and closed the door behind her.

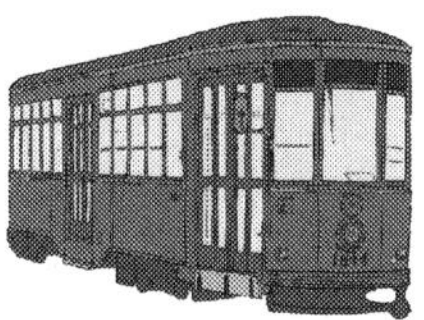

41

A few minutes later, Nick took the first chart of the day from its rack. He was glad to see that Charles Monroe had returned. He walked into the treatment room and saw him, beautifully dressed as always, reading the *Wall Street Journal*. The older man rose to greet him and extended his hand. "Good to see you, doctor. How've you been?"

Nick shook Charles' hand and motioned for him to sit. "I'm fine, Charles. But that's not the question. How are you doing?"

"If I were any better, I'd be twins."

Nick chuckled at the familiar remark and moved to the side of the exam chair. He carefully removed the bandage from behind Charles's ear and studied his reconstruction. Nick had fixed the hole by creating two flaps of skin in an asymmetrical "O to Z" reconstruction. The larger half of the Z used the more mobile neck skin below the wound. A smaller, triangular flap had come from the tighter scalp skin above. Nick had been careful to make the upper flap smaller so as not to distort the shape of Charles's hairline. The two healing flaps came together in a horizontal line of stitches. Nick knew this was the area where he had placed the most tension on the healing skin. He eyed it carefully to make sure there was no separation.

"Charles, you're healing well."

"Glad to hear it, Doc, but I had no doubts. I knew you'd fix me up."

"That's my job," Nick answered, reaching into a drawer for instruments. He removed every other suture from the healing cuts, leaving the rest to support the repair. When he was finished, he placed antibiotic ointment and a clean dressing over the site, then stepped back and nodded. "That should do it for now. I'd like to see you back in four days to remove more of the stitches."

"That's a deal," Charles replied. "So, how's everything else going?"

"Pretty well. I'm staying busy."

"Are you dating anybody you like?"

Nick laughed. "Would I date anybody I didn't like?"

"You might if she was good-looking enough."

"You have a point, Charles. I was seeing a drug rep. She's quite a bit younger than me, and you're right—she's good-looking enough to be with no matter what she's like. It turns out she's a great girl. But she made it clear to me that she's looking for a younger guy to start a family with. She met someone, and so that was that."

Charles nodded. "Been there, done that. But it sounds like you were both straight with each other, so no harm, no foul, right?"

Nick was scribbling a note in the chart. "I guess so. I've just started seeing someone more age-appropriate; another great girl. We'll see where it goes."

"Sounds good, buddy. I'll tell you, in my experience, the early romances after a marriage breaks up rarely work out. You're kind of damaged and not ready. But it's a necessary part of the process. And I suppose there are exceptions."

Nick set the chart down on the counter. "Like you said, I plan to be completely honest with whomever I date. That's one thing my divorce brought home to me—in the end, what you really owe each other is honesty."

"Yup."

"What about you, Charles? Anybody special in your life at the moment?"

"Not really. Remember Tiffany from the party? We've been out a few times; we're more friends than anything else. Still, she's someone to do stuff with. Like The Eagles said: 'Late at night, the big old house gets lonely.'"

Nick registered surprise. "Don't tell me *you* get lonely, Charles. You're my idol of bachelorhood. My Yoda. If you get lonely living the perfect bachelor life, what hope is there for mere mortals like me?"

Charles laughed. "Yoda, huh? That's good." He paused, and his face took on a more serious expression. "I'll tell you something, Nick. That melanoma diagnosis shook me up. I got online and learned about what it can do, and I was scared. I mean, really scared. Thank God that node biopsy came back negative."

Nick nodded. Charles continued, "One thing that struck me was how alone I am. I mean, I have plenty of buddies to do things with; you know, scheduled things, or partying when we can get together. But there's too much time in between. And no one's really there for me when the good times aren't rolling."

Nick looked him in the eye. "I hear you, Charles. But you're a great guy and I think you'd find that when the chips were down, your friends would step up for you. You impress me as the kind of person who would be there for them."

"That's nice of you to say." The older man took a deep breath. "I guess what I'm saying is that I'm lonely. I'm retired, so I spend most of my time by myself. Don't get me wrong; I enjoy my alone time. But there's too much of it. I'd like to have a woman in my life who I can care for and who would return the favor."

Nick winced slightly. His patient had touched a chord within him, raising a small but anxious fear; the specter of being alone forever. "I get that. I've been logging quite a few nights by myself at home lately. It's peaceful and relaxing, but, you're right." He chuckled. "Listen to us—what's a pair of lonely bachelors to do?"

"I know what I'm doing," answered Charles. "As soon as you give me the all-clear, I'm going to have an adventure. Shake it up a little bit. After all, what can you do when you can't dance, it's too wet to plow, and the drummer's on vacation?"

Nick smiled. "My dad used to say that."

Charles nodded. "Mine too. I think I'll do some traveling. Somewhere beautiful or exotic to celebrate not having a killer melanoma."

Nick rose. "Sounds like a great idea. I want to see pictures when you get back."

"You got it, buddy."

"You should be able to travel in a couple of weeks. Give it that long in case we have any setbacks with your healing."

Charles rose and shook his hand. "Will do, doctor. And you won't have to remind me to pack my sunscreen."

Nick came back out into the hall to see Ginger carrying a large basket of muffins toward him. It tottered back and forth as she stepped from one stiletto heel to the next. He detected a fresh-baked smell. "Just out of the oven?" he asked.

"You bet. I'm bringing them up to the break room. Your friend Rachel just dropped them by."

Nick grinned. "Did she now?"

"Yup. She's a nice girl, boss; and quite nice looking."

"I noticed that."

She giggled. "I bet you did. I told you it wouldn't be long before you'd be on the prowl."

He let that one go.

"That girl's in love with you, you know."

He shook his head. "No, I don't think we're quite there yet."

"You may not be, but she is. You should have heard her: 'Nick this' and 'Nick that'. She even called you Nicholas one time."

"Really?"

"Yup. I've got a sixth sense for this type of thing. That woman is head over heels."

She continued down the hallway. Nick snagged a warm blueberry muffin from the basket as she passed. He bit into it thoughtfully. *What if Ginger was right*, he wondered. He hadn't spent any time considering the strength of Rachel's feelings toward him. He searched his own. He cared for her and enjoyed being with her. But love? It didn't feel like love to him. *Maybe down the road, after I've had more time to get past the divorce*, he thought. Nick thought about what Charles had said about early romances. He resolved to take things slower with Rachel, and at that moment an ominous feeling came over him. They were already having sex, very good sex, so he recognized they were pretty far down the road. He certainly didn't want to end it. Was that weakness on his part? Maybe he just needed more time for his feelings to develop. He knew that what he owed her was complete honesty and the thought shook him. He took another bite and headed down the hallway.

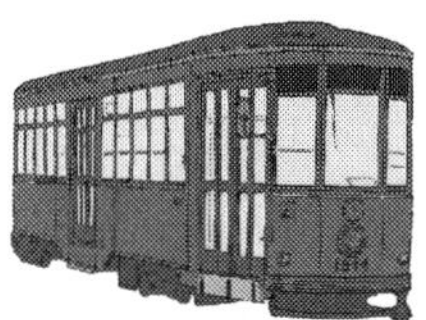

42

They turned down Washington Avenue with the convertible's top open, and pulled up next to Lafayette Cemetery Number One. The necropolis was deserted in the early evening. Concrete tombs and marble spires cast long, weird shadows on the ground. Nick made a U-turn and stopped in front of Commander's Palace, one of New Orleans' oldest and most beloved restaurants. A valet took the car, and the couple stopped a moment to look at the beautiful old home. It was a Victorian delight: striped awnings, gingerbread trim, ornate columns, and a big corner turret. First time visitors always wanted to know about the military history of the place, but there was none. In 1880, a man named Emile Commander established the restaurant in the Garden District, and the name had stuck.

An impeccably dressed manager greeted them and showed them to a corner table. The large room was beautifully decorated; ornate but not over the top. Fresh flowers adorned the tables. Nick always felt happy here, like he was in a lovely private home that just happened to be full of people eating. They ordered drinks.

Rachel wore a blue and white print dress that clung to her athletic body. Nick thought she looked gorgeous tonight. He told her so, and she smiled at him. The drinks came. "To a good end to a long day," she said as they clinked glasses. Each took a deep sip.

Nick leaned back in his chair. "Aaaah, that's good. Was it a long day for you?"

She looked up at him, her big green eyes partially obscured by brown and blonde bangs. "Oh yeah. I learned more about trucks today than I ever wanted to know."

"Really? What happened?"

She sipped again. "We had two of them break down, both during deliveries to shelters. One of them is still blocking traffic near the Superdome."

"That sounds bad."

"Well, we dealt with it. I had to rent another truck and find enough guys to transfer the food before it spoiled. The good news is that the groceries made it to where they were needed, so people got to eat. That's the main thing."

Nick reached across the table and took her hand. "You are such a do-gooder."

She smiled at him. "Well, you are too. You make people happy."

He grinned. "I guess so, in my own way. But I just make them look better—*you* keep them alive. You're better than me. You win."

She laughed. "No, I'm not." The waiter brought menus and a napkin-covered basket. "Anyway, it's not a contest, is it?"

Nick chuckled. "I suppose not." He moved the napkin, uncovering the famous Commander's garlic bread. "But if it were, there's no doubt you'd win." He bit into a piece of the toast. "Delicious," he said through a half-full mouth. "If it was a contest to see who could eat more of this, I think I'd win." She giggled as he held the basket out to her.

Conversation flowed easily between them, as it always did. Beneath the tablecloth she extended one leg, then put her foot on his knee. He absently massaged her calf as they talked, running a finger over the now-healed cut on her foot. "How's this doing?" he asked.

She wiggled her toes. "Great. You can barely see it. Of course, I had a great surgeon."

"You're too kind."

"And you're too modest. Just keep rubbing."

They finished off a sumptuous dinner by sharing the signature bread pudding soufflé and a cappuccino. Nick paid the bill, then took Rachel's hand. "Let's walk around a bit before we leave. I love this old house." They made their way through the foyer to two large wooden doors marked YES and NO, and chose the correct one to enter the restaurant's kitchen, passing through the warm, busy space to the main bar. Nick ordered them an aperitif, Frangelico on ice. They took turns sipping the sweet hazelnut liqueur. "This is perfect," Rachel said, giving his arm a squeeze.

Nick looked down and saw her lick a droplet of the drink from her lower lip. "It could be even more perfect," he said, taking her hand, and leading her from the bar through an open glass door. "Let's check out the patio."

It was late now, and they were alone in an illuminated stone courtyard filled with wrought iron tables and chairs. He bent down to her, his lips brushing her hair. "There's a little garden over there," he whispered, indicating a hedge to the side of the patio.

She turned to him and kissed him lightly on the mouth, tasting of hazelnut. "Hmmm. Maybe we should go see it," she whispered.

They found a small path between the bushes and strolled to the far corner of the garden, where a tree shielded them from the overhead light. Rachel was in his arms now, her light, strong body pressed against his. They kissed for several minutes, both fully aroused. His hand slipped beneath her dress, and he squeezed her firm ass. She stroked the front of his thigh, trailing a finger over his erection, and he moaned. Breathing heavily, Nick looked into her eyes. He could see desire, and something else, longing maybe.

For what, though? He hoped they wanted the same things. A light sense of dread came over him. He felt afraid. But of what? He pulled her closer. She felt perfect. *Hell, she is perfect*, he told himself. She held on tightly. The night was quiet save for the sound of dishes and pans being washed somewhere nearby. “We really have to get a room,” Rachel whispered, kissing him again.

43

The long afternoon was fading into twilight as Nick drove up St. Charles Avenue with the convertible top down. Work that day had been hectic but satisfying. The radio played a Go-Go's song from the eighties. He softly sang along—"*we got the beat; we got the beat*." Remnants of sunshine danced through the branches of the ancient oaks all around him, and a bright green streetcar clanged by. He reflected for the zillionth time that he loved New Orleans.

Turning left on to State Street, his mood changed. He normally enjoyed driving up to his house, but now things were different. It reminded him of what he had lost. He pulled into the driveway and turned off the engine. Nick looked at his house. It wasn't nearly the largest one on the street, but it was one of the prettiest. And he felt so comfortable there. But these days, lonely too. Nick dreaded that feeling.

Nick put his key in the lock and opened the cut glass front door. There was a scrambling sound as Roquefort rounded a corner at the back of the house, crashed into a doorjamb, and rushed across the hardwood floor. Nick knelt down and the pudgy animal rolled onto its back, thrusting four paws in the air. He rubbed the dog's belly, and Roquefort responded with a grunting, gasping purr. "You really are man's best friend," he said giving the tummy a final pat. The bulldog gurgled at him, and Nick laughed, grateful for the little beast's presence.

The evening sun was coming through the front windows, striking the crystal chandelier. Colors danced on the wall behind it; each crystal acting as a prism for the rays of light. Nick recalled the many times he'd been asked if he was moving out of this place. How many times had he heard the words, "All alone in that big house," said to him by a concerned friend or acquaintance? It was like he was morally obligated to relinquish his home to a happy family and take his rightful place in a condo or townhouse. But that wasn't going to happen. He was staying. Perhaps in time he'd find someone new to share it with. And this wonderful new love would make him put away the trappings of bachelorhood that were already starting to accumulate, the guitars and the video game console and such, and make the house beautiful again. And he would complain while loving her for making him do it. *Please*, he thought, in silent prayer.

He walked through the foyer and living room to his study. On his way he looked around. What he saw made him sad. Elizabeth had taken much of the furniture and most of their possessions with her, but there were reminders of her everywhere, which brought back memories of the good times they had shared, and of the misery they had suffered at the end of their marriage.

A painting they had bought together on a trip to California hung over the fireplace. *Man, we were in love then*, he thought as he continued through the room, past bookcases housing photo albums, crammed with countless pictures of the perfect couple together somewhere.

To Nick the house now felt like a monument to something doomed that had once been great. For months after they separated, he'd woken here each morning temporarily forgetful of the crisis. He'd had to remember every day that his marriage was dying. Waking not from, but to, a nightmare. He didn't do that anymore. Their love was dead, their marriage over. He wondered who Elizabeth was dating, and if she was happy. He hoped she wasn't. The thought made him feel petty. He thought of other romances from his past. The love he had experienced with Holly Spencer as an intern and how strangely it had ended, more recently his infatuation with Lovely, brief and intense as it was. Now there was Rachel; would she soon be another reminiscence?

Filling a glass with bourbon, he entered the study and sat in his favorite chair, where only a few months before he'd sat alone, taking Percocet, and drinking by himself to keep the anguish at bay. His isolation had brought him nothing but crushing anxiety. Nick looked down into his glass. Well, at least he was off the pills. He took a big sip of bourbon with a sigh.

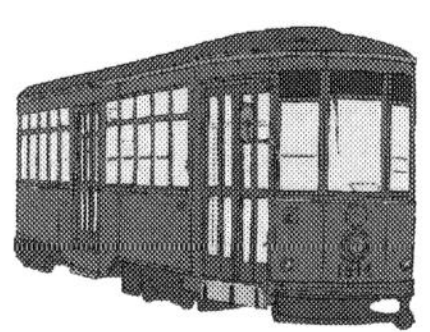

44

Later that evening, Nick's cell phone rang. He muted the television and answered. "Hello?"

"Nick? Thank goodness. It's Sandra," she said, sounding emotional.

"What's up?"

"It's Dave. Have you seen his face?"

"Not, recently."

"He looks like a lizard."

"More like a lizard than usual?"

There was a pause. "Not funny. It's those skin care products."

Nick rolled his eyes. "Okay, tell me what happened."

"Well, I've been out of town, and I just got back. I came in the house and could hear him walking around upstairs. I called up to him, but he didn't come down. He just stood at the top of the stairs, and I could see his feet but not the rest of him. So, I went up to see him."

"Uh-huh."

"And when I got up to our bedroom, he scurried into the bathroom and locked the door."

Nick giggled involuntarily.

"Are you laughing?"

He choked back the giggle. "No."

"Good, because this isn't funny."

Nick took a deep breath and regained his composure. "What happened then?"

"I talked to him through the door. I could hear running water, and he kept dropping things, like he was trying to do something quickly. Finally, he said, "You might as well see," and opened the door. There were little bottles and tubes all over the floor. His back was to me, and he told me that he'd had a problem with the skin care products, that he didn't think he was using them correctly. Then he turned around, and, oh gosh, Nick, he looks like he'd been dragged through the street on his face."

"Tell me what it looks like exactly."

"Well, his skin is very red and it's scaling and peeling. It's super-red around his eyes and mouth, and then the redness fans out across his cheeks, like in little waves. His eyelids are swollen and there are deep creases in his temples and around his mouth. A few sores on his forehead and cheeks are oozing a kind of clear fluid."

Nick was concerned now. "Yuck."

"Yuck is right. I asked him what happened, and he showed me what he'd been using. Nick, he's been using super-strong glycolic acid and the ACE bomb two or three times a day. I use it once or twice a year! I told him I couldn't believe that Felicity put him on that routine, and he admitted that she hadn't. Finally, he told me that he'd lied to y'all and said he was buying these things for me."

"Oh, man."

I washed off all the products and put some Vaseline on which made him feel better immediately."

"That was the right thing to do, Sandra. Do you want to bring him over? Or I can come look at him."

"No, it's late. We'll call Felicity in the morning and get her to see him." She sighed. "He looks like a Gila monster, Nick."

"Yeah, but he's your Gila monster." They were both giggling now.

At length, Sandra spoke. "I asked him why he did it. At first, he told me that the products Felicity gave him didn't seem to be doing much, and he wanted stronger ones to get more effect."

"Uh-huh."

"But when I asked him again why he felt he needed to use them at all, I mean he's a handsome guy, do you know what he told me?"

"What?" Nick asked.

"He actually paid you a compliment. He said that he's got a young-looking wife, and he feels he has to keep up."

Shortly after Nick hung up with Sandra his cell phone rang again. He looked at the number and saw that his accountant was calling, which was strange at this time of night.

"Hello?"

"Hi, Nick, it's Kevin. I'm sorry for calling this late."

"That's okay. What's up?"

"Nothing good, that's why I'm calling. I just went over your quarterly expenses and receipts, and I hate to tell you that you're losing money."

Nick paused, taking it in. "I knew we were down, but actually in the red?"

"Yep, especially for the last two months. Your income is down and your supply expenses are way up."

This was not good. Nick felt a weight in the center of his chest. "I see."

"Has anything changed that you think could be causing this?"

In his mind's eye, Nick could see Greg grinning at him, and the thought made him angry. "I think I know what the problem is, and I'll soon be taking steps to correct it."

"Well good, because if not, you'll probably have to cut salaries or lay somebody off."

"It's that bad, is it?"

"Yup."

"I understand, Kevin. Believe me, I'm on it. Thanks for calling."

"Sure, and sorry to give you that kind of news. Call me if I can help." The accountant hung up.

Nick looked at Roquefort, who was lying on his side near the TV snoring softly. "Buddy, we got problems," he said. He thought about having another drink and decided against it. It was strange, he reflected, but facing up to the divorce had given him a new perspective—a certain immunity against lesser pain. It was as if anything short of that emotional catastrophe was just not a big deal. The business was having problems, yes, but he had a good reputation and a strong following in New Orleans. It would be okay because he would make it okay. He knew that Greg was a big part of the problem, maybe all of it. He sat up late that night, thinking hard about how to put things right.

45

Nick and Rachel carried their dishes and cups from the backyard patio into the house. They had used Nick's decidedly low-key grill to cook up steaks and sweet white corn. Rachel lost control of a blue plastic Mardi Gras cup that made a loud noise as it bounced on the tile of the kitchen floor. "Whoops," she giggled, trying hard not to lose the plates and silverware still in her hands. While the food was cooking, they had consumed a cold bottle of Riesling, and they were both feeling the effects.

"I got it," called Nick from somewhere behind her. She laughed as she heard the clanging of a platter and barbeque tools in the living room. A moment later, Nick came into the kitchen, grinning. Roquefort trailed behind with steak juice staining his jowls. "He tripped me up, then licked up the tray," he said, giving the porcine dog an affectionate look. They dumped everything into the sink. She turned to him. "You cooked, so I'll get the dishes."

"You wash, I'll dry," he said, and kissed the top of her head.

They finished the easy chore and moved into the main room together. "So, what do you want to do now?" she asked, looking up at him coyly from under wispy bangs.

Nick put his arms around her. "Well, that was quite a bit of effort, you know, what with the drinking and eating and dishwashing and such. Maybe we should go up to my bedroom and rest."

She laughed and squeezed up against him. "And how much rest do you think we'll get, doctor?"

He felt himself starting to get aroused. "I predict not much for a while, then a good nap." He took her hand and led her up the stairs.

Their lovemaking was fast and passionate. She climaxed first and a few moments later Nick did as well, savoring the delicious feeling of being one with her. It was a warm night, and their naked bodies were wet and hot against one another. He rolled off of her panting, and she snuggled close to him, her head resting on his shoulder.

"Listen," she whispered, "I want to say something. I've wanted to say it for a long time. And you don't have to say it back, but I have to get it out."

Nick was half asleep. "Okay," he murmured.

"I love you." The words came out of her like a musical sigh, as if they'd finally been released from a tight space after a very long time.

Nick was silent. His thinking felt slow and awkward; he didn't know what to say. Finally, he replied with the only answer he could think of: "Thank you." He realized how bad it sounded the moment he said it.

She turned to him, and he looked into her eyes. He could see she was hurt. “You don’t love me?” she said in a very different tone, almost a whimper.

Nick turned onto his side to face her and put both arms around her. “The truth is, I don’t know.”

“You don’t?”

“I know that I enjoy being with you and that we’re good together. And I care for you, a lot, really.”

“But you don’t love me?” She sounded like a little child.

“Look, living through the breakup of my marriage messed me up.”

“Yeah?”

“Yeah. And I have feelings for you, but they’re not what I remember being in love was like. I honestly don’t know if I’m ever going to love anybody again.”

She was crying now. Fat tears coursed from her lovely green eyes. He could feel her body shaking against his. She gasped for breath. He tried to pull her closer to him. “No,” she said, and broke free of his embrace, wiping her eyes and gathering the sheets around her. She looked at him sideways. “I feel so stupid. I thought you were ready. I thought the signs were there. I really misread them.” She started crying again, her head bent to her knees. He couldn’t see her face now.

“I’m so sorry,” he said, trying to think of what more to say. “I’ve always been honest with you. I’m just not there yet. Can you understand?" She nodded, but was fighting the crying too much to speak. She shook her head when he tried to embrace her again, pushing him away. Nick got up and walked around the bed to sit on her side. "What can I do?"

"Nothing," she said, hugging her knees to her chest, "just leave me alone."

In the darkness, Nick rose from the bed and found his shirt and shorts on the floor. "I'll be downstairs when you're ready to talk," he said, closing the door gently behind him. He walked to the living room window and looked out at the streetlights and front gardens across State Street. He felt terrible; he had inflicted pain on someone he truly cared about, someone who it turned out, loved him. He felt an overwhelming sense of guilt; it felt bad and raw and miserable and was a different kind of anguish than he'd felt during the separation and divorce. Rachel had done nothing to deserve this; it was his fault. For a moment he wondered if Elizabeth had ever felt this way in her dealings with him.

Twenty minutes later Nick heard the bedroom door open. Rachel came down the stairs. He met her in the foyer. She was dressed, and her eyelids were swollen. She moved to him and gave him a long hug. "It's okay, Nick. You can't make yourself feel what you don't. Maybe I rushed it." She kissed him on the cheek and pulled away. "You don't have to worry about me. I'm a strong person. I'll be alright," she said, her voice trembling.

He took a step towards her. "Let me drive you home."

She shook her head. “No, I need to be alone. I’ll be alright.” She walked to the door and gave him a little smile. Her puffy eyelids crinkled. “You take care of yourself, Nick. I hope you find someone who makes you happy.” Before he could answer she was gone.

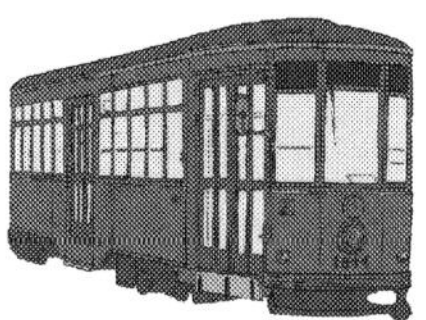

46

Nick lay awake in the dark. It was four-thirty in the morning and he couldn't sleep. He had barely slept at all since Rachel left. He heard a streetcar moving far away on the avenue and absently felt the rough patch of skin at the base of his finger where his wedding ring used to be. The callus was still there; it didn't seem to be changing at all.

Drawing a deep sigh, he finally sat up in bed. All he could hear was the sound of Roquefort breathing. He got out of bed and dressed in his running gear. Five minutes later, he was jogging on St. Charles Avenue.

It was quiet and very dark in the spots between streetlights. He took care not to trip on ruts in the grass between the streetcar tracks. As he made his way uptown, the houses got bigger. Many of the mansions were lit up at night. The indirect lighting made the old homes look even more beautiful. He kept going, running at a more regular pace, until he crossed Calhoun Street and saw the park come into view.

Nick ran frequently in Audubon Park, but he had never seen it at this hour. He could just make out the large asphalt path that looped for almost two miles around the interior of the park. He ran past the Gumbel fountain and straight towards a group of statues titled "The Travelers," which looked strangely primitive and somber to him in the darkness. He continued his steady jog in a counterclockwise direction and thought about what had happened.

He had dated a perfectly wonderful girl and broken her heart. Had he led her on? He searched his mind and could think of nothing he'd said that wasn't true. He'd had a vague awareness that she wanted to take their relationship to a more serious level, but hadn't known what that might mean. Ginger had warned him that Rachel was in love with him. He'd discounted that, but he'd sensed that Rachel was further along the path to love than he was. He remembered hoping that his feelings would catch up to hers; thinking that the divorce had made him more guarded than she was. Could he have saved her this pain by telling her about his feelings sooner? *Maybe so*, he thought, and the idea made him miserable. He coughed in the darkness, passing an old man walking a dog.

And why *didn't* he love her? They'd been dating for a while, and he'd enjoyed every minute of it. They had compatible personalities and tastes. Their physical chemistry was off the charts. So, what was it? Was he not capable of loving anyone? Had the death of his marriage killed something inside of him? *Maybe it had.* Maybe he was broken and would never mend. Not fully, anyway. A heaviness came over him and he found the running harder.

Nick made the long turn along Magazine Street and started back towards St. Charles. To his left, in the middle of a long slender lagoon, was Bird Island. The park had been dead quiet, but now he could hear chirps and squawks. Above the tops of cypress trees to his left and oaks to his right, the sky was starting to lighten. He took a deep breath and tried to let the tension go out of him.

He was scared for Rachel. She'd told him not to worry, but he couldn't help it. He wondered if she was capable of hurting herself. His gut told him that she wasn't. She was a strong and resourceful person. She had dedicated her life to helping other people; people that depended on her. That would give her perspective. If he could recognize that fact, so would Rachel. She was at least as smart as he was. *No,* he thought, *she won't harm herself.* The realization made him feel a little better. Still, he had hurt a really good person; someone who cared for him. There was no way around that. She would have to deal with the pain, and he would have to live with the guilt. An*d that sucks for both of us*, he thought, as he took a deep breath and kept running.

The question kept coming back to him—If he couldn't love her, basically the perfect woman, could he ever love anyone again? His feet made a rhythmic pounding noise on the pavement as he considered that question. He knew himself; he was fifty years old for crying out loud. He knew he would do everything he could to try. Time would tell. The death of his marriage had been a soul-searing experience, and it had scarred him. No, he thought, it had *wounded* him. He was a surgeon; he knew wounds came before scars. Wounds took time to heal and scars took much longer to form. His healing was just beginning. What would be left after the healing would be the scar. He resolved to live his life, to heal in such a way, that the scar that would form in his soul could accommodate a new love one day.

Nick realized he was running faster, much faster in fact. He reached the fountain and slowed to a walk, taking in huge breaths of the cool morning air. He turned for home, walking alongside the outstretched arms of ancient oak trees. Their damp leaves glittered in the morning light. His step felt lighter as he went. It would take time, but Rachel would be all right and so would he. Life would be good again. It might even be great.

Part Three
Lifting

"There is no point in simply working on the outer layer. For the lift to endure, the deeper structures must be intact and secure."

—*Terry Johnson, MD to his residents, 1989*

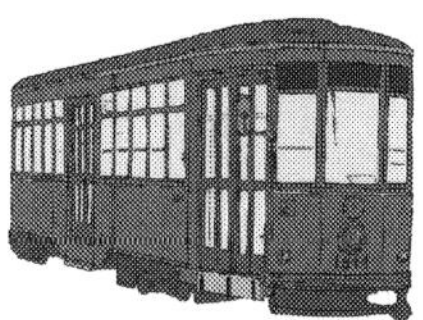

47

Sandra McGloughlin opened the front door to Nick's office and motioned for her husband to enter. Dave came up the front stairs with all the enthusiasm of a reluctant dog about to be bathed. He entered the waiting room wearing a hooded sweatshirt and a pair of Sandra's oversized Gucci sunglasses, which hid most of his face from view.

Nick walked up and shook his friend's hand. "You look like Ted Kaczynski in that outfit," he said.

"Who?" asked Ginger. Her bright red lips formed an inquisitive pout.

"The Unabomber," Dave answered. "Your insensitive boss just compared me to a domestic terrorist."

They heard Felicity from down the hallway before they could see her. "Where is he?" she called playfully. She entered the reception area and got an eyeful of Dave in his bizarre outfit. "You look like the Unabomber," she said, suppressing a giggle. Nick laughed. Sandra took hold of her husband's elbow and began pushing him up the hallway. "Oh, he looks worse than that," she said, giving the aesthetician a lord-help-us look.

They continued to the skincare treatment room at the back of the office, with Nick trailing behind. On the way, Dave was gently berated by both women at once for misusing the products he had bought. Felicity patted the spa bed. "Hop up here, Sweetcakes, and let's take a look." The beleaguered man sighed and slowly took off the glasses, then reached to peel back the sweatshirt hood. "Here goes," he said revealing himself to them.

Dave McGloughlin looked like a scalded armadillo. The areas of redness and peeling had coalesced into distinct patches, like the skin of an ancient soccer ball. His eyelids were swollen and open sores wept from his cheeks. Sandra was distressed to see that on top of it all, he had developed hives, which gave the angry skin an oddly three-dimensional look. "Oh baby. It's worse," she said softly.

"Wow," Felicity said, stepping back. "You've really done it. This is the worst reaction I've ever seen." She looked over her shoulder to Nick.

Dave let out an ironic chuckle. "I always try to overachieve."

"First time you actually did," Nick said from the doorway. Even he was taken aback by his friend's appearance.

"That's enough from the peanut gallery," Felicity said, walking around him now, peering at his face from the side. "Does it itch?"

"Like crazy," Dave replied.

"And what are you putting on it now?"

Sandra answered her. "We started out with Vaseline, but last night Dave began using an aloe gel that we have for sunburn. He's been slathering it on."

Felicity seemed fascinated. She continued looking; "I think the Vaseline was a good call. I'd go back to that. You might have sensitized yourself to aloe if you used a lot of it. Let's see your hands, Dave."

He held them up and the two women could see that they were irritated and swollen. Felicity nodded, "Yup, your skin is so fired up that it will react to almost anything now." She picked up a soft cotton towel and a bottle of cleanser. She dabbed the goo from his skin with gentle strokes. When it was dry she used a large Q-tip to apply a clear ointment to his face. "This is Aquaphor; it's very similar to Vaseline. This will give you some cover for now." She looked at Nick, "Do you agree, Doctor Jordan?"

"I do," he responded coolly.

"You know," Dave said to Felicity, "he'll never let me live this down."

Sandra took her husband's hand and gave it a squeeze. "Nor should he," she said sweetly.

Nick walked forward and looked closely at Dave's face, 'Plenty of time for that later," he said. "Right now, I just want to get you better."

Dave gave his friend a ghastly gloppy grin. "Thanks, pal."

Nick turned to Sandra. "I'm sorry you're living with the Creature from the Black Lagoon, but we'll get him right." She gave him a warm smile.

Nick looked at Felicity. “Call him in a prescription for triamcinolone cream, point one percent. The big sixty-gram tube. He can use it twice a day—morning and night. And if he’s itching, Benadryl will help him sleep and not scratch. Have him come see us at the end of the week, sooner if any new problems arise.” He looked back at his friend. “And for God’s sake, stop putting all that stuff on your face.”

Dave nodded “Will do.”

At the front desk, Nick told Ginger to make a return appointment. The receptionist had gotten a brief glimpse of Dave’s face and was purposely avoiding looking at him. “We’ll see you on Friday at eleven thirty, sir.” she said, using one fingernail to push an appointment card across the counter towards him.

Sandra picked up the card. “Thank you, sweetie,” she said, taking her husband’s hand, and rolling her eyes. “Ready, Freddy?” she asked.

“Huh?” he replied.

Nick leaned in close to him and whispered loudly enough for all to hear. “I think she means Freddy Krueger, you know, the horror character.”

The women laughed and even Dave smiled. He turned to Nick. “Normally I’d tell you to go screw yourself, but for once you’re right.”

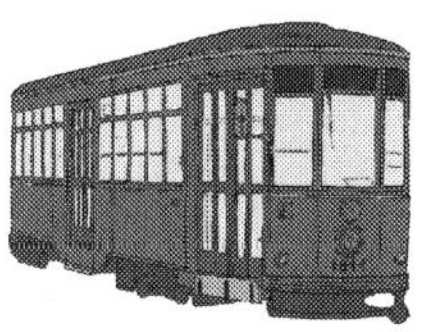

48

Nick came out of his office into the hallway and heard someone shouting in anger. He moved to the partially open break room door and listened.

He recognized Greg's voice yelling, "*What the hell do you know about it*?" It surprised him because he had never heard his assistant shout before.

Then he heard Felicity respond, "I know that, like the rest of you, that moustache is utterly repellant." Nick peeked through the space between the door and the frame and could see her and Greg. His short stature and her thick pink clogs put them eye-to-eye.

The little man's face cracked into a nasty half-smile; "What I know is that this place is bleeding money, and sooner or later someone's going to get the ax. And that will be you, because frankly, Scarlet, you're useless."

"What the hell are you talking about?" she yelled.

Nick rushed in and said, "Both of you, be quiet, now! A patient could hear you. We'll discuss all this later. Right now, we need to get to work."

"Yes, Boss," Felicity said, turning to walk back to her room. As she passed Greg, she whispered, "Prick" under her breath. The wiry little man looked pleased with himself.

Nick looked at him. "Get that stupid grin off your face. I can't have that kind of crap in my office."

"Yes, Boss," he replied, mimicking Felicity.

Nick shook his head and took off down the hallway. He paused in front of the first exam room door, nodded to Greg, and the two men entered the room together. An attractive woman in her late forties was seated in the large examination chair holding a hand mirror. She alternately knit her brow into a frown, then raised her eyebrows in mock surprise. "There are just too many lines, Doctor Jordan."

Nick gently took the mirror from her and placed it on the counter. "Martha, I know we don't have the effect we're looking for yet, but it's still too early for a touch-up. Your treatment was only six days ago."

"But I want the touch-up now."

"I know, but remember, we don't see the full effect of Botox for two weeks. If I give you more now, it might be too much for you. You don't want to walk around looking tired and angry for three months because you can't move your brow, do you?"

"I know, I know. I'm just impatient."

Nick smiled "I get that. But you have to remember that here you're called a patient, not an impatient."

"My favorite kind of flower," she said, then sighed dramatically. "Well, you've disappointed me again, Doctor."

Nick patted her arm on his way out the door. "What can I say? Keeping it real is part of the job. Come see me in another week, and we'll do a touch-up if you need one." He handed the chart to Greg and left the room.

A few minutes later, Nick came out to the reception desk to fill out prescriptions for a patient having surgery next week. He was completing the forms when Martha joined him at the counter. She spoke to Ginger. "Doctor Jordan is cruelly denying me a touch-up today. He wants to see me in a week." Nick nodded absently, still working on the scripts. Martha reached into her purse and withdrew a business card. She placed it on the counter and slid it away from her saying, "Oh, by the way, the young man who works for you gave me this. Whoops." The card fell off the edge of the granite surface on to Ginger's computer keyboard. She looked up at Martha in surprise. The patient smiled at her and said, "I don't need it."

Ginger picked up the blank white card and turned it over. She read the name and saw the phone number. It made no sense to her. She read it again, then spoke under her breath but loud enough for Nick to hear: "Holy shit."

Nick stopped writing and looked up. "May I see that, please?" he said, reaching for the card. Ginger handed it over like a bomb about to detonate. He read it once, then read it again to be sure. The card listed Greg's name and a phone number in fancy script. On the bottom, in block letters, was written:

SUPERIOR FACIAL INJECTABLES AT DEEPLY DISCOUNTED PRICES

COSMETIC SURGERY REFERRALS TO QUALIFIED PLASTIC SURGEONS

BY APPOINTMENT ONLY

There was no address. Nick let out a low whistle. The last piece of a puzzle had fallen into place. He turned to Martha. "Could we talk privately for a few minutes?"

She smiled, an intelligent sparkle in her eyes. "I thought you might want to chat, Doctor."

Nick turned to Ginger. "Don't speak to anybody about this, especially Greg." Ginger nodded. Her sculpted eyebrows were at full alert. "Let my next patient know I'm running fifteen minutes late," he said, guiding Martha into the office manager's office.

Lesli was on the phone when they entered. She waved them to two seats across the desk from her and quickly finished the call. "Hello, Martha, how are you?" she said warmly, then looked quizzically at Nick. It was unusual for her boss to sit in her office in the middle of a busy day.

"Martha was given this card by Greg," Nick said, handing her the business card. "I thought we might discuss how that came to happen."

Lesli's face changed as she read the card. She took a deep breath and let it out slowly then whispered, "That fucking snake." She looked at the patient, "I'm so sorry, Mrs. D'Aubusson, I didn't mean to…"

Martha laughed. "No worries, dear—I think fucking snake about covers it."

Nick turned to her. "Can you tell us how he came to give you this?"

"Yes, I can," she said, looking at Lesli. "Doctor Jordan had just been in the room to tell me that I wasn't ready for my Botox touch up yet." She gave the doctor a playful scowl. "And that fellow, Greg, remained after he left."

The office manager nodded. "Go on."

"I was gathering my things to leave, when he said, "It's a shame it didn't come out quite right, but that sort of thing happens from time to time." I was taken aback at how forward he was, and a little offended too. I tease Doctor Jordan, but he knows he has my complete confidence."

"Uh-huh."

"So, I told your strange assistant that it was my understanding from the doctor that we would have to wait longer to see if it's right or not. The young man appeared to agree with that, but then he said, "Yes, of course, but in *my* experience, which is extensive, you know whether or not you got it right by this point."

Lesli shook her head. "You're kidding."

"I'm afraid not, girlfriend. Then I asked him if he had extensive experience injecting Botox, and he told me that he did. He said he had been the principal injector at another plastic surgeon's office for years, a Doctor Rose, I believe."

Nick bit his lip. Martha reached out and gave Nick's hand a playful squeeze. "So, I decided to play along. I told him it was a shame he wasn't doing the injections himself. He came closer to me and asked me if I could keep a secret. He has awful breath, by the way."

Nick was shaking his head. "I can't believe this happened in my own office."

Martha gave his hand another squeeze. "It's better to know, so you can deal with it. Anyway, I assured him that I could keep his secret, and that's when he gave me his card. Then he told me that he does his own injections off-site. He said that I would receive the same quality Botox at half your price, and that the results would be better."

Lesli looked like she wanted to kill somebody.

"I was completely stunned. All I could think to say was, 'Thank you'. I wanted to be out of that room as soon as possible—it felt dirty. As I was leaving, he grabbed my arm and made me promise not to tell anyone."

Nick turned to her. “I’m so sorry you had to experience this, Martha. I can’t tell you how grateful we are to you for letting us know.”

She smiled. “If it were my business, I would want to know.”

“Believe me, we will deal with this very soon. And Greg won’t be able to undercut my price for your next treatment. It will be on the house.”

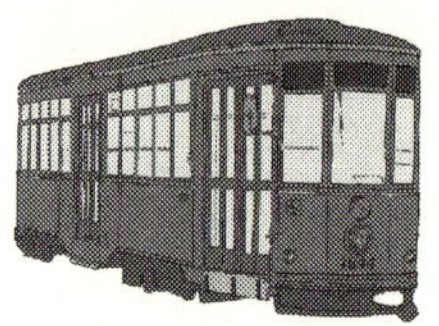

49

Later that day, Nick sat at his desk flipping through *Plastic Surgery News Review*, a colorful throwaway magazine that came unbidden to the office every month. A doctor he had never heard of was touting the benefits of a new machine for removing cellulite *and* wrinkles without pain or downtime. The physician said that the device was FDA cleared, and that the clearance meant it had to be effective. Nick's opinion was that the FDA very correctly prioritized safety over efficacy when evaluating lasers and other machines. He had seen many expensive devices over the years that bore the agency's stamp of approval but did little to nothing to justify the money that doctors and their patients spent on them. Eventually they were recognized as trash by the marketplace and went away.

He heard a tap from the doorway and looked up to see Lesli standing there. She closed the door slowly and deliberately, then walked over to his desk and sat down opposite him. "Can we talk about Greg's treachery now?"

He set the magazine down. "Yup. It seems our new medical assistant is quite the entrepreneurial fellow."

"He's also quite the backstabbing bastard. I'd like to skin him alive."

"And I would love to watch you do it. But let's go over what we know. Greg's doing Botox, and from his card, I'm guessing other injectables like fillers, too. It has to be somewhere out of the office. We don't know where." Something clicked in Nick's mind. He remembered the letter from an anonymous colleague. It made sense to him now. The guy had thought he was padding his income by having his assistant do cut-rate treatments.

"Uh-huh."

"And I think this explains why our Botox profits are down."

Lesli's eyes opened wide. "Because he's stealing our patients?"

"Well yes, maybe in part, but I think he's stealing more than that." He looked at her, waiting for the penny to drop. She stared at him.

"You told me our patient numbers are fine. We're doing plenty of treatments. I doubt many of our regulars would go to him. But our inventory costs are way up."

"He's stealing the Botox!"

"Right." He stood up and paced back and forth. "He must be stealing it. You have to be a physician to buy Botox. Allergan doesn't sell it to just anyone; at least not in this country. He could be impersonating a doctor's office, but that seems implausible because he'd need a DEA number and a medical license, and the company probably checks on those to make sure they're genuine."

Lesli nodded. "I see."

"So, he's stealing it from us. Not full bottles, because I'd notice, but partially used ones. I'm sure that's what's happening." Nick paused. "And if he's got a key to where he used to work, he could be stealing from there, too. But I doubt it. He's mentioned Doctor Rose to a couple of our patients. And I saw a suspicious series of texts on his cell phone that seemed to be about getting patients to go somewhere else. I'm sure he's diverting our patients there, especially those who want surgery. Hell, Fiona said our office told one of her patients that we don't do eyelids anymore. And I think she said we referred them to Dr. Rose. I thought it was some kind of weird misunderstanding. But now it makes sense."

Lesli was on her feet. "Oh my God…."

"Which is why our overall income is down. It has to be that."

"So, getting back to the Botox, the reason our profits are down is not that we're doing less of it, but that we're buying more. Because weasel-boy is stealing it."

"Right."

"Please, Boss, let me fire him."

Nick shook his head. "We will fire him. But there's a more permanent way to deal with him. I've thought of a way to catch him in the act, but it's going to take time to set up properly."

Lesli groaned softly. "It's going to be so hard to work in the same office without tearing his face off."

Nick laughed. "I know, but for right now I want you to wear the mask. If he can do it, you can do it. I don't think Greg will realize you know. He doesn't seem to be too attuned to the feelings of others."

Lesli nodded. "That's for sure. Do you want me to lock up the Botox?"

"No, don't lock it up. Don't even change where it is." He paused for a moment, then looked back at her. "But inventory it. How many bottles came on which date, lot numbers on the boxes, all of that. We'll compare that information with how much we actually use. It will help prove the theft when he's arrested."

"Arrested—I like the sound of that. So, you're going to trap him, huh?"

"I'm going to try, and I think I've figured out how to do it."

50

The following Friday morning dawned surprisingly cool in New Orleans. Summer was nearing its end. Nick paused outside of an exam room and read the name on the chart: Lolly Boudreaux. He knocked lightly and entered, followed by Greg. Greg seemed to stand a little taller than usual in his new blazer from Rubenstein Brothers, a local high-end men's shop. Nick now knew how he got the money to shop there.

Lolly and her husband were dressed for the occasion as well. One look confirmed that she did indeed dress her spouse. The old woman was wearing a soft purple sweater set and a long, dark skirt. Douglas, whose wheelchair sat in the same spot as the last visit, wore pants that matched the color of her skirt, a white dress shirt, and a lavender dickey. Nick's eye lingered on the dickey. *You don't see that every day,* he thought as he greeted them.

Lolly's face displayed a peeved expression and a bandage over her left temple. "I can see that Dr. Espinoza has removed something here," Nick said, pointing to the white patch. "Do you mind if I have a look?"

"That's why we're here," she said in a tone that confirmed her exasperation. "I must tell you that I'm very disappointed.

The hole is much larger than I thought it would be." Douglas looked at Nick with a fearful expression.

"She's been a bit, uh, anxious since the removal," he said quietly. It was the first time Nick had heard him speak. There was pleading in the man's eyes: *this has been hell—please fix this.*

Lolly glared at her husband. "You'd be anxious too if someone cut off half of your head, Douglas."

He almost spoke again and was silenced with a scorching look.

"Let's have a peek," Nick said, gently peeling back the tape. Her attention turned to Greg, who was opening a bottle of peroxide. The old woman's brow furrowed. "Nick, why do you let your assistant wear a horse blanket to work?" The doctor followed her gaze to Greg, who looked stricken.

Nick bit his lip but couldn't quite suppress a smile. "Now, Lolly, that's not very nice. I'm sure Greg's coat is very fashionable." He wanted to laugh, but managed to give his assistant a somewhat reassuring look.

Lolly turned back to Nick, causing her half-attached bandage to flutter. "There's a difference between *fashion* and *style*." She glanced towards Greg. "Fashion can be quite idiotic; style endures. Even Shakespeare knew that."

Let's concentrate on you right now," said Nick as he removed the dressing. The roughly triangular wound on her left temple was the size of a large tortilla chip and very close to the outer corner of Lolly's eye. Red and brown granulation tissue, sometimes called "proud flesh", shined in the base of the hole. Nick was pleased to see it as he knew it would help provide a blood supply for his repair. He took a step back and looked at the area carefully. His mind raced through the various options for reconstruction. Allowing it to heal on its own would yield an unacceptable result. Simply bringing the skin edges together would distort the eyelids and leave ugly bulges, known to surgeons as "dog-ears", at the ends of the inevitable scar. He would either have to move tissue into the defect as a flap, or graft it with skin from somewhere else.

He liked the idea of a graft. It would minimize distortion of the facial features around the hole and give him a thin window of skin to monitor in the unlikely event that the tumor recurred. This was important because no removal technique was one hundred percent effective. Most of the time a skin graft looked good, but if the result was not excellent, he could consider doing a flap there in the future. Nick wondered where he could find skin thin enough. Nowhere on her tightly pulled face, that was for sure. He continued to look at Lolly.

"Well?" she asked, sounding annoyed.

"I'm thinking, please give me a moment," he replied, and continued to scan her face and neck. *Her neck.* Something clicked. She had come to him complaining of sagging on the right side of her neck, the side opposite from the hole in her temple. Her neck skin was no good to him as a graft. It was too thick and sun-damaged to use. But he knew that the skin behind her ears would be perfect. It had never seen the sun. He recognized that he could do the lift she wanted on the right side which would move her neck skin upward and backward, behind the ear. That would give him more than enough looseness there to take a graft big enough to fill the hole on the other side. Lolly would get her neck lift and the best reconstruction he could think of. It was a win-win. *He would make something good, better, in fact, out of something bad. How cool.*

"What are you smiling at?" Lolly asked in an offended tone.

He put a hand on her shoulder. "Lolly, I've figured out the best way to fix this and you're going to like it. I'm going to repair that hole in a way that will give us the best possible result and you're going to get the neck lift you wanted at the same time."

For a moment she was silent and then she looked up at him. Her commanding scowl was gone. "That would be wonderful," she said in a soft voice.

He turned briefly to Douglas and nodded at him. The other man's eyes shone with relief and gratitude. There was an unspoken understanding between them. It was going to be all right.

Nick guided the couple to Lesli's office to schedule Lolly's procedure, and then turned to the nearest exam room door where a chart waited in the rack. He read the name, then threw the door open and entered the room. “Well, look who’s here. David McGloughlin—in person. Let’s see how the devastated area is coming along.”

Dave turned to him. Nick could see that his face had improved considerably in five days. The skin was still red and peeling, but the open sores and crusting had gone. It looked far less irritated. “You don’t look radioactive anymore, buddy,” Nick said, peering closely at the face from side to side. “You’ve been using the steroid cream.”

Dave nodded “Sure have. And the itching is much better too.”

Nick gestured towards chairs, and they both sat down. The doctor began writing something in the chart. Dave cocked an eyebrow. “You still write in charts, pal? I thought it was all electronic these days.”

Nick kept writing. “Ah, yes, the electronic medical record. That’s true for most practices. Fortunately, the state hasn’t mandated it for all of us yet. I hope they never do. It’s not like I bill insurance or Medicare for the stuff I do, you know.”

“Got it. So, for now you still write. You are old school, my friend.”

Nick grinned at him. “No school like the old school.” He looked in the chart. “Dave, it looks like you’re on the mend. You can cut back the triamcinolone cream to once a day. After a week you shouldn’t need it at all.”

“Great.”

“And avoid getting sun—your skin is very sensitive right now.” He looked up to make sure his friend was paying attention. “The skin’s still dry, so at night cake on some Vaseline or Aquaphor. Felicity can tell you which moisturizer to use during the day, so you won’t look greasy.”

“Okay.”

Nick pointed his pen in an accusing gesture. “And no more going nuts with the skincare products. I don’t know why the hell you did that in the first place.”

Dave was silent for a moment and then let out a sigh. “I do.”

“You do what?”

“I know why I did it.”

Nick put the chart down. “Why?”

“It’s related to something else I wanted to talk to you about.”

Nick could see he was serious. “What’s up?”

Dave pinched the skin in the middle of his neck between two fingers and shook it side to side. “I want you to get rid of this.”

Nick looked at him in disbelief. “You want a neck lift?”

Dave moved his hand up to his jaw line and grabbed the loose skin there. “I want you to get rid of these jowls for me, too.”

“Are you serious?”

"As a heart attack."

Nick stared at his friend. "But you're always telling Sandra what I do is unnecessary, a waste of time. At least that's what she tells me. 'Catering to the vain and the weak-minded,' isn't that what you said?"

Dave let out a sigh. "Yeah, I said that. I didn't really mean it. I just didn't want her to have surgery."

"But you know I'd never do anything she didn't need. I wouldn't do that for anyone, but especially for her. I love you guys."

"I know. You do a great job." Dave shifted in the chair and looked down at the floor. "I guess I just don't want her to be any more beautiful."

"What?"

"Because I could lose her."

"If she's more beautiful, you mean?"

"Yeah."

Nick shook his head. "That's crazy talk, man."

"I don't know that it is. I didn't know it at the time, but when I married Sandra, I won the freakin' lottery. We've been married twenty-two years. We've had our ups and downs, but I always know that she's there for me. And I haven't always been there for her."

"Have you been unfaithful?"

"No. I know there've been rumors, but I've never screwed around on her. What I have done is taken her for granted. I always put my business first, like nothing else mattered. And she deserved better."

Nick nodded. "That's an easy mistake to make. I did the same with Elizabeth."

"Easy and stupid. And she's a good-looking woman. I see other guys looking at her. Some of them are rich, and I mean like super rich, and could give her anything she wants."

"But she's not like that."

"I know; believe me, I appreciate the person she is. Talk about a heart of gold—she's got one. I'm the luckiest guy on earth."

"Have you told her that?"

"I have. She just laughs when I say it."

Nick took a moment to take it all in. "So, you're afraid that since I've made Sandra look younger, you could lose her? Is that why you're talking to me about a facelift?"

Dave leaned back in the chair, hands behind his head, and stretched. "Let's put it this way: I want to stay on the first team. Why do you think I went crazy with all that skincare stuff?"

They both chuckled and then were quiet for a moment. Nick spoke. "I'm no marriage counselor, more of a marriage fuck-up, but I've come to look at the male-female relationship like a little flame that you have to keep going. I mean you need to protect that thing with everything you've got from the howling winds all around. It's obvious to me that you're willing to do that. And I'm sure she knows it. I think you guys are secure."

Dave cocked his head to one side. "I never thought of it like that." He smiled at his friend. "You know, sometimes you're not the dumbass everyone thinks you are."

"That's the nicest thing anyone's ever said to me."

Dave rose from the chair. "Happy to help. So, no facelift for me?"

"Not right now. But if you get any uglier, we're going to have to do something."

They laughed and shook hands. Nick walked him down the hall and into the lobby. "You take care, and say hi to that beautiful wife of yours for me."

Dave gave him a wink. "Will do."

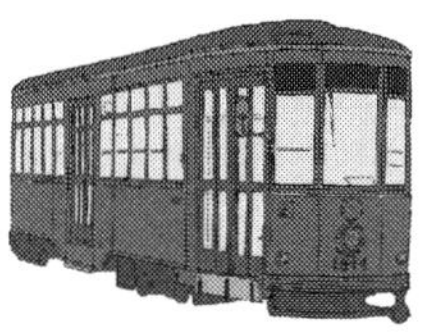

51

It was 5:30 in the afternoon and the bar at Rosie's was nearly empty. Long shafts of light crossed the dark wooden planks on the floor. Nick sat down and signaled the bartender. A cold draft beer appeared, and he took a deep swallow, his reward at the end of a long day.

He heard "Hey buddy, where y'at?" and turned to see Eddie Marquez taking the barstool next to his. Nick signaled the bartender. Eddie's usual Abita appeared in front of him. They clinked bottles and each took a swig. Eddie let out a satisfied sigh. "This is what I needed. S'been a ballbuster of a day."

Eddie rarely complained about anything. "What happened?" asked Nick.

"We had a pipe burst under the shop, right before the lunch rush. I had the plumber and one of my cooks under the restaurant workin' on it all afternoon. There was a mini-Lake Pontchartrain right in front of my place that people had to walk around just to get in the door. They tracked mud all over the place. It was a mess. I just finished cleaning up."

Nick grimaced. "That sounds rough. So, tonight's on me. Oysters?"

"You bet. And get some of dem fried shrimp, too."

"You got it, buddy." Nick waived the waiter over.

Eddie sat back in his stool. "So how was *your* day, dear?"

Nick chuckled. "Just making New Orleans beautiful, one face at a time."

The oysters arrived on a well-used aluminum platter. Eddie took one and spooned cocktail sauce and ground horseradish onto it. He tilted his head back and brought the half shell to his mouth. Gravity did the rest. "Ummm, d'ats good," he said in his best New Orleans accent, smacking his lips and reaching for another mollusk. He turned to Nick, who seemed lost in thought. "What's going on with you, man? You still our most eligible bachelor?"

Nick gave him a half-smile. "I'm a bachelor for sure. It's been two months since I signed the divorce papers."

"No shit? Time flies. You doin' alright?"

Nick took a swig from his bottle. "Yeah, I guess. I mean, it's sad in a way. You go back in your mind to figure out what went wrong, when it went wrong, that type of thing."

Eddie nodded. "I can see that. Did you figure anything out?"

"Well, when you're going through the break-up, especially if you don't want it to happen, I think you tend to blame the other person, at least I did. But now I see my part in it too."

"It always seemed like you were a good husband."

"In many ways I was. I cared about her and did the husbandly things, taking her places and buying her things. But I didn't pay attention to what was going on between us. I just assumed we had a rock-solid foundation. My marriage was the most important thing in my life, and I neglected it."

Eddie nodded.

"I just wasn't paying enough attention. Deep down, I must have known that something was wrong, and I didn't try to fix it. I just assumed that in marriage the good feelings come and go. Because that's the way it felt to me. But her love for me just left and never came back. If I were more mindful of what was going on, maybe I could have done something early on to save it."

"Maybe, maybe not."

"I guess I live more in the future. I think most doctors do. We spend our twenties working our asses off, putting off things other people enjoy, thinking we'll have time for them later, after our training is done. Then training ends and we have to work just as hard to get our practices started. That's the mindset."

"And thinking that way makes you neglect what's happening now?"

"Exactly."

"I can see that. I always gotta live in the now. It's not like I can wait 'til next Tuesday to fix that broken pipe. I have to do it right away to limit the damage."

Nick smiled at him, "Nice metaphor there."

“I do what I do.”

The bartender brought new beers. Eddie looked at his friend. “I’m sure there’s truth in what you’re sayin’, but don’t beat yourself up too much. I mean, it takes two to tango, right? Was she checking in with you to see if you were happy with the marriage?”

“No, she didn’t. And that part’s on her. If she felt her feelings for me slipping away, she should have said something, or tried to get us to a marriage counselor sooner. But she didn’t. She just let it all go. She said she wasn’t even aware it was happening. She just stopped loving me.”

Eddie gave him a sympathetic look. “That’s a sad story, pal.”

“Yeah it is, and in the end, the divorce had to happen. She was right.” Nick leaned back and looked at his reflection in the mirror behind the bar. For a moment, his face seemed deflated and old.

“So, ending it was a good thing? Now you can go out and find somebody you can connect with.”

“That’s true I guess.”

“Of course, it is, but that doesn’t make it feel any better.”

“I just really miss what we had. Back in the beginning I mean.”

Eddie clapped him on the arm and squeezed hard. “I hear what you’re saying.” He released the grip. “Keep your head up. Life has a funny way of surprising you. And if someone does come along and knock you on your ass the way Elizabeth did all those years ago, think of how sweet that will feel."

"That's right. You're a good friend Eddie."

"I'm not blowing smoke up your ass. It could happen. Probably will."

Nick nodded and reached for an oyster. "I hope you're right." He tasted the combination of salt and fire as it went down. "Man, these are good."

"Best in the city."

"In the meantime, I've got to figure out how to forgive Elizabeth."

Eddie took another pull at his beer. "For blowing up your marriage?"

"Yeah. I'm having a hard time forgiving her. She was right; we couldn't stay married and be happy. But I spent so much time and effort trying to save the marriage. It was like I was standing there with my arms spread wide, begging her to love me, and she just kept saying no. I resent her for it."

Eddie looked at him. "I can see that. I mean how could you not feel that way?"

"I'm trying to get over it. I've been reading about forgiveness. There's this guy named Thich Nhat Hanh…."

"The Vietnamese monk?"

Nick looked at him in astonishment. "You've read his stuff?"

"Sure, he's a famous guy. He watched his freakin' country get torn apart by war, and now he's a voice of reconciliation there. He's even brought American GI's back to Vietnam to heal the wounds on both sides. The guy is right on."

Nick shook his head. "You never cease to amaze me, Eddie. Beneath that crusty exterior lies a crusty but, dare I say it, intellectual interior."

Eddie laughed. "Don't tell anybody."

"I won't. They'd never believe me, anyway. So, you remember how the monk talks about forgiveness being a practical, even selfish act. It benefits the giver the most, and right away. He talks about a wave of peace coming back to you, washing over you as soon as you forgive."

"Yeah. It makes a lot of sense."

"I want to think of my time with Elizabeth as a positive thing again. She'll never be the kind of positive she was when we met and fell in love, of course. But I want to lose the resentment."

Eddie nodded "I'd say you're on the right track, buddy. You know it's the right thing to do. And where the mind goes, the heart will eventually follow."

Nick reached for another oyster. "Huh. You're probably right."

"So, any new ships on the horizon?"

"You mean other women?" Eddie nodded. "No, I told you what happened with Rachel. That hit me pretty hard.

It showed me I've still got a long way to go. To feel close to somebody again, I mean."

"Yeah, I can see that. Still, you fall off the horse, you get back on. How about that beautiful dermatologist?"

Nick shook his head. "Like I told you, we're just friends. I'd hate to date her and screw that up."

"You know, you might not screw it up. I know you have a thing for her, and you're both doctors; you two speak the same language."

Nick shook his head. "I know. But hurting Rachel like I did showed me that I'm still getting my act together emotionally. I'm not ready for prime time yet. So, for now we'll just speak the same language over the phone."

Eddie chuckled and they ordered another beer.

Later that evening, Nick was at home reading in his study. Roquefort made slurping sounds as he transformed a rawhide dog treat into a pulpy mess. Nick looked up from his book to a large, decorated platter mounted on the wall he was facing. The colors were vibrant and beautifully painted to represent a garland of leaves. He thought about the shop in Italy where he and Elizabeth had bought it.

He remembered how much fun they had together on that trip and was surprised to find himself smiling a little.

He thought back to his conversation earlier that night with Eddie; the part about how forgiveness benefits the forgiver the most. He had many happy memories of time spent with Elizabeth. The best thing would be to hold onto them and, as much as possible, let the bad memories go. She was part of his journey and had helped to shape him. It hadn't turned out the way he expected, but a lot of it had been good. He saw now, more clearly than ever, that the positive feelings were the ones to take with him on the next part of his journey.

With a loud snort, Roquefort rose from the vanquished chew toy and scratched at Nick's leg with a forepaw, signaling that it was time to pee. Nick got up quickly and walked to the back door of the house, Roquefort following closely on his heels. He lingered in the doorway to make sure that the bulldog made it off the patio and onto the grass to do his business. Nick looked up at the stars, picking out the few constellations that he knew.

He heard a garbled grunt at his feet and looked down to see Roquefort had returned. He moved to let the dog enter, and then closed the door. It stuck halfway open, and Nick had to lift the handle and pull it to him hard to make it close all the way. He knew this was from the wood swelling in the summer heat, and that each year it would get a little worse until all the doors in the house would have to be sanded down. He felt annoyance rising inside of him, and then he checked it. The house was beautiful, but it would never be perfect. It would always need work. He had to accept that.

52

The next morning Nick sat at a table under the striped awnings of the famous Café Du Monde in the French Quarter. He could see almost all of Jackson Square with Saint Louis Cathedral behind it, and for a while he just took in the view. The place was quiet now except for artists setting out paintings to sell; the tourists were still in bed. Nick looked down at the *Times Picayune* and then up to see Fiona Espinoza waving at him from across Decatur Street. He rose and motioned for her to come over. Fiona was wearing a short skirt and leather boots, topped off by a fuchsia blouse; the ensemble showed off her beautiful figure. The morning sunlight made her long auburn hair shine. *Damn*, Nick thought as she came to his table and gave him a hug.

She smiled at him. "Shouldn't a man about town like you be sleeping it off at this time of morning?" she said, looking around for a waitress.

"Nope. My doggie has already been walked. He has zero heat tolerance, so I have to take him out early," Nick replied. "I already ordered us coffee and doughnuts. I hope that's okay."

“Perfect,” she replied, settling her purse and sunglasses. “So tell me, what’s this secret project? I’ve been wondering about it since you called.”

“After the doughnuts,” Nick said, winking at her.

Moments later their waitress appeared bearing hot chicory coffee and beignets. Together they bit through drifts of powdered sugar into the hot, fried doughnuts, the white powder spilling all over the table. “Don’t sneeze,” Nick said, and Fiona nodded. Sneezing near a beignet sent sugar flying everywhere. The coffee was fresh and strong and balanced the outrageously sweet pastries perfectly.

“These are delectable,” Fiona said, reaching across the table to wipe sugar off Nick’s face. “But, oh my God, they’re fattening. We must walk after this.”

Nick swallowed and took a sip of coffee. “You’ve got a deal. We’ll walk on the levee. And when we do, I’ll tell you about the special project.” He gave her a conspiratorial smile.

She cocked her head. “What are you up to, doctor?”

He took a napkin, dipped it in water, and carefully wiped a bit of sugar from her sleeve. “Finish up and I’ll tell you.”

“Thank you,” she said, and Nick thought he saw a little twinkle in her eyes.

After paying the check, Nick took Fiona’s hand and led her out of the restaurant and up steep steps to the top of the levee. They walked over train tracks and looked across the Mississippi River towards Algiers Point.

"It's magical up here," Fiona said, clutching his hand tighter in the wind. Her hair was blowing around her face and Nick thought it made her look like a kid.

"I know," he replied. "Look how much higher the river is than the city. You can see how it would flood if the levee failed."

"In school, we learned that this whole place was a swamp before they started building here."

"I know, right? I mean, who would do that?"

She considered the question, then at length answered, "People filled with hope."

They were strolling along the river now, and still holding hands. Nick was struck by how natural it felt. "Do you come up here often?" Fiona asked.

"Every once in a while, on weekends," Nick replied. "I like to walk up Decatur Street to Central Grocery and get half a Muffuletta sandwich. I can usually find a bench, and I'll sit up here and watch the ships and barges go by. It's a great way to have lunch."

"I could see that," she said, watching a child throw bread crusts to a group of birds. She turned to him. "Now, tell me about this secret project."

Nick told her all about what Greg had been doing. When he finished, her shapely brows were bunched in an angry scowl. "Unbelievable. What a treacherous asshole."

He grinned and nodded. "Yup. And I want you to help me set a trap for him."

"Me?" she smiled, "What do you have in mind?"

Nick gave her the business card that Martha D'Aubusson had turned in at the front desk of his office. He told Fiona what he wanted her to do.

Fiona looked excited. "Okay, I'm in. Do I get to use an accent?"

"Can you have an accent?"

"*Mais oui, monsieur. Je parle français très bien.* Perhaps you didn't know that I studied in Paris for a semester at the Sorbonne?"

Nick cocked an eyebrow at her. "Two things: no, I did not know that and, wow, the way that you do that accent is really working for me."

She giggled. "Good to know. So, can I speak that way and not ruin your plan?"

Nick nodded enthusiastically. "That would be better in fact. I think you should lay the French accent on thick and tell him you're from out of town and won't be here long. He'll like that. He's bound to be suspicious of anyone he doesn't know, and that will put his mind at ease as far as getting caught."

"What should my name be?"

"Hmm. Something exotic sounding. Any ideas?"

She ran a finger playfully down his chest. He felt it all the way to his bones. "I think I will be Veronique. *J'aime bien* the sound of that."

Nick felt tightness in his throat. "Works for me," he croaked.

He produced a pay-as-you-go phone he had picked up at an electronics store on Canal Street. "It has its own number, so he won't be able to trace it back to us," he explained. They practiced what she would say during the call a few times, with Nick acting the role of Greg. When they were both satisfied with her performance, Fiona dialed the number on the throwaway phone. A nasally voice answered on the third ring.

"Hello?"

Fiona straightened abruptly, almost dropping the phone. Nick made a calm down motion with his hands.

"*Allo, Monsieur* Greg please."

There was a pause. "Ummm, this is Greg. Who's calling?"

"*Oui*, my name is Veronique. I was given this number to call."

Another pause. "Who gave you my number?"

"A friend gave it to me. She suggested I call you for a.... service."

"What's your friend's name?"

Fiona hesitated. "She asked me not to say. She said you are *très*, how do you say, careful with information, and she asked me to be the same."

"I see," Greg hesitated, then continued. "And how can I help you?"

"*Merci*. I am away from home, I live in *France*, and have not been able to get my Botox treatment. I was told you are excellent."

Nick nodded to her enthusiastically. He knew Greg would eat up the praise.

Greg's voice sounded more reassured. "Well, yes, I am known to be one of the best in the city. Will you be coming with your friend?"

"*Ah, non*, she has now left for vacation." She looked at Nick. "But I will bring my husband. He may want a treatment as well."

Greg hesitated, but only for a second. "That will be fine. We can make an appointment if you'd like. You should know that I only accept cash."

"*Oui*, cash is not a problem. I am so happy you can help me."

They chose a day and time, and Greg gave her directions to the meeting place. He spoke quickly before she could disconnect the call. "One more thing. It's okay if you want to bring your husband, but please be discreet; tell no one else about me. I want to reserve my services for a select few."

"I understand, *Monsieur*. We will be, as you say, discreet."

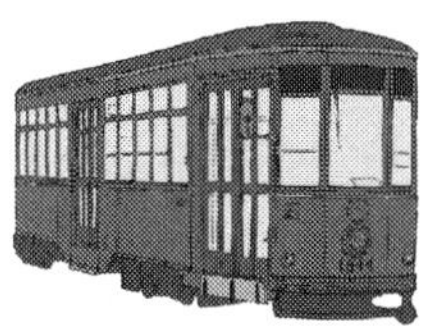

53

Nick heard a tapping at his office door and looked up from his desk to see Lesli holding two large shopping bags. He waved her in.

"I think I got it all," she said, placing the bags in an armchair. She sounded excited. Ever since he had told her about his plans for Greg, she had been an eager collaborator.

Nick came around the desk and began to go through the bags. "Let's see what you got," he said, extracting a long gray wig. He laughed. "You've got to be kidding."

"No, that's the best part," she replied, looking like a child opening presents on Christmas morning. "Try it on!"

"Wait," he said, reaching into the bag again. "I want to see what else you got." He reached down and picked up a black felt Fedora from the top of one of the bags. "Nice," he said, putting it on his head and looking at himself in the mirror. "Like Frank Sinatra, minus the looks and talent." He withdrew a pair of gold-rimmed sunglasses with large black lenses and a camel-colored overcoat from one of the bags. In the other, he found a well-worn men's suit with huge lapels and a loud white pinstripe. He glanced over at Lesli. "This is perfect; I wouldn't be caught dead in it." Finally, he retrieved a wildly colorful necktie with a chrysanthemum motif and a surprisingly tasteful silk pocket square.

"Where did you get all this stuff?" he asked, arranging it on a chair.

"Bloomin' Deals on Freret Street," she answered, practically hopping up and down. "Try it on!"

Nick went to his office door and closed it. "Alright," he said; "I'll try on the pants later." He removed his tie and put on the floral extravaganza. It smelled vaguely of mothballs. "Do they fumigate this stuff?" he asked, reaching for the pinstriped coat.

"It's a nice place," said Lesli. "I'm sure everything's been cleaned."

Nick put the coat on. "This is a little big for me," he said, "but I can get the sleeves taken up and wear an undershirt for bulk. It should work." He folded the silk square into his left breast pocket, allowing part of it to protrude for a splash of color. He put on the overcoat, and then reached back toward his office manager. "Hand me that wig, would you?" he asked.

Lesli giggled. "I never thought I'd hear you say *that*."

Nick laughed. "Well, we *are* in New Orleans. Just hand it over." He scrutinized the interior of the hairpiece carefully. "I don't *see* anything crawling around in there." He lowered the wig onto his head and smoothed the tresses away from his face. In place, the hair didn't seem as long. He looked at himself in the mirror again. "That's different," he said. Lesli bit her lip to keep from laughing.

Nick put on the sunglasses and hat and regarded himself in the mirror once more, then turned to Lesli. "Well?" he asked.

His office manager was laughing hard. When she recovered, she said, "Boss, I've known you forever. Take it from me, there's no way anyone would recognize you like that."

He turned back to the mirror. Maybe she was right, but he couldn't be too careful. "It's good, but I'll need it to work for more than a few seconds. I want to catch him red-handed and that will take time. There's one more thing it needs."

"What?" Lesli asked. She honestly couldn't imagine how the costume could be better.

Nick tilted the sunglasses down and looked at her over them. "Get Doctor Espinoza on the phone please."

She gave him a puzzled look and was halfway out the door, when Nick called her back, "Oh Lesli, one more thing: is your brother still on the force?"

She nodded. "He is."

"Let me talk with him, too."

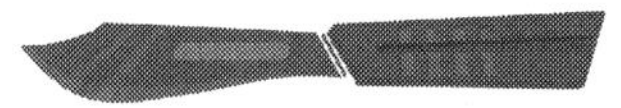

Later that afternoon, Nick took the Metairie Road exit from the Pontchartrain Expressway and headed west. It was a beautiful fall afternoon, bright and clear with just a hint of coolness in the air. He parked in front of a modern-looking office building that Fiona shared with a prominent local dentist. After giving the receptionist his name, he was immediately brought back to Fiona's private office, where she sat waiting for him in a blue and white dress that showed off her legs and somehow went well with her doctor's coat. She smiled as she gave Nick a quick hug and said, "I still can't believe you want me to do this."

During a telephone conversation earlier that day, Nick had filled Fiona in on the next step in his plan to catch Greg red-handed in his traitorous business enterprise. She had been hesitant at first, but finally agreed. She looked at him now and said, "It's going to hurt, Nick. Can I at least put some numbing cream on you and let it soak in while I'm seeing my last few patients?"

"Sure," he answered, "I have no particular fondness for pain."

"No?" she said playfully. "Too bad."

"And just to be sure, this is only temporary, right?"

"Yep. It'll be gone in a week."

He grinned at her. "Alright. Let's do it."

She reached into a cabinet and came out with a small white bottle. She squirted a generous amount of whitish cream onto her gloved fingers and then began applying it to Nick's face. Her fingertips glided over his cheekbones, his forehead, and his chin in small light circles. He closed his eyes and let his head fall back. "That feels good."

She smiled and kept working the anesthetic into his skin. "Glad you like it, doctor."

Her fingers were on his neck now, stroking it up and down, coating it evenly with the shiny cream. He swallowed hard and felt his Adam's apple move under her hand.

"Give me your hands," she said at length, and applied more cream from the bottle onto the back of each one. Slowly and firmly, she rubbed it into the skin of his hands, making circles with her thumbs.

"I need this after surgery every day," he said, opening an eye to look at her.

"You couldn't afford me, baby," she said, still smiling.

When she finished, she removed the gloves. "Let that work for a while, Nick. I'll go see some patients. If I don't get out there soon, there'll be a riot."

"Take as long as you need. I'm just going to bask in the afterglow." She laughed and blew out of the room, off to fight the good fight against skin disease.

Thirty minutes later Fiona returned, took off her coat, and threw it over a stool. Nick looked up at her from his smartphone. "All done?"

She took a deep breath and collapsed into the chair next to him, closing her eyes. "I am. Totally done. Stick a fork in me."

Nick smiled. “I know exactly how you feel. It’s like you’ve been on stage doing a one-person play for eight hours. Exhausting.”

“Exactly,” she said. She slowly opened her eyes and turned to him. “Are you numb?”

A single loud beep signified that the laser was activated. Fiona used the hand piece to fire circular beams onto Nick’s face as the machine hummed loudly. “Is that hurting much?” she asked.

“It stings a little, but not bad,” Nick replied. “I know you don’t want to hurt me, Fiona.”

“No,” she said, her tone softening. “I don’t want to hurt you at all.”

Nick couldn’t see through the protective goggles she had put on him. He extended a hand towards her voice, and Fiona took it in hers. He squeezed for a moment and then released it.

“Okay, let’s keep going. I’m going to use a light to medium power setting and overlap the laser shots in places to make them look irregular, like freckles.” Her foot pressed a pedal to fire the laser, and each time she did a tiny circle of frosty ash appeared on Nick’s skin. When she had covered his face and neck completely, he directed her to do his hands. “Whatever floats your boat,” she said and continued the treatment.

After another fifteen minutes she hit a button on the machine’s console to put the laser on standby. “I think that should do it,” she said, rising to retrieve a hand mirror, which she passed to Nick. Lying on the treatment bed, he regarded his face for a long moment in the glass. He was covered in fine dark blotches of varying shape and intensity that did indeed look exactly like age spots. “Fiona, you’re a genius,” he said.

“And you’re undatable,” she said, smiling. “So, what’s the plan from here?”

He sat up on the gurney. “Meet me at my office at ten tomorrow morning and we’ll drive over to Magazine Street together.”

“Okay.”

“Oh, and try to dress—how do I want to put this—provocatively.”

She laughed, “Can you expand on that?”

“Well, I’d like him to be a little distracted by your natural, umm, gifts.”

“My gifts?”

“You know, your uh, body, and all.”

She grinned and shook her head. “I see. Go on.”

Nick blushed, “You might, well, uh, put him off of his guard, you know, is all I’m saying.”

She moved toward him. “Turn him into a sort of bumbling idiot, you mean?”

Nick felt the room getting warmer, which seemed odd since the machine had been turned off. “Just wear something that shows off your beautiful figure.”

She took another step closer. “Do you really think I have a beautiful figure, doctor?”

His face flushed and he felt the front of his pants tighten.

Fiona was looking directly into his eyes now. She took another step closer, “Do you?”

Nick turned away quickly, sending a wheeled stool into the wall with a loud crashing sound. He was in full panic mode.

Without looking back, he said, “Uh, thanks so much… I’ll see you tomorrow, Fiona,” and hurried out of the room. A giggle followed him down the hall.

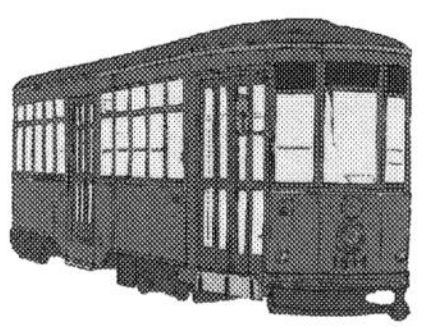

54

Nick parked off Magazine Street and stepped around the car to open Fiona's door. He looked around to make sure no one was watching, then removed a shopping bag from the back seat. He was already wearing the thrift shop suit. Item-by-item, he put on the rest of his costume. Fiona looked nervous, but still had to suppress a laugh. "I know, I know," he said. "But tell me, would you recognize me in this?"

"Not in a million years," she answered, removing his hat and smoothing wayward tufts of hair on the wig. "*Bon*," she said, "you're ready to go."

He replaced the fedora, put on his big dark sunglasses and looked at her. She was wearing high heels, a chic Diane Von Furstenberg wrap-around-dress that clung to her figure, and expensive jewelry. "You look perfect," he said.

They walked on broken asphalt and crushed shells until they reached the main street, then turned down the sidewalk towards the address that Greg had given Fiona. A faded sign over the entrance read, **RAY-RAY'S HAIR DESIGN**. Nick took a deep breath and pushed the door open. "Here we go," he said under his breath, "just like we planned."

The shop had been furnished in the 1950's, and nothing had been done to it since. The floor, walls, and ceiling were varying shades of faded yellow. A scarred wooden church pew rested against one wall for customers to sit on while waiting their turn. Four well-used brown leather barber chairs formed a row on the opposite wall. Stylists exhibiting various levels of boredom occupied three of the chairs. An old man with a bad comb-over, presumably Ray-Ray himself, talked on a cordless phone in the first chair. He didn't bother to look up. The two other stylists were reading magazines. One looked at them and nodded. The other, a pleasant looking middle-aged woman, rose from her chair and approached them. "Can I help you folks?"

Fiona replied in a thick French accent: "*Oui,* Madame, we are here to see *Monsieur Greg.*"

The haircutter looked puzzled. "Misshure Glaig?" she asked.

"*Oui, Monsieur Greg,*" Fiona answered giving her a brilliant smile. A moment later Greg hurried out from an opening in the back wall. Nick noticed that he was wearing the new blazer.

"It's alright, Marie," Greg said, coming forward. He gave the couple an appraising look. The woman's appearance was ideal; she was attractive and fashionably dressed. He sensed money. Greg unconsciously flicked the tip of his tongue across his upper lip. He took a long look at her husband. He seemed too old for her and was dressed for the dead of winter, not a mild New Orleans Fall day. "A little warm for a topcoat, isn't it, buddy?" He asked. Nick looked back at him through sunglasses and shrugged. *Probably her sugar daddy*, Greg thought. He smiled and extended his hand, which the man in the fedora shook with a weak grip. Greg noted the mottled appearance of the man's skin and wondered how such a fine-looking woman could stand to be touched by the owner of that hand.

Greg turned back to Fiona. "You must excuse the shabby appearance of this place." He ignored an indignant snort that came from one of the barber chairs. "It's only temporary until I get my own. I'm in negotiations to lease a beautiful office in the Garden District. Please come with me, won't you?" He led them through an opening in the back wall into a kind of break room and storage area. Clear plastic bins packed with hair care products were stacked around the room. There was an old water cooler and smocks hung on pegs next to the rear exit door. A dilapidated kitchen table, its oak veneer cracking, occupied the center of the room. It had been cleared of napkins, silverware, and condiments, which were lying on top of a small refrigerator. On the table Greg had placed a stack of gauze pads, and two piles of wrapped syringes and needles, which Nick had no doubt were stolen from his office.

Fiona shuddered involuntarily at the sight. "Chilly in here, *non*?" she said quickly. Greg shrugged and offered them two of the chrome and fabric office chairs that surrounded the table. He took the seat opposite, then leaned forward with his hands folded together and began. "Now, I'm glad that you're here. I'm going to take excellent care of you. I have top grade Botox," he said, pointing at an Igloo cooler on the floor, "that I'm able to offer to you at half the price it would cost you elsewhere." He looked at Nick. "But I do have a few requests. First of all, I have limited quantities at this point, so I'll ask you to speak of this to no one."

Nick nodded back. He almost said, "I understand," but stopped himself at the last moment. *Holy crap*, he thought, *my voice could blow this whole thing. I should have thought of that*. Nick leaned back in his chair signifying that he would let Fiona do all the talking.

Greg continued, "Secondly, I only deal in cash. Your treatment today will be three hundred dollars. Is that acceptable?" Nick nodded again, then withdrew a clip of hundred-dollar bills from his coat pocket and placed three of them on the table near the syringes. His traitorous assistant smiled. "Thank you," he said reaching for the cash, which he moved to his side of the table.

Greg moved closer to Fiona and examined her forehead and the area around her eyes. He asked her to squint, then smile, and finally to raise her eyebrows in surprise. He nodded gravely, giving the impression that he had reached a carefully considered diagnosis. "I know just what you need, my dear," he said, withdrawing a small glass bottle with a purple label from the cooler.

Nick watched him as he opened a syringe and attached a needle to it, then stuck it through the rubber seal at the top of the bottle. He noted that his assistant had neglected to clean the stopper with alcohol first; something Nick always insisted he do in the office.

Greg turned the bottle upside down, and slowly the syringe began to fill with clear fluid. He was aware the old man was watching him intently, far more closely than patients usually did. He glanced away from the bottle toward the man in the hat. Was there something familiar about him? *I don't know anyone that old*, Greg thought, as he resumed filling the syringe.

On the other side of the wall, a bell tinkled, as the front door of the salon opened, and a large policeman entered quietly, holding a finger to his lips to silence the stylists. Ray-Ray looked up with an exasperated expression and ended his phone call. He started to speak to the officer, but was silenced by an urgent gesture. The policeman walked softly to the rear of the room and stood next to the wall, where the people in back couldn't see him.

Greg approached Fiona, holding the Botox bottle in one hand and the syringe in the other. He asked her to frown again, then moved the needle closer to her forehead. She recoiled from him. "Don't be scared, sweetie," Greg grinned. He seemed to enjoy the position of power. "This only hurts a little."

Nick stood up and closed his hand around Greg's wrist. This time his grip was strong. The needle stopped in mid-air. In a loud, clear voice, Nick said, "Officer, please come in." Greg looked bewildered; Fiona collapsed into her chair with relief.

"What the fuck is this?" Greg shouted, as he saw the policeman enter the back room. Nick wasn't speaking to him. "Please notice that he has a loaded syringe with a needle in one hand and a medication bottle in the other."

The officer nodded. "I can see that."

Nick snatched the bottle from Greg's left hand then gave it to the officer. "You'll need this for evidence," he said. The policeman held up the small bottle, looking at the liquid inside. Greg put the syringe down on the table. He seemed to be searching for words. Nick capped the needle and handed it to the officer, who produced a small plastic bag and carefully placed the bottle and syringe inside it.

Greg finally spoke. "I don't know who you people are or what you think you're doing, but I'm a licensed medical assistant, and I have every right to be doing this."

The policeman glared at him "Really? I thought you had to be working with a doctor to inject medicine into people."

A bit of Greg's confidence returned. "Well, Officer, I do work with a doctor. So, you see, whatever kind of a trap you weirdos have set for me won't work."

This seemed to give the policeman pause. "And the doctor knows you're doing this? In the back of Ray-Ray's?"

Greg drew himself up to his full five feet seven inches. "Of course he does."

The policeman took out a notebook and pencil and began writing. "Well, for your sake, I hope he backs you up." The cop seemed to be trying hard not to smile, which Greg found infuriating under the circumstances. "Name and address of the doctor?" the officer asked, not looking up from the notebook.

"Doctor Nick Jordan, Saint Charles Avenue," Greg responded in a confident voice. He'd figure out some way to spin this, he thought. He just needed time. He looked at the policeman, who was now grinning broadly. "Something funny, officer?" he asked in a nasty voice. "Doctor Jordan will vouch for me, and you won't be laughing anymore. Matter of fact, I'll file a complaint against you. Maybe you'll lose your job. See how funny you think that is."

"What's funny is how screwed you are, sir. With all due respect."

"Oh yeah? How do you figure that?"

Nick rose slowly from his chair, removed the felt hat, and placed it softly on the table. He took off the overcoat and draped it over his chair. "No, Greg, I don't think I'll vouch for you," he said. Using both hands, he took off the wig and sunglasses in a single gesture.

Greg was stunned. He'd never seen the eyes of his boss look so cold and hard. His mouth worked but no sound came out. The officer let out a loud laugh.

"This doesn't prove anything," Greg sputtered. "I could have gotten that bottle anywhere. I could be working with another doctor."

Nick looked at him and nodded. “I think you are working with another doctor, Greg. But not today. I’m certain you stole that Botox from me.”

Greg gave him a defiant look. “You can’t prove that.”

Nick turned to policeman. “Officer, would you mind looking at the bottle that I took from this man?”

The policeman reached into his pocket and retrieved the bag with the vial. “Not at all, sir.”

Nick turned back to Greg, but continued to address the officer. “And on that bottle is there a white and purple label that identifies it as containing one hundred units of Botox manufactured by the Allergan Corporation?”

“Yes, sir,” replied the cop.

Nick looked directly into Greg’s confused eyes. He could tell his assistant still didn’t get it.

“And also on that label is there a bar code, serial number, lot number, and expiration date that positively identifies which bottle of Botox it is?”

The policeman spoke slowly. “Yes—there seems to be.”

Nick looked at Greg. “You see, I’ll be able to prove from invoices at the office that I bought this specific bottle. It belongs to me. And of course, the Allergan Corporation will be able to confirm that fact. And in my statement to the police, I’ll make it very clear that I didn’t give it to you and certainly didn’t authorize you to take it out of the office.” Nick looked at Fiona, who had recovered from her near miss and was listening with great interest. He put a hand on her arm and gave it a squeeze. "And, Greg, I don't think you'll get a judge and jury to believe that I gave it to you to inject into my colleague, Doctor Espinoza here, for three hundred dollars in the back of Ray-Ray's. She will be a highly credible witness against you when this goes to court." He leaned towards Greg's now stricken-looking face and said, "You stole it." He pointed to the medical supplies on the table. "You stole all of this from me, and we both know it."

Greg's confusion turned to panic. His eyes veered helplessly toward the back door. "I wouldn't try it, friend," said the officer, taking a step forward. "I'm fast when I need to be."

Nick gathered up the items of his costume, then gently took Fiona's hand to help her up. She rose and smiled at him; her eyes were sparkling. He turned to the policeman. "Will you take a statement from him and file a report on this, Officer?"

The cop nodded. "I will."

Nick looked at Greg, who now slumped in his chair. "I should tell you that you'll have to answer for this in a court of law, Greg. I will be pressing charges."

Greg looked up at him, hatred in his eyes. "Fuck you."

"I'm not the one who's fucked here, Greg. And don't think I don't know about the surgeries you've been diverting from my office. The patients you've been directing to your old boss. What are you getting from that? A finder's fee?

"That's none of your business," Greg answered with a nasty sneer, and then added, "actually it could have been your business."

Nick knew the man was upset and decided to push him. "Well, it couldn't have been much business anyway."

Greg gave him a hard look; "It's not a crime to recommend someone else, so I'll tell you. I've cost you about half a million bucks so far, I think."

Nick nodded. "Then you hurt me a lot there Greg."

"Payback is a bitch, isn't it?"

For the first time, Nick was surprised. "Payback? For what?"

"For something that happened a long time ago."

"What?"

"Remember the summer Medical Scholars' Program? At Charity Hospital?"

"No."

"Of course, you don't because you're an arrogant prick. But I do. I was in high school working in the ER with hopes of going to medical school one day. I got caught doing something I shouldn't have, and they arrested me and kicked me out. That got me suspended from school too. Which was not very helpful when applying to college. So med school was out."

"What's that got to do with me?"

"I got kicked out because a young doctor called security to arrest me. They caught me in the act. Ringing any bells now?"

Nick searched his memory and suddenly it connected. "Wait… were you that kid breaking into the narcotics cabinet?"

"Yup. And you were the narc who ruined my life. So, when I saw a chance to get in with you and ruin yours, I jumped at it."

"You wanted revenge?"

Greg looked right at him, "Damned straight I did. I saw you were advertising for a medical assistant, and I knew it was my opening. It was like I'd been given a gift."

"I can't believe it. After all these years," Nick said, shaking his head. He looked up at Greg. "But you know, it was really you that ruined your life the first time, and now you've done it again."

"Go fuck yourself."

Nick moved closer. "Yeah, I hear you. Now hear me. You will be prosecuted to the fullest extent possible. I'll make sure of that. And I'll also take this up with Doctor Rose and the state medical board. That scumbag might lose his license for good. Especially since you said what you did in front of a police officer."

Fiona spoke up, "I should think he would."

Nick continued, "You'll be let go from my practice for cause. Which means you won't be collecting unemployment." He looked at the expensive fabric of the man's coat for a moment, then directly into his eyes. "After you've dealt with your legal problems, which will begin immediately, I think you'll find it impossible to find a job in New Orleans. I'm going to make sure word of what you've done gets around. You'll find it easier to look for a job in another city."

Greg looked down at his hands. He appeared to be on the point of crying. "Fuck you all" he whispered.

"Not nice…*monsieur,*" Fiona said, leaving the back room.

Nick and the policeman turned away from the sniveling assistant and moved toward the doorway. "Thanks, Robert," said Nick under his breath to the larger man.

"No problem," the cop whispered back. "Give Lesli my best."

At the doorway, Nick turned to look at his assistant one last time. Their eyes met. Nick's were still cold as he fired his parting shot. It felt good to say it.

"And Greg, just so we're clear, you're fired."

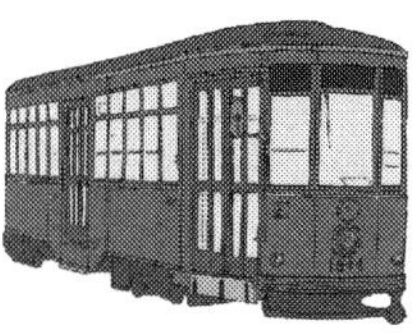

55

A few days later, Nick let out a sigh as he closed his laptop and pushed away from his desk. Few people, he knew, realized that doctors in private practice had to think like small business owners. He worried over profits and cash flow, taxes and new regulations, and what his competition was doing, just as if he owned a shoe repair shop or operated a grocery store. Nick had spent the last hour calculating the practice's month-end tallies and determining what staff bonuses would be for the quarter. It was tedious work, and, in the wake of Greg's influence, the numbers looked grim. But it had to be done.

He left his office and was turning off hallway lamps, when he noticed a light coming from the break room upstairs. Nick trudged up to turn it off as well, and was surprised to see Felicity sitting at the big round table by herself, staring glassily at her cell phone. Her eyes looked puffy, and he heard a sniffling noise. She heard Nick's footstep on the threshold and looked up.

"Hey, Boss," she said, managing a half-smile.

"Hey, yourself," he said, sitting down next to her. "What are you doing here so late?"

She sniffed again. "Nothing. Just getting ready to leave."

He reached over and gave her a hand a squeeze. "What's wrong?"

"Nothing," she replied lamely, dabbing at the corner of her eye with a balled-up clump of tissues in her other hand.

"I know you way better than that, sweetie. You don't look like this when nothing's wrong. Do you want to tell me about it?"

She looked down at the ball of tissues and sighed. "Oh, it's just my stupid love life."

Nick nodded, and got up to go to the refrigerator. "I've got a secret stash here," he said, crouching down and reaching to the far back of the fridge. "Want a beer?"

"Sure," Felicity said, and blew her nose into the tissue ball.

Nick came back with two beers, opened them both, and placed one in front of her. "So, I take it you and Muffy have hit a rough patch?"

She turned the bottle slowly on the table. "Really rough. We're broken up."

"I'm sorry to hear that. You seemed happy with her."

She took a small swig of beer, then wiped her mouth. "I was the happiest I've been in a long time. I really loved her, damn it."

Nick nodded. "Any chance of putting it back together?"

"I don't know. She says she wants to try, and deep down so do I. But you know what I'm like when I get stirred up. I say stupid things in the heat of the moment, and they can't be taken back."

Nick smiled. "Yeah, I've seen that side of you a few times." He paused and took another gulp, then looked into her eyes. "But you know, I've always loved you anyway."

She reached over and pinched his cheek. "That's because you're a big sweetheart." She looked down at her beer and her face changed. "But this really feels like the end. I mean, I'm already mourning what I've lost. It hurts like hell."

"I know exactly how you feel."

"I know you do."

Nick took a long sip, draining his bottle. "I guess you've just got to be honest with yourself and with her. If this relationship is what you want, do your best to save it. If things don't work out, you'll know you did everything you could."

Felicity sighed. "I know you're right, it's just hard to climb down. I was such an ass."

"Yup. I guess for you that'll be the hard part. But think of what you'll be climbing down to. Happiness, right?"

"Potentially. Or humiliation if she won't take me back."

"I get that walking away now might seem easier. I know how stressful hanging in there and trying to make it work can be. I went through three years of it with Elizabeth."

Felicity tilted her head and looked at him sideways. "God, three years. How did you get through that?"

"Well, I had great friends, you among them, who I knew would be there for me no matter what. And I saw a therapist for a while. It helped me to talk about what I was feeling."

"And what did the therapist tell you?"

"She did more listening than telling. But she did help me to realize that if your partner truly doesn't want you, she's doing you a favor by separating from you. It ultimately sets you free."

Felicity nodded. "That doesn't make it hurt any less, but it's probably true. Anything else?"

"Yeah. She helped me to see that either way things went, eventually they would be okay." He looked at her. "And I think that applies to you, Felicity. If you patch things up with Muffy, great, but if not, painful as it is, ending it gives you the chance to get on with your life. In time you'll have another relationship, maybe even a better one."

"I doubt that; this was the best relationship I've ever had."

He nodded but didn't say anything.

"Did she tell you anything else?"

He thought about it. "I remember one more thing. It was strange how she put it. She suggested I vigorously avoid self-pity. She called it a trapdoor leading to a pit of despair."

She nodded. "I agree. That's one thing you won't have to worry about with me. I'm not one to feel sorry for myself for long."

He stood up and bent down to put an arm around her shoulders. "I know you're not, babe," he said, giving her a little hug. "I don't know how things will turn out with Muffy, but I do know what a wonderful person you are. I'm proud to be your friend."

She returned the hug. "Stop it. You're going to make me cry more."

"Good luck and let me know what happens."

She gave him a little kiss on the cheek and whispered, "Will do."

Nick picked up the two empty bottles and dropped them in a wastebasket. "So, you're coming to the party, right?" he said.

"Oh yeah" she sighed, "wouldn't miss it. Maybe I'll go stag. It never stopped me before."

Nick turned to her as he headed out the door. "Either way you'll be among friends."

"I know," she answered and blew him a kiss.

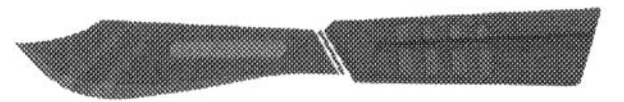

The following morning Nick saw patients in the office. His new assistant was Annette, a transplant to New Orleans from New England who possessed a winning smile and Yankee good sense. Nick had already found that her intellect and attitude made her a big improvement over Greg. She was helping him by holding a patient's hair out of the way as he inspected facelift incisions. He was pleased to notice that the scars in front of the ears had faded to the point where they were unrecognizable as anything except very fine lines, essentially identical in appearance to other tiny wrinkles there. He looked behind the ears, where the healing always took longer. The scars were slightly thicker, but well on their way to disappearing as well. He examined the minute scar in the midline under her chin and noted that it was virtually undetectable. Satisfied, Nick stepped back from the patient.

"Betsy, I don't think it's possible to heal any better than you have. Do you like the way you look?" Nick knew that this was the main question. In the end, it didn't really matter if he was pleased with the work. The patient had to be happy for the operation to be a success.

"I love it," she responded. "My friends have been telling me how good I look, but they can't figure out why." She giggled. "I've been saying I lost a few pounds and I'm doing my hair differently. It's just what I wanted." She rose from the chair to leave and gave him a little hug at the door.

"That's what it's all about," Nick said, with a broad smile, and gently returned the hug.

Annette wiped down the chair cushion and counter with an antibacterial sponge. "It's nice when they're pleased like that," she said. "It seems like all of them are."

"Not all, but most," he said, handing her the chart. "Who do we have next?"

She retrieved a folded paper schedule from her pocket and scanned it. "Let's see," she said, looking down the list of names. "Next is Mr. Charles Monroe."

Nick smiled. "Send him in."

Annette went to retrieve Charles, and a moment later he bounded into the exam room grinning broadly. "Doctor, how've you been?" he said, extending his hand.

"I've been fine, Charles," Nick replied, shaking it. "You seem unusually chipper today—like the cat who swallowed the canary."

Charles laughed. "I guess I am. It shows, huh?" Nick nodded. "My new girlfriend's out in the waiting room. Do you mind if I bring her in?"

Nick was surprised. "Of course not. But Charles, did you really just use the word girlfriend?"

"Uh-huh."

"So, someone finally corralled the wild stallion of Saint Charles Avenue?"

Charles grinned. "Happens to the best of us," he said, and was out the door.

A moment later he returned, holding a wrapped gift and a familiar woman by the hand.

Nick stood staring at the two of them, unable to speak. Finally, he spluttered, "Jane?"

She giggled and put an arm around Charles's waist. "Can you believe it?"

"But how?"

"We met on my cruise," she gushed. "We literally saw each other across a dance floor under the stars, and he came right over and asked me to dance."

Nick pointed to seats and pulled up a stool. "Tell me all about it. You're my last appointment before lunch, so we've got plenty of time."

They sat down together. Nick noticed that Jane immediately took Charles's hand in hers. Charles just grinned at him. "Okay," she said, "where to begin?"

Charles chimed in, "On the cruise ship, honey."

"Right. So, I was on the cruise ship with my friend Beth and there was a party, the Soiree under the Stars, they called it. We went up to the top deck to check it out. It was a beautiful night. The sun was setting, and they had strung lights up on poles over the dance floor. We were surrounded by the sea."

Charles broke in. "If you've never been to the Amalfi Coast, Nick, you must go. It's ridiculously beautiful."

Jane continued, "They had this great retro band, all dressed in tuxedos. I remember they were playing a song Sinatra used to sing…"

"It was *The way You Look Tonight*," Charles said.

She gave him an adoring look. "Right, Honey." Nick couldn't get over how happy they both were. Charles looked ten years younger.

"The music was playing and the lights were twinkling and a wonderful little breeze was coming off of the ocean. I think I told my friend Beth that I was never coming home. And then I looked across the dance floor, and there he was. His back was to me, but there was something kind of familiar about him. He was silhouetted against the island…"

"We were anchored off the coast of Capri," Charles said.

"And he turned around, and I knew I'd met him before. But I couldn't remember where."

"At first, I didn't recognize her, either. Then it came to me."

"I could see that he knew me. He walked towards me, looking very handsome in his suit, and when he reached me, he introduced himself. I remembered the name Charles Monroe, but I still couldn't place him. Then it hit me."

Charles smiled broadly. "She dated my college roommate at Tulane. And boy, did I envy him. I had the biggest crush on her. Seeing her, what, forty years later, just blew my mind. I couldn't get over how great she looks, how little she'd changed."

Jane giggled. "Well, I did confess that Nick had something to do with that."

Nick shook his head. "You brought the beauty, Jane, and I just helped refresh it a little. But please, go on with the story; this is great."

"Then he asked me to dance, and we were out on that dance floor for the rest of the party. We caught up on each other's lives, and it was just perfectly romantic, swaying there together under the stars."

Charles nodded. "We really couldn't have picked a more perfect setting."

"After the band stopped playing, we took a long stroll on the deck, and, well, one thing led to another," said Jane, blushing a little.

Nick clapped his hands together. "I'm so happy for both of you. You're two of my favorite people, and to see you together like this blows my mind. It restores my faith in the universe."

Charles beamed at him. "Thanks, buddy. It proves happiness is out there. You've just got to go find it." He turned to Jane. "Do we have something for our favorite facial plastic surgeon?"

"Oh yes, sweetie, I forgot. We saw this and thought you should have it."

Nick carefully took off the wrapping paper, and found himself looking at the back of a framed painting. He turned it over and saw that it was a lovely rendering of a small seaside town and its harbor. The colors were bright and beautifully blended. Small boats bobbed in the clear water. "This is gorgeous," he said.

"It's a painting of one of the towns in a place called *Cinque Terre*," Charles said. "They're five little villages on the Mediterranean that you can hike between. We went there after Capri. It's a magical place."

“I’m overwhelmed,” Nick said. “I’ll treasure this. Thank you.”

The couple got up and hugs were given all around. Nick carefully examined each of them and found they were both healing well from what he had done for them. He scribbled a note in each of their charts. Then something occurred to him. “Hey,” he said, “we’re having a small party tomorrow night. It’s our office anniversary dinner, and I’d love it if the two of you would join us.”

“That’s very kind of you, Nick,” Jane said, “But we don’t work here. Wouldn’t we be out of place?”

“Not at all,” Nick replied. “My office staff is coming, of course, but some friends of the practice will be there too. And you’re both certainly that. We’re meeting at Galatoire’s at eight. I spoke to Casey, who takes care of me there, and he’s getting us a big table. I hope you’ll come.”

Charles looked at Jane, who smiled and nodded. “Sounds like a plan, Doc,” he said. “We’re looking forward to it.”

Nick watched the two of them leave the room hand in hand with a deep sense of satisfaction. He thought about how far they’d all come.

56

Friday evening was cool and clear. Nick navigated through the narrow, crowded streets of the French Quarter and found a parking garage on Bienville Street across from the Acme Oyster House. The sky was getting dark, and the storefront lights and neon signs of the Quarter were coming on. The streets were busy with people wandering past brightly colored bars, strip clubs, and souvenir shops. A street-corner saxophonist provided background music.

Nick took Fiona's hand, and together they walked to the corner of Bourbon Street. He leaned his head closer to hers and said, "In case I forgot to mention it, you look beautiful tonight."

She turned to him. "Thank you, kind sir. You're not bad yourself."

He caught a warm sparkle in her eyes, and leaned in closer. Their lips met tenderly, and they held the kiss. Nick felt a thrill go through him. "Wow," he whispered.

Fiona smiled. "That was our first real kiss." He nodded, still overcome by the feeling. She squeezed his hand. "Stay tuned. More to come."

They looked across Bourbon Street to see a line of people waiting on the sidewalk outside of Galatoire's Restaurant, looking exactly as it always did. In a city where nothing changed quickly and tradition was valued above all else, Galatoire's seemed to stand still in time. Many of the people in line sipped from to-go cups containing potent cocktails from surrounding bars.

The couple bypassed the line and walked into the restaurant. Nick nodded at the Maître' D who had been there for several years, having succeeded one who had been there forever. He turned to the right and entered the large dining room, spotting a long table in the center, which he knew to be his. The restaurant took no reservations unless you knew somebody and then they'd save you as big a table as you wanted. Nick resolved to give Casey a large tip at the end of the evening. The waiter had been "helping him"—that was the way they always put it—for years. To get a waiter at Galatoire's you either ate there frequently enough to become known, or more commonly, inherited one from your parents.

Each time Nick arrived at Galatoire's, he felt as if he'd been transported back in time. There was electric light, but beyond that it could easily have been a hundred years ago. The large room was lined with thick ivory moldings suspended above mirrors set in tall wainscoting. Brass and wood ceiling fans glistened overhead. White tablecloths contrasted with black café chairs. The elaborately tiled floor and fleur-de-lis patterned wallpaper complemented one another perfectly and completed the classic appearance of the restaurant.

Although it was only seven in the evening, the noise level was already approaching stupendous. Nick felt lifted by the air of happiness that always seemed to pervade the restaurant. It was so familiar; always the same. He saw families dining together and knew that even the oldest people sitting at these tables had been here as children for special occasions. They had returned as teenagers on prom nights and now were here with their spouses, children, and grandchildren. The thought warmed him.

Approaching the table in the center of the room, Nick noted that most of his guests had already arrived. At the far end, he saw Lesli with her husband and Ginger with a date accepting drinks from a large tray. He gave them a little wave, and Ginger blew him a kiss back. Casey, looking dapper in his black tuxedo uniform, handed the tray to a passing busboy and greeted Nick warmly. "Doctah! How you doin'?"

The men exchanged a hug. "I'm good, Casey," Nick replied. "How've you been?" They chatted for a moment, and Nick introduced Fiona. The waiter kissed her hand, gave Nick a congratulatory grin, and left to take more drink orders. Annette arrived with a date and made introductions. Nick made his way around the table, greeting his office staff and stopping to say hello to Virginia and her husband and to Herb Shear and his wife Bonnie.

Casey brought him a bourbon and ginger. Nick moved to the head of the table, where Fiona was sitting with Dave and Sandra. Next to them were Charles and Jane, who were deep in conversation with Eddie Marquez and his young-looking date. *Good for you, old dog,* Nick thought as he took a pull at the bourbon, then placed his drink next to Fiona's and sat down. She patted his arm, welcoming him to her side.

Just that little gesture, how naturally it came and how comfortable it felt, hit Nick. He glanced over at Fiona; she was looking stunning tonight in a gold Chanel skirt and jacket. A profound sense of gratitude came over him. He was happy to have her with him, to have her in his life. They were taking things slowly, but he hoped they would be lovers. He could see himself with her for a long time. He covered her hand with his and gave it a gentle squeeze. She continued talking with Sandra, but he saw a smile animate the corner of her mouth, and he knew it was for him. It was all he needed. He felt like he'd come home.

Nick looked around the table to see who was missing. *Felicity, of course.* He hoped she was just running late and hadn't decided to stay home. Dave, who was sitting to his left, leaned over and nudged him. "Who's the cutie?" he said, looking down the table at Annette.

"That's my medical assistant. She's the new Greg."

"New and improved," Dave said suggestively.

Sandra gave them both an exaggerated eye roll. "What happened to the old Greg?"

Fiona chuckled and looked at Nick "Let's just say that Monsieur Greg is at liberty, at least for the moment."

Nick nodded. "That's right. I understand he has a court date next week."

That caught Charles's attention and Eddie's as well. "Court date? What did the boy do?" Charles asked.

Nick, helped at intervals by Fiona, told the story of Greg's bad day at Ray-Ray's. When he came to the part about the costume they roared with laughter. "I'm picturing the dirty old man from Rowan and Martin's Laugh-In," Charles choked. Eddie's date, who looked to be in her early thirties, was puzzled. "What dirty old man?" she said. Eddie put an arm around her waist. "Before your time, Darlin'," he said; "but I've got a DVD of it at home. We'll watch it, and you'll laugh your ass off."

Nick continued with the story. When he came to the end, Jane turned to Fiona. "But weren't you scared to let him hold a needle so close to your face?"

"Actually, I was terrified—I didn't want that that foul little man to touch me," she acknowledged, putting a hand on Nick's knee; "but I knew my knight in shining armor would protect me."

They heard laughter from further down the table. Virginia and Herb were telling a story from the operating room. A group of servers appeared bearing appetizers on large silver trays: spice-boiled shrimp with perfectly seasoned *remoulade* sauce, oversized oysters Rockefeller on the half shell, fried oysters wrapped in bacon *en brochette*, and fresh lump crabmeat *maison*, accompanied by a light and tangy sauce of the restaurant's own invention. Small white plates bearing torpedo-shaped French bread, hot from the oven and lighter than air, were set down at intervals for the diners to enjoy. There was a murmur of approval from the table as its occupants dug in.

Nick got up and made his way to the restroom at the far end of the restaurant, entering a small hallway. To his left was the bustling kitchen, and opposite it was an alcove near the door to the ladies' room. He was walking past when his attention was caught by a couple that stood close together, talking and giggling. It took him a moment to register what he was seeing.

"Excuse me, Muffy," he said, "but every time I go to a party you seem to have your arms around my aesthetician."

The two women turned towards him. They were smiling as well. Muffy looked embarrassed but happy and Felicity was positively beaming. "Fancy meeting you here, Boss."

"Uh-huh," Nick said, mock seriousness on his face. "And why aren't you two at the table?"

"Oh, just waiting for the loo," Felicity replied. "It takes us girls longer. We have to sit to do our business."

Nick smiled. "Too much information" he stepped forward and hugged the two of them. "I'm glad you're both here." He stepped away and continued towards the men's room. He looked back at the couple; Felicity was smiling at him. He gave her a wink and turned away.

When he returned to the table, Felicity and Muffy had found their seats and were chatting away with the group. The main courses arrived; a wide variety of delicious preparations of fish and shellfish accompanied by savory vegetables. Smaller torpedo shapes, the restaurant's famous pommes soufflés, accompanied the entrees. Nick bit into one and sighed with pleasure. Fiona looked at him. "Are those your favorites?"

"Since I was a little boy. There was a restaurant called Chasen's in Los Angeles that we used to go to, and I'd always have them there. These taste just the same."

She leaned towards him. "I bet you were so cute," she said, and kissed him lightly on the mouth. Then her lips brushed his ear. "You still are," she whispered and gave his hand a squeeze.

Nick felt the warmth of the gesture and smiled at Fiona. Absently, he ran his thumb over the bump at the base of his ring finger. The skin was smoother now; the callus was almost gone. He looked around the table and took it all in. The people he loved most were there—happy and enjoying one another. The feeling inside him was overwhelming. His eyes filled with tears.

Later that night, after he'd brought Fiona to her home and returned to his own, Nick lay in bed, reaching to turn out the light. The empty spot on the wall caught his attention and he stopped, struck by an idea. He got out of bed and carefully stepped over Roquefort, who lay on his side snoring lightly, all four legs extended. Nick walked downstairs and retrieved the painting Jane and Charles had given him from his study. He brought it upstairs and over to the lone nail on which Elizabeth's bridal portrait had been suspended. He hung the painting carefully and stepped back.

The vibrant colors transformed the room, giving it a warmth that he realized had been missing for a long time. He looked up and saw that the picture hung straight but was off from the slant of the molding above it. For the first time he saw a kind of perfect harmony in the way the house had aged and settled over the decades.

He got back into bed and looked at the painting once more, then switched off the light. In the darkness, just before slipping into a deep, healing sleep, Nick Jordan whispered one word:

"Better."

Call to Action

Thank you for reading *Fighting Gravity*. I hope Nick's journey through the challenges of divorce, dating, and second chances brought you moments of laughter, recognition, and inspiration about the possibility of starting over at any stage of life.

Having now completed two novels in the Nick Jordan series, I'm more committed than ever to continuing this literary adventure, and I would love to have you along for the ride. Here's what you can do to help me to keep writing stories for you to enjoy:

1. You are cordially invited to join *The Literati List*, my treasured group of readers who receive occasional updates from me on the progress of my writing and may also receive complimentary reading content. It would mean a great deal to have you join us at msgodin.com.
2. Please visit the retailer's website to leave an honest review of the book you purchased. Reviews are vital to authors and book sellers these days, and your thoughts help other readers discover stories they might love.

3. If you'd like to get in touch with me with questions about my books, the medical world, or the meaning of the universe in general, please email me at mgodinwrites@gmail.com. I'll do my best to respond in a timely manner.
4. And finally, if you'd like to read the prequel to the book you've just finished, please order *The Big Prick* from your favorite retailer or through this link: www.msgodin.com/the-books.

THANK YOU !!!

Michael Godin

What's Next

The adventures of Dr. Nick Jordan continue! While I can't reveal too much about what's ahead, I can tell you that Nick's story is far from over. His journey through midlife, medicine, and matters of the heart will continue to evolve in unexpected ways.

If you haven't yet read Nick's origin story in *The Big Prick: Surgery, Surfing, and Survival in 1980s San Diego*, I encourage you to discover how this remarkable journey began. You'll meet a younger Nick navigating the terrifying early days of the HIV pandemic while learning to surf and trying to become a surgeon.

For updates on future Nick Jordan novels and other projects, please visit msgodin.com and join *The Literati List*. I promise to keep you informed without overwhelming your inbox.

And finally, I'd love to have your opinion on where to go next. I can write a "bridge book" telling Nick's story between his 20's (*The Big Prick*) and middle age (*Fighting Gravity*) OR I can write a sequel to the book you just read, following *FG*'s characters on their next set of adventures. I plan to do both, but which should I do first? You get a vote, so please let me know at mgodinwrites@gmail.com.

Acknowledgments

I couldn't have written Fighting Gravity nearly as well or as enjoyably without all kinds of help. I want to thank both my family and friends, and the writing and publishing professionals who helped me along the way.

Jeff Feldman, Stella Tabassian, Nicole Colgrove, and Martha and Bobby Speight are all dear friends who were kind enough to look over various FG drafts and offer not only their insights, but enough encouragement to help keep me going.

Ashley Farley, Heath Hardage Lee, Joni Davis, Autumn Woods, and Irene Ziegler are very talented writers who looked over the manuscript and gave their two cents which proved to be far more valuable.

I'm grateful to my wife Christina, for providing comfort, support, nourishment, and keeping the dogs out of my study as well as anyone reasonably could so I could write.

I'd like to thank Chloe Hoang, one of my many brilliant nieces, for taking the time to look over the final draft of FG, just as she did for my previous novel, especially since it will coincide with the time she's beginning medical school.

I haven't asked her yet and she hasn't agreed to this, but I'm hopeful.

I want to shout out to my dear friends in New Orleans who made the city such a delight for me that I had to set a whole novel there.

A special thank you goes to my first-grade teacher, Ms. Margy Eisenberg, who became my email friend approximately 58 years after she literally taught me how to write.

I wrote Fighting Gravity approximately 15 years before its prequel, *The Big Prick: Surgery, Surfing, and Survival in 1980's San Diego*. I decided to release TBP first to learn about the book business and find out if anyone actually enjoyed my writing. It turned out to be a good move. I did and they did. So now let me go way back in time to thank editor Rachel Sherman, who advised me on an early version of FG and taught me the virtues of third-person close narration in darkest Brooklyn.

Sarah Duckworth and the folks at Gatekeeper Press were very helpful in launching TBP and teaching me about the publishing world. I'm enjoying working with Lexi Tebet at Gatekeeper now, and she's doing an excellent job of allowing me to do things at my own pace while keeping me on track.

I want to especially thank Kristen Kasza-Wise and Maira Pedriera at PRESStinely in New York (and Portugal) for their wise guidance and hard work in helping to make my first novel a success and hopefully this one a bigger one. If you're an author looking for excellent marketing help from nice people, look no further. But please, they have to take my call first ☺

I want to thank the fantastic bookstores and literary places that were kind enough to host me and my first novel at events and/or encourage their customers to check out my writing. They include:

Warwick's in La Jolla, CA, The Book Jewel in Los Angeles, CA, Book People in Austin, TX, Book No Further in Roanoke, VA, Apothec in Richmond, VA, and author Jeffrey James Higgins's Elaine's in Alexandria, VA.

In closing, I want to thank my dear friend and professional collaborator Betsy McClearn. Betsy was kind enough to throw me a fantastic book launch party in a prohibition-era speakeasy in the bowels of a fancy old hotel. It was easily one of my most enjoyable evenings. Betsy—let's please do it again!

And finally, I want to thank you, my reader, for spending a bit of your valuable time with the characters it's been my joy to create. It means the world to me. Please stay tuned for more.

Michael Godin

Richmond, VA

July 2025

About the Author

Dr. Michael Godin is a facial plastic surgeon with a passion for storytelling. While he loves the world of plastic surgery, he also has a creative side that has been developing since childhood. By combining these two areas and drawing on his personal experience, having been on both sides of the knife and the needle, he writes books that take readers inside the world of medicine and surgery in a fascinating way.

Godin comes from a family of avid readers, and in a sunny upstairs bedroom of a solidly middle-class home in Los Angeles' San Fernando Valley, his love of literature flourished. He was captivated by the adventures of Dr. Dolittle, Frank Merriwell, The Hardy Boys, and *Lad: A Dog*. He received Alfred Hitchcock's Spellbinders in Suspense as a birthday gift, and he loved it, reading the short, scary stories over and over. Roald Dahl's *Man from the South* was one of them, and through it he learned the power of a story to haunt its reader. Then he read Dahl's *Charlie and the Chocolate Factory,* which became his favorite book. A lifelong love of reading had been established.

What Godin didn't know at the time was how much learning to write persuasively would help him in his medical career. He has written over 20 scientific articles and a bestselling surgical textbook. While he always found time to write, Godin's ultimate goal was to create works of fiction. He survived surgical training during the 1980s at the beginning of the HIV pandemic, experiences that inspired his debut novel, *The Big Prick*. He learned to operate and surf, continued to write, and took good care of his patients. The year's experiences culminated in his creation and release of *Surgery Survival Guide: A Manual for Interns and Precocious Medical Students*, which sold at medical bookstores throughout the US and Canada.

His debut novel, *The Big Prick: Surgery, Surfing, and Survival in 1980s San Diego*, received critical acclaim and enthusiastic reader response. Building on that success, Godin has now released *Fighting Gravity*. This romantic comedy explores the challenges of midlife, divorce, and modern dating through the eyes of a New Orleans plastic surgeon. Drawing from his decades of experience in medicine and his understanding of human nature, Godin brings authenticity and heart to stories about second chances and personal transformation.

Dr. Michael Godin practices facial plastic surgery in Richmond, Virginia, and Southern California, and enjoys living on both coasts with his wonderful wife, adult sons, and two dogs. One is very good, the other *still* not so much, but he loves her more than ever.

Godin is delighted that his books bring joy, laughter, and enlightenment to his readers, and he looks forward to continuing to combine the worlds of medicine and literature in future novels.

Made in the USA
Middletown, DE
03 February 2026

27529899R00269